WHAT DOESN'T CURE YOU

STACEY DIGHTON

First published by Stacey Dighton (2025)

ISBN: 978-1-0369-0882-9

Cover illustration by Dan Gogerly (Instagram - @dangogerly)

For Jo, Jayden and Harley

Prologue:

Thursday, 3rd August:

St. Pancras, London

Paul Karin had the last of his great epiphanies as he prodded at the sludgy remains of his double-shot americano with a wooden stirrer. He'd been thinking about string. String was the problem. The whole shit-show was a tangled ball of the stuff. Life, love, the pursuit of wealth. You picked at one thread, a knot formed in another. You pulled at a loose end, everything else became snarled up. Sure, you could go at it with scissors, a knife, but then you were just cutting away little sections of who you were, abandoning plans that you thought would define you, snipping away people that you considered important. People like Manny, Renee, Uncle Barnaby. Julie. In the end, you ask yourself, why bother? Why even try? If everything was so difficult, so damn hard, why not just stop? But you never do. You never will. You can't.

He checked himself in the smeared haze of the coffee shop window, contemplating his last big assault on that damn ball of twine, but knowing it would all mean nothing if he couldn't get this thing over the line. He glared at his crooked tie, mop of dark curls and awkward stance. He'd borrowed the suit from his part-time dad almost four years ago, and he'd only ever worn it that one time. That was to his granddad's funeral, the last time he'd seen his old man. His mum too. It wasn't a pleasant memory, but then none of them were. If only they could see him now.

He pinched himself beneath his shirt, twisted the skin. He needed to be together. The people he was meeting expected a certain type of presentation, an element of normalcy. It was okay. He knew what he was going to say. Every line had been meticulously crafted, every syllable clipped and enunciated in his cockney-cum-east-Kent twang. It was about as perfect as it could get. He just had to remember to keep his mouth in check, another knot he was yet to unpick.

A barista appeared, a lop-sided smile over yellow teeth. 'Another coffee, sir?' she asked, her voice laced with a heavy Gaelic accent. Paul thought she looked like his grandma, but without the hand rolled fag clamped between her lips.

'No thanks,' he replied. 'I have a big meeting this morning.' He gave a nod towards the gleaming building across the street.

'Harkers?' she asked. 'Impressive.'

'I like to think so.'

'They can be pretty tough in there, you know?' Her tone was mildly patronising. 'I've seen them swallow kids like you whole.'

'Well, with respect, I ain't a kid, and I'm not planning on being swallowed, either.'

She gave a nonchalant shrug. 'So you're the big fish, eh?'

'What's that supposed to mean?'

'That you're the one who's going to make it upriver.'

The thought of hundreds of slowly suffocating salmon floundering in shallow water made his skin itch. 'Nice analogy.'

'Hey, no problem. I'm here all week.'

He felt the eels of darkness stirring in his stomach. The sharp scratch of the woman's claws was beginning to irritate him.

'Listen,' she said. 'It takes guts, a great idea and a lot of luck to make somebody like David Harker sit up and take notice.' He groaned. She was a kink in his string, an agent of chaos. 'But as a proud Kerry girl, I'll offer you this. Go n-eirí an t-ádh leat.'

He shook his head. 'I have no idea what that means.'

'It means good luck, son. Good luck to you. You're going to need it.'

'Luck is for the lazy.' He patted his case. 'This stuff sells itself.'

'That's what they all say.'

He glanced at her name badge. Brionie, like the poisonous vine.

'And what is it you have in there? Gold?'

'It might as well be.' He gestured towards the TV. 'I suggest you keep watching that news channel. You could be seeing my face up there very soon.'

He enjoyed the change in her expression, the belittling pity. He didn't care. She'd realise soon enough.

He opened the door and crossed the street. He knew his friend, Manny, would be totally against what he was doing, but in his view, there was no excuse for narrow mindedness. His pal lacked vision. There was no point in having the key to the universe if you were too afraid to open the door? Paul wasn't afraid. He'd kick the damn thing down if he had to.

'Good morning,' he beamed as he entered the plush building. 'Paul Karin. I have a nine-thirty appointment with David Harker.'

'You're early,' the young, male receptionist replied, barely looking up from his tablet.

Paul checked his watch. It was nine-fifteen. 'Well, you know what they say, better to be—'

'Mr Harker?' the receptionist interrupted, holding up his hand. 'Your nine-thirty is here. Yes sir, I told him that. Would you like me to ask him to wait? Okay. No, that's fine. No sir, that's completely fine. Yes. I'll do that.' He gave Paul a cursory glance, clocked his blue, polyester suit, and raised an eyebrow. 'He'll see you now,' he said. 'But Mr Harker asked me to remind you that he only has ten minutes available in his schedule. He's a very busy man.'

'But I'm fifteen minutes early,' Paul objected, before catching himself. 'I mean, of course. That's no problem at all. Ten minutes will be plenty.'

'Very good. Here's your name-badge. Mr Harker is on the fifth floor, second office on the right. The lifts are dead ahead.'

Paul felt the hairs on his arms bristle in anticipation. He gave a half-hearted smile as he waited for the elevator doors to open.

The ride up was slow. Tiny beads of hot perspiration began to gather on his forehead. He dabbed at his brow and checked his body odour. The pressure was almost unbearable. All eyes were on him. His Punjabi friend's voice bounced around in his head like a misfired projectile. *We need to keep this under wraps, Paulie. Those bigwigs in the city will never understand what we have here. Before you know it, they'll be exploiting it for themselves.* Manny had been wrong. He'd never been good at seeing the bigger picture. Things had moved on. The seeds of something new had germinated, and Paul had allowed the saplings to grow. Adapt and survive, that was the way it had to be.

There was a loud ping, and the door slid open. Three smartly dressed Zoomers stood waiting, laptops held open like snapping turtles. A girl with her hair in a tight updo shot him an impatient glare.

'I'm sorry,' he said, before navigating around them.

There was a babble of noise and chatter.

'Guys, check out the suit.'

'TK Maxx has a lot to answer for.'

'Hey pal, the nineties want their hairstyle back.'

He ignored the jibes, pausing in the gangway to take in the

office layout. It was modern, open plan, bustling with conversation and nervous energy. Dozens of flittering eyes studied him, the newcomer in cheap threads. He didn't care. They all looked like Apprentice rejects, fake and full of bullshit. He glanced at himself in the tinted glass partition, a very small tadpole in a pond full of toads. That was fine by him. He was used to being the underdog.

He walked with a brash confidence to the second office along. It was a spacious, glass fronted room. The furnishings were minimal. A smart dressed man stood behind a height adjustable desk, fingers hammering on the keys of an ergonomically designed keyboard. Paul tapped on the glass.

'Come!'

He pushed the worst of his emotions into the pit of his stomach and stuck his head through the open doorway. 'Mr Harker?' he asked.

'That's what the name plaque says. And you're?'

'Paul Karin, sir.' He strode in and thrust out a hand. 'I've come to talk to you about—'

'Take a seat, Karin,' Harker replied, leaving him hanging. 'Did the receptionist tell you I only have—'

'Ten minutes? Yes, he did. And that's fine. I really appreciate you taking the time.'

'Well, I didn't really have a choice in the matter, what with my wife being good friends with your…aunt, is it?

'Aunt Angela.'

'Mm, yes. That's the one.' He folded his arms. 'Well, Karin? Let's have it. Show me what you got.'

Paul lifted his case and thumbed the key code. He withdrew a slim folder and a little vial containing a thick yellow liquid. He handed the paperwork to Harker. 'It's all in there,' he said. 'The projected annual revenues, production costs, likely market, and a very conservative estimate of the sort of annual profits your company could expect to make.'

Harker glanced through the slim document. 'It all looks very healthy,' he said, 'if it's to be believed, which in my experience, it hardly ever is.' He closed the file, set it on the desk and folded his hands. 'You claim to have a product that can slow the ageing process. Is that right?'

Paul clenched his hands. 'Well, sort of.'

'Because I've got to tell you, Karin, there are a million-and-one companies out there selling cosmetic products that claim to do exactly the same thing, and most of them do it pretty poorly if you ask me. It's a very, *very* saturated market with little space for a breakout product.'

'I understand that, but—'

'I'm not sure you do, otherwise you wouldn't have gone to all the effort of pulling this business plan together and travelling all this way for a ten-minute appointment with me. Look, I at least have to show willing—I promised my wife as much—but in my opinion, you have no USP here, and even if you did, we're not a beauty products company. We sell medicine, stuff that cures people with actual, real-life illnesses.'

'I don't think you appreciate what this is, Mr Harker. If I could just—'

'I don't know what to tell you, Karin, other than to go back to the drawing board and see if you can't come up with something a little more compelling. Nobody's going to buy a supplement that claims it stops you from getting old. People just don't believe that crap anymore.'

Paul could feel himself beginning to unravel. It was like the guy hadn't read the brief. His whole speech had been culled at birth. Why had Harker even agreed to see him if he didn't know what he was offering? 'But that's not what we have here!' he blurted out, struggling to control his escalating tone. 'I mean, with respect, that's not our product.'

Harker suppressed a laugh. 'And I'm guessing you're going to tell me that what you've invented is something that nobody else can provide. Something that no other scientist, an expert in his or her field, has been able to come up with, despite you only having worked as a junior biochemist at —' he thumbed through his notes, 'Matax, is it?'

'That's right.'

'A company that's on the verge of going into administration.'

Paul's mind was racing. The meeting wasn't going to plan. He had been so sure of himself, and yet here he was, on the verge of losing out on what he knew would be a global clamour for a product that nobody else could possibly have. It would be a travesty, an unqualified disaster. He thought of his little ball of string, of the loose ends that hung just out of reach. If only he could stretch a little farther, try a little harder. In his desperation, he grabbed the yellow vial and held it out in front of him, allowing Harker a better view. Inside, the crystalline cells danced against one another, causing the plastic casing to vibrate. 'This will change people's lives.'

'And how will it do that?'

He took a moment to compose himself. 'I'm not claiming that we can slow the ageing process, sir. We would never make such a bold statement.' He handed Harker the vial. 'And with respect, old age doesn't kill anybody. Dying of it is a fallacy, much like the urban myth that you can catch a cold, or that rubbing a sliced potato on a burn helps heal the wound.'

Harker's poise was dented. 'Where the hell are you going with this, Karin?'

'I'm trying to clarify our USP.'

The executive eyed the vial. He exhaled through his teeth

before setting it down on the desk. 'Okay. If you're so smart, tell me. You've got me intrigued, if nothing else. What exactly is it that you're offering?'

'We have the cure.'

'The cure for what?'

Paul leaned across the desk and tapped the vial.

'Mr Harker, we have the cure for everything.'

Part One: Black Spring

Sunday, 28th May:

Ogof Ffynnon Ddu (Cave of the Black Spring), South Wales

They were in a narrow crag, situated about halfway along the central section of the Great Oxbow Series of the Black Spring cave network, known locally as Ogof Ffynnon Ddu, or OFD for short. The slim cavity was carved out of black limestone, hard and jagged, dripping with cold groundwater. The place was something else, filled with rocky crags and unnatural shapes that made it look like the set of a Peter Jackson movie. Paul had never ventured such a long way beneath the surface before, almost two hundred and thirty metres underground. Down there, some of the colours appeared otherworldly, as if they didn't exist anywhere else on Earth. The smell of the place was intense, too: the crispness of freshwater, the saltiness of iron, the dense, earthy smell of underground plant life.

He and his friend, Manny, had hired all the best gear before embarking on that weekend's pot-holing trip, spending a small fortune on waterproof jumpsuits, Kevlar hardhats with carbon headlamps, plastic mountaineering boots, heavy duty knee and elbow pads, waterproof backpacks, static ropes, clips, and at Manny's insistence, chocolate.

'You okay back there?' Paul yelled, glancing over his shoulder. Manmeet Davi, or Manny, was a year older than Paul and around four stone heavier. His family were Sikh immigrants who had moved to the UK from Jalandhar, India in the late eighties. The two of them had been best pals since sixth form when Manny had rescued Paul from a particularly nasty beating at the hands of the school hardman, Gary Coates.

'You struggling to get your fat arse through that narrow crack?' he laughed.

'Oh, very funny!' Manny replied. 'A fat joke! How original. Next you'll be slipping in some casual racism.'

'Hey, don't be so sensitive. You know I save that sort of stuff for when we're out with our mates.'

'If only you were joking. Anyway, don't you worry about me. I might be a little overweight, but I'm pretty bendy. Didn't you see me pull myself up that five metre chimney back there.'

'Yeah, I did. It was like watching Kung Fu Panda climbing a tree.'

'Honestly, Paulie, you should try standup comedy.'

The fissure was just over half a metre high and three metres wide, and the conditions were cramped and claustrophobic. Every now and then Paul would be overcome by the unsettling sensation of the walls moving towards them. When this happened, it would feel like his throat was beginning to close, slowly starving his lungs and brain of oxygen, and he would frantically fumble in his pocket for his inhaler.

They were around two miles from where they'd started, with a long way to go, but Manny had assured him the climb down was perfectly safe. However, Manny knew as well as he did that things could pivot within a micro-second. It had happened before, and it would happen again.

'How much further did you say this thing was?' Paul asked.

'Oh, not far. Another fifteen minutes, maybe.'

'You've been saying that for the past hour,' Paul shot back, only half joking. 'I'm not a kid anymore, you know? I can handle the truth.'

'Okay, Jack Nicholson. How about this? I don't actually know.'

Paul shook his head. 'How shocking. I never would have guessed.'

Usually, he didn't mind how long their expeditions took, but his bouts of asthma had been coming a lot more frequently recently, and the thought of lying there, unable to breathe when the nearest medical staff were a thirty-minute drive and a three hour climb away, set his teeth on edge. More importantly, it was approaching six in the evening, and he was craving a beer.

Julie, Paul's girlfriend of just over a year, hadn't been keen on him spending three days in South Wales with little to no contact. 'What if there's a rockfall?' she'd asked. 'Or you lose each other? Just because you've been on a family day out to Wookey Hole doesn't make you an experienced potholer, you know?'

He'd told her to stop being so ridiculous, and that he and Manny weren't idiots and would take the necessary precautions, but what he didn't tell her was that he'd actually fallen four metres during a routine caving expedition two years prior and had broken his arm in two places.

'That's odd,' Manny said, tapping Paul's leg. 'You see that? Just up ahead. I think it's an opening.'

Paul peered into the gloom. The light from his headlamp only illuminated the ground up to seven metres ahead of them. Beyond that, everything was about as black as a bucket of liquorice.

'It's a cave, Paulie,' Manny hollered. 'I told you, didn't I? I said we were nearly there.'

'Yeah, I guess, but just because I won a tenner on the lottery, doesn't make me an investment banker.'

'No, but I could think of something that rhymes with it that describes you perfectly.'

Paul slowly pulled himself along the crag's slippery limestone floor and edged towards the precipice. He took in his surroundings. It was a cave alright, and a pretty enormous one too, easily the most impressive they'd encountered so far. He estimated it was around twelve metres high, fifteen metres wide and approximately twenty metres long. Bands of milky stalactites hung from the ceiling, twisted and gnarled. The air was dank and warm. A pool of greenish-blue water covered over half the ground beneath them. They sat with their legs dangling over the edge of the crevice, peering down at their own reflections.

'I'm knackered,' Manny said. 'Starving, too. You want some chocolate?'

'No, I'm okay,' Paul replied, waited to catch his breath while he watched Manny pull a family sized bar of Dairy Milk from his backpack.

'Beautiful,' his friend said. 'Don't you think?'

'Yeah, I guess.' Paul eyed the chocolate bar. 'That thing doesn't stand a chance against you, does it?'

Manny shook his head, snapped off an entire row and shoved it into his mouth.

Paul reached into his pocket, extracted his inhaler, and took two deep drags.

'You okay?' Manny asked.

'Yeah. Chest just feels a bit tight.'

'We don't have to go any further.'

'No, we've come this far. You've sold me on Marble Showers. I wanna see it.'

He breathed in and out slowly, letting the medication do its work, concentrating on his lungs, his chest, his throat, the way his doctor had advised him. His asthma was a part of him now, an unwelcome guest that simply refused to leave. It followed him around like a giant zeppelin. No matter how hard he tried, he'd never been able to slip out from beneath its shadow.

That was when he saw it. The hole. It was nestled in a cave wall to their left, barely visible beyond the pallid glow of his head lamp, a narrow crack surrounded by fallen rock and stone as if there had been some sort of landslide. That wasn't particularly strange—they had been warned that there had been quite a large earth tremor the week before they'd arrived—but what was odd was the eery green glow that pulsed from within the darkness.

'What do you reckon that is?' he asked.

'What's that?'

'Over there. Look.'

Manny crunched the last remaining piece of chocolate between his teeth and turned.

'I can't see anything.'

'Not over there, you idiot.' Paul grabbed his head and twisted it around.

'Ow, that hurts.'

'Then stop focussing on eating your body weight in confectionary and look where I'm pointing.'

Manny peered into the darkness. He grunted. 'That's weird.'

'Yeah, that's what I thought.'

'Fluorescent anemone, maybe?'

'What? Underground?'

Manny shrugged. 'I dunno. Do I look like David Attenborough?' He huffed through his nose like a bull. 'I bet you want us to go take a look, don't you.'

'Yeah,' Paul replied, hitching his backpack and dropping to the cave floor. 'I do.'

Sunday, 28th May:

'The Hope and Anchor', Faversham, Kent.

Julie Harbor watched as the rock band, Pickled Cabbage, packed their gear into their dilapidated, barely-white Transit van. The group were all in their fifties and played eighties and nineties rock covers—the kind of music Julie's mum used to play to her over and over again when she was a kid—but the pub had been almost empty, and because of that, the night had dragged. She'd found herself wondering what the hell she was doing there. It wasn't that she disliked the place or her job for that matter—in fact, most of the time she quite enjoyed it—but it just wasn't what she'd spent an exorbitant amount of money on a university education for, leaving herself in the kind of debt that she could probably never fully repay. It certainly wasn't what her father would have wanted, either, not that he knew much of anything anymore.

'You heading off, Jules?' Bobby asked. The landlord was a big bear of a bloke with a scraggly beard and a patchwork of tattoos on his forearms and neck.

'Yep. I'm just finishing up.'

'You good for tomorrow night? We have The Whistleblowers in, and you know how much this lot love those old folkies.'

Julie groaned. She hated folk music, and she hated working on the bank holiday. 'Yeah, sure. Why not.' She grabbed her keys, silently seething.

The walk home wasn't far, but she decided to take the scenic route for a change. She needed the air. Things at home weren't good. Her dad had been diagnosed with stage five dementia in

January. He had been sixty-two at the time. His decline had been rapid, and now her mum was struggling to keep up with the demands of his care. Julie, an only child, was finding herself pitching in more and more. The endless, soul-destroying hours were teaching her one thing—that she wasn't cut out to be a full-time carer. She couldn't deal with the emotional rollercoaster of it all. She just couldn't handle it. She hated to admit that to herself, but it was the truth. Her dad would go from being the father she knew, the dad that had been her idol, her rock, to being this angry, sometimes violent shell of his former self, rambling nonsensically and regularly lashing out. It was draining, and what's more, it was damaging to her mental health. She'd been mulling it over for days, playing it back and forth in her mind, but she knew there was only one sensible solution to her problem. She had to get away, even if that meant abandoning them both. She just couldn't be there anymore.

Her phone buzzed in her pocket, snapping her out of her tortured thoughts. It was Paul. He was video-calling her, which was something he'd only recently learned how to do.

'Hey,' she said.

'Hey, it's me.'

'No shit.' He had a habit of stating the bloody obvious. 'How did you get on today? Did you…find any interesting rocks?'

'Are you alone?' he asked, looking harried. 'I mean, are you by yourself?'

'Yes, of course.' She held the phone up. 'I'm walking along North Lane. See? There's the brewery, there's the grocers—'

'I need to talk to you about something,' he cut in. 'It's just that me and Manny, well, it's sort of weird, but we discovered something in the caves. It was way down in some new part of the network. It's not even on the maps, which is odd. We just seemed to stumble upon it. Anyway, I'm going to need you to go with me on this, but—'

'Paul, Paul!' she said. 'Just slow down a bit, will you? I'm struggling to keep up here.'

'I know, I know. Sorry.' His eyes were wild.

'Have you taken something?'

'No. What?'

'You just look…weird.' She'd never seen him like that before, not when he was sober.

'Yeah, I guess.' He peered at his selfie image. 'I do look a bit strange, don't I?'

'A bit? Are you kidding? I'd say a lot.' She laughed. He laughed back.

'It's really exciting, Jules. I don't even know where to begin or how to explain it. It's like nothing I've ever seen before. Even Manny was lost for words, and you know how he can get.'

She did. The guy never shut up. 'Well, come on then. Spit it out. I'm cold and I need to pee.'

Paul set the screen down and stooped to the floor. She could see his room behind him. It was a mess.

'Hurry up,' she said.

'Just wait a sec.' He was just out of shot.

'Paul, I really need the toilet.'

'Just give me a minute.' His face came back into view. He was holding something. It was a large container filled with a yellow, viscous liquid.

'What the hell is that?' she asked.

'That's just it,' he replied. The material's reflection glowed like butterscotch against his skin. 'We don't know. We just don't know.'

Tuesday, 30th May:

University of Canterbury, Canterbury, Kent

'So, what do you think?' Paul asked.

'Difficult to say,' the lab technician replied. She was a petite redhead with a distinctly French accent named Renee Douglas, a second year PhD student studying Biomedical Science. She also happened to be an ex-classmate and ex-girlfriend of Paul's. 'It's extremely viscous, crystalline in nature and with a cell construction that I've never encountered before. It's almost too complex to fully appreciate. This movement, the energy it contains, I've never seen that. It's almost as if it's alive, which, of course, is quite impossible.'

'Because?'

'Because it has no muscle, no cerebral tissue, nothing that would identify it as anything other than a liquid. It really is quite a bizarre material. Where did you say you found this stuff again?'

Paul shot Manny a furtive glance. 'I don't think we want to disclose that just yet.'

'It's on a need-to know basis, I'm afraid,' Manny added, tapping his nose.

Renee's mouth twitched. 'I'm going to need to run more tests to see what we're dealing with here. Could you leave it with me for, say, a couple of days?'

Paul ushered Manny to the corner of the room. 'What do you think?'

'I don't really want to let this stuff out of our sight,' Manny replied.

'I suppose I could examine it at home, but I don't have the equipment, and Renee's really good at this kind of thing.'

'Do you trust her?'

Paul watched as the young scientist poked the gelatinous liquid with a scalpel, making notes as it appeared to shrink against her touch. 'I think so. I mean, yeah, I do. I do trust her.'

'Okay, but she has to be sworn to secrecy. Legally, I mean. This can't get out.'

'Yeah, right.' Paul laughed before realising his pal wasn't joking.

'I'm serious,' Manny said. 'I'm not kidding around.'

Paul had an idea. He grabbed a sheet of plain paper from the printer and a pen from the stationary drawer. He started to scrawl:

I, Renee Elizabeth Douglas, agree not to disclose, in any form - verbal, written or otherwise - details regarding the yellow liquid substance handed to me by Paul Karin and Manmeet Davi on the 30th May, to any other Party or Parties. This Non-Disclosure Agreement is binding, worldwide and in perpetuity.

Signed:……………………………………Renee Elizabeth Douglas

Date…………

'Classy,' Manny chirped, squinting at the clumsy script. 'It's convenient, your uncle being a lawyer, isn't it?'

Paul handed the document to Renee. 'You okay to sign this?'

She set down her scalpel and looked over the wording. 'Is this really necessary?'

'It's just a precaution.'

'You must be really serious about this stuff.' She took the pen. 'How did you know my middle name?'

Paul grinned sheepishly. 'I used to copy your work,

remember?'

She smiled. She'd always had a pretty smile. He subconsciously fiddled with the asthma pump in his pocket. She didn't notice. He wouldn't miss the inhaler, the drawers filled with as many refills as he could afford, the preventative pump he used at night to reduce the risk of a sudden attack while sleeping. The thing was, he and Manny had brought back way more from their trip to Penwyllt than a Tupperware container filled with a strange looking liquid. They'd brought back something he'd never had before, something he'd dreamed about every day since he was a little boy.

The ability to breathe.

Sunday, 28th May:

Ogof Ffynnon Ddu (Cave of the Black Spring), South Wales

Manny staggered across the uneven cave floor. His foot caught in a crag, and he almost toppled into the underground pool. He was holding the laminated map of the network.

'I've been looking,' he said. 'This place isn't shown anywhere on here.'

'Maybe you're reading it wrong.'

'Not likely. I've been down these tunnels loads of times, remember?' Paul knew that was true. Manny and his father, Rabinder, were keen pot-holers.

They clambered up the slope and stood at the edge of the jagged opening. The crevice in the rock emitted a warm odour, like out-of-date oysters.

'It looks pretty deep,' Manny said. 'Probably wide enough, too. You wanna go in?'

Paul took a long drag on his inhaler. 'Sure. Why not.'

The diagonal shaft led downwards, the ground broken but slick. The walls were coarse and sharp, like really rough sandpaper. The slim fissure looked as though the rock had literally been ripped open by a lateral movement in the Earth's crust. Paul held his hand to the wall.

'It's vibrating,' he said.

'It's what?'

'Here, see for yourself.' He grabbed Manny's hand and held it against the rough granite. They stood there for a moment in silence. The rapid throb was subtle but real.

'That's strange. What do you think it is?'

Paul shrugged. 'No idea, and that glow is odd, too. You think there's someone down there?'

'Could be. These caves are pretty popular.'

They walked further along the tunnel. The deeper they went, the more intense the light became. An uneasy feeling crept up on Paul. There was a sense of inevitability, a darkening finality. It was the strangest sensation, as if a warning siren was going off inside his head. There was no logical reason to fear anything, but that was exactly what it was. It was primal, feral.

The tunnel came to an abrupt end. They stepped into a slightly smaller cave. The walls were made out of the same dark material, but the ground was completely submerged in grey water. From within the pool, just below the surface, came that dull-green, pulsing glow.

'It's under there,' Manny said. 'Whatever's creating that light.'

Paul peered into the pool. His reflection was distorted and stretched. He looked like a monster, an extra-terrestrial emerging from a mothership.

Manny took a deep breath and plunged his hands into the liquid. 'I think I can reach it.'

Paul grabbed his arm. 'Wait! I mean, are you sure about this?'

'Yeah. I thought you wanted to know what it was.'

'I do, but—'

'Then just stand back'

Paul reluctantly obliged.

'I can feel it. It's, like, metallic or something. It's heavy, too. You might have to help me here.'

Paul stepped into the pool and plunged both his hands into the warm water. He could feel the murky liquid pulsing just like the walls, except the sensation was much more intense. His hands found smooth metal coupled with a strange sort of plasticity. He blindly reached out to find the object's edges, but whatever it was, it moved away from him. He slipped into the pool.

'Paul, be careful.'

'It's moving. It's like it's alive or something.'

'I can feel it, too,' Manny said. 'Maybe we should get out of the water.'

Paul was transfixed. He couldn't take his hands away. His fingertips tingled. His whole body felt charged with energy. He stepped further into the pool, the water now up to his waist. The moving, shifting thing began to back away slowly. Paul followed its smooth motion, walking with his hands held against its body, his feet slipping within the silt beneath him. Manny was no longer in his thoughts. He wouldn't have been able to hear his friend if he was. It was just him. He and the unseen thing beneath the surface, symbiotic, conjoined.

His foot struck a rock and his leg buckled. He stumbled forwards, tipping face first into the water, his body landing on top of the creature's back. It instantly began to thrash around beneath him. Something struck his cheek, throwing him backwards, and then there was a sound like a high-pitched keening. He was underwater now, deep within the pool, the silty, gritty liquid turning bright yellow as the creature jettisoned something from its lower torso. Some of it slipped into his mouth, and there was a hot, burning sensation in his chest. He reached for the edge of the pool, but the liquid was in his eyes, stinging his retinas. He couldn't breathe. His lungs were on fire. No matter how much air he pulled into his body, none of the oxygen was reaching his brain. An arm slipped beneath him, pulling him upwards. Within seconds, he was lying on the rocks, bubbles of yellow saliva spurting from his parted lips.

'Paul!' Manny yelled. 'Paul, are you okay?'

Paul was panicking. He frantically reached inside his pocket for his inhaler, but his fingers just found thin, sodden material. His thoughts were consumed with how much he needed to breathe, and how he was going to suffocate right there on the cave floor, miles from help. Everything started to cloud over, his vision now a shrinking circle in the centre of his view. His body was thrashing and his lungs bursting. Above him, Manny was shouting at him, his hands in his mouth, trying to open his airway.

Just as Paul was about to lose consciousness, something shifted inside him as if his lungs had tipped onto their sides somehow, and then gradually his frantic, urgent gasps began to ease. He rolled onto his front and tried to get up, but he was vaguely aware of Manny telling him to '*stay down! Just stay the hell down*!'

Paul didn't know if he was okay or not. He didn't know what the thing in the murky water was. He didn't know what he would tell people if he was asked. But he did know one thing. It was as clear as the sight of Manny's round face bearing down on him, his eyes painfully wide, his lips stretched open, his mouth screaming words he could barely hear.

Whatever the yellow liquid was, it had saved his life.

Tuesday, 30th May:

Sittingbourne, Kent

He was fully submerged, but somehow able to breathe. The water was warm and calm. It felt oddly smooth against his naked torso. Above him, he could see the faint strains of the day's fading sunlight, a pinprick in the rolling tide. Below, the ocean was vast and empty. The abyss beckoned him. Something enormous caught his eye, and he turned to face a huge sperm whale. Its impressive mass hovered above him like the hull of a ship. Its blue-grey skin rippled against his fingertips. Paul swam alongside it before letting it drift away, watching as it disappeared into the distance, silent and ethereal.

A hand touched his foot, and he looked down to see his girlfriend, Jules, floating beneath him. Bubbles spurted from his lips as he gasped. She was clutching her throat and gulping in huge mouthfuls of seawater. Her eyes were bulging, her neck and shoulder muscles strained. He reached for her, but his fingers only grazed her flailing arms. She was drowning.

He tried to yell, to cry out, but it was useless. He had to find help.

Something rose from the depths of the ocean. It was as though the seabed was rising to meet them. Its surface was sleek and gleaming like stainless steel. At its centre was a wide, yawing mouth-like hole. It was filled with a yellow, gelatinous substance. Blue and green lights flashed at its circumference. Dark grey, multi-limbed creatures stood behind its many windows, their dull, yellow eyes glaring at them. He tried to pull Jules with him, but the draw of the vessel was too strong, and they were sucked downwards towards its open mouth. A sea of yellow bubbled and swirled beneath them. Tentacled limbs reached for their tumbling bodies. They were engulfed by its thick, undulating flesh. Paul eyed one of the creatures. It had become something else entirely. Something eerily familiar.

Manny stood on the deck, grinning. He opened his mouth and devoured them.

Wednesday, 31st May:

Fernando's Coffee Plaza, Faversham, Kent

'I had the strangest dream last night.' Paul sipped his coffee, trying to shake that morning's nightmare.

'Oh really? What was it about?' Julie held her mug of chai latte beneath her lips and eyed him over the rim.

'I have no idea, but it scared the living crap out of me.'

They were sitting outside Fernando's Coffee Plaza in the centre of town. The little café was located just off Market Square, the town's central hub, a favourite destination for tourists and sightseers with its famous brewery and eighteenth-century clock tower. It was mid-morning on a Wednesday, however, so the place was almost deserted.

'Any news from Renee?' she asked.

'No, not yet. I'll probably take a drive over there tomorrow morning and see what she's managed to find.'

She swirled her latte. 'You think it's dangerous?'

'What? No. I mean—' he shrugged. 'No. Definitely not.'

'You found it underground, Paul. Like, way underground. It could be toxic, carcinogenic, anything.'

'You worry too much.' He played with his phone. 'Look. We took precautions. We were wearing gloves almost the whole time.'

'And your nose and mouth,' she asked. 'I bet you didn't think to cover them.'

'It doesn't smell of anything, Jules. I'm sure it's not airborne.'

'I still think you should take it to somebody, like the Office of

Environmental Health or the police. Somebody who actually knows what they're doing.'

'Renee knows what she's doing.'

'Oh, come off it, Paul. You only took it to her because she was your—'

'Because she's a bloody good scientist.'

'Because she was your girlfriend.' She took his hand. 'Look, I'm worried. I know you believe this stuff somehow cured your asthma, but can't you see how weird that sounds? You don't just accidentally drink some contaminated water and, hey presto, a condition you've suffered from since birth miraculously goes away. Somebody needs to know about this.'

He shook his head. 'Not until we know what we're dealing with. Not until *I* know.'

'It's not your secret to hide.'

He turned away. It totally was. He'd found it. He'd had the balls to go down there and search for the source of that eery green glow, and he'd been the one who'd fallen into the pool and swallowed a mouthful of the stuff. He'd earned the right to keep it a secret, at least for a little while longer.

'Do what you want,' she said, 'but I want you to know I'm worried about it.'

'Your concerns are noted.'

She folded her arms and glared at him. 'Anyway, enough about what you got up to at the weekend. I need to talk to you about something else.' Her expression shifted. 'It's about my dad.'

He mentally kicked himself. 'Yeah, your dad, sorry. I've been meaning to ask. How is he?'

'Not good. He's dying. Maybe not in the near future, but this disease is incurable. It will kill him.'

'I know. Yeah, it's awful. I'm so sorry.'

'I can't handle it,' she said. 'I can't stay there.'

Paul swallowed a mouthful of black coffee, burning his tongue in the process. 'Okay, I understand that, totally. So, you need to move out?'

'I do. I really do.'

'Where are you, er—' he dabbed at his scalded mouth with a napkin. 'Where are you planning to go?'

She leaned across the table. 'I was sort of hoping that I could stay with you for a while.'

'But there's no room.' He winced, realising he'd answered way too quickly.

'What do you mean? In that flat? There's plenty of room. You're swimming around in there all by yourself.'

'But there's all my stuff, and you know, it's a long way from the pub. How would you even get to work?'

'It's two stops on the train. It's, like, a ten-minute journey.'

'Yeah, but then there's the cost of travel to consider. Train ticket prices have shot right up.'

'Jesus, Paul. Don't you want me to move in with you?'

'I didn't say that. I—' He tried to think of the right words. It wasn't that he didn't want Julie to move in with him eventually. He just wasn't ready to make that kind of life-changing commitment yet. They'd only been together for just over a year. 'You know I'd love it, Jules, but—'

'But you don't want me in your personal space. Is that what you're saying?' She stood and grabbed her bag.

'Well, I guess—'

'Thanks a bunch, Paul.' She tossed a napkin at him. 'It's good to know where I stand.'

'Jules, wait, I—' he tried to go after her, but he clumsily knocked his coffee cup on its side, spilling hot liquid all over the crotch of his jeans. 'Shit, shit. Oh, bloody hell.'

The phone in his pocket started to buzz, and he answered it, realizing Renee was video calling him.

'Paul,' she said, her face erupting onto the screen. 'I need to see you as soon as possible.'

'I'm sort of in the middle of something here.'

'Whatever it is, it can wait. This is important.'

He groaned, watching Julie depart into the distance. 'I think my girlfriend just broke up with me.'

'Oh, that's too bad. I liked the two of you together. Anyway,' she held a vial up to the screen. 'You're going to want to see this.'

Wednesday, 31st May:

University of Canterbury, Canterbury, Kent

Paul peered through the microscope, one eye open, the other squeezed tightly shut. 'Okay, so what am I looking at here?'

'There,' Renee said, leaning forward and twisting the dial. 'How about now?'

He waited for his eye to focus on the multitude of tiny polygonal, star-shaped cells, and was confused for a second. What appeared entirely yellow when viewed as a gelatinous liquid was actually a multitude of colours under intense magnification. The cells flickered and sparkled, creating a rainbow mosaic.

'They're stunning,' he said. 'I didn't expect that.'

'Neither did I.' She handed him a pipette filled with a light-brown liquid. 'Caught me off guard, too. Here, take this and place a couple of droplets onto the petri dish.'

He studied the slim tube. 'What is this? Dirty water?'

'Sort of, but not quite.'

'If this is a joke, I don't get it.'

She shrugged. 'Had a little accident late last night.'

'Gross,' Manny yelped from behind them, screwing up his nose. 'That's not what I think it is, is it?'

'No!' Renee's cheeks turned pink. 'Nothing like that, stupid. I knocked my espresso over. Spilled it all over the sample.'

'I don't understand,' Paul said. 'Are you telling me there's coffee in here?'

She nodded, grinning. 'You should have seen what happened. The cells became really agitated, crashing against each other, creating this really intense friction. Some of the cells conjoined, others literally disintegrated. The dish became hot, too. Like, really hot. I decided to pair back on the caffeine, see what happened. It took me quite a few attempts to get it right. There's barely any in there at all now, just the smallest amount. That's a 25 ml pipette you have in your hands, and there's only 0.42 ml of caffeine contained in the mix.'

'What makes up the rest?'

Renee held up her plastic bottle of Evian. 'Just good old mineral water.'

'Sounds pretty tame.'

'You won't say that when you see what happens.'

'I can't believe you've dragged me all this way to literally pour coffee all over our discovery.'

Renee folded her arms. 'You want to see what I've found, or what?'

Paul reluctantly stooped to the microscope and lowered the pipette to the dish. He squeezed gently on the rubber teat, causing a single droplet to emerge. It slipped soundlessly from the tiny hole and fell onto the sample tray. As the brown liquid came into contact with the star-shaped cells, they started to vibrate, slowly at first, but then increasing in velocity until they were literally fizzing around the shallow container.

'Woah.'

'Keep watching.'

'What's happening?' Manny asked, but Paul didn't reply. He was too busy watching the cells start to mutate and grow, becoming almost oval in shape, and then thinning out at the centre until the larger cell split into two single star-shaped cells, and then those individual cells grew and split in half, and those new cells did the same. Soon, there were tens of new cells, then fifty, a hundred. He pulled his head away and glared at the petri dish as liquid spilled over the top, spreading across the bench and dripping like honey onto the tiled floor.

'It's multiplying,' he said. 'And it's not diluting, either. It's…it's creating itself.'

Renee nodded. 'And it doesn't need a lot of activating liquid, either. Just one drop turns a few millilitres into a few litres, so imagine what a hundred litres of caffeinated water could do to it, a thousand.'

'You'd never run out,' he said, thinking about the possibilities. Ingesting just a small amount had cured his asthma. What if it could cure other things, incurable things? What if they had an endless, ever-multiplying supply? A thousand-and-one thoughts began to swirl around in his head. 'We need to run more tests. On live subjects this time. Can you do that?'

'Paul,' Manny said. 'What are you thinking here?'

'Just bear with me on this.'

Renee shook her head. 'There are rules about that sort of testing. Procedures. You of all people should know that.'

'Don't worry. I'll get the subjects. I can get them for you.'

Her mouth fell open. 'Paul! Are you asking me to conduct unsanctioned testing on human subjects? Really?'

'No, he's not,' Manny said, turning to Paul. 'Are you?'

'Don't you see?' Paul replied. 'We need to know what this stuff can really do.'

'And there's a strict protocol for that,' Renee fired back. 'You can't just jump straight to human trials. It's unethical.'

Paul bit his lip. She was right. He couldn't ask her to get involved.

'Okay,' he said. 'I'm sorry. I don't know what I was thinking. That was a stupid idea.'

Except it wasn't. It wasn't stupid at all. And he knew exactly who he could call.

Friday, 2nd June:

Sittingbourne, Kent

Manny arrived with the beers in a tatty Asda's bag-for-life that looked like it didn't have much life left in it. He'd promised his friend Wade a six-pack of Beavertown Neck Oil if he volunteered for what Paul described as a "clinical study". Wade was a school friend of Manny's from way back when they attended South Street Primary together. A good friend. When he was very young, Wade contracted a particularly bad case of mumps which severely affected his hearing and eyesight, leaving him almost completely deaf and as blind as a one-eyed bat. Manny had never heard him complain, however. Not once.

'Cheers,' Wade said as Manny handed him the cans. 'I'll sink one or two of those later on if you don't mind.'

'I don't mind at all,' Manny replied, patting Wade on the shoulder, making sure he could read his lips. He turned to Paul. 'You, er, got a minute?' he asked.

'Yeah,' Paul said. 'Of course.'

They stepped into the kitchen and Manny closed the door behind them.

'I don't know about this,' he said.

Paul shrugged. 'What's not to know?'

'Look, I know you think this stuff cured your asthma, and that's great, but—'

'But what?'

'We don't know what side effects there are yet. And Wade? Well, he hasn't been dealt the best hand in life, has he? He lives at home with his poorly mum, doesn't have a great job, and he can barely see or hear. What if…?'

Paul grabbed Manny by the shoulders. 'You mean, what if we cure his hearing loss so at least that part of him works properly? Or fix his eyesight? Is that what you mean? Because I can tell you something I do know, Manny. Employers don't exactly come looking for people with disabilities, even though they'll publish their taglines and statistics, telling everyone who will listen how diverse their workforce is. Can you imagine how hard it is to get a job when you can't answer the phone or look down at a document without seeing a jumbled picture of blurred lines? Can you? And what about getting someone to go on a date with you? You say that Wade has had it tough. Well, I agree with you. He has. He really has, but this stuff—' he held the little vial to Manny's face. 'This stuff just might be able to change that for him. Maybe it can make him better. Don't you think he wants that? Don't you think that's the first thing he thinks of when he wakes up in the morning, praying that his hearing has returned or that he somehow has perfect vision? He doesn't need that beer, just like he doesn't need you and I fussing over him. What he needs is a break, and maybe, just maybe, this stuff can give that to him.'

Manny stared at him, mulling it over. When Paul was in mid-flow, he was hard to say no to, and this was one of those times. He knew that even if they explained all the risks to Wade, he would take the chance regardless. Who wouldn't want to have their imperfections fixed, their disabilities erased?

'Okay,' he said. 'But if this goes south, Paul—'

'It won't.'

'But if it does—'

'Trust me.'

He watched as Paul opened the door and approached Wade,

the little vial of yellow liquid in one hand, a teaspoon in the other. 'Now, my old mate, here's the stuff we were talking about earlier. I promise, it doesn't taste as bad as it looks.' He ushered Wade to a chair and gestured for him to sit. He opened the vial and squeezed the contents onto the spoon. Wade looked up, eyes like saucers.

'Open up and say aah.'

Friday, 2nd June:

Ospringe Road, Faversham, Kent

Julie hadn't spoken to Paul in three days. She just couldn't bring herself to do it. Although he'd been a prick—nothing new there—she had kind of sprung the whole idea of moving in together on him. She hadn't picked the best moment either. His asthma had only just been cured. Had she made enough of that? Had she been as excited as he was, as over the moon? No. And why not? Because she'd been thinking of herself, as usual. What made it worse was she hadn't even been thinking about her dad, or even her mum for that matter. All she'd been obsessing over was how difficult it was to be at home with her sick father, a man who had done absolutely everything for her every single day of his life, until he'd got so sick he'd become unable to carry out even the simplest of tasks. She shouldn't be mad at Paul. She should be ashamed of herself.

'He's having one of his good days today, dear,' her mother said, handing her a hot cup of tea. 'He's eaten his dinner. He's even drunk his coffee. He hardly ever does that anymore.'

'That's great, mum.'

Her parents' house wasn't big. Far from it. It was a two-bedroom, mid-terrace property that had been built in the late nineteenth century. They'd only had gas-fired central heating installed when Julie was in her teens, and even so, the house still got terribly cold in the winter. Julie's father refused to move, even though both her parents had good jobs with decent pay, citing the ridiculous fees charged by 'those crooked estate agents and bloodsucking solicitors' as his primary objections. Julie didn't mind. She loved her bedroom. It had a quaint charm and held wonderful memories for her. She'd hated moving to London to study economics at the Imperial College, and she hadn't hesitated to come back home when she'd finished her three years there. Her friends said she was such a daddy's girl, and they were probably right. She'd had a happy childhood, after all, and she wasn't going to be shamed into hiding it.

'He's been asking for you, you know?'

She glared at her tea, the hot liquid swirling like a cyclone in her cup.

'He misses you, when he remembers.'

Julie gazed out the window, remembering how her dad used to play football with her in the garden, even though she'd always been awful at it. He never minded, didn't even complain about constantly hopping over to the house next door to recover the ball when she regularly booted it over the fence.

'He'll miss you when you're gone,' her mother continued. 'It won't be the same here without you.'

'I know Mum, but—'

'You don't have to go.'

'I can't stay here. I just can't.'

'I don't understand. Why not?'

Julie shook her head, unable to put her words together.

'Look,' her mother said, touching her hand. 'If you're dead set on going, at least say goodbye to him.'

'Mum,' Julie scoffed. 'I'm not leaving town. I'll be right around the corner.'

'Julie, please.'

She let out a sigh of resignation and placed her teacup on the coffee table, standing and smoothing herself down before trudging up the stairs. She knew she owed it to her mother to do as she asked. She was abandoning her, leaving her to pick up the shattered pieces of their little family. Every day, her mother attempted to glue the tiny fragments back together like a patchwork of broken China, only for her father to pick it up and smash it again. Break, mend and repeat. It wasn't his fault, it just wasn't, so why the hell did Julie always feel like it was?

'Hello Dad,' she said, entering the bedroom on feet like jelly. 'How are you feeling today?'

Her father was sitting in the upright chair by the window. His skin was grey, the flesh around his cheeks pulled tight across the bones. 'Ah, there you are,' he replied. 'Jill…er…Julie I mean. Oh, I can be such a thickhead at times.'

She smiled. It didn't matter. Her mum was right. He'd remembered. 'Mum said you've been eating well.'

'Have I? I guess I have. You know your mother. She's such a good cook. I always said that she should be on one of those television programs, the ones where all those daft people try to cook something posh for those two loud blokes. You know the one I mean?'

'I do, Dad,' she said, laughing. 'We used to watch it together, didn't we. The three of us.'

'Yes, that's right. You'd always guess which imbecile was going to be kicked off the show, and nine times out of ten, you were right.'

Julie felt tears blossoming in the corners of her eyes. She tried to hide them.

'I have something to tell you, Dad, if that's okay.'

He leaned across to her, took her hands. 'Of course it is, Julie. You can tell me anything. You know that, don't you?'

'Yeah, yeah, Dad. You've always listened to me.'

'Always,' he said, smiling. 'What have I always told you?'

A tear slipped onto her cheek. 'That that's what dads are good for. Ears for listening and—'

'—hands for fixing.' His skin was so cold, his bones fragile like glass. 'Go on, Julie. What was it you wanted to say?'

She took a breath. She could feel her heart in her throat like a thick ball of hair. 'I, er, I'm moving out for a while, Dad. Just to the other side of town. With Vicky. You know her, right? From work? She has a spare room, and it'll help her out with the rent. Her landlord's such a conman, so, you know, it's kind of a win-win.'

Her father's smile faded. 'But your mother. What about your mother?'

'What about her? She'll have you here with her. She won't be on her own.'

'Yes, she will. Of course she will.'

'I'll only be five minutes away.'

'Oh, and that's okay, is it?' His voice became coarse. 'Have you seen me lately, Jules? Have you seen what I'm becoming—what this damn disease is doing to me? You both think I don't know—that one minute I'm here and the next minute I'm somewhere else—but in reality, I'm here all the time, Jules, even when my mind is playing tricks on me, confusing me, telling me things that I know not to be true. I'm a liability, a burden to the both of you. That's why you're leaving, isn't it? That's why you're running away?'

'No, Dad, it's not that at all. I—' but she caught herself. Is this what she was going to do? Lie to her sick father? Was she really going to stoop that low? 'It's just hard, Dad. Seeing you like this. It's really hard.'

He took her hands in his. 'Don't you think I know that, love? But if it's hard when there's two of you, think what it will be like for your mother without you here?'

Julie felt her head sink into her shoulders. The tears came and she had absolutely no way of stopping them. Her dad being back with them in the present, as if nothing was wrong, was somehow making it harder, because she understood that it couldn't last.

'Whatever happens to me, Julie,' he said, stroking her hair. 'Always remember that I love you. Ever since that first moment in the hospital when the midwife gave you to me and I cradled you in my arms while you sucked on my knuckle. You gazed into my eyes as if I was the most magical, wondrous thing you'd ever seen. I knew then that whatever happened to us, whatever this life threw at the three of us, everything, every bloody moment, would be worth it.'

She looked into her dad's eyes, at the smile on his lips and the deep lines in his face, at the mischievous glint that was hardly ever there anymore. She wondered if she was making a mistake, a truly horrible error of judgement. This was her dad, the man she adored. She thought about calling Vicky and telling her she'd changed her mind, that her dad's condition wasn't as bad as she'd thought, but then, as if it had never really been there at all, the life seemed to drain from his face.

'Dad?'

'Who are you?' he said. 'What are you doing in my room? Where's Jerry?' Jerry was her dad's older brother. He'd been killed by the Argentine army in the Falkland's conflict. 'Jerry! They're here again, trying to steal our things. Get Dad, he'll sort them out. Jerry!'

'Dad?' Julie said, standing. 'It's me, Dad?'

'Piss off!' he yelled, spit flying from his lips. 'Piss off, the lot of you! Get out of our house! Get out! Get the hell out of here!'

Julie span round, her heart kicking her in the ribs. She saw her mother standing in the open doorway. 'It never lasts,' her mum said. 'However happy he is, it never lasts.'

Julie pushed past her and ran downstairs, grabbing her bag

from the hallway before stumbling out into the street. 'I'll call!' she yelled, but she barely believed her own words.

Saturday, 3rd June:

Queenborough, Isle of Sheppey, Kent

Paul supped his beer and pondered their situation. Manny stood at the bar, waiting to order their lunch. The Wade experiment had gone perfectly, almost too perfectly. So well, in fact, that Paul had absolutely no idea how they were going to keep everything under wraps, even though he'd got Manny's pal to sign a much more professional looking Non-Disclosure Agreement, something he'd robbed off the internet. Wade had even managed to sign the document without wearing his glasses because he now had 20:20 vision and perfect hearing. The effect had been almost instantaneous. The wonder, the pure, unsuppressed joy had spread across Wade's face like a sunrise. It was a heart-warming, head-thumping, gut-churning, slam-dunk of a moment; one that Paul would never forget.

They'd both sat with him and explained the likely side-effects. Paul told him how he often felt a little nauseous and sometimes a touch light-headed, but he found that drinking lots of water helped. He also explained that the benefits afforded by consuming merely a teaspoon of the yellow liquid lasted for around thirty-six hours, two days at the most, and so daily doses were needed. When Paul had initially realised that simple fact, he had been worried they would run out of the limited quantity they'd brought back from the cave, but his pal Renee's little discovery had completely solved that conundrum. They'd bought three chest freezers from Amazon and set them up in Paul's front room, immediately setting about reproducing stocks until the refrigeration units were almost completely full. Right now, Paul estimated they were sitting on eight hundred litres of the stuff. A dose was around five millilitres, so they had approximately 160,000 doses, enough to last both he and Wade up to 80,000 days each, or two hundred and nineteen years, give or take.

What they hadn't been able to ascertain yet was what other conditions the stuff could cure, which meant they needed to carry out wholesale studies, potentially on hundreds of live subjects. Paul couldn't ask Renee to risk her place at the university, but he was more than willing to risk his job. Why wouldn't he? He and Manny were sitting on a goldmine. All they needed was the right plan, the right resources, and just enough balls to get it ready for commercial release. People would pay a tidy sum to have perfect hearing and perfect eyesight for, like, forever. Their bright yellow goo would put Specsavers out of business in an instant.

'Do you think they'll go for it?' Manny asked, eyeing the white-bricked building that occupied a long stretch of Queenborough seafront.

'Not a chance,' Paul replied. 'But they won't need to know, will they?'

Manny sat down and handed Paul his cutlery. 'Fish and chips, mushy peas,' he said. 'That's what you wanted, right?'

Paul nodded, barely listening. 'I mean, I've got a badge, I have open access to the labs, and there's thousands of rodents in there. No-one's going to miss a couple of hundred.'

'I don't know about this,' Manny said. 'I don't like the idea of hurting innocent animals.'

'We won't.' Paul lowered his voice as a young couple took the table across from them. 'You've seen what this stuff has done for me, and how happy Wade was after he took it. If anything, we'll be helping the little fellas.'

'My mum's a veterinarian, Paulie. If she finds out we're

participating in live animal testing, she'll string me up. I'll never be allowed in the house again.'

'Then don't let her find out.'

Their lunch arrived and they ate in silence for several minutes. A song came on the jukebox, 'Hold Back The River' by James Bay. Paul found himself tapping his feet, relishing the distraction. He'd been thinking about Jules. He missed her. She hadn't called, but then again, neither had he. It had been such a stupid, ridiculous argument. He'd heard on the grapevine that she was moving in with her friend Vicky, and he wondered how her mum had taken the news. Not well, he guessed. He hoped Jules was okay. She loved her parents, which was something he'd always been a little envious of. His own mum and dad were useless. He felt like he was an inconvenience to them, but Julie's parents? They were the real deal. At least they gave a shit. He thought about her dad, Roger, and how sick he'd become. It was completely consuming Jules's life, causing her so much stress and anxiety. What if—

'Maybe we don't need the rats,' he muttered, almost choking on a mouthful of battered cod and ketchup.

'What's that?' Manny asked, devouring his burger.

'I said, maybe we don't need the rats. To do the testing, I mean.' The couple on the table across from them looked up, and Paul shot them a leering grin.

'I'm not following you, Paulie. I thought you just said—'

'I know what I just said, but I've had a better idea. An idea that could potentially help out someone in dire need and give our ambitions a big shot in the arm.'

He'd have to figure out how to broach the subject, but he thought she'd go for it, even if it only had a tiny chance of success. What did they have to lose? He was going to die anyway, and at least this way they could say they'd tried everything.

'Jules's dad,' he said through a mouthful of chips. 'We're going to cure Jules's dad.'

Sunday, 4th June:

Whitstable Road, Faversham, Kent.

'You're asking me to do what?'

Julie and Paul were sitting in the front room of the flat she now shared with Vicky. It was a tiny place, much smaller than she'd anticipated, and her stuff was haphazardly scattered across the little kitchen diner while she figured out where the hell she was going to put it all. She knew that Paul didn't think the place was big enough for her, but what did he care? He'd made his feelings about the two of them living together abundantly clear.

'I'm not asking you to do anything,' he replied. 'I'm just asking you to consider it.'

'Consider what? Consider giving some crap you and Manny found two hundred metres beneath the ground to my terminally ill father?' She couldn't believe him sometimes. He was so impetuous, so self-righteous, so bloody selfish.

'It works, Jules,' he said. 'Or at least it worked for me. And it worked for Wade, too. You can ask him if you want.'

'I don't know this Wade, Paul, and I don't care what you say, either. You've got no evidence this stuff is even safe, have you? For all you know, it could be doing you more harm than good. It could be killing you.'

'Do I look ill to you? Do I look even remotely unwell?' He pulled his inhaler from his pocket and pressed the refill capsule. 'It's empty. I haven't needed it at all since Black Spring. With just a tiny, daily dose of this stuff, I won't ever have to use these bloody things again.'

'You don't know that.'

'True, but so far so good, right?'

Julie stood. 'I think you need to leave. This isn't my place, and Vicky's due back any minute.'

'Oh, come on.' Paul grabbed her hands. 'What if it can cure him? Just, what if? Aren't you even curious?'

She was. Of course she was. She would do anything to bring her dad back from the edge of that black hole, but did that mean she should risk his health, his life, on some speculative, unvalidated theory? Was she willing to go that far? Was it even her decision to make?

'I won't put him at risk, Paul.'

'You won't have to. I'm living, breathing proof of that. You love him, Jules. He's always been your hero, I know that. I can never, ever get close to the pedestal you put him on, and I'm okay with that, but I can't watch you suffer like this. It's eating you up inside, and this…this stuff that we found? It might be able to fix all of that. It won't just cure your dad, it can heal you, too. And your mum. You can be you again. We can be—' he paused, 'we can be us again.'

Julie felt the tears starting to come. What was he doing to her? Was he manipulating her? Would he stoop that low? She didn't know the answer to those questions, which was a pity, but she did know that the picture he was painting was everything she wanted, everything she'd dreamed about. If only.

'Mum will need to make the decision,' she said. 'Not me.'

Paul nodded. 'I understand.'

The room fell silent, neither of them willing to make the next move. The gravity of what she was contemplating suddenly felt like the universe resting on her shoulders. She wanted to curl up in a little ball, pull the rug up over her head and sleep until she no longer felt tired. Just as she was about to crumple under the burden, the front door burst open.

'Hey guys.' It was Vicky, all blue hair and tattoos. 'Woah,' she said, dropping her shopping bags. 'Who died?'

Monday, 5th June:

Ospringe Road, Faversham, Kent

'Hey, Dad,' Julie said. 'I've brought someone to meet you. You remember Paul, right? And his friend, Manny?'

'Is it Jerry?' he asked. 'Where's Jerry?'

Julie's mother touched her arm. 'That's the only person he seems to remember, love,' she said. 'I have no idea why. Jerry's been dead for over forty years. From what I can recall, they didn't even get on particularly well. I can't get through to him. He's getting worse. Every day it's like he's moving further and further away.'

'Don't worry, Mrs Harbor,' Paul said. 'If this works, you could have your husband back to just the way he was in no time at all.'

'Paul!' Julie cried. 'We spoke about this!'

He held up his hands apologetically.

'Mum, there are no guarantees,' Julie offered. 'The chances are, this will do absolutely nothing at all, but like we both agreed, it's worth trying.'

'What have we got to lose?' her mother said. 'He wouldn't want to be like this.'

'Exactly,' Paul added, eyeing Manny. 'That's the right attitude, Mrs Harbor, and so far, the results have been very promising.' He held up his phone. 'Are you okay if we film the proceedings? Just for the benefit of our research, of course.'

'Yes. I guess that's fine.'

Paul handed his phone to Manny. 'Ready?' he asked.

Manny offered a curt nod.

'Okay, so the date is the 5th of June, and we are in Faversham, Kent, at the property of Roger and Barbara Harbor. Roger has been suffering from dementia, caused by Alzheimer's disease, for some months now, and due to a rapid deterioration in his condition, he is now at stage—'

'Five,' Julie said. 'He's at stage five, although we think he's quickly approaching stage six.'

'Okay, so shall we say stage five and a half?'

Julie shrugged. 'Does it really matter?'

Paul looked at Manny. 'What do you think?'

'Let's go stage five and a half,' Manny said. 'Sounds more accurate.'

'Okay,' Paul continued. 'So, Roger Harbor is currently suffering from stage five and a half dementia, and his condition is worsening day by day. In this controlled experiment, we will be witnessing the effects of administering a five-millilitre dose of a medicinal remedy we call—' he paused, 'Amrita.'

He shot Manny a knowing wink. His friend had come up with the name while they'd been sitting in the Silver Harp pub, supping on what must have been their sixth round of Spitfire real ale.

'You know,' Manny had said, his words a little slurred, 'this stuff reminds me of a story my dad used to tell me about Garuda.'

'Garuda?' Paul had replied. 'Sounds like a sexually transmitted disease.'

'No, stupid,' Manny scowled. 'Garuda is the name of a half-man, half-bird creature in the Hindu faith.'

'What? Like Superman?'

Manny shook his head, wiped beer froth from his upper lip. 'No, not really. More like a harpy, or one of the birdmen from Flash Gordon. Anyway, it doesn't matter. The point is, in the scriptures, the Nagas, or evil serpents, imprison Garuda's mother,

Vinata, and in order to get her back, Garuda has to bring them the nectar of immortality, a potion that is heavily guarded by a band of demons known as devas.'

'You've been reading too much Harry Potter, mate,' Paul scoffed. 'This all sounds a bit far-fetched to me.'

'Believe what you want,' Manny replied. 'But it's no more far-fetched than the parting of the Red Sea or an ark that can somehow rescue every creature on Earth from a global flood. My point is, this nectar of immortality, or Amrita as it was known, was said to give anybody who consumed it the gift of eternal life. That's kind of what we have here, isn't it, Paulie? Something that cures everything? If we're right, perhaps we can give that gift to people. The ability to live a very long, very healthy life.'

Paul thought the name was perfect. It was exactly the kind of thing they needed for the marketing concept he was beginning to visualise.

'We are filming this experiment so that we may accurately assess the positive effects or otherwise of the Amrita on Mr. Harbor's deteriorating condition,' he said, turning to his girlfriend. 'Jules, the Amrita, please.'

Julie pulled the vial from her coat pocket and handed it to him. 'It's a dumb name.'

'Okay, Mr. Harbor, I'd like you to take this medicine, if that's okay. It will make you better.' Paul poured the liquid onto a teaspoon.

'I don't want it,' Julie's father replied. 'Where's my brother? He said he'd make me a sandwich.'

Paul peered sympathetically into the camera. 'This is a clear example of Mr. Harbor's symptoms. In fact, our subject's brother was sadly killed during the 1982 Falkland's conflict, the events of which appear somewhat erased from Mr. Harbor's fragile memory.' He approached him again. 'Mr. Harbor, could I please ask—'

'I said, where's my sandwich?' Julie's father lunged at Paul, shoving him backwards. The spoon flew from his grip, spraying yellow liquid all over the walls and carpet.

'Bugger!' Paul cried, trying to regather the tumbling spoon.

'Wait,' Manny said. 'Mr. Harbor, I have something you can eat. I don't have a sandwich, but I have this.' He held out a bar of chocolate. 'I was saving it for later, but you can have it if you want.'

'Jerry!' Roger cried, reaching out. 'You came.'

Manny's eyes snapped to Julie, but she nodded for him to continue.

'Yep,' Manny said. 'Yep, it's me. Your brother, Jerry.'

'What took you so long, you silly sod? Mother's been looking all over for you. Dad's even walked down to the police station to see if you'd been arrested again.'

'Yeah,' Manny said. 'I know. I'll…I'll go and talk to them in a bit. Look, I brought this for you, brother. Do you want it?'

Paul watched as Julie's dad took the chocolate bar, peeled back the wrapper and took a large bite. He grinned as chocolate and wafer biscuit spilled from his grey lips. 'That's lovely, that is,' he said. 'Bloody delicious.'

Paul turned to Julie and held out a hand. She huffed and reluctantly withdrew a second vial from her pocket. He traded positions with Manny and took the camera phone from his hands, passing his friend the spoon and vial.

'Mr. Harbor,' Manny said. 'I mean…Roger. Mother has asked me to give you your medicine. Are you okay if I—'

'Of course,' Roger said. 'As long as you apologise to her for running off the way you did.'

'I will, I promise. Just as soon as you take this.' He poured the yellow liquid onto the spoon and held it out to him.

'Is it bitter?' Roger asked.

'A little, but it's okay. It's just a tiny spoonful. It'll be gone in no time, and then you'll be well again.'

Paul held his breath. The anticipation was hot in his stomach. At first, he didn't think Julie's dad was going to go for it, but then his expression shifted from suspicion to reluctant acceptance. Gradually, he opened his mouth. As he clamped his lips around the spoon, Paul heard Julie let out a tiny gasp.

'Whatever happens,' Julie's mother said. 'We can always say that we tried.'

Paul forced a smile, but in truth, he could no longer feel his legs.

'Ugh!' her father cried. 'It is bitter. You lied, Jerry!'

Julie eyed Paul anxiously, but he signalled for her to give it time. She took a glass of water from the side table and handed it to her father.

'Here you go, Dad,' she said. 'Wash it down with this.'

Her father looked up at her, something missing in his vacant stare, and then took the glass, glugging it down as if he were thirstier than he'd ever been in his whole life. Within no time at all, the water was gone.

'How are you feeling now?' Julie asked, crouching on the floor.

There was water dribbling down her father's chin, a look of dejection in his eyes. His skin was just as grey as before, his cheeks as sallow, his body as frail. Paul heard Julie's mother crying somewhere behind him, could see the disappointment in Julie's face. Her dad really was too far gone, however hard that was for anyone to accept. Apparently, not even the Amrita could save him.

'What are you doing down there on the floor, Julie?' Roger asked. 'You look like a ragamuffin. Barbara, tell her what she looks like, will you?'

There was a tiny cry from Julie's mum as Paul grabbed the back of the chair to steady himself.

'I think it worked,' he whispered in disbelief.

'What worked?' her father replied. 'And what the bloody hell are you all doing in our bedroom? I mean, just look at the state of me.' He covered himself with a blanket and headed to the bathroom. 'At the very least, let me take a shower.'

They all stared at each other in silence, wondering what had just happened. Paul was the first to move, flipping the phone camera to selfie mode and throwing his arm around Julie's shoulders.

'Looks like the experiment was a resounding success,' he said. 'A bloody fantastic success!'

Tuesday, 6th June:

Matax Pharmaceuticals, Queenborough, The Isle of Sheppey, Kent

Paul stood outside his boss's office, wondering what he was going to say.

'Hey, Dean. Have I got an idea for you?'

'What's up, Deano. You'll never guess what I did at the weekend?'

'Morning boss, did you hear that one about the flying birdman from India?'

He shook his head. It all sounded ridiculous, which he knew was exactly what it was. The fact of the matter, however, was that it was all true. For one, he could now breathe normally; for two, Manny's friend Wade had perfect vision and hearing; and, for three, the dementia that had been crippling Julie's dad for so long had simply disappeared. It was the kind of cure the drug companies would kill for.

'Morning, Paul,' his co-worker, Sandra said, emerging from the kitchen with a fresh cup of tea. 'How was your holiday? I see you managed to avoid hurting yourself like last time.'

He smiled. 'Thank God. I don't think I could stand the humiliation twice.'

She winked and passed him by. He shuffled his feet. He knew he couldn't just stand there like a lummox all day. He tried to summon his usual bravado, but for some reason, he didn't feel like he had any in the tank.

He glanced at the office wall. The company, Matax

Pharmaceuticals, was renowned for its world-beating designs of drugs that helped people with disabling conditions: multiple sclerosis, arthritis, fibromyalgia; the kind of afflictions that put people in wheelchairs. There were long lines of patent certificates hanging on the partition, each with a summarized description of the invention the company had protected. Some were older than twenty years and had therefore expired, but most of them were still alive and kicking. That meant that once Matax had passed their fully tested and certified design to a drug manufacturer, and that drug was then sold to the mass market, the board of directors simply sat back and waited for the royalty cheques to come in. Paul knew those cheques could amount to millions, even hundreds of millions. The Amrita could cure all those conditions, and at close to zero cost, too. Once their secret came out, the drug companies wouldn't know how to deal with it. It would shake the pharmaceutical industry to its very foundations.

That's when it struck him. Their little secret. He couldn't believe he had almost made the most stupendously idiotic mistake of his life, and one that could have cost him a sizeable fortune.

He held his phone to the wall and took a photo, firing the picture off to Manny. An answer came back almost immediately. *Why are you sending me a picture of a bunch of frames?*

Paul quicky replied. *It's not the frames, idiot. It's what's in them.*

There was a moment's pause, and then his phone pinged again. *Do you even know how to get one of those?*

No, Paul didn't. But his uncle did.

Wednesday, 7th June:
Temple, London

Paul and Manny sat on the couch, their hands tucked between their legs, looking like a couple of kids waiting outside the headmaster's office. Paul's Uncle Barnaby had always had that effect on the pair of them. It was something about the way he dressed: tweed suit, cotton shirt and a paisley bowtie, although his tall, wiry frame, white hair and long beard made him look a little closer to a wizard. Barnaby Karin was a well-respected lawyer in the city and had represented some of the UK's largest corporations in multi-million-pound cases. He was approaching retirement age now, but Paul's envious dad had always declared to anyone that would listen that his brother Barnaby would work until they plucked the smouldering pipe from his cold, dead lips. Rumours abound that he played free and loose with the law at times in order to successfully defend his clients, many of whom were less than saintly, but his legal mind had outwitted the best prosecuting lawyers in the country, as well as a long list of well-respected judges. It was only his reputation as a bit of a cantankerous rogue that had prevented him from making it onto the King's honours list, and had definitely blocked his accession to the House of Lords.

'How's that brother of mine?' Uncle Barnaby asked. 'Is he still playing with trains?'

Paul nodded. 'He still works for the railway, yeah.'

'And your mother?'

'She still works with him, even though they're separated. It's their company now. They do private contracting for Southeastern Railway, mainly.'

'And that's working out for them, is it?'

Paul shrugged. 'Wouldn't know. I don't see them that often.'

'So, nothing's changed then?'

Paul shook his head. No, nothing had changed.

His uncle switched subjects. He had always been good at sensing the mood of a room. It was one of the things that made him such a good barrister. 'So, tell me about this invention of yours.'

'It's not an invention as such. More like a new discovery.'

'And you don't know the chemical composition, you say?' He paced the room.

'I would say it's more like a...natural ingredient.'

'A new natural ingredient,' Manny added. 'One that's never been seen before.'

'So, it's a scientific discovery,' Uncle Barnaby offered, continuing to pace. 'Difficult to patent something like that, not without claiming it has a particularly novel use. Although, even then, you can't patent an ingredient that is therapeutical in nature. The Europeans really don't like that. Tell me, is this material mineral or biotic?'

Manny shrugged and glanced at Paul.

'He's asking if it comes from a living organism,' Paul said. 'Yes. Yes, it does.'

'What kind of organism?'

Manny shrugged again.

'A fresh-water animal,' Paul replied, recalling the dark water, the enormous, alien creature, its plasticised, metallic skin. 'We don't know what, exactly. It was dark, and it got away before we had time to—'

'So, there's a chance that someone else has encountered this organism before?'

'I…I don't know.'

Uncle Barnaby tapped the contents of his pipe into an ashtray and filled the bowl with thick strands of dark-brown tobacco. The scent was so familiar to Paul, like the dense odour of a musty room, or the smell of a good curry house. 'But there's a chance. You can't rule it out.'

'It's possible,' Manny replied, catching a glimpse of Paul's expression. 'Well, it is, isn't it? We can't be the only people to have ventured that far into the cave network.'

Uncle Barnaby lit the tobacco and sucked furiously, blowing little clouds of yellow smoke. 'This is all a little irregular,' he said, 'and, therefore, my advice will be speculative at best.'

'Speculative's good,' Paul said. 'Speculative's great, actually.'

'Well, then I would say your best bet here is to play with the rules a little.' He sat in his leather chair and blew another billowing cloud. 'If you truly are the only people in the whole world who have this material in their possession, then I suggest you keep the location of your store secret. Guard it like you might guard an item of fine jewellery or a family heirloom. If anybody else obtains this…ingredient, then they will be able to do with it as they please, just as you might do the same. However, if you claim—and prove with some degree of certainty, I might add—that mixing this material with some other substance in a unique and novel way creates something that nobody else has, then perhaps you can patent that formulation or method, thereby protecting you from another party or parties coming along and stealing the whole bloody thing from underneath your noses.'

Manny's eyes narrowed. 'But we just add water and a little caffeine to make more of it.'

Uncle Barnaby smiled. 'And there you have it,' he said. 'Just write that down, young man. Embellish it somewhat, be creative, tell a few white lies if you like, and then when you're ready, come back and see me.'

Monday, 12th June:
Sittingbourne, Kent

Paul woke at around four that morning. He had a lingering feeling of dread that was twisting his gut into a hard knot. The sensation had wrested him from his dreams. He glanced at Julie, who was sleeping peacefully beside him, and pulled back the covers. He wondered if he was just thirsty. He'd had a lot of salt with his dinner.

He shuffled like a zombie into the kitchen and grabbed a glass from the counter. It was still dark, but he could just make out the layout of the room: the breakfast bar up ahead, the kitchen cupboards to his right, the sink beneath the window. He made his way across the linoleum, its smooth surface cool beneath his feet, and turned the tap on full while he waited for the water to run cold. He filled the glass, glugged it down in one go, re-filled it, and then drank some more. His throat really was as dry as brick dust.

There was a clattering sound from behind him and he turned to face it. A tall shadow loomed in front of the door to the living room. It was thin with long, branch-like arms and sinewy legs. A layer of fine, wispy hair covered what seemed to be its body. As it shuffled forwards, Paul's breath caught in his throat. He took a step backwards, bashing clumsily into the corner of the worktop.

'How did you find me?' he asked, his voice listless. The shadow approached, its lythe presence looming over him, long, hooked talons covering the length of its limbs. Paul tried to turn and run but he was frozen to the spot, as if someone had nailed his feet to the floor. He tried to cry out, to warn Jules, to tell her to get out of there as fast as she could, but all that came out was a wheezing rasp. The thing closed the distance between them in one swift motion, and Paul knew it was going to make him pay for what he did. For what he and Manny did. He recoiled, holding his hands in front of his face, shielding his eyes, but then the shadow-creature's fingers began to come apart, and its arms blurred, disintegrating like ash. As its legs frittered away, its body seemed to become thin and translucent, and within an instant, it split and fractured into tiny pieces, drifting into the air like coal dust.

Paul set down the glass and bent over, his hands on his knees. He drew in a bunch of deep breaths, expecting the light-headedness to come, the tightening of his windpipe, the vicelike, suffocating grip that only his inhaler could alleviate, but it never did. He shook his head and bit down on his bottom lip. He had to get a grip. He fought to gradually piece back together his grasp of reality.

What the hell was wrong with him? Everything was going well, wasn't it? Jules's dad was his old self once more, his own asthma had been wholly and entirely cured as far as he was concerned, and the patent application had been drafted. He had to focus on that. He had to dwell on the positives. There were so many of them. He and Manny were going to be rich beyond their wildest dreams. Hell, they were probably going to be famous, too. Insanely famous. No more working long hours for crap money, no more eking out every pound of his meagre food budget just to make sure he could afford his rent at the end of the month, and no more rainy holidays at rubbish, rundown caravan parks on the coast. No way. He was done with all of that. By the end of the year, he and Jules would be bathing in the sunshine on a beach in some tropical location, listening to the exhilarating sound of money pouring like rain into an offshore account.

The incident in the cave, that horrible, lung bursting experience, was just a distant memory now, an inkblot on an otherwise perfectly white canvas. Nothing was coming for him. No creature from an underground lagoon, no bloodthirsty horde of inhuman creatures. They'd repelled the monster that had crept out of that tunnel, and they'd blocked the entrance with as many rocks as they could lay their hands on. It couldn't get out, and even if it did, it would never find them. Nothing, and nobody, was ever going to take away what they had. This was his future now, his fate, and he planned to grasp it with both hands.

Friday, 16th June:
Sittingbourne, Kent

Manny pulled the van into the car park of the playing fields and pitched his cigarette. Paul reached into the bag Manny's mum had given them and dished out the food—four large vegetable samosas, two aloo tikka chaat patties, four chicken pakoras and two cans of Coke.

'Cheers,' Manny said, taking a bite from a piping hot patty. 'I've been looking forward to this all morning.'

'It never ceases to amaze me, you know?' Paul said, eyeing his pal's bulging waistline.

'What's that?'

'How much you can put inside you. You're practically a food warehouse, mate.'

Manny grinned and gulped a mouthful of cola. 'What can I say? I'm a Sikh. We like to eat.' He looked out over the playing fields. 'I've been meaning to ask. This Amrita,' he held up his half-smoked pack of Lambert and Butler's. 'You think it could help me quit smoking?'

Paul shrugged. 'Who could say? Let's face it, we don't really know the true extent of what it can do, but one thing's for certain, we need to find out.'

Manny took another bite before grabbing a napkin and wiping oil from his chin. 'How do we go about doing that? Without trying it on everyone we know, I mean?'

'Well, as it happens, I've been thinking about that. Firstly, we need to protect what we've got. Uncle Barnaby will file the patent document with the International Patent Office. That's going to cost us a few hundred quid.'

'Which we don't have,' Manny said.

'No, but he said he'll sub us the money. Then, once it's in, we publicly declare our invention as patent pending. Once that's done, we can stop worrying about people stealing what we have, and we can take it to the big boys.'

'Such as?'

Paul scrolled through his phone and pulled up a picture he'd saved. It showed a gleaming, twenty storey building in the middle of a bustling city. He shot Manny a toothy grin. 'Go big, or go home, my friend.'

'That's Harker's Pharmaceutical!' Manny said, half-choking on a samosa. 'They're massive.'

'Exactly.'

'We'll be way out of our depth. People get eaten alive in there.'

'Rubbish. Don't forget, we have the upper hand here. Our drug is so good, it can cure the uncurable.'

'They'll rip us off.'

'We won't let them.'

'They'll do it anyway.'

Paul clenched his teeth and waited for his idea to sink in. He knew his friend would take some convincing, but that was okay. Paul had always been the ideas guy in their relationship, the blue-sky thinker. When he'd come up with the plan to sell counterfeit Ring doorbells to the nearby council estate, Manny had practically hyperventilated. He was the sceptic in their little duo, the conscience. They balanced each other out.

'We have to think about the immediate term,' Manny said.

'What do you mean?'

'Well, we need to find a better storage location than your front room, for a start.'

Paul had to agree. He knew it wouldn't take much for some random hooligan to break into his flat, open the chest freezers and steal their stock. Without the Amrita, they were dead in the water. Any debate about what to do next was pointless if they had nothing to sell.

'I've been thinking about that, too' he said. 'Storage Explosion. You know the place?'

Manny raised an eyebrow.

'I called the bloke yesterday, and he said he could offer us a hundred square-foot room for only two-fifty a month.'

'Two-fifty? Paul, I don't have that kind of money.'

'No, neither do I, but—'

'I know, I know. Your Uncle Barnaby does.' Manny glared out the window. 'I don't know about this. I mean, I realise he's your uncle and everything, and he's been good to us, but isn't he going to want something in return? His money back, at least?'

'Maybe, but if this stuff is really as good as we think it is, there'll be more than enough to go round.' Paul tried to suppress his excitement. He was finding it increasingly difficult to contain himself. If he was right about what they had—or, even if he was only half-right—he and Manny would literally be rolling in an ocean of banknotes before the year was out.

Manny set his pakora down on the dashboard. 'Do you ever think about—'

'What?'

'That thing.'

'Nope,' Paul lied. 'Never. Why would I?'

'I still wonder whether we should tell someone.'

'And say what? That I fell into a pool of dirty water and got squirted by a giant alien creature? Give me a break, Manny. We'd get ridiculed in the street.'

'I don't mean that. Well, I guess I do, but not just that. The thing that attacked us, Paul. That weird…animal thing. What if there's more of them?'

'But there wasn't.'

'I know we didn't see any, but what if they were down there? In that tunnel? We don't even know where that thing led. It could literally come out anywhere in those hills. People go caving in Black Spring all the time. What if the cavers get attacked, and then the authorities find out we knew about what was down there all along? What if people die?'

Paul grabbed him. 'Look mate. We killed it, didn't we? We wounded it, at least, and we blocked the entrance, too. We took care of it.' He crumpled the bag and threw it in the back of the van. 'Nobody needs to know anything about what we saw. All they need to care about is what we found, and what it can do.'

He could see Manny was less than convinced, but he didn't care. Someone in their little endeavour had to have the balls to take it to the next level, and he already knew exactly how to do it. His uncle had filled him in during a midnight phone call. As it turned out, there were people out there with the ways, the means and the resources to set certain things up without having to go through all the red tape and stifling bureaucracy. It cost money of course, and you needed the right introduction, but that was exactly the kind of thing his uncle was good at. Making connections.

The guy Uncle Barnaby had recommended was a Scandinavian entrepreneur called Petra Gunderson, and apparently, the trial—the clinical trial, no less—could start as early as the end of the month. Once they had the certificate in their hands, the meeting with Harker's would be a walk in the park. The only snag was, in order to kick the whole thing off, they had to go to Norway.

Wednesday, 14th June:

Temple, London

Barnaby Karin sat back in his chair and stuffed tobacco into the bowl of his pipe. His phone was pressed between his ear and the crook of his neck. It rang for thirty seconds or more before the intended recipient picked up.

'Petra, it's me, Barnaby Karin…yes, I'm fine, thank you for asking. Look, I wouldn't normally call so late, but I've just been given something you might be interested in.'

He had no idea if his Gatling gun of a nephew's find had any merit, but both he and his Indian friend had seemed convinced enough. It was hardly proof, but it was enough to pique his interest. He'd been in the business long enough to know that when a gift horse trotted into the office, only a fool would turn it away. Something as world beating as a cure for the incurable was a thoroughbred of an idea, even if it turned out it was only ten percent of what his nephew claimed it to be. If nothing else, it was worth a wager.

He had known who to call almost as soon as he'd learned the full extent of what the find was. Barnaby and the Norwegian entrepreneur had been friends for a long time, long before he had helped Petra set up the little enterprise in the mountains. Because of that, he maintained a finder's fee, one which had kept both he and his wife, Angela, in the lifestyle they were accustomed to.

With the meeting agreed, he placed the phone back in its cradle and slowly drew the tobacco into his lungs. He let it swirl inside him for a few moments before exhaling.

If everything worked out the way he hoped, he could retire, and then he and Angela could head off into the sunset, maybe build a house somewhere on a distant shore, miles away from his idiot of a brother and his equally small-minded offspring. Did he feel bad about luring his nephew into a deal with someone as cut-throat as his business associate? No, not really. Paul had always been the runt of the litter, and runts were only good for one thing. Feeding to the pigs.

Wednesday, 21st June:

Ospringe Road, Faversham, Kent

Julie watched her father mow the lawn and then stoop to tug little strands of bindweed from the flowerbeds. He was singing some old pop tune to himself, unaware that she'd brought him out a cup of tea, blissfully ignorant of how magical just watching him do the gardening was for her. She still couldn't get over what had happened. One minute he was almost gone, completely on the verge of being lost to them forever. The next, he was out there in the sunshine, moving sprightly around the garden like a man half his age, as alert as he'd ever been. She'd been wondering what the catch was, what sort of awful problem would bite them on the backside, but so far there just hadn't been one. It had worked. Completely and utterly.

Keeping the secret from her parents had been hard. Of course they had questions. Where did Paul get this stuff? What was it made from? Was it even legal? Were there likely to be any side-effects? Why wouldn't Paul accept any money for it? Surely, it had to cost something.

Julie had fielded them as best she could, using the pre-planned lie that she'd agreed with her boyfriend—the drug was a ground-breaking, experimental treatment that had been created by the company Paul worked for, Matax Pharmaceuticals, and his bosses had agreed, after some persistent pressure from him, to allow her dad onto the clinical study phase as long as his next of kin signed a waiver, absolving them of any liability (a document that Julie had drafted on the home computer and that her mother had dutifully signed). It was a perfectly convincing story, and one which her parents had accepted without question, but Julie knew that as soon as their extended friends and family network started asking, or perish the thought, her father's GP got involved, then the whole thing would unravel pretty quickly. That was why they needed to move at pace to get the Amrita certified, which was difficult given the suspicious nature of it. She didn't like Paul's idea of heading to Norway to meet up with some crooked medical certification agency, but what choice did they have? No reputable drugs company was going to touch a chemical of unknown origin unless they had a compelling body of evidence. Regardless, Julie had to know what was going on. She needed to find out if her dad really was taking any risks, if they were all just sitting on a ticking timebomb.

Paul wasn't helping with her anxiety. He'd been keeping something from her ever since he returned from Black Spring. She knew him too well for it to go unnoticed. It was the little things, like the way he gave her the side eye as if he was constantly suspicious of what she was thinking. He wasn't sleeping well either, which was always a tell-tale sign with him. She could hear him yelling in the middle of the night, telling someone to leave him alone and then screaming at Manny to 'shut it in, shut it in!' Something had happened down there, that much was obvious, and the thought of it made her want to be sick.

'What you doing, love?' her mother asked, catching her off guard.

'Just watching him,' she replied. 'He looks so well. I keep wondering if it's all too good to be true.'

Barbara Harbor sat down on the patio chair. 'Something I've learned, Julie, is to take the wins when you can, and accept them for what they are. This time last week you didn't have a father, not one who knew who you were. Now look at him. He's a new man, the man I married, and if that lasts for ten minutes or ten years, so what? It's time that we didn't have, and time I plan to cherish. You should, too.'

Julie smiled. Her mum was right. This was a lottery win. She knew she shouldn't question it, but she just couldn't help herself.

'Will you be okay with him? When I go, I mean?'

Her mother nodded. 'You're only a phone call away.'

'It's just the weekend. I should be back on Monday.'

'Take all the time you need, love. You deserve it.'

Julie was planning to. Paul and Manny were leaving for Norway that Friday morning. As soon as they were gone, she was going to get into her car and head west. She'd already hired the gear and gleaned as much knowledge as she could via You Tube videos. She was as ready as she would ever be. Black Spring was beckoning.

Friday, 23rd June:
Oslo Lufthavn Airport, Norway

The flight from London Gatwick to Oslo was uneventful, with the exception of Manny's snoring and the awful quality of the brown swill the airline company called coffee. They collected their luggage and entered the arrivals lounge on the stroke of 1 pm.

'Do we have any idea what this guy looks like?' Manny asked.

Paul shook his head. 'I don't think he's too keen on having his face plastered all over the internet. The most I could get on him was that he made his money on the crypto currency exchange before investing in a property portfolio and backing a few successful startups.'

'I don't like the secrecy. People with secrets are usually up to something.'

'Oh, relax,' Paul said, peering along the long line of waiting taxi drivers and chauffeurs that stood patiently at the concourse. 'Uncle Barnaby says this guy comes with a solid reputation, and that's good enough for me.'

As they approached the end of the queue, a tall woman with a narrow face and long blond hair approached them. She wore a charcoal grey suit and a red scarf, and was holding a clipboard with their names printed in large capital letters.

'See,' Paul said. 'This guy's got class. No grimy, old-bloke chauffeur for us.'

'You're not kidding,' Manny replied.

'You must be Paul,' the lady said. 'And you're Manmeet, I presume.'

Manny held out his hand. 'You can call me Manny. Only the Granthi calls me Manmeet.'

The lady smirked. 'Then Manny it is. You can call me Marla.'

They each shook hands. Paul was surprised to find the woman had a strong grip.

'Welcome to Norway,' she continued. 'We have quite a drive to the facility, so I took the liberty of buying you both coffee and pastries. I assume you like coffee?'

Paul nodded and nudged Manny.

'Good. Well, they're in the back of the car, so if you'd like to follow me, it's right this way.'

The vehicle that Petra had sent was a brand new, metallic red, S model Tesla. As they collapsed onto its black leather seats, Manny turned to Paul. 'Whew. This car's easily a hundred grand, right? The guy must have some serious wedge.'

'I told you,' Paul said. 'We're in good hands. Hopefully, now you'll be able to chill.'

'You ready?' Marla asked, eyeing them in the rear-view mirror.

Paul took a bite from a sticky Danish pastry and grinned. 'As ready as we'll ever be.'

Friday, 23rd June:

Milton Creek, Sittingbourne, Kent

Wade was drunk. Blind drunk, barely able to walk drunk, constantly in fear of regurgitating his lamb bhuna drunk. He was so happy. So deliriously overjoyed. He'd been partying pretty much solidly since Manny and his friend had given him the vial of magical, yellow liquid, and now all he could think about was how much time he had lost, and how much living he needed to do to make up for it. The day after he'd been fixed—because being fixed was how he thought of that unbelievable moment—he'd decided to go clothes shopping and had revamped his wardrobe in one ridiculously expensive afternoon. Gone were the tracksuit bottoms and Primark T-Shirts. In came the River Island jeans and Hollister, slim-cut polos. He had a pretty good body after all—he wasn't overweight, and he was quite tall—so now that everything else about him was functioning properly, he intended to show off what God had blessed him with.

That night he'd gone to his local, The Railway Arms, sunk around eight pints of Stellar, and headed off to a nightclub—Toxicity—where he'd somehow managed to pull a pretty brunette. When he'd woken up, hungover and in a strange bed in a flat he didn't recognise, he knew it couldn't have all been a dream after all. It really was happening. His fortunes had changed for the better, and it was all because of the Amrita and his pal Manny. He and Paul Karin were saints, angels, bloody gods. They'd changed everything for him, turned his whole life on its head. He just couldn't believe how lucky he was to have been chosen like that. Everything had been so hazy since that afternoon. It had all been a mad blur of a rollercoaster ride.

'Tell us more about this drug you've been taking, Wade,' a little bloke called Ted said to him. Ted was a nice fella. He'd introduced Wade to cocaine, and cocaine was fantastic. It made his nose sting and his brain jump.

'I tole you already,' he replied, feeling the effects of the vodka. 'It made me see again. Made me hear again, too.'

'Yeah, yeah. I know you told us that,' Ted continued. 'And that's great. But you haven't told me where you got it from.'

Wade held a finger to his lips. 'Itsh a shecret,' he said. 'I shigned a piesh of paper.'

They were at a private party at a rundown house located in what had once been a residential neighbourhood by the creek. Now the place just sat on its own, waiting to be demolished by the council in favour of what they were optimistically marketing as riverside apartments, another project to fulfil a misguided government quota. The whole building was covered in bindweed and ivy, and the rotten-egg stench of brown, sludgy water was overpowering, particularly when the weather was hot. The houses either side had already succumbed to the wrecking ball.

Ted had invited Wade back to the house while they were both downing sambucas. Sensing an opportunity to further his ambitions with the opposite sex, he had agreed. However, as soon as they'd arrived, he'd been dismayed to learn that the other party goers were mainly big, muscle-bound blokes with ultra-short haircuts and pissed-off expressions. The only thing that had convinced him to stay was the fact that the music was loud and the drugs were free.

Ted rounded the sofa and slumped next to him, a tumbler of vodka-on-ice in each hand. 'Look, Wade old mate. It's just that I told a couple of these blokes that you were the guy to talk to about this…Amrita, wasn't it?' He handed him his drink.

Wade took the glass, sipped the cold, sharp liquid and cringed. Had he really told Ted the name of the drug? He was pretty sure he wasn't allowed to do that. 'Uh-huh,' he replied.

'Well?'

'Well what?'

'Are you the guy to talk to? Only, I don't really want to be embarrassed in front of my friends. You wouldn't want that, would you, Wade?'

Wade nodded slowly, because too much movement made him feel sick. He didn't like the way that Ted was talking to him. Sure, the guy was shorter than he was, perhaps a little younger, but he was stocky, and he talked fast, which in Wade's experience usually meant he could handle himself. In any case, Wade didn't want to fight Ted. He liked him.

'Good, good,' Ted continued, gesturing to one of the big blokes. 'This here is Rami, and Rami's mother is really poorly. Like, really ill and stuff.' Rami perched on a stool beside them. 'And all he wants to know, for the sake of his terribly sick mother you see, is how quickly you can get him some of this Amrita and what the cost of it is per litre. He wants to buy in bulk. For his sick mum. That's right, Rami, isn't it?'

Rami nodded. He had a face that looked as though it had been hit by a truck, and a neck that resembled a concrete pillar. Wade knew that the Amrita wasn't for Rami's mother, sick or otherwise. He didn't look like the mother-caring type, and Ted suggesting they wanted to buy it in volume was a signal that he had more of a commercial proposition in mind.

'I—' Wade waited for the room to stop spinning and considered his words carefully. 'I guess I could have a word with my ashoshiates.'

Ted slapped him on the back. 'That's the spirit, mate. I told

Rami I could rely on you, didn't I Rami?'

Rami nodded again before reaching into his ridiculously tight jeans and pulling out a large bundle of twenty-pound notes.

'Here's a little sweetener,' Ted said. 'Just to show you what good friends we all are.'

Rami plucked out five notes from the bundle and handed them to Wade.

'And we are good friends, Wade, aren't we?' Ted asked, pulling him in close, so close their noses almost touched. There was the stench of marijuana and vodka on his breath. 'Because we're the type of friends you need to keep on your side, my old son.'

Friday, 23rd June:
Penwyllt, Ogof Ffynnon Ddu National Nature Reserve, Wales

Julie arrived at her hotel in the middle of the afternoon. She was staying at a little three-bedroom B and B, just over a mile away from the uppermost entrance to the Black Spring cave network. She'd recalled what Paul had said to her shortly after he'd returned from his trip.

'We were in the Great Oxbow section of the caves, but decided to be a little adventurous and took the right-hand tributary, just before you reach Marble Showers.'

Julie hadn't known what any of those words meant, but she'd scrawled them down and looked them up on the internet. The jumbled mess of tunnels that sprang to life on her laptop looked like someone had taken a big pile of cooked spaghetti and dumped it onto her screen. She thought she was never going to be able to navigate her way through the complex, mind-boggling maze. She was completely inexperienced, mildly claustrophobic, and totally afraid of the dark, which weren't exactly the ideal ingredients for a successful caving expedition. However, she was determined to know the source of the Amrita. She needed to know for her dad—she felt she owed it to him—and despite initially planning to go it alone, she'd accepted her own limitations and decided, somewhat reluctantly, to invite someone along who knew exactly what they were doing.

'I can't wait to get down there,' her cousin, Ellie, said, grinning like a kid with a brand-new Xbox. 'I've never been to the OFD before, but I've heard great things about it.'

Julie shook her head. 'The OFD? What's that when it's at home?'

'Oh Jules,' Ellie replied. 'You really don't know anything about caving at all, do you? It stands for Ogof Ffynnon Ddu, which is Welsh for The Cave of the Black Spring.'

Julie smiled and sipped her wine. She and Ellie were sharing a bottle of Malbec. Her cousin was diminutive in height, topping out at four feet, ten inches, but she had the physique of a trained athlete and the sort of smile that seemed to make everything feel okay. She was a little older than Julie at thirty-two, but she was as fit as a fiddle, and what's more, she'd been potholing with her dad since she was five or six. Julie felt bad about not telling her cousin the truth about the purpose of their expedition, but she didn't see the point in widening the net of confidentiality until she knew exactly what they were facing.

'Well,' Ellie said. 'I for one am going to take a shower and make the most of a double bed, all to myself. We have an early start tomorrow.' She leapt up, grabbing her cousin by the arms. 'An evening without two kids hogging the duvet. I can't wait.'

Friday, 23rd June:
Spiterstulen, Norway

The drive was long and the road seemed to stretch out for hundreds of miles, reaching into the distance like a long, grey tongue. With Manny snoring beside him with crumbs from his demolished pastry scattered over his chest and heaving stomach, Paul had some time to think about their imminent meeting.

Petra was as mysterious as his reputation. There was almost nothing about him on the internet, and what Paul had managed to find out suggested the man's background was more than a little unsavoury. He had lied to Manny about how Petra had earned his wealth. It hadn't been through crypto currency or property investments at all, and for all he knew, the guy didn't own any start-up companies, either. However, he did apparently possess an expansive portfolio of exclusive leisure complexes, most of which were rumoured to be inhabited on a semi-permanent basis by many of the world's most dangerous criminal elite. Snippets of news reports alleged that The Elysian Field resorts were located in top-secret locations scattered around the globe, but that the headquarters lay some distance north of Oslo, Petra's hometown. There were stories about the place. Some suggested it was a large complex near Lake Mjosa, while others said it was a modest little shack much closer to Geiranger Fjord. Paul's guess was that the resort was located somewhere much more remote, in a place that was far more difficult to reach.

As if to prove his point, the car rounded a long, sweeping bend, and a huge, snow-capped mountain range loomed up ahead.

The sight took Paul's breath away. He'd never seen anything like it before. Dark clouds kissed the snowy peaks, a thick cotton skirt of mist hanging around its torso.

'Is it far?' he asked sheepishly.

'No,' Marla said, pointing. 'It's just up there.'

'In the mountains? Really? I haven't brought any clothes for that sort of weather.'

'Oh, you don't need to worry about that. We won't be going outside.'

So, we're underground, Paul thought. Interesting. 'Will Petra have time to meet with us today?'

'I'm sure that can be arranged. I understand you and your friend have something very special that you want my boss's help with.'

He felt his muscles tense. How much did this chauffeur really know? 'Just a business proposition,' he replied. 'I think it's something that will make Petra very happy.'

'That's what I heard. You've travelled a long way for this meeting, so I naturally assumed that Petra is the only person who can provide you with what you need.'

'Oh, we have a few interested parties,' Paul lied. 'But we like the anonymity that Elysian Field can offer us. We're not ready to go public. Not yet, at least.'

'Then, I think you've come to just the right place. Petra hates publicity, as I'm sure you realise. Elysian Field is a very private company, with clientele that like to keep their affairs very secret.'

Yeah, right, Paul thought. From what he'd heard, they were the sort of customers who couldn't particularly afford public scrutiny. 'Exactly. That's the reason we flew all the way out here.'

The road climbed steeply into the mountains and headed in the direction of a town called Spiterstulen. Paul had no idea where that was, and was starting to become increasingly preoccupied by the steep descent that fell away just inches from his side of the car. He imagined the Tesla hitting an ice patch and careening off the road, tumbling and spinning down the side of the mountain, its bonnet crumpling like cardboard, sharp rocks penetrating the canopy and ripping them to shreds.

'Where are we?' Manny asked, rubbing his eyes. 'Woah, it's almost five in the afternoon. You weren't kidding when you said it was a long drive.'

'Norway's a big country,' Marla explained, 'with some of the most beautiful scenery in the entire world. It's lucky for you, Manmeet, that you stirred just as we reached the best part of the ride.'

The view truly was breath-taking, with white dusted summits, steep glaciers, ice covered valleys and tumbling streams. The roadside was sparsely littered with tiny wooden cabins, but as they neared the town of Spiterstulen, the cabins grew in number and size, and more and more traffic began to pass by on the road.

'Are you taking us on a site-seeing trip?' Paul asked.

'Not quite.' Marla laughed, before taking a sharp, lefthand turn. The road was a single track and covered in gravel. It rose steeply through the mountain range towards a place called Galdhøpiggen.

'I know this place,' Manny said, sounding excited. 'It's the largest summit in Europe. It stands almost 2,500 metres high. Apparently, it's an absolutely jaw dropping spectacle.'

'You certainly know your geography, Mr Davi. I'm impressed.'

Manny shot her a blushing smile. 'I read a lot. Mountains are kind of my thing.'

'Well, I'm glad you approve. And what about you, Mr Karin? Do you approve?'

'I just want to meet Petra. If that means we have to head to a place somewhere in the clouds, then so be it.'

'It's just a shame we had to get on that plane,' Manny groaned.

'He doesn't like flying,' Paul said to Marla. 'He doesn't think it's natural.'

'But you flew out here,' Marla commented. 'Maybe you are overcoming your fear.'

'I don't think so. I just took a Valium. By the way, I don't like narrow roads, either.' Manny glared out the window as the crumbling track wound through the mountain range, the trail skipping past them as the car desperately fought to maintain its grip on the road.

'Where are we going?' Paul asked. 'This seems kind of remote.'

Marla didn't reply. Sharp, black rock rose like dark stalagmites either side of them as the track swept through what appeared to be a deep ravine. The sky overhead became a narrow sliver as the mountains stretched upwards and out of sight, a white, billowing blanket masking its summit. Paul was beginning to feel mildly claustrophobic.

'Exciting, isn't it,' Manny chirped beside him.

'If you say so.'

'I mean, Galdhøpiggen. I never thought I'd get to come here.'

Before Paul had a chance to respond, the narrow road opened onto a wide, snow-covered plateau that hung hundreds of metres above the valley floor. The wide vista stretching out before them looked unreal, as if it was an artificially enhanced image. Marla swung the car beside a small, wooden shack and turned off the engine.

'Gentlemen,' she said. 'Will you follow me?'

The air outside was cold and sharp. Paul pulled the collar up on his jacket to shield his face from the rapidly plummeting temperature. He cursed his uncle. If he'd told him where they were headed, he would have dressed appropriately.

He eyed Manny as Marla opened the door to the cabin. His friend looked animated, which was a concern. They'd already agreed that Paul would do most of the talking. Manny was a good pal, but he was no diplomat. He was there to stop Paul from letting his enthusiasm run away with him. He knew that he wasn't really the "play it cool" type, so he often used Manny as his counterbalance.

'Gunthar,' Marla hollered. 'Will you pour some coffee. My friends and I have had a long drive.'

A tall, well-built man with blonde hair and neatly trimmed beard set a steaming jug of brown liquid down on the coffee table. 'How do you like it?' he asked.

'Decaf for me,' Paul replied, thinking of the way the Amrita had reacted to just a small amount of caffeine.

'I'll take mine strong with milk and three sugars,' Manny said. 'This is some place you have here.'

'We like it,' Gunthar said, shooting them a warm smile. He poured the drinks and stirred three heaped teaspoons into the coffee.

'Do you live here?' Manny asked.

Gunthar glanced at Marla before running his hands down his apron and descending a staircase that disappeared into darkness.

Paul took in their surroundings. The shack was small but tidy and was built from what looked like cured pine. A small kitchen sat at its farthest corner and a series of burgundy sofas lined the edges. Tall bookshelves stood against the walls, stacked with dusty paperbacks, all with titles that Paul couldn't even hope to translate. Through a large window, the snow-capped mountain range stretched into the distance.

'Take a seat, gentlemen,' Marla said.

Paul shook his head. 'I'm okay, thanks. I need to stretch my legs.'

'As you wish. What do you think of the view, Manmeet?'

'It's quite something.'

'One of the greatest landscapes in the whole world,' she said. 'Maybe even the very best. It's truly amazing what our planet can tell us, if only we would listen. As a race, we take from the Earth, rob it of everything it has, even fighting with each other for the right to take that which never really belonged to us. We rarely give anything back, of course. Before too long, there will be nothing left, and our children's children will be left to pick what's left of the carcass. It's very sad.'

Paul stifled a groan. 'You sound like Greta Thunberg. Isn't she from around here?'

'Perhaps,' Marla replied, reclining on one of the sofas. 'And no. She's Swedish.'

'Will Petra be meeting us soon?' he asked, sipping his coffee.

'Tell me about this Amrita,' she said, ignoring his question. 'What can it actually do?'

Manny spoke first. 'With all due respect, Marla, you've been very nice to us, and you brought us here safely, but what we have to say is really only for Mr Gunderson's ears. He signed a strict confidentiality agreement and—' he glanced at Paul, 'you really shouldn't have been told the name of our invention.'

Marla ran a finger across her lipstick. 'Of course. But you see, Petra tells me everything. Yes, he and I are very close. We've known each other since we were very little, from way back when we both lived in the same village in the north of the country. He rarely makes a move without my approval, which I find quite flattering, of course.'

Paul shook his head. 'Be that as it may, this topic is of a very confidential matter. Please don't be offended, but we'll only be disclosing the details with Petra.'

Marla's lips thinned. 'It is no bother. I rarely think of such things. We are who we are, and the way someone perceives another person's behaviour is just a matter of opinion. You want to protect your invention, and I want to know more about it. If you don't want to tell me, that's fine.'

Paul eyed her over the rim of his cup. If they'd offended her, so be it. There was no way they were disclosing their secrets to a jumped-up cab driver.

'I suggest you grab something to eat,' Marla said, standing. 'And perhaps another cup of coffee. It's a long drive back to the airport.'

Manny shot Paul an anxious glance.

'What?' Paul said. 'I thought you'd brought us here to meet Petra.'

'He's changed his mind. You're not who we thought you were.' She grabbed her car keys. 'If you would follow me.'

'Wait!' Paul cried, grabbing her arm.

'I suggest you remove your hand from me, Mr Karin, or I'm afraid this might become a very impolite exchange.'

'I'm sorry,' he said, lifting his hands. 'It's just that we've come such a long way. We were told that Petra was the right man to see, that he would understand what we were trying to achieve here. Maybe we were wrong.'

Marla turned to him. 'Are you smart, Mr Karin?'

Paul shook his head. 'What?'

'It's a simple question. Do you and your friend here believe you are men of intelligence?'

'I don't know what you—'

'We're smart enough to have created the Amrita,' Manny replied, his fists clenched. 'Smart enough to file a patent to protect it. Smart enough to find you lot at Elysian Field. So yes, we think we're men of some intelligence.'

'That will be your downfall,' she replied sharply. 'Come. We have a long drive.'

As the door opened and the cold air rushed in, Paul sensed their one big opportunity racing away from them. He thought fast.

'We're not smart,' he said. 'We're pretty naïve, actually. Look, Marla, I don't know who you are or why Petra sent you to screen the two of us, but I do know that we are way out of our depth here. We have no idea what we have or how powerful it might eventually be, so we need the help of someone like Petra to figure this thing out with us. If that means he gets a slice of our pie, then so be it. At the moment, the pie's not in the oven. The pastries not even rolled flat. It's worthless. We want to get the Amrita tested, we want to get it approved, and we want to get it to market. We need Elysian Field. We need what you can bring to the table. Without your help, this thing will die on the vine. I beg you, if you could just see in us what we see in ourselves, then you'll close that door and let us have our meeting.'

Marla let out a long sigh. A white plume erupted from her lips, a dragon's breath in the ice-cold air. Eventually, she turned to him, letting the door shut behind her.

'Gunthar will take you to your rooms,' she said. 'Get some rest. Tomorrow will be a busy day.'

Saturday, 24th June:

Canterbury, Kent

Wade sat in his mum's Fiat Punto. The engine was running. He had a pounding headache and was in a foul mood. Dried blood caked his upper lip, and a purple egg-shaped swelling was visible just beneath his right eye. His nose was sore too. He thought it was probably broken.

The day had started so well. He'd woken at around ten, swallowed a couple of paracetamols, devoured a large McDonalds breakfast, and finished off by smoking a joint. By mid-day he'd started to feel almost whole again and had decided to do the job that Ted had requested. Although the events of the prior evening were still a little fuzzy, he remembered that particular conversation quite clearly. After some back and forth in his head, he'd decided what the hell. What would his friend Manny care, anyway? Surely he would see the business opportunity in it, even if it did mean he'd be peddling the stuff through some dodgy blokes.

Wade had decided to call first, but there had been no answer. Frustrated, he made the decision to cut out the middleman and go straight to the source. He knew the freezers were kept at Karin's place, so he headed there. The problem was, Karin hadn't been home either, and with the two of them being completely radio silent, it meant he had to get creative. The lock on Karin's flat was pretty basic—any wannabe burglar could get past it with ease—and within a minute or two, the door was open and he was inside, as calm as you like.

The shades were drawn and so he felt along the wall for a light switch before realising that Karin's girlfriend could be at home. He crept along the hallway, cautiously checking the tiny bathroom and cluttered bedroom, before peering into the front room. The shades were drawn. He let out a long breath before turning on the lights. What he saw made his heart sink. The freezers were gone. All of them. There were just deep, rectangular indentations where they had once stood.

'Shit,' he'd said. 'Shit, shit, shit.'

He'd called Manny's mum, who'd informed him, very politely, that her son was out of the country for a few days with his friend and that she didn't know when he was going to be home. Mrs Davi then asked how he had been, and told him he could come round any time to visit. He'd replied by telling her how much he appreciated it, and swiftly hung up the phone. Manny's mum had always been nice to him, but nice wasn't what he needed right now.

With the pair's absence confirmed, he'd reluctantly decided to go and see Ted. It wasn't a rendezvous that filled him with happiness. Giving Ted Barker the bum's rush was the equivalent of telling Jeffrey Dahmer you'd love to go up to his apartment for coffee.

As predicted, Ted hadn't taken the news particularly well, and he'd got one of the big, ugly goons from the riverside house to remind Wade just how important his request was—his particularly urgent request. Semi-conscious and bleeding on the floor, Wade had received the message loud and clear.

Those events had led to him being in this one spot with a bruised face and a crushed ego, waiting patiently for a specific person to show up. Alone in his mum's car, parked beside a long row of terraced houses, he thought of the woman he was hoping to find. She was someone he knew the boys had been in contact with because he'd overheard them talking about it in Karin's kitchen.

'We can't rely on Renee anymore,' Karin had said. 'I think she's done everything she can for us. Canterbury Uni' really only has a limited budget, and if she's caught spending it on something like this, she could lose her scholarship.'

Wade hadn't known who this Renee was, or what she'd done for Manny and his pal, but a quick flick through Karin's Facebook page had brought up the pretty face of one Renee Douglas, a biomedical science student who was currently working on her doctorate. A flick through her own social media sites (*really*, he thought, *people should learn how to use the privacy settings on their social media pages*), and all of a sudden, Wade had a street address. It was in the background of one of the pictures she'd taken with two of her friends on moving in day.

Pilgrims Way. Number thirty-two.

He didn't know what time Renee would come home, or even if she was already in the house, but he knew sooner or later she would show up at the front door.

When she did, he would be waiting.

Saturday, 24th June:

Penwyllt, Ogof Ffynnon Ddu National Nature Reserve, Wales

Julie and Ellie stood at the top entrance to OFD II, the central section of the cave network. They were under a rocky overhang, trying in vain to keep out of the rain. It seemed to be coming down in sheets.

'This is sod's law, isn't it,' Julie said, holding her hand out, feeling the heavy downpour.

'It's no bother,' Ellie said, checking her phone. 'We'll be underground in a bit, anyway. Bob from the OFD Cave Association says we have to wait until nine before we can go in. Apparently, there's a group already down there and they don't want us getting in their way.'

Julie shook her head. She'd been hoping to get in an out by lunchtime.

'How long will it take?'

'To get to Marble Showers? Oh, a good few hours of caving, I'd say. It's going to be a little tricky working our way down, but stay close to me and you'll be fine.'

Julie felt a headache coming on. A good few hours? That meant they'd be lucky to be out by dinnertime. Maybe this wasn't such a good idea after all.

'Perhaps we should just leave it,' she said. 'If they already have people down there, I mean. We can try again later in the year.'

'I don't think so, Missy,' Ellie replied, cocking her head.

'You're not getting out of it that easily. You said you wanted to see the Cave of the Black Spring, and I for one am going to make sure you get a bloody good look. After all, we've come all this way. Are you telling me you want to bail at the first hurdle?'

Julie shrugged. 'I don't know. I—'

'It's all yours,' an older man said. He had a greying goatee and serious eyes. 'Sorry it took a little longer than we expected. I'm Owen, by the way, and you must be—'

'Ellie,' Julie's cousin replied. 'And this is Julie. I'm taking her down into OFDII.'

Julie grinned at the party of four younger cavers that emerged from the cave mouth. They looked exhausted.

'Jeez,' Julie exclaimed. 'What time did you set off?'

'Oh, we started at about four-thirty, just as the sun was coming up. That's the beauty of caving. No daylight required.'

'I guess.' Julie said, a pang of uncertainty swilling in the pit of her stomach.

Owen waved on his group. 'Anyway, come on you lot. We have bacon sandwiches waiting.' He turned to Ellie. 'Enjoy. The Falls are looking pretty spectacular today.'

As they departed towards the carpark, Ellie shot Julie a satisfied smirk. 'Did you see him? What a dish.'

'Ellie, you're married.'

'Doesn't stop me window shopping, does it? Gotta keep your options open.'

Julie laughed. 'You're a nightmare.'

She felt anxious. She'd spoken to Paul the night prior, and he'd seemed a little off. When she'd asked him about his meeting with Petra Gunderson, he'd said they'd only actually met with his driver and some other bloke called Gunthar. Julie said she thought that sounded suspicious, but Paul had been insistent that he and Manny were in control of everything and that they expected to meet the boss today. She hoped he wasn't kidding himself. He had a habit of being overly optimistic. He could get so caught up in the moment, he couldn't see the truth if it stood stark naked in front of him

'You ready then, girl?' Ellie asked, tapping Julie's hard hat.

'I guess I am,' Julie replied, although she felt anything but.

'Then, let's descend! In the immortal words of Amy Lee, we're going under.'

Saturday, 24th June:

Galdhøpiggen, Norway

Paul sat up in bed, a black, tentacle resting on his shoulder. He glanced at it, watching as the long waxy finger caressed his cheek.

'Get off of me!' he yelled, pulling back the covers. 'Get away from me!' He skipped across the floor, flapping at the air.

'What the hell are you doing?' Manny cried from the next bed. He reached for his glasses and peered at his watch. 'You woke me up. It's only…five-thirty in the morning.'

'Sorry,' Paul said, peering at the corners of the room. 'I guess I had a bad dream.'

'Maybe it's all the stress.' Manny pulled the sheets up to cover his hefty man boobs. 'You know? What with what went down in the cave, everything with Julie's dad, and then flying out here. It's been a lot to process.'

'Yeah. I guess you're right.'

The door opened and Gunthar walked in. He was dressed in pleated trousers and a flannel shirt. He wore leather, open toed sandals on his feet.

'Ah, good' he said. 'You're up. Petra asked that I make you an early breakfast. What would you like?'

Manny's eyes lit up. 'This may sound a little cliché,' he said, 'but a full English would be perfect.'

They took their food into the basement's kitchen. There were no windows, so Paul had absolutely no idea what the weather conditions were outside. He sincerely hoped they weren't going to get snowed in. Their flight was first thing the next day, and he really didn't want to miss it. He had a strong, unexplainable urge to get home and check on their stock.

'This is great,' Manny said, devouring a thick, greasy sausage. 'Delicious.'

Paul pushed congealed egg-yolk around his plate and thought about their chauffeur. She'd been odd, elusive, but as sharp as a steak knife too. 'Who do you think she is?' he asked.

'Who?' Manny replied, bean juice on his chin.

'The blonde lady. Marla. She's obviously not just a driver, she even admitted as much. Why do you think Petra sent her to meet us? I mean, what's his game?'

'I guess he wanted to check us out before our meeting. If she's really known him since they were kids, he must trust her judgement. Let's face it, we were about ten seconds away from blowing it back there.'

Paul sipped his tea. He'd figured Marla's reaction had been a negotiation tactic. Perhaps Petra was trying to make them so desperate that they'd agree to anything. Fair play. It had almost worked. In fact, if Marla had pushed on the point, he thought he would have probably done something rash and signed a whole chunk of their revenues away. For some reason, however, she'd backed off and let them sleep on it. She was a smart cookie, there was no doubting that. It made Paul realise that he and Manny needed to be on top of their game. If they were off, even by just a little, the chances were they would get their arses handed to them.

'Are you finished?' Gunthar asked. 'I'll clear the table and take you to HQ.'

'Is it far from here?' Paul enquired, handing him his plate.

'No, not far at all'

'Will Petra be there.'

Gunthar forced a smile. 'I'm sure the meeting will be fruitful. You have nothing to worry about.'

Paul chewed his lip. If anything was going to make him worry, it was a tall, bearded bloke in a flannel shirt and open toed sandals telling him not to.

After the table was cleaned, Gunthar led them down a long hallway that descended a gradual slope. The walls, floor and ceiling were painted in a dark, forest green, with bronze, LED lanterns hanging at head height. There was only one door that sat right at the very end. It looked like it had been carved from a giant slab of quartz. There was a camera inset into the right-hand side of the door. Gunthar bent down and placed his eye against it. Within a second, there was a high-pitched ping, followed by the sound of large deadbolts retracting.

'Through here,' Gunthar said. 'Follow me.'

The room on the other side was spacious with a tall, domed ceiling, held aloft by giant marble pillars. An expensive looking chandelier hung from its apex. Up ahead, there was a sweeping staircase that curved over a semi-circular, oak desk. Large, sixty-inch TV screens hung from the walls, each displaying different news channels from all over the globe. The room smelled of vanilla and jasmine. The lighting was crisp but not too bright, and everything appeared immaculately clean. Two armed guards stood at the entrance. They patted Paul and Manny down before allowing them to proceed.

'Right this way,' Gunthar said. He proceeded to the desk, behind which were seated two male concierges. 'I have our visitors. They're from England.'

'Ah, Mr Karin and Mr Davi,' the man closest to them said. He had small brown eyes with high cheekbones, and he wore a black jumpsuit and white running shoes. 'We were expecting you yesterday.'

'Yeah, sorry about that. We got a little waylaid.'

'No bother at all. I'm Yaz, your host for the day. Here are your name badges.' He handed them two magnetic name cards. 'Please display them at all times. The guards can get a little forceful if they suspect you to be an intruder.'

Paul eyed the two heavies. They looked like something out of a Warhammer graphic novel, all shoulders and neck.

Yaz flapped a hand. 'They're pussycats really. All bark and no bite.' He turned to Gunthar. 'You can leave them with me. I'll take it from here.'

'Very well. I'll be seeing you,' Gunthar said, turning to Paul. 'I hope the meeting goes the way you planned.'

Yaz ushered them both towards an opaque glass door.

'Right this way gentlemen.'

Saturday, 24th June:

Pilgrims Way, Canterbury, Kent

Wade had been sitting outside the building for four hours. He'd smoked two spliffs and sunk a whole flask of strong coffee. He was jacked up and bored, and what's more, he was starving. What was it with students? They were always either down the pub spending their lavish grants on cheap alcohol, or sleeping all the damn day long. He was getting twitchy and pissed off, so he decided to take matters into his own hands.

The house was a two storey, mid-terrace on a busy street, so breaking in through the front door wasn't really an option. He decided to take his chances and walk to the end of the road, risking Renee leaving the house without him noticing. He had to find a way around the back. Inaction wasn't exactly working out for him.

The day was overcast with the odd shower, making everything seem damp and grey. He grabbed his jacket, locked the car and headed downhill towards the T-Junction.

He knew he'd made a big mistake spending an evening with Ted and his pals. What had he been thinking? He'd just been cured of two significant disabilities, and now, rather than enjoying what he had, he was chasing his tail, trying to coerce a student into giving him access to somebody else's property. As he silently seethed, he rounded the corner and bumped into a pretty young woman with red hair, knocking her bag from her shoulder and spilling the contents of her purse all over the floor.

'Oh, sorry,' he said, dropping down to scoop everything up.

'I'm so sorry, I wasn't paying attention. I didn't see you.'

'That's okay,' she said, picking up her lipstick, vape and credit cards. 'I didn't see you either. It's just one of those things.'

Wade handed the woman her stuff and tried to hide his astonishment. He couldn't believe he'd gotten so lucky. It was her. It was Renee Douglas. 'Here,' he said. 'I think that's everything.'

She smiled. 'Thank you. Woah, what happened to your face.'

'Oh, that?' He'd forgotten about the way he looked. 'It's a long story.'

'Hopefully not a painful one.' She shook her purse. 'Anyway, thanks.' She turned to walk up the hill.

'It's Renee, isn't it?'

'How do you know my name?' She studied him through narrow eyes.

'I'm a friend of Paul Karin. I've seen a picture of you two together.'

She pondered his response. 'Odd, but okay. How is he? I haven't heard from him for a couple of weeks.'

'Yeah, he's fine. He's out of the country at the moment with another friend of mine. Manmeet?'

'You mean Manny?'

'Yep, that's him. The big Indian fella. I've known him a long time. We used to knock about together when we were kids.'

'Cool,' she said. 'Look, it's nice to meet you, but I really have to go. I have a paper to write, and my day started out a little haywire. Sorry for throwing my things at you.' She went to leave.

'The yellow liquid,' he said. 'I've taken it.'

She stopped in her tracks.

'It cured me. Before that, I had severe hearing loss, and my eyesight was shocking. These were disabilities I'd had for years, but now they're gone.'

Her eyes widened. 'That…that can't be possible.'

He pulled his thick spectacles from his jacket pocket. 'Well, I don't need these anymore, so make of that what you will. You're the scientist.'

She shook her head, her eyes fixed on his glasses. She took them and held them up to the light. 'These are very fat lenses. They must be greater than -6.00 diopters, which means—'

'—the sufferer has high myopia. That's right. As I said, I could barely see.'

'And you claim you no longer need them?'

'Might as well throw them in the bin.'

Renee shook her head. 'That's amazing.'

'Thanks. I guess that's a complement.'

She paused and handed them back to him. After a moment, she rifled through her purse for her keys. 'I'd like to talk to you some more,' she said. 'Get some more details. Are you free at the moment? Right now, I mean? I have a pretty decent coffee maker.'

Wade smiled, thanking his lucky stars. 'I never turn down a free coffee.'

Saturday, 24th June:

OFDII Cave Network, Wales

'This is so beautiful,' Julie said, gazing at the blue-green rocks that surrounded them. Large stalactites hung like unfinished pillars from the roof of the cave. 'I really had no idea what to expect. It's pretty spectacular, isn't it?'

'It sure is,' Ellie agreed, adjusting her hard-hat. 'It's certainly one of the more eye-catching cave networks I've had a chance to explore. Thanks again for the invite.'

They had been working their way along the tunnels for a couple of hours. Julie had been perfectly fine all the while they were walking upright, despite occasionally losing her footing on the slick rock, but once they'd had to get on all fours and squeeze through the tightly constrained crevices, she'd started to feel a mild sense of panic, brought on by her burgeoning claustrophobia. All the while she kept telling herself that she was doing this for her dad, but her self-reassurance seemed to have little effect. She remained petrified.

'How far is it now?' she asked. 'To Marble Showers, I mean.'

Ellie glanced at her laminated map. 'I'd guess we're around an hour or so away. No more than two. But I have to warn you, the next section is a little more difficult.'

'What? More difficult than that?'

'Well, it depends on your point of view. How are you with heights?'

Julie shook her head. She hated heights even more than she hated being hemmed in on either side by giant slabs of limestone and granite. Just as she started to think things couldn't get any worse, her headlamp started to stutter, and the shadows on the walls began to bend and stretch.

'That's odd,' Ellie said. 'I charged those batteries before we left.' Then her headlamp went out completely and the cave was plunged into a strobing, flitting darkness.

'What's going on?' Julie cried out. Her heart was doing the macarena in her chest.

Ellie removed her helmet and slammed her hand against the side of it. 'I have no idea.' The strobing light made her look like some sort of animated mannequin.

'Ellie? Don't tell me we're out of batteries.'

'Of course not.' She reached into her yellow backpack. 'I'm not an amateur, you know?'

'Thank Christ for that.' She sat down on a rock and watched as her cousin pulled out a lithium-ion battery pack, removing the failed unit from her headlamp before swapping them.

'Hang on,' she said. 'That's not right.'

'What's not right? Tell me, what's not right? Isn't it working?'

Ellie shook her head. 'Let me try yours.' She clambered over the rocks.

Julie removed her own headlamp and handed it to her. Ellie held it beneath her chin, which turned her face into a stuttering death mask.

'Hey, stop kidding around.'

'Sorry,' Ellie laughed. 'I'm only joking.'

'Do something with that thing, won't you?'

'I'm going to have to take this battery out to put the new one in. Which means we'll be in complete darkness, but don't panic. It'll just be for a moment. Are you okay with that?'

Julie shrugged. She really wasn't, but what choice did she have?

'Okay. Here goes.'

Instantly, the cave was thrown into a dense black. It was so dark, so completely and utterly devoid of light, that it almost felt to Julie as if she no longer existed, as though she were nothing but a conscious thought drifting in the eternal blanket of death.

'Are you there?' she whispered. 'Ellie, are you there?'

There was the sound of heavy breathing and feet pressing against rocks, followed by a loud clatter.

'Shit!' she heard Ellie cry.

'What? What's going on?' Julie's terror rose in her throat and every hair on her body stood on end.

'I dropped the bloody battery.'

'You've got to be kidding me! Can you find it? Do you know where it is? Ellie, please tell me you haven't lost it.'

'Jules!' Ellie yelled. 'Will you stop freaking out and just let me concentrate.'

She held her breath and gripped the rock beneath her. She felt like she was floating in space, like she was on a meteor that was rushing through the galaxy at a billion miles an hour, the utter nothingness of the universe compressing her into a tiny, compact ball. She felt something brush against her shoulder and she whirled around.

'What was that?' Her body froze.

'What was what?'

'Something touched me.'

'It's just your imagination,' Ellie said. 'Just give me a minute. I think the battery's just between these two rocks.'

Julie peered into the nothingness. She was sure there had been something there. There was a warmth on the nape of her neck, like a breath, followed by a damp, musty odour.

'Ellie,' she said. 'There's someone in here with us.'

'No there isn't. It's just your anxiety playing tricks with you.

I'm almost there. Just wait a second.'

Julie knew Ellie was right. They were deep underground in a cave where nothing grew, let alone breathed, but she also knew that Paul and Manny had found something down there, even if the very notion of that seemed crazy to her. She was sitting there encased in a darkness so deep, she could almost feel its black, dripping blanket draped over her.

Something touched her hand and crept up her arm, and then she was being pulled backwards against the cave wall.

'Whoah!' she cried. 'Ellie, something has me! Help!'

'I've got it!' Ellie yelled.

Her body was slammed against the rock, her hard-hat coming into contact with the bottom of a sharp stalactite which broke away and sliced her cheek. Something wet sucked at her body before wrapping itself around her neck. It felt like a snake or a greasy eel. It began to compress her windpipe with a force so powerful that bright pinpricks of light burst inside her retinas, as if the celluloid film of her life was melting away before her very eyes.

'Ellie!' she half screamed as her larynx was being crushed inside her throat. 'Ellie! Help me! Please!'

Her consciousness began to dwindle, but just as she felt herself slipping away, the cave was bathed in a bright white light as her headlamp sprang back into life, followed by Ellie's own torch.

'There,' Ellie said, grinning. 'Got it.'

She turned to Julie who was slumped between a raised outcropping and the cave wall, blood trickling from her cheek where the stalactite had pierced her skin. 'What's up with you?'

'There was something here,' Julie said, still breathless. 'Something attacked me.'

'Like what? We're alone down here?'

'I don't know, do I?' Julie dusted herself down and wiped the thin smear of blood from her face. 'I didn't just throw myself at that stalactite for laughs, you know?'

'I think somebody is a little afraid of the dark, am I right?'

She shook her head. It had felt real enough. Somebody or something had tried to choke her. Maybe it had all been her imagination, but if it had, it had felt bloody real. Too real. 'I was sure something was here.'

Ellie handed over the headlamp. 'It can do that to you. The darkness. These caves. Don't worry. It's happened to us all, even the most experienced cavers.'

Julie's cheeks flushed with the prickly heat of embarrassment. She tried to shake herself out of it. She was usually so calm, so assured. It was something she'd learned from her father. The memory of her dad made her think. Perhaps that was it. With everything that had been going on in her life these past few months, compounded by her disabling claustrophobia and the sudden loss of light, it was very possible she'd had a panic attack. A real big one, too. It seemed plausible enough.

'I guess you're right. I was just being stupid. I'm sorry.'

'Don't be silly. It's just one of those things.' Ellie stood, her hands on her hips. 'Now, about that vertigo.'

Saturday, 24th June:
Elysian Field HQ, Galdhøpiggen, Norway

The swimming pool was Olympic sized. There was a swirling fountain at its centre and palm trees along the edges. Two fully stocked tiki-bars occupied either end, and three large whirlpools were spread evenly around its perimeter. At the far side of the room there was a sauna nestled within three neat rows of plush, cushioned loungers. UV lamps were inset into the ceiling, interspersed between LED daylight lamps. Upbeat dance music played from a hidden speaker system.

'Welcome to the Ambassade,' Yaz said, gesturing with an open palm.

'The Ambassade?' Paul asked.

'Yes. It's the name Petra gave to our residential complex for those that require what one might call permanent discretion.'

'You mean, somewhere to hide from the authorities.'

Yaz offered a thin smile. 'Something like that. We have around seventy guests here at Galdhøpiggen, all of whom pay handsomely for the privilege this facility affords them.'

'What kind of numbers are we talking about?' Manny asked.

'Those details are a matter of confidentiality,' Yaz replied, 'but you would be surprised what wealthy entrepreneurs are willing to pay to protect their ongoing liberty.'

Paul puffed out his cheeks. 'It certainly is something.'

'That's very kind of you to say so. This particular area is what we refer to as The Caldarium, a rest and relaxation space designed to allow our clients time to recuperate. As you can see, we've had to be a little innovative in order to replicate sunlight. Our residents still expect suntans, even though we can't give them the real thing.'

'Doesn't it feel a little too…artificial?' Paul asked. 'After a while, I mean. You can't really beat the great outdoors, can you?'

'Our clients are happy to trade fresh air and the beach for, how can I put it, their personal wellbeing. There are people out there who would love nothing more than to incarcerate many of our members for an indeterminate amount of time. In some cases, indefinitely.'

An older guy with wiry muscles and a litany of tattoos on his chest and neck stood up from one of the tables and headed for a sunbed. He shot them an unsettling glare as he passed.

'He didn't look too pleased to see us,' Paul said.

'Oh, don't mind him. Tiggy can be a little cold with newcomers. He was actually one of our first clients.'

'Really? How many years ago was that?'

'Oh, about thirty,' Yaz replied, the smile barely leaving his cheeks. 'Many of them have forgotten what it's like to live above ground, but they don't care. They love it here, and who can blame them? It beats spending the rest of their days in a maximum-security prison.'

'But isn't this just the same?' Manny asked. 'They can't leave, they're permanently stuck indoors, and they're constantly mixing with the same people, day in, day out. It must be like going on a cruise, but never being allowed to leave the ship.'

'Oh darling,' Yaz exclaimed. 'There aren't many prisons in the world that can boast Michelin star meals every evening, the best live entertainment money can buy, and the complete freedom to partake in whatever drug, alcohol or sexual activity you most desire.'

They exited the pool area and entered another corridor, and

Paul realised they were heading further and further into the belly of the mountain.

'This place is huge,' he said. 'It's like a labyrinth. How do you ever find your way in and out?'

'Oh, you get used to it,' Yaz replied. 'Trust me, it's not as haphazard as it may at first appear. There is a logic to everything. Petra makes sure of it.'

'How long have you worked here?' Manny asked.

'All my life. I was actually born here.'

'In this complex? Really?'

Yaz turned. 'Oh, yes. It's quite normal for the residents to conceive children that perhaps they had not intended.'

'So, your parents were criminals?'

'Must you be so contrite?' he sniped. 'My mother trafficked high end cocaine for a number of the world's largest drug transportation networks, and my father?' He shot them a wry smile. 'He was the paid help.'

Manny raised an eyebrow. 'He was a prostitute?'

If Yaz was offended, he didn't show it. 'Once again with the cutting remarks. You really are quite the straight talker, aren't you, Mr Davi.'

'I just say it as it is.'

'Is that so? Well, now you know me, I think it's time for Petra to learn all about you.'

He ushered them to a set of double doors, stopping to present his eyeball to the scanner before the doors slid silently open on steel tracks. They revealed a glass encapsulated foyer, and beyond that, a large, immaculately white hall containing rows of lab benches, glistening equipment, and dozens of lab technicians, dressed head to toe in white coveralls and face masks.

'Welcome to our laboratory, gentleman. This wing forms part of Petra's diversification into the medical industry.'

'Diversification?' Paul asked. 'So this is all new?'

'Covid taught us all a lot of things, Mr Karin. Principally, how much money could be made from being the first to market with a drug that saves millions of lives. Petra is a visionary, asserting, quite rightly, that if something like that can happen once, it will eventually happen again. We plan to be the first to the table next time.'

'Jesus!' Manny cried, turning to Paul. 'He's hoping for another pandemic.'

'That's an interesting way to put it,' a female voice from behind them interrupted. 'But my view is that we would be foolish to be ill-prepared a second time.'

They spun round to face a woman in a charcoal grey suit and peach blouse. Her face was thin, her hair long and blonde.

'Marla,' Paul exclaimed.

'Marla was my mother's name,' she said, holding out a hand. 'My actual name is Mrs. Gunderson. Petra Gunderson, to be precise.'

Saturday, 24th June:
Pilgrims Way, Canterbury, Kent

Wade sipped his coffee, which he thought was delicious. The flavour was dark roast with a hint of hazelnut. Renee had been right. Her machine, a Delonghi Barista, really did deliver an excellent cup of the brown stuff.

'This is nice,' he said. 'Really good.'

'Oh, that thing's not mine,' Renee replied. 'It's my flatmate, Rosa's. Her parents have money, but that's another story. I'm more interested about what you were saying earlier. About the yellow liquid.'

'The Amrita,' he replied unconsciously, belatedly realising he'd once again breached the terms of his NDA.

'Is that what they called it?' Renee laughed. 'What does that even mean?'

Wade shrugged. 'I've no idea.' He studied the room. 'I heard you did some checks on the stuff for Paul and Manny. On the quiet, that is.'

'Oh, they mentioned that, did they?'

Wade nodded, trying to look sincere.

'Well,' she said. 'I shouldn't really say too much about it. They made me sign an agreement.'

'They made you sign one, too? I put pen to paper as well. I mean, what do they think we're going to do? Shout about it all over the county?'

'I know, right?' The air of mistrust between them seemed to evaporate. 'Well, as we're both in the same boat, I guess there's no harm in telling you what I know, although, I have to say, I don't really know much at all. I haven't had a significant involvement. They wouldn't let me. I just carried out a little structural analysis for them. You know, it really is a strange material? It's like nothing I have ever seen before. It's crystalline—almost a solid, but not quite—and the cells themselves do not conform to anything currently contained within the elemental table.'

Wade was no scientist, but that sounded bizarre. 'You mean this material is completely unknown?'

She offered him a chocolate bourbon. He took two. 'Well, as I say, I didn't have it for long so I couldn't be sure, but from what I witnessed, yes, that's exactly right. This material is apparently brand new.'

'So, it's alien.' Wade couldn't help but think about the teaspoonful he was willingly ingesting every day.

'Maybe not in the populist version of the term, but in as much as it is completely separate from our known earthly materials, then yes.'

Wade could feel the coffee and chocolate biscuit swirling around in his stomach.

'In your view, could this substance be toxic?'

She shook her head. 'Hard to say. It's possible.'

He felt a belch rise in his throat.

'Are you okay?' Renee asked. 'You seem to have lost your colour.'

He stood, feeling a little unsteady on his feet. 'I just need a minute. Can I use your loo?'

'Sure. It's right through there, at the back of the house.'

He didn't wait for a second invitation. He pushed through the kitchen door, stumbled across the linoleum, and crashed into the bathroom. He flipped the lid, dropped to his knees, and threw up into the bowl.

'Are you okay?' Renee yelled.

'Ung,' he groaned. 'Fine. Urgh! I'm, urgh, fine.'

'Do you need some water?'

'No. I'm, urgh, okay.'

As the flow of thick vomit subsided, leaving yellow, stringy bile hanging from his lips, he grabbed a towel and cleared the sweat from his cheeks and forehead. He just kept thinking about the Amrita in his stomach and what those strange alien cells were currently doing to his insides. Worst case, they were eating away at him, sucking at the lining of his intestines, tearing hungrily at the meat and tissue, causing him to die a slow and painful death as his veins ruptured. Best case, they were totally benign and would be absorbed into his body like any other material, his organs using what they wanted and then evacuating anything that was useless. He hoped for best case, but suspected reality was somewhere south of that.

When he returned to the lounge, Renee had poured him a glass of juice and had even added some ice cubes.

'It always helps me,' she said.

'Thanks.'

'How are you feeling?'

'Better,' he lied.

They sat that way for a minute or two as Wade sipped his drink and Renee finished her coffee.

'You know?' she said. 'I'd really like to take another look at it. Just to satisfy my scientific curiosity.'

'They didn't leave you with any?' he asked, a little surprised.

'No. I don't think they trusted me.' She ran a finger along the rim of her cup. 'You obviously have some. I mean, you're taking it daily, right?'

'Thanks for the reminder.'

'Sorry. I know I probably had something to do with your little incident there, but there really is nothing to worry about. Probably nothing, anyway.'

Wade didn't like the caveat. Probably wasn't good. Probably was fifty-fifty at best.

'I could come to you, collect some samples and do some experiments to put your mind at rest,' she added. 'If you want that, of course.'

He shrugged. 'I don't have much of it. So far, the guys have only given me enough for a month or so. I need that to, you know?' He pointed to his eyes and ears, and now it was his turn to blush.

'Of course, but that's okay. We could just make some more.'

Wade's ears pricked up. What was she talking about? 'Make some more? How could we do that?'

'You know? With the—'

He shook his head.

'They didn't tell you, did they?' she laughed. 'I can't believe they didn't say anything.'

'What?' He laughed along without knowing why. 'What didn't they tell me?'

'You never wondered about the formulation?'

He was getting annoyed. 'Well, yeah, but that was their business, not mine.'

She grinned and picked up a pod from beside her flatmate's machine.

'Wade, do you know what they say about caffeine?'

He shook his head.

'It makes the world go round.'

Saturday, 24th June:

Marble Showers, OFDII Cave Network, Wales

The clamber along the elevated stretch of tunnel that wormed its way towards Marble Showers from the Oxbow section of cave was probably the most terrifying experience Julie had ever had in her life. The path wasn't a path at all. It was a ledge, either side of a thirty-metre drop that fell to a bubbling stream below them. One wrong move and they could have slipped and fell the whole way, or possibly worse, got trapped in the narrow gap, breaking an arm or a leg and incapacitating one or both of them. It was horrendous. Julie could hear herself half-gasping for breath the whole way while she fought to prevent herself from crying. If it hadn't been for Ellie yelling words of encouragement and telling her exactly where to put her feet and hands, Julie would have just curled up into a tight little ball and waited to die down there.

When they'd clambered onto the shelf a metre or so above them and found a firm footing, Julie grabbed her cousin and planted a huge kiss on her lips. Sure, she knew she had to go back the way she had come, but she was so relieved to have made it, that for the moment, she didn't care.

'Marble Showers is just this way,' Ellie said. 'Oh, Julie. You should be so proud. You've never done this before, but here you are. Just think of what you've achieved.'

Julie nodded, smiling, but she was frantically trying to recall what Paul had told her.

'We took the right-hand tributary, just before you reach Marble Showers.'

She looked along the long section of tunnel which was narrow and twisting. She couldn't see an opening of any kind. What if they'd been wrong? What if it hadn't been this way at all? What if their long, excruciating journey had just been a complete, painstaking waste of time.

'Something up?' Ellie asked.

'No. I'm fine. Come on. Let's keep going.'

The tunnel was roughly human height, so the going was relatively easy. She ran her hands along the cool rockface and listened to the soothing hiss of the tumbling stream up ahead. At that moment, the thought of putting her head under cold running water seemed like the best thing in the whole world.

Her hand reached the end of the wall to her right, which was odd because the tunnel was still stretching off into the darkness.

'Wait!' she cried. 'Ellie, just wait a minute.' She peered at the deep crack and looked down at what seemed to be a small tunnel. 'What's that?'

'What's what?'

'This hole. Look. Can you see it?'

'That's interesting,' Ellie replied, holding out her map. 'It's not on here.'

Julie stooped down. 'That's a bit strange, isn't it?'

'Very.'

'Shall we take a look?'

'But I thought you wanted to see Marble Showers.'

'I do,' she replied, trying to hide her excitement, 'but I'm sure this won't take long. We can just take a peek and then come back this way. What do you think? It might be kinda fun.'

Ellie looked down at her, her lips tightly pursed, her arms folded, and Julie was suddenly convinced that her cousin wasn't going to go along with her request. A sickening dread consumed her as she realised what that meant. She would have to belligerently head down the slim cavity on her own. She peered into the darkness, wondering what could possibly be waiting for her down there. She raised a hand to her throat, recalling the snake-like limb around her larynx. She wanted to turn around and go back to the relative comfort of her parents' house, but she knew that wasn't an option. She had to see this through to its natural conclusion. She chanced a glance at Ellie and saw the broad smile that was now painted on her full lips.

'Well,' Ellie said. 'You've changed your tune. One minute you're almost hyperventilating over that little clamber along the ledge back there, the next, you want to go all Lara Croft and start exploring tiny tunnels that don't appear on any map.' She stooped down and peered into the hole before pushing her body into the tight crevice. 'I like this new Julie. I like her a lot.'

Saturday, 24th June:

Elysian Field Laboratories, Galdhøpiggen, Norway

'Why didn't you tell us it was you all along?' Paul asked. 'I feel like such an idiot.'

He and Manny were now dressed in hooded white coveralls with white face masks, white gloves and elasticated overshoes. He thought he looked like a ghost.

'You would be forgiven for not knowing who I am, Mr Karin,' Petra replied. Her suit was lime-green, which Paul guessed signified her status. 'Most people who have simply heard of the myth of Elysian Field believe the person who created it to be a man. It is the common assumption, is it not? That power belongs to the male?'

'I guess.'

Yaz beckoned them to a glass doorway. 'Shall we? This is what you've come here for, after all.'

He led the group towards the end of the passageway. Along the far wall, there stood a display case filled with petri dishes. Each contained a different coloured chemical. Paul eyed each of them in turn.

'These are our experimental drugs,' Petra said. 'Cures for mutating strains of bird flu, Ebola, the Marburg virus, and of course, Coronavirus. We are working on hundreds of live projects at any one time, all with varying degrees of success.'

'What sort of degrees?' Manny asked. 'I mean, have you actually achieved anything yet?'

Petra offered a wry smile. 'No, we haven't. Not yet. We've

made progress, we've seen promising signs, and all these samples have, at the very least, lessened the effects of the deadliest viruses currently threatening the continuing existence of our species; but I will confess, at present we are yet to find a cure.'

'And what if you do? How will you ever release it to the public? Particularly given the type of organisation you are.'

'And what type of organisation are we?' Petra asked. 'What exactly do you think Elysian Field is?'

'You house criminals among other things,' Manny replied, shrugging. 'Your operation is illegal, and that makes you a criminal yourself.'

Her eyes narrowed. 'I don't see it as that, but then I formed the company from nothing, dragging it up by the scruff of its neck as I navigated my way through a million dark alleyways, hampered by so much unnecessary bureaucracy. You want to know how I see Elysian Field?'

'We'd love to hear it,' Paul said, glancing at Manny. 'Wouldn't we?'

Manny shrugged.

'We're an antidote,' she said. 'Just like the chemicals you see behind the glass. Elysian Field is a remedy for common misconceptions, for unfair bias, and for discrimination in all its many forms.'

'I'm sorry, but I don't get it,' Manny said. 'Are you trying to tell us that the criminals you host are all the victims of discrimination?'

'Yes, why not? What gives you the right to say what is right and what is wrong?'

'I don't. The law does.'

'Who's law?'

'The government's law.'

'Who's government?'

'Any government!' Manny cried.

'What he's trying to say,' Paul interrupted, 'is that criminality is a well-defined term. What one country finds illegal is typically illegal in most countries.'

'But who writes the rules?' Petra asked, raising a hand to one of the lab technicians. 'Who gets to say if the rules are right or wrong? Not you or I. Not anybody in this lab. Not ninety-nine percent of the population of the Earth, and yet we dutifully abide by these laws as if they were created by God herself. Don't you find that a little odd?'

Paul raised his eyebrows.

'Look,' she continued. 'I'm not saying that many of our clients aren't dangerous people. They are—of course they are—but that doesn't mean what they do is wrong, just as you are not doing anything wrong in trying to shortcut a dreadfully antiquated drug approval system. We are all doing what we think is right, even if the people who have managed to attain power assert that it isn't.' She stopped and turned to them. 'Do you know how utilised the prison system is, Mr Karin? Mr Davi? Would you hazard a guess?'

Paul shook his head. 'I've no idea.'

'Sixty percent of all prisons in the UK are overcrowded. The Norwegian prison system is so oversubscribed, we are now sending convicts overseas. The United States has 2.2 million people in its prison system, which is a hundred and five percent utilised. The system is broken, and the rehabilitation rates are unsustainable.'

'So, you're doing your civil duty,' Manny said, smirking. 'Is that what you're claiming?'

'Exactly,' Petra replied. 'We hold no ill-will, we offer no judgement, and we create a win-win situation for all involved. Our governments get to build less prisons, saving the taxpayers billions, and our clients? Well, let's just say they are afforded the kind of welcome they would not receive in Belmarsh or San Quentin.'

'Wow,' Manny sniped. 'That really is some fucked up way of justifying what is, in essence, a free ride for some of the worlds' worst offenders.'

Petra whirled on him as Paul glared at Manny over his mask. He jumped in before his friend could do any more damage.

'Look,' he said. 'We're not judging. This is your business, and I must say, you have a very impressive place, but we're not here to talk about the rights and wrongs of the criminal justice system, are we Manny?' He raised his eyebrows. 'Are we?'

Manny bit his bottom lip. 'I guess not, but I don't have to like it.'

Paul turned to their host. 'Look, Petra. This lab looks like it's exactly the kind of thing we need, and the drug we have, the formulation we've created, is going to be world-beating. There's no doubt about that. We want you to help us bring it to market, and we're willing to discuss the details of what we consider to be a very generous deal.'

She ran a finger across the edge of her lipstick. 'Oh, I think there's been some misunderstanding here. You see, there's really nothing to discuss.'

Paul shook his head. 'I don't understand. What do you mean there's nothing to discuss?'

'I mean just that. If we did talk about your so-called deal, it would be a very short conversation.'

Paul glared at his partner. 'But I thought—'

'Yaz,' Petra interjected. 'Before we waste any more time, will you take Mr Karin and Mr Davi to the conference room and show them our offer?' She turned away. 'And to be clear, it's non-negotiable.'

Saturday, 24th June:

The Railway Arms, Sittingbourne, Kent

Wade sat in the pub and nursed what remained of his pint of Stella Artois. He had a headache and his teeth hurt, which usually signalled the onset of a migraine, although he'd hoped that his improved eyesight would have put paid to his elongated bouts of extreme pain and general miserableness. He had to pull himself together. Ted was going to arrive in around five minutes, and Wade knew he was going to have to be on top of his game. One wrong move and either the deal would go cold, or worse still, he'd be taken down a dark alleyway by one of Ted's goons and beaten to a pulp. Again. Neither of those scenarios appealed to him.

He thought of Renee. She had proven to be such a spark, such a firework of colours. They'd spent the majority of the day together. It had been an enjoyable, stress-free, full of laughter kind of day. The type of day Wade couldn't really remember having before, not since he was little anyway. Sure, it was all under the guise of making more of the Amrita, but it had turned into so much more than that. They'd had lunch together, watched a little TV, and they'd even chatted about mundane things, like what songs they liked, what their favourite game shows were, and what football team they supported. Renee had shown Wade how a precise mixture of water and caffeine could be used to multiply the Amrita almost instantaneously. He'd never seen anything like it. Just a few drops of good old-fashioned coffee—cold coffee, at that— and suddenly five millilitres of the Amrita became fifty, and fifty millilitres became half a litre. The possibilities were endless, as was the amount of money someone could make. *He* could make. When Renee had poured some of the yellow substance into her flask and said she needed to leave, Wade had felt a pang of bitter disappointment that he really hadn't expected.

'Will we see each other again?' he asked. 'I mean, to talk about what you find?'

'We probably should keep this on the down low for a while,' she replied. 'I don't want to lose a friend in Paul. If I find anything significant, I'll let him know, and then perhaps I can suggest we bring you in on whatever the next step is.'

He tried to suppress his emotions. 'Sure. I get it. We signed those confidentiality agreements, after all.'

She grabbed her keys. 'Right. Those.' She smiled. 'Well, I really must be off. I still have that assignment to finish.'

'And I still have TV to watch. This has been…nice. You know?'

She blushed, her coat folded over her arm, her petite hands clasped together. 'It has. It really has.'

When she left, Wade felt an awful sense of loss, like he'd found something phenomenal and then it had been wrenched away from him at the last second. He really liked Renee, even if his intentions in meeting her had been far from pure. He slid down the wall and slumped onto the carpet, not wanting to be anywhere or do anything.

He sat that way for a moment, listening to the sound of the clock on the mantel, but then there was a tap on the door.

'Who is it?' he called out. 'I don't want to buy anything or sign up for any charitable donations.' When he opened it, he wasn't confronted with a salesman or a door-to-door canvasser. It was Renee, and she wore the look of someone who was more than a little flustered.

'Here,' she said, handing him a slip of paper.

'What's this?'

'It's my number. Maybe...well, maybe we can have dinner sometime. Whenever you're free, if you want to, that is. At least, I hope you do. I'll...I'll cook.'

He felt his chest tighten. 'I'd love that. It sounds...well, it sounds perfect, actually.'

She blushed again. 'Okay. Good. Anyway, I'd best get going.' She paused before reaching up and kissing him on the cheek. Then she turned hastily and departed. He reached out a hand to touch the spot where her lips had met his skin, wondering if it had really happened. Her actions had caught him off guard in the most spectacularly awesome way. The smile that spread across his cheeks almost cleaved his face in two. He felt on top of the world, on top of the universe.

It did mean one thing, though. There was no way he could betray her trust and sell the Amrita to Ted and his bunch of roadmen. He had to shut it down, which was a road fraught with danger. He wasn't a drug dealer, and he certainly wasn't a gangster. After an hour of pacing his apartment, ruminating over the best way to broach the topic, he'd reluctantly called Ted and asked to meet him at the Railway Arms. He'd suggested 7 pm, a time he'd hoped the pub would be full of regulars. Much to his disappointment, when he arrived he learned that the majority of the locals had gone to Margate on a pre-arranged outing, which meant that, aside from Tracey the barmaid and an old drunk nicknamed Shandy Kev, the place was empty.

Wade glared at his lager. He was nervous. He'd done a little digging about his new drinking buddy and found out that Ted Barker ran a couple of highly illegal, highly dangerous enterprises in the area. He was the go-to guy for Class A drugs, although he always ensured there were several layers between himself and his dealers. On top of that, he also ran a few illegal gambling syndicates. He'd gotten so good at it that other rival gangs had started to put the pressure on him, which was why he paid Rami and his eastern European pals to act as his muscle-bound security team. Apparently, so rumour had it, Ted had gone from a pisshead nobody who squandered his money at the bookies on a regular basis, to a very rich crime-boss in less than five years.

Wade was distracted from his thoughts by a sudden movement, and he glanced at the door, half-expecting Ted to be standing there. Much to his surprise, he found the place was still empty, but there was something. A shadow in the corner that he hadn't spotted before. It was almost too dark, too artificial. It had an unusual shape, like a starfish but with more limbs. He shook his head and sipped his beer.

'You alright over there, Wade?' Tracey asked. 'You look a little off-colour, my love.'

'I'm fine,' he said, smiling. 'I probably just need to get some sunshine on my face.'

'Well, now's the time. The weather forecast is looking good for next week, and it's a bloody good job n'all. All this rain has been keeping the punters away.' She held out a hand. 'As you can see.'

'Careful what you wish for,' he replied, keeping one eye on the odd-looking shadow. 'You know how you hate it when it gets too busy.'

'It's better than being bloody bored. I've been standing here watching the clock for the last two hours. It doesn't move any faster, you know.'

There was a slippery, sucking sound as the shadow began to move. It inched along the wall, sliding between the coat rack and the fruit machine like a giant spider. He closed his eyes, hoping the apparition was just a figment of his imagination, but when he opened them again, it was still there.

'You put something in this beer, Trace?' he asked.

'Not that I know of.'

'You've not slipped me a Ruthie?'

'No offence, but you're not my type, love,' she laughed. 'You're too nice.'

'No offence taken.'

'I've got a mate who's on the lookout for a fella, though. If you're interested, that is.'

'Depends on the mate,' he replied, but he couldn't take his eyes off the dark, ill-defined shape. It was completely flat, as if it were part of the wall, but not part of it at all. A black appendage grew from its mid-section and crept slowly across the fruit machine, working its way steadily towards him like a rapidly spreading strand of cobweb. Little, dark finger like protrusions grew from this new limb, accompanied by a squelching, pulling sound, as if each finger had tiny rubber suckers.

As the shadow moved closer, Wade saw the early signs of what appeared to be a face: yellow eyes bulging from an oval shaped head, a beak-like mouth with grey lips, two rows of sharp, black teeth. He looked up at Tracey, but she was busy cleaning the bottles of booze, and Shandy Kev was half asleep in his chair. He was alone with this strange, unsettling thing, and now it was just centimetres from him.

The door burst open and both Ted and Rami wafted in like a bad smell. The shadow instantly evaporated.

'Wade, my old son!' Ted cried out, sitting down on a stool. 'What do you have for me?'

Wade tried to collect himself. 'Er...that's kind of what I wanted to talk to you about.' He glanced anxiously at the fruit machine. 'I don't have good news, I'm afraid.'

Ted's expression was unmoved. 'Oh dear, oh dear. That really has put a dampener on an otherwise fine day. You said you had contacts.'

'I told you, they're not in the country.'

'Other contacts then.'

'They couldn't help me.'

'Oh, couldn't they? Really?'

Wade nodded.

'Cos Rami here says he saw you with some pretty little bird earlier today.'

Wade stiffened. They'd been watching his flat.

'She's got nothing to do with this,' he said. 'She's just a friend.'

Ted grinned. 'I bet. I'd be very friendly with her too, if you know what I mean.'

Wade clenched his fists beneath the table.

'Look, Wade, old son,' Ted continued. 'I gave you a day to sort this out, which I thought was very generous, but you see, I really can't wait any longer. Rami's mother is feeling very unwell indeed. Another day and the poor old girl could croak.'

'I don't know what to say, Ted,' Wade replied, feeling hot beneath his shirt. 'I feel bad for your mum, Rami, I really do, but I just can't help you. Not until my associates return from overseas. I've got no way of getting you any of this Amrita until then.'

Ted nodded, running a hand slowly across his chin, staring at him through black, soulless eyes. Wade tried to think of something to say to alleviate the tension, but before he could open his mouth, Ted stood and reached for the door. 'Message received loud and clear. If you can't help me, you can't help me. It's disappointing, but it is what it is.' He turned to his bodyguard. 'Rami, my friend, I guess we'll have to go and tell your poorly mum the bad news.'

Rami grunted.

'I'll be seeing you around,' Ted said as Rami opened the door.

'Take care of yourself, mate. Look after that handsome face. I'd hate to see anything happen to those plump little ears or those newly working eyes of yours.'

Wade raised a hand and attempted a wave, but as the door closed, he knew he hadn't got away with it, not by a long shot. Ted was pissed off, and his little farewell had been a thinly veiled threat. There was a better than average chance that Rami and the other goons would be sitting outside, waiting for him to leave. He decided quickly that he had to go, right that second, and not through the front door.

'Tracey? You still have that problem with the sink out back?'

'Yeah, we do love,' she replied. 'Now you've got your sight back, didn't you say you were going to take a look at it for me? I'm still waiting, you know?'

'I'll do it right now,' he said, returning his pint glass and coming around the bar. 'Where's your spanners?'

'Underneath the sink. Knock yourself out, sweetheart.'

He gulped, imagining Rami's dinner-plate sized fist smashing into his cranium. The sink could wait. Right now, he had to get out of there before he had his arse handed to him. The back door to the pub was usually locked, but he'd spotted Tracey nipping out for a fag earlier. When she came back in, she'd locked up and placed the key on the windowsill. He grabbed it, slipped it into the lock and retracted the latch as quietly as he could. With that done, he pulled the handle, placed the key back on the windowsill, and slipped outside.

'See you Trace,' he whispered. 'Sorry.'

The backdoor opened onto a little outside storage area where the pub kept empty beer barrels, crates and other assorted junk. The plot was only four metres square with a two-metre fence surrounding it. There was a gate at the back that had seen better days. He went to it. He slid the two bolts away from the frame and unlatched it before peeking through the gap and checking that no-one was there. Thankfully, the alleyway behind the pub was deserted. He stepped out into the open, closed the gate behind him, and slid along the pub wall. He poked his head around the corner, and sure enough, Rami and his mates were standing by the outside tables. They looked shady. Wade let out a long breath. He needed Manny and Paul to come back home as soon as possible. He might be able to slip away unnoticed tonight, but that type of escape act only bought you so much time.

He turned towards the alleyway which snaked between the rear gardens of two terraced streets that backed onto each other. The track was narrow and dark, and the path was uneven and strewn with litter. Despite the empty condom wrappers, discarded fag packets and slowly hardening dog shit, he cherished the isolation the rear exit afforded him. It was a much safer journey than the way out front.

He crept along the alleyway as his thoughts shifted to other things. He wondered how soon was too soon to call Renee. He thought about phoning her that night but realised that was definitely too soon. Tomorrow, though? That could work. He started to visualise what she'd cook for them. She was French, so he thought the food would probably be pretty damn good. Maybe she'd knock up a coq au vin or a beef bourguignon. He salivated at the thought. He was so distracted by the excitement of their first date that he didn't notice the shadow that unattached itself from the fence to his right, or the long, snake-like arm that reached for his throat and constricted his windpipe until it was too late. When the tentacle wrapped itself around his neck and pulled tight, Wade didn't feel his neck break or his nerves shear as all conscious feeling left his body. He was still thinking about Renee.

Saturday, 24th June:

Marble Showers, OFDII Cave Network, Wales

Julie watched as Ellie pulled herself from the mouth of the crevice and swung her legs over the edge of the drop.

'Outstanding,' she said. 'This isn't on any of the maps, and yet here it is. Another cave, and a big one too.'

Julie grabbed her hand, swinging her lower section out from within the shallow crack. A pool of water lay beneath them. It glistened with the green and blue colours of the granite and limestone overhead. She peered into the darkness, searching for a clue, anything to give her hope that they were at least in the right place.

'Good on you, Jules?' Ellie continued. 'Hundreds of cavers come down here every year, and as far as I know, not one of them has ever found this place. I'd say that makes you the discoverer, which means you get to name it.'

Julie shook her head, thinking of Paul and Manny and how they'd secretly fallen upon the mysterious cave just one month prior. 'Yeah, I guess it does.' She grabbed her water bottle and sipped eagerly. 'Well, as we found it together, how about we call it The Cave of Jewels, but we'll spell it J-U-E-L-S. You know? As in Julie and Ellie.'

Ellie doubled over, laughing. 'That's so cheesy it's good. I love it.'

Julie dropped down onto the cave floor, taking care not to step into the water.

'What are you doing?' Ellie asked.

'Having a look around. I mean, we've come all this way, so we may as well have a good nose. As you said, as far as you know, nobody's ever been down here before. There really could be hidden treasure.'

Julie circled the edge of the pool, marvelling at the beautiful mosaic of colours that shimmered off its smooth surface. The water was completely still and dark, like black onyx. Julie imagined herself skating across the pond, the blades of her ice-skates cutting shallow scars into the gleaming stone. She felt like walking into the centre of the pool and dipping her head into its cool depths. She imagined the liquid to be soft and soothing, like the freshest mineral water. Perhaps it too would be healing, like the Amrita.

As her eyes traced the edge of the water, she spotted a large, diagonal fissure in the wall. There was a faint green glow that looked out of place. She knew instantly that they needed to head down that crevice. It was exactly the kind of thing Paul would have done.

'Look, Ellie. It's another opening.'

'Where? I can't see.' Ellie dropped down beside her. 'Oh, yeah. Well, would you look at that. It's weird, isn't it?'

'Yeah, and there's that green glow, too. What do you think that is?'

Ellie approached. 'I don't know. I really don't. The limestone, maybe? Some form of luminous vegetation?'

Despite her excitement, Julie could feel every molecule in her body screaming at her to leave immediately, to climb back into the narrow tunnel and to scramble back to Marble Showers, and then, preferably, back to the safety of their hotel rooms as quickly as possible. Everything about the cave felt wrong. It felt dangerous.

'We need to tell the authorities about this, Jules,' Ellie said.

'We don't know what we're dealing with, here. We have no idea where this tunnel goes, or even if it's safe.'

Julie knew her friend was right. She also knew that if they had an accident and they were both incapacitated in some way, no-one would ever find them. They hadn't told anyone about their little detour. They would die there, hundreds of metres beneath the surface of the earth in the darkness without food. It would be the most painful, desolate death, and one which terrified her more than anything, but she also knew that she had to find the source of the Amrita. She had to know what Paul and her father were wilfully ingesting. There was no way she could leave without uncovering the truth.

'Oh, come on Ellie,' she said, her voice faltering. 'What do you always say to me? Live a little?'

'I do. But this is different. If we go down there, we're really stepping into the unknown.'

Julie took a deep breath and approached the dark hole. 'I know. Exciting, isn't it?'

Saturday, 24th June:

Elysian Field Laboratories, Galdhøpiggen, Norway

Paul and Manny sat in the conference room and glared at the thick bundle of documents they'd both just skim-read.

'This can't be right,' Manny said. 'Does this say what I think it says?'

Yaz had handed them the official file as soon as they'd walked through the door and told them to take their time in reviewing everything. The conference room they'd been directed to was large, expensively furnished and divided in half by a free-standing screen. A long, teak table occupied the centre of the room which was filled with pastries and fresh fruit. A Tchibo coffee machine stood by the door, which seemed to offer every caffeine concoction known to man. Paul ignored Petra's hospitality, however, and dived straight into the file.

'Forty percent,' he said. 'She wants forty percent of the profits, and worldwide distribution rights, in perpetuity.'

'She can take a running jump off a short pier,' Manny replied, gruffly. 'Forty percent? That's ridiculous.'

'I know.'

'I mean, does she think we're stupid, or something? Do we look that dumb?'

Paul pushed the paperwork aside. Maybe they did, and maybe she was right. He'd been so bullish about this whole trip, so supremely confident, so cock sure of himself. The problem was, in the face of someone smarter, someone with more power, more connections, what was he really? Just a bloke with a bit of mouth who worked in a lab, barely scraping a salary above minimum wage, living in a shitty flat in a small town that wasn't really much of anything.

He approached the coffee machine, deciding he needed something after all. He was feeling pretty overwhelmed: the top-secret location of Elysian Field, the severe lack of daylight, the mysterious Petra Gunderson, the cloak and dagger way they'd been introduced, and the gleaming white brilliance of the underground laboratory. And now this deal that was both unfair and apparently not up for debate.

'I reckon this is it,' he said. 'I think it's this or nothing.'

'Nonsense. I say we walk out of here with our pride intact and see what other ideas your uncle can come up with.'

'I don't think he's awash with options, Manny.'

'Then we'll find someone else. Someone who really knows what they're doing.'

Paul waited for the machine to mete out his decaf Americano. 'What does it matter?'

'What do you mean?'

'What does any of this matter? Look, if we're right about this stuff, we're looking at making billions here. Probably tens, maybe hundreds of billions. Once word gets out about what the Amrita can do—the diseases and conditions it can cure—the world won't be big enough for it. We'll be churning it out by the lorryload. We'll have more money than we can handle, Manny. More than we could ever imagine. So what if Petra gets forty percent of that? We'll still be the majority shareholders, and we'll be making so much money, we won't think twice about what we're giving away.'

'But what is she doing for it, Paul?' Manny hissed. 'We found the stuff. We risked our lives in extracting it from that cave. What is she actually bringing to the party?'

'We can't do anything with it without a clearance certificate,' Paul replied. 'Without that, it's worthless. It'll just sit in our storage container and rot. We need her. She has the key to the vault. Our riches are no good if we can't get access to them.'

Manny paced the room, the pulse in his thick neck twitching. Paul let him walk it off. His friend was feeling cheated, which was understandable. Paul didn't feel great about it either, but sixty percent of something was worth a hell of a lot more than a hundred percent of nothing. He needed the money, he needed the freedom, and what's more, he needed to know what the hell they were dealing with. Sure, the Amrita had cured his condition, Wade's and Julie's father's too, but was it permanent? Were their side effects? Was it even safe? And the giant creature and that grotesque monstrosity that had crept out of the tunnel? What were they? Were they real? Were they known by science? Was there some big secret that those in power were keeping from the general population? He had to believe that if Petra and her team of scientists at Elysian Field could determine the molecular make-up of the Amrita, then perhaps what had happened to him and Manny in the cave could be explained in some logical, less terrifying way.

Manny sat down at the opposite end of the long table, a cinnamon bun gripped between his fingers.

'I think this deal is crappy, Paul. Really crappy. I reckon we're being taken advantage of, and not in a good way.' He set down his bun. 'But I also happen to think you're right. We have no option. As much as I don't want to admit it, that's the truth. In the grand scheme of things, sixty percent is still a big slice of a huge pie.' He took a bite and let the crumbs tumble from his mouth. 'I say we get your uncle to look over the document, and if he's happy—and only if he's completely happy—then we sign.'

Paul allowed himself a smile. 'Well, then I guess this is it.'

'I guess it is.'

Petra emerged from behind the screen. She was holding a bottle of Dom Perignon and three glasses.

'That really is wonderful news,' she said. 'You have made the right choice, believe me. May I suggest a celebration.' She uncorked the wine and filled three crystal flutes, handing a glass to each of them. 'To the start of a beautiful partnership.'

Paul sipped the champagne and smiled as the bubbles slipped down his gullet. She was right. It was going to be a stunning, life-changing union. He just hoped they wouldn't come to regret it.

Saturday, 24th June:

Marble Showers, OFDII Cave Network, Wales

The stench coming from the end of the tunnel was putrid, like a barrel of fish that had been left out in the sun for too long and allowed to fester. Julie held a finger to her nose. The green glow was dull and undulating. The walls were dark and glistening with a strange, slimy seaweed-like substance that clung to its smooth surface. Everything smelled damp. The stench of mildew assaulted her senses.

'I don't like this, Jules,' Ellie said. 'This isn't normal.'

Julie barely heard her. She had the bit between her teeth now. This was what she had come all this way for. This was what was going to give her answers; answers that she should have pursued before allowing Paul to give her father that greasy gunge.

'Jules, are you listening?'

She approached the pool. It was a dark khaki shade of green with an oily substance floating just beneath the surface. It looked like the pool had once been more substantial. A tide mark was visible a foot above the current waterline, and something long and sleek lay stricken, half in and half out of the liquid.

'What the hell is that?' Ellie asked, but Julie was already moving towards it. It appeared to be wide and flat, about the size of a small truck. It had a smooth, metallic appearance, the colour of pewter, but with a green tint. Its underside was barely visible, but Julie could see that finger like protrusions jutted from its belly, like coral, but each of the protrusions contained tiny hairs with black buds on the ends of each. In the middle of its flat surface was a gelatinous opening, the size of a large window, with a group of tiny clear ball-like structures with black slits at their centre. It was as though the cavity was filled with tiny eggs. The thing smelled awful.

'I think it's dead,' Julie said. 'Whatever it is.'

At the other side of the small chamber, a group of rocks had been pushed together to block what appeared to be another much smaller tunnel. Julie thought the groundwater must have originally emerged from that opening, and the placement of the rocks had the effect of cutting off the supply of what little liquid was available. Had Paul and Manny done this? Had they killed the creature deliberately or had it been dying anyway? Did they do it to get to the Amrita? If so, where was it? Was there some secret compartment on the other side of the rocks? She bent down to get a closer look.

'Jules,' Ellie said. 'For God's sake, stay away from that thing.'

'It might still be alive.'

'I know! And that's all the more reason to keep your distance. We don't even know what it is.'

'It could just be wounded.' Julie ran a hand along the creature's back. Instantly her mind flashed to somewhere black, somewhere damp and silent. There was a horrible groan followed by the slurping sound of wet flesh in shallow water, the scurrying of claws on hard stone, fingernails scraping against clumps of soil and flint. Julie pulled her hand away and fell back into the pool.

'Jules, you okay?' Ellie cried. She was suddenly behind her, thrusting her hands beneath Julie's armpits and pulling her onto dry land.

'Holy shit,' Julie said, breathless. 'That was odd.'

'What happened?' Ellie handed her a water bottle.

Julie took a large swig. 'Thanks. I saw something. Something in the dark. I don't know. It sounded like something was digging.'

Ellie glanced at the blocked tunnel. 'You mean, in there?'

'I don't know.'

'Come on, we're getting out of here. This is getting way too creepy. I say we go back to the hotel, have a hot shower, order a couple of large gin and tonics, and then tell Bob and his professional caving pals about what we found. They can deal with it. They're much better equipped than we are.'

Julie didn't like the idea, but she was too stunned to argue. The creature had once lived and breathed—of that there was no doubt—but she had no idea what it was or what she had just seen. Getting away from the caves seemed like the right thing to do, but it still didn't answer her questions. Where had the Amrita come from, and what were Paul and Manny hiding?

Julie gradually got to her feet, her arm around Ellie's shoulders. 'Thanks again,' she said. 'And I'm sorry. I shouldn't have dragged you down here.'

'It's no problem, really,' Ellie replied. 'It's been an adventure. A strange one, but an adventure nevertheless.'

Julie yearned for soap and hot water on her skin, her robe wrapped around her aching body and a hot cup of tea in her hands. She was exhausted and confused. She felt like she could close her eyes and not stir for a dozen hours, maybe more.

They started to walk up the shallow incline when Ellie suddenly stopped.

'Oh wait,' she said. 'You left my bottle beside the pool.'

She walked back to the water's edge where Julie had left it. It lay against a cluster of small rocks, its base still in the shallow liquid. Ellie bent down and grabbed the polished steel container. 'My husband will never forgive me if I lose this. It was an anniversary present.'

Julie smiled, watching as Ellie turned back towards her, the bottle in her hand like a trophy. She stumbled a little on the wet rock and stepped backwards with one foot to steady herself, inadvertently treading on something in the water. As Ellie wheeled her arms to regain her balance, the motionless form of the creature rose up behind her like an enormous hand, it's coral-like fingers now rigid and taut. Its body was wide and undulating, and it stood erect on thick limbs that ended in squirming toe-like appendages. It was enormous. As its skin rippled, a thick yellow liquid ejected from black buds at the ends of what she guessed were its arms, covering the cave walls and dousing Ellie's head and torso.

'Eurgh!' she screamed. 'What the hell?'

Before Julie had time to react, Ellie was enveloped within the creature's huge bulk and shoved to the floor as its enormous body folded around her. The muscles beneath its hard skin tensed, crushing Ellie inside its thick, pungent mass.

'Ellie! No!'

Her cousin peered back at her, her face barely visible. Her mouth was open in a silent scream, her eyes wide and bloodshot. When Julie heard the sound of Ellie's bones fracturing, and saw her head crushed to a red mess of skull and meat, she turned and ran. She ran for her life.

Part Two: Storage Explosion

Sunday, 25th June:

Sittingbourne, Kent

Paul exited the taxi and looked up at his first floor flat. You couldn't miss it. Tatty, white-plastic window frames, fading yellow paint and a streak of grey sludge that drew a line from the creaking guttering to the pavement beneath. It wasn't much, but it was all he could afford. What's more, it had a bed. He'd been awake for over thirty-six hours and needed to sleep. Badly.

He paid the fare, grabbed his backpack, suitcase and jacket, and climbed the steps to the ground floor entrance. Fumbling for his key, he dropped it twice before jamming it home. He took the lift to the first floor (he was too exhausted to climb another flight of stairs) and trundled along the hallway to his door. Number thirteen. Unlucky for some.

His stomach was growling and his throat was dry, but none of that mattered right now. His head needed to hit a pillow, and fast.

After they'd shaken on the deal at Elysian Field, he, Manny, Yaz and a few of the others had gotten pretty drunk. It had hardly been professional, but the alcohol was free, the music was loud, and Petra and her employees were very receptive hosts. Paul could barely remember how the night had ended. He hadn't even been sure if it had been night-time at all. There were no bloody windows at Elysian Field. Little, fractured snippets kept coming back to him. None of them were good. Drinking absinthe from the bottle, dancing on a tabletop in his underwear, taking his boxers off and jumping in the pool, Manny snorting something from another man's bald head.

Petra had merely sipped cognac and watched everything unfold around her, a smile kissing her immaculately painted lips. In hindsight, it made perfect sense. He and Manny had danced to the well-dressed CEO's tune the whole time they had been there.

He tossed his suitcase into the cupboard, dropped his backpack on the floor and kicked off his shoes. His feet hurt and his eyes were burning. The flight home had been horrible. Manny had thrown up in the sick bag while Paul's head pounded the whole way. Passport control was a disaster, and they'd had to stand in a queue for what seemed like hours. The taxi they'd booked hadn't shown up, so they'd had to scramble around, looking for another cab-firm to collect them, eventually settling on a ridiculously expensive Uber. The M25 had been nose-to-tail all the way back, the needle barely reaching twenty miles an hour, and then to boot, there had been a three-car pile-up on the M20, and they'd sat completely still for forty minutes. If luck was a disease, he and Manny had proven to be ridiculously healthy.

His phone buzzed in his pocket but he decided to ignore it. He couldn't face speaking to anyone, let alone dealing with any more bullshit. He looked at the collection of post on his doormat but kicked it to one side. Again, he didn't need to look at bills and takeaway menus. He needed to study his eyelids, and for a good few hours, too.

He pulled back the sheets from his bed, slumped onto the mattress and blinked.

*

Nine hours later, he opened his eyes. The room was dark and deathly silent. He checked his watch. It was three a.m., which he knew was four a.m. in Norway. It was still far too soon for him to be awake, even if he had crashed out at a ridiculously early hour.

His throat was dry and his stomach was screaming for him to eat. He swung his legs over the edge of the bed and headed for the kitchen. He reached into the fridge, opened the milk and instantly pulled his nose away. The cow juice was way past its sell by date and smelled of pungent cheese. He bent down and rummaged through the shelves, looking for anything cold to drink. There was one bottle of Heineken buried under a mass of curled vegetables and dehydrated mushrooms. He reluctantly accepted it as his one and only option. He withdrew a small vial of the Amrita from his bag, opened the lid and swallowed. He scrunched up his nose. The bitter taste wasn't exactly appealing. They would have to work on that. He reached into the drawer, grabbed a bottle opener, and flipped the top from his beer, glugging four mouthfuls in quick succession. He found a block of cheddar to make himself a sandwich, groaned as he realised his bread was mould-infested, so decided to cut a big hunk from the nose of the cheese, instantly devouring it along with what remained of a chorizo sausage. His hunger sated, he grabbed his beer and walked back into the bedroom.

That's when he saw the shadow. It was lying on his duvet, its long arms folded across its lythe, muscular body. Yellow unmoving eyes glared at him from deep indentations in a malformed face. Paul reacted instantly, curling his fingers around the beer bottle and throwing it as hard as he could. It hurtled towards what he imagined to be the creature's misshapen head, but the bottle seemed to pass straight through it, as if the thing lying on the mattress was a ghost. It shattered harmlessly against the rear wall. The room was immediately covered in beer and glass fragments. Breathing fast, Paul reached for a lamp and flicked the switch. The room was bathed in yellow light, but the shadow was no longer there.

'Shit,' he groaned. 'I'm so tired.'

He heard his phone buzz again. It was on the floor. Paul stared at it for a moment, still processing what had just happened. When his mind came back into focus, he saw Julie's image glaring up at him from the brightly lit screen. He stooped down, glanced once more at his bed and collected the phone.

'Hi Jules,' he said. 'What's up?'

'What do you mean, what's up? I've been trying to get hold of you since yesterday!'

'Sorry, I've been travelling. The ride home was a nightmare.'

The line went silent.

'Why don't you come over?' he asked, trying to break the tension. 'I can make us something to eat.'

'Paul, it's three in the morning.'

'Yeah, oh yeah. You're right. Sorry. Jetlag.'

He could hear the sound of Julie sobbing down the line as the signal quality started to break up.

'Julie, are you okay? What's wrong?'

'Why...tell me...Black Cave…Ellie…the thing.'

Had she said Black Cave? What did she know about that? He'd been economical with what he'd told her about the caving expedition he'd taken with Manny. 'Jules, I'm only getting every third or fourth word. Can you say that again?'

'Horrible…Ellie…coming home…tell somebody.'

He paced the room, trying to find a spot in his flat where the signal was stronger, but when he glanced at his screen, he saw that it showed a healthy four bars. 'I think it's your end, Jules. Can you call back on a landline?'

'Coming home,' she said again. 'Three hours…maybe less…I'll come over.'

'Okay,' he said. Where had she been? What had she done? 'Call me when you get in. Come here, or I'll come to you, whatever. Just call me.'

They were cut off and Paul was left standing in silence in nothing but his beer-soaked underpants. He eyed his bed, which was drenched, and caught a reflection of his sorry self in the mirror.

'Shower,' he said eventually. 'I need a shower.'

There was a hard rap on his door. Paul stood still, hoping the visitor would go away. After a few seconds, there was another loud knock, followed by a man's voice.

'Open up, it's me.'

'Who's me?' Paul asked. 'It's three in the bloody morning.'

'Four, if you're in Norway,' the voice replied.

Paul reached for the lock and opened the door. 'Jesus. Shouldn't you be in bed?'

Manny pushed past him. His face was grey, the skin dark beneath his eyes.

'I got a call,' he said. 'It's bad.'

Paul tried to shake off the remains of exhaustion. 'What's up?'

'It was his mum. She sounded a bit frantic at first, so I cracked a joke to calm her down. I could barely understand her.'

Paul had no idea where this was going.

'She started to talk about her son in the past tense, and that was when it clicked with me, what she was trying to say.'

'I don't get it,' Paul said. 'You've come over here in the middle of the night to talk about a chat you had with some bloke's mum. Is this some kind of sick prank?'

'Listen, Paul. Don't be a prat. I'm trying to tell you something here.'

'Then why don't you get on with it, because right now you're making absolutely zero sense.'

Manny grabbed his shoulders. Paul could smell the absinth and airline coffee on his breath. 'It's Wade,' he said, his voice wavering. 'He's been murdered.'

Sunday, 25th June:

Pilgrims Way, Canterbury, Kent

Renee rose at around eight, took a shower and hastily got dressed. Her housemate, Rosa, was in the kitchen making coffee. Another woman was slouched on the sofa.

'Morning,' Renee said. 'I see you have company.'

Rosa, her dark hair hanging across her face in thick, untidy curls, held up a hand and moved her fingers towards her thumb.

'Keep it down a bit,' she half-whispered. 'I had a bit of a heavy night.'

Renee grinned. 'Who's the blonde?'

'I can't really remember.'

'You're going to get yourself into a lot of trouble one of these days,' she scoffed, pouring some of the coffee into a travel mug and grabbing her keys. 'By the way, I can't make breakfast at Wetherspoons today, but by the looks of it, neither can you.'

Rosa shook her head, sipped her cappuccino, and slumped onto the kitchen counter.

Renee unchained her bicycle from the back gate, threw on her backpack and pedalled along the cobbled streets. She hadn't slept well at all. She kept thinking about Wade and their afternoon together. He'd claimed the Amrita had cured his hearing loss as well as his chronically poor eyesight. There was no medicine known to man that could do such a thing; nothing even came close. Short of complicated, unreliable procedures, the only productive methods that science had come up with were reductive in nature. That is to say, they reduced the symptoms, perhaps even slowed deterioration to a degree, but there was no prevention, no cure. If proven to be scientifically true, this yellow crystalline material, this alien gunk, could fundamentally change the way the scientific community viewed medicine. It could potentially cure ailments that, as yet, were incurable, unfixable. The possibilities were endless. Sure, she'd signed an NDA to prevent her from discussing it, but how could she keep this quiet? She had friends, family members, who could potentially benefit from taking just a small amount of it daily. An uncle with stomach cancer, a cousin with painfully acute arthritis. What if the Amrita could rid them of their conditions? Could she sit back and let them suffer, potentially die, knowing all the while that she had something in her possession that could make it all go away?

She'd mulled it over while tossing and turning in bed, sleep avoiding her like a lottery win, and she'd eventually come to a decision. She had to get to the lab to do more tests. After all, she now had a flask full of the stuff, with the ability to make an infinitely greater quantity if needed.

She planned to get to the bottom of what this strange remedy was, and what it could do, all of it, whether Paul Karin liked it or not.

Sunday, 25th June:

Cobham Motorway Services, M25, Surrey

Julie sat in the service station on the M25, her head in her hands. Ellie was gone, crushed to death by some otherworldly creature, her body left to rot hundreds of metres underground in a terrifying, claustrophobic darkness, hours from daylight. It didn't seem real. It was like a bad dream. The worst kind, except this was real.

She couldn't shake the look her cousin had given her just before that monster had squeezed the life out of her broken body, her eyes pleading for her to save her. Julie had frozen in the moment, unable to move, unable to think. That awful instance of petrified inertia would never leave her. Ellie had come to Black Spring to help her, her best friend, and yet Julie had been unable, perhaps even unwilling, to reciprocate when it had mattered the most. Ellie would never see her husband again, would never see her sons, Bailey and Harper, reach adulthood, go to school, get married, start families of their own. *Oh God*, she thought, the tears flowing once more. What would she tell them? What could she possibly say?

Julie sobbed until her body ached and her throat was hoarse. Her shoulders and torso shuddered behind the steering wheel, hot, salty tears trickling from the point of her chin. Passers-by glared at her through the window, but none of them stopped to check if she was okay. She was grateful for that. What would she even say? That she and a cousin had gone on a field trip to the Cave of the Black Spring to find the source of an alien material that could cure previously incurable conditions, only to come up against some sort of giant, subterranean water creature that could stand upright, stretch out its serpentine limbs and literally crush the life out of a human being? They would think her mad, high or both.

The climb out of the caves had been difficult and terrifying, but Julie could barely remember details. There were just flashes of images as she took wrong turn after wrong turn, almost slipping through the gaps in the rock and constantly losing her footing as she clambered across uneven platforms and ridges. When a shaft of daylight fell on her cheek, she'd barely registered it. She had felt numb, her body on autopilot, her mind on a different plane entirely.

Owen had been standing by the cave entrance when she emerged from the gloom, a group of amateur cavers waiting dutifully behind him. She was surprised by the huge upswell of emotion she felt at the sight of another living, breathing human being. She'd almost blurted everything out right there and then. When Owen almost nonchalantly enquired after Ellie, it had caught her off guard. A switch inside her had flicked, and somehow she had come up with a story, explaining how Ellie had had to leave a little early for a family emergency, allowing Julie, after some persistent and belligerent pleading on her part, to stay back and take some photos. Her ability to lie under such pressure repulsed her. How could she be so cold?

Owen had called his boss, Bob, who had been incensed at the thought of an inexperienced caver such as her being left alone in what was, after all, an extremely treacherous place, and he'd vowed to call Ellie later that day to give her a piece of his mind. Julie hadn't argued. She'd just wanted to get out of there. Now that some time had passed, however, she realised she'd made a dreadful mistake. She'd allowed those poor kids to go down into those tunnels, knowing that a deadly creature lurked within their shadowy depths. She thought about them being attacked, right at that very second, but convinced herself it was unlikely. The creature had been dying when they'd found it, and its last tragically fatal act had been more of a muscle reflex than some ingenious trap. It was the unseen things that bothered her. The things beneath. The ones that scratched, clawed and dug furiously at the earth. Where were they? *What* were they?

She knew she had to get home. She had to talk to Paul.

She sat upright in the seat of her car and wiped snot and tears from her cheeks and lips. She glanced at herself in the rear-view mirror. She looked and felt shocking. Her eyes were dark holes, her lips thin and cracked. Her skin was covered in cave dust and grime, her hair matted. It clung to her face like tar. She didn't care. The nightmare had to end right now. With a grunt, she started the car and shifted it into first gear. She was an hour from home. An hour from answers.

Sunday, 25th June:
Sittingbourne, Kent

Wade had been strangled to death, or that was what his mother told them. The flesh around his neck was purple and mottled, his windpipe had been crushed, and his vertebrae had been severely fractured. The cause of death was currently unconfirmed, but the working hypothesis was asphyxiation. Someone had literally choked the life out of him.

Paul and Manny had decided to buy flowers and took them to Wade's mother's house. She lived at the far end of town in a little terraced place with an overgrown front garden, window boxes that hung empty and rotten, and thick, black smears of car exhaust deposits that tinted the flaking paintwork. The woman had looked as grey as the exterior walls when she eventually came to the door.

'I just can't believe it,' she repeated over and over as they perched in the sitting room, each nursing a milky cup of sweet tea. 'Who would do this to him, and why? He's always been such a nice, shy boy. He wouldn't even say boo to a goose when he was little. You remember that Manmeet, don't you?'

Manny nodded. 'That's right, Mrs Hughes. We had to make him laugh to get him to talk. He was a great friend, though. A good mate.'

Paul sat silently. He hadn't known Wade that well. Until now, he'd just thought of him as one of their experiments. He felt pretty bad about that.

'All those years being barely able to hear or to see,' she continued. 'He suffered at the hands of bullies almost all his school life—name-calling, mostly—but now, when he miraculously seemed to have grown out of his conditions, and he could see and hear again, and we could talk to each other and make each other laugh, well, now it's all been taken away from him, hasn't it. It's just so, so—'

Paul watched as the old woman broke down. He nodded in silence as he nursed his cup. He peered across at Manny who was sitting uncomfortably on the sofa beside her. They shared a quiet exchange. The timing hadn't gone unnoticed on either of them. It had been mere days since they'd convinced Wade to take the Amrita, and now he lay in a morgue, his neck broken and his windpipe crushed. It seemed more than just an unlucky coincidence.

'I had to identify him,' Mrs Hughes continued. 'I had to go in there and…' She took a deep breath. 'I had to look at my son like that, all bruised and lifeless. No mother should ever have to see their child in that state. It's not right for your children to die first.' She broke down once more and Manny shuffled closer to her, putting his arm awkwardly around her shuddering shoulders.

'There, there Mrs Hughes,' he said. 'Let it out.'

When they left the house, they both sat in Paul's car, Manny smoking furiously, neither of them speaking.

'What are you thinking?' Manny eventually asked.

'I don't know,' Paul replied. 'That it's just one of life's tragic mysteries?'

'It can't be anything to do with the Amrita, can it? I mean, the poor bloke was strangled. The Amrita can't do that, can it? Tell me it can't, Paul.'

'Well, I'm still here, aren't I? And I've been consuming that stuff far longer than Wade. And what about Julie's dad? As far as I know, he's been okay.'

Manny nodded. 'So, it's as you said. Just a tragic coincidence.

It's just one of those things.'

'I guess so. There's no other explanation for it.'

What they were saying made sense, but Paul couldn't help feeling there was more to it than that. He just couldn't figure out what. He didn't say anything, and neither of them discussed Elysian Field or what their next move was. It wasn't the time or the place. Paul dropped Manny back at his flat and returned home.

Back on the first-floor landing, Paul approached his door and noticed something he hadn't spotted when he'd first arrived back from Norway. The lock to his door—it had a gouge in it, like someone had gone at it with a knife or a screwdriver. He tried the handle, which held firm, and his own key turned in the lock, maybe a little more clunky than before, but the door opened, nevertheless. He stood on the threshold, unnerved and skittish. Wade had been murdered, and so he had to consider the possibility the killer could be hiding behind a door or lurking in his wardrobe among his crumpled shirts and faded jeans. He turned the key in his palm and pushed it between his fingers, creating a makeshift blade.

He closed the door behind him and stepped into the lounge. The room was empty and looked precisely as he'd left it, a bowl of cereal on the coffee table and two empty mugs beside the sofa. His backpack was still on the floor where he'd left it. He circumnavigated it before peering into the kitchen. There was no-one inside, but there was a space behind the door where he couldn't see. He placed a hand on the doorknob, which was unnaturally cold, readied his makeshift blade, and pulled the door towards him, leaping into the kitchen and thrusting the key out in a jabbing motion. It wasn't long before he realised the only thing behind the door was a mop and an empty bucket. He shook his head, marvelling at how pathetic he looked.

The bathroom proved to be empty, as did the in-built cupboard where his suitcase lay, still unpacked. He knew the last possible hiding place for an intruder was his bedroom, the place where his bed still lay soaked in beer and covered in shards of glass. The door was closed, which he thought odd—he hardly ever closed it—and there was a noise like something scratching against it; clawed fingers against hardwood, tip-tapping like stilettos on a dancefloor. His heart raced. Could there really be someone in there? Could it be Wade's murderer coming for him?

'Hello?' he called out. 'Is there someone there?' He cursed himself for sounding so juvenile. 'I'm coming in,' he added, attempting to sound at least a fraction more adult.

His hand reached tentatively for the door just as the tip-tapping stopped, and he stood back, waiting for the door to shatter outwards as a black beast with yellow eyes and clawed hands tore through its wooden structure and launched itself at him, gouging at his flesh and jabbing hard talons into the soft skin around his eyeballs. He shook the image away and re-set himself, aiming a foot at the door before kicking out, forcing it to swing violently inwards.

He clenched his fists, took a deep breath and charged into the bedroom, swinging wildly at the darkness. Something ran towards his legs, and he skipped to the side, missing his footing before smashing his hip into a corner table and toppling sideways onto the carpet. 'Shit!' he cried out before his shoulder connected with the floor and hot pain erupted in his cheek from a shard of beer bottle glass. 'Fuck, fuck.' He pushed himself up onto his knees, pulling the glass painfully from his face and kicking backwards, half expecting something to grab his feet and pull him towards the open door.

But there was nothing in the room. It was just as he had left it.

Blood trickled down his neck and he dabbed at it with a finger while he rose gingerly to his feet. He shook his head. There in the doorway, perched on its haunches, the hint of a smile on its fur covered lips, was the tabby-cat, Jesus, from the flat next door.

'Jesus!' he cried out. 'You'll be thankful for a crucifix if I ever lay my hands on you.'

The cat merely yawned, turned and sauntered into the kitchen.

'Oh no you don't,' he said. 'You're not making yourself at home.' Paul closed the bedroom window. He cursed himself for leaving it open and allowing the neighbour's cat yet another opportunity to invade his personal space. He scooped up Jesus and ushered him out the front door. 'How many times do I have to tell you, you don't live here.'

As the cat sauntered along the hallway, its white and brown tail raised high in the air, deliberately giving him a clear sight of its exposed anus, Paul glanced at the barrel of his lock. It was there alright. A definite gouge at the key entry point. He peered along the hallway towards the fire escape and glanced at the white, spherical object connected to the ceiling above. Five blue LED lights blinked at him from within a dark, circular lens. Paul recognised it as the landlord's cheap CCTV system. That gave him an idea. If someone really was out to get him, he was going to find out exactly who it was.

*

As Paul locked the front door and exited the flat, a stranger watched silently from within the shadows. He had heard the idiot Wade had been killed, but he was sure it hadn't been by one of his own staff. Rami and the other guys had sworn to him they hadn't even known that the devious little shit had made his escape out the backdoor. He knew that could only mean one thing. Karin must have found out that Wade was planning to sell a chunk of the yellow stuff to him, and he'd obviously been unhappy about it. So unhappy, in fact, that he'd seen fit to have one of his own friends rubbed out right under their noses. That wasn't very nice. Not very nice at all. If Paul Karin and his fat, Indian mate with the loud mouth thought they could get one over on Ted Barker, they had another thing coming. They obviously didn't know who they were dealing with, and how important, how well respected, how *downright lethal* Ted had become in the past two years. He was a veritable overlord now. A man of well renowned ill-repute.

He salivated at the thought of the money he was going to make once he got his hands on Karin's stash of Amrita. The deal with Wade was off, but that was fine by Ted. He hadn't wanted to part with any of his hard-earned cash anyway. What he really wanted was to take what he now thought of as rightfully his, and he wasn't planning on paying a single penny for it either. He was no longer happy to settle with just a few pitiful litres of the stuff. He wanted the lot. He wanted everything Karin had.

As Ted turned to leave, he heard footsteps ascending the stairway to the second floor, and he hastily hid himself in a store cupboard, leaving the door open just a crack. The footsteps stopped just outside, and Ted wondered whether Karin had spotted him on his way out and decided to come back and confront him, rather than run away from him like the wet blanket that he was. However, the scruffy haired lab technician wasn't the one that stepped into the corridor at all. It was someone far more interesting, and better looking to boot. This was a person that Wade had told him all about while he lay semi-conscious on the sofa during the party at the house by the creek a few nights ago. She was medium height, slim build and with long dark hair. He thought she had a nice body, too—very nice, although she looked like she was in dire need of a good wash. He retrieved his phone from his pocket and scrolled through Karin's contacts on Facebook, grinning smugly when he found her profile picture. It was an accurate likeness.

The woman paused halfway along the hallway and opened her handbag. She rummaged around in it for a few seconds before retrieving what she was searching for. With barely a moment's hesitation, she pushed the key into the lock and opened the door to Karin's flat. Ted couldn't believe his luck. It was like the good karma fairy had delivered him a little gift, not that he was owed anything. As she entered the room, he hastily exited the store cupboard, bounded with padded feet across the hallway, and placed the toe of his shoe between the door and the frame, preventing it from latching shut. After glancing along the corridor to make sure he wasn't being watched, he pushed the door open and followed Julie Harbor inside.

Sunday, 25th June:

Elysian Field, Norway

Petra Gunderson sat in her office, picked at a nail and recalled her discussion with the British wannabe billionaires the night before. The party had all been carefully stage managed, of course. She'd wanted to know everything about the Amrita, realising the moment she met them that neither were qualified scientists or physicians, and that there was absolutely no way they could have possibly created the potentially life-changing cure for all manner of debilitating conditions by chemical means. Her working hypothesis was that they had chanced upon it. She'd come to that conclusion less than thirty minutes into the drive from the airport to Galdhøpiggen. It was her usual strategy. Fool the client into believing she was a lowly driver working for Elysian Field, probe with a little small talk, and gradually prise open their lips. It worked every time. It was also why, prior to any formal introduction, she had clients stay overnight in a room that was the equivalent of the Big Brother TV studio, bugged to the hilt and fitted with 4K high-definition cameras that captured every angle.

Karin had been the first to leak the source. She had guessed that would be the case. Davi was obviously a cynic and less inclined to fall for the manipulation of strangers, however subtle. A few glasses of rum had been enough to loosen Karin's stoic demeanour. Even then, he hadn't given her everything, but it had been enough; enough for her to reach out to her ever-reliable sources and send them on their investigative errands.

'This is going to be a good contract for Elysian Field, mark my words,' he had slurred while they reclined on the large, leather sofa that occupied a space in the VIP section of the Caldarium. In front of them, the other residents of the Ambassade cavorted and writhed to a mix of pounding house music that had been carefully put together by their resident DJ.

'I have no doubt,' she'd replied, sipping on cold tea that was made to look like a tumbler of whiskey.

'We're going to make billions, Petra. Billions.'

'I sincerely hope so, Mr Karin.'

'Call me Paul.'

'Okay, Paul it is. Tell me—' she leaned forward and placed her hand on his knee, knowing after many years of dealing with hundreds of needy clients that the best way to build a trusting relationship was to be as tactile as possible, '—how did you even come up with this stuff? It's eluded the whole world for thousands of years, and yet here you are, claiming to have the great panacea, the holy grail, the elixir of life.'

Paul grinned and folded his hands behind his head. 'Well, that would be telling, wouldn't it.'

'Oh, come now. Your uncle tells me that you have worldwide patents pending, which means you are legally protected from a wanton copycat attempting to steal and replicate your work. I can assure you, Paul, that Elysian Field is no wanton copycat.'

Karin seemed to think this over. Eventually he stood, holding out his hand and grinning.

'I love this song,' he said. 'Let's dance.'

She obliged, which was completely out of character for her. She hated house music, she hated dancing, and, above all, she hated intimacy, particularly with men who had consumed far too much alcohol and far too many drugs. After several minutes of hip shaking, arm waving, and insincere whooping and giggling, they flopped back onto the sofa, breathless and sweaty.

'I could get used to this,' he'd said, eyeing his friend who was slow dancing with one of the residents, a woman in her sixties who had been a madam of a well renowned brothel when such things had been illegal. Karin held up a glass in salute.

'Back to what we were discussing,' she'd said, continuing to push. 'I don't want to know all your secrets, of course, but it would seem sensible for me to have at least an understanding of what I'm dealing with. That would be in both our interests, would it not?'

'Let's just say we don't need to be concerned about the competition. There's only three people that know about the real source of the Amrita, and two of them are right here.'

'And the other one?'

'Back home, and you don't need to worry about her. She's solid.'

'Solid, as in trustworthy? Or solid, as in you have protected your investment by making this person sign a bulletproof contract that means that if she breathes a word of anything about this to anyone, then her life would not be worth living?'

Karin paused, a glass of rum pressed to his lips. 'Er, the first one, I guess.'

'In my experience, Paul, trust is a flawed concept. I've found that even the most loyal of individuals can be bought for the right price. It's human nature, I'm afraid. The dollar, or in your case, the pound, is king.'

'No way, Jules wouldn't sell us down the river.'

Petra never forgot a name, and she had no plan of making this the exception.

The music suddenly flipped to seventies disco, causing the whole place to turn into a frenzy of tangled bodies, and Karin's partner, Manmeet, opened the top three buttons on his shirt, revealing an unruly crop of dark hair. Karin fell into a bout of hysterical giggling as Petra suppressed a groan.

'He can be such an idiot at times,' Karin said, trying to control his laughter. 'Just look at him!'

'Quite. I can see why you like him.' Petra placed her hand on his. 'But tell me, Paul, what is it that this woman knows? Surely if you have shared things with her, secret things, then wouldn't it be foolish to not let your new business partner in on just a little of what you're protecting?'

Karin seemed to consider this.

'I'm not sure,' he said. 'I need to talk this through with Manny.'

'I thought you were in charge.'

'Me? No. At least, I don't think so. We're a partnership. We split everything right down the middle.'

'Except you don't, do you? I overheard your conversation in the board room. Manmeet didn't want to sign the deal, but you saw what he couldn't see. You saw the opportunity. You were aware of the bigger picture.'

Karin's eyes widened. 'Well, yeah, I guess I did.'

'You know how huge the Amrita will become once it's cleared for mass consumption, and you are not closed to the idea of joining forces with an organisation like ours and giving up what is, let's face it, a sizable share of your company. As you said in there, sixty percent of the profits is still a hell of a lot of money.'

'I did say that,' he said. 'Yeah, I guess I did make that decision, didn't I?'

'Which means you are a leader, Paul. A natural leader.'

He shook his head, but Petra could see that his consumption of drugs and alcohol was catching up with him. His pupils were severely dilated and his eyelids were sagging. She realised that if she was going to get anything out of him, she had to do it before he passed out.

'We didn't set out to find it,' he said. 'It was just supposed to be a lad's weekend away, you know?'

She nodded enthusiastically, deciding not to interrupt.

'It was just down there, in the water. We didn't even know what it was, but then I fell into the pool and some of it went into my mouth, and all of a sudden, I felt different, somehow. Like a new man, or something.'

His head lolled to one side as he drifted off, but Petra gave him just a little nudge to bring him round.

'Woah, what happened,' he said.

'You fell asleep a little, I think.'

'I'm so tired.'

'Here,' she said, hastily cutting him a line of high-grade cocaine on the glass table. 'Try some more of this.'

She pushed Paul forward and tilted his head towards the white line, and he clumsily grabbed a tube and snorted. He jolted backwards as if he'd received a particularly sharp slap, and then he was in the room once more.

'That's better.'

Petra placed an arm around his shoulders. 'You were saying? Something about your fall into the water, and about how it made you feel.'

'Like a new man,' he repeated. 'I felt like I had been reborn.' His mouth fell open as he pushed Petra away. 'It came at us. Out of the shadows, yellow eyes, weird looking tentacles. It looked sick, as if it was old or dying or something. It tried to drag me with it into the tunnels, but Manny jumped it, hit it with a rock. It backed away then, but I think there were more of them down there. I didn't see them, but I felt something, you know? As if that tunnel led somewhere.' He grabbed hold of Petra's shoulders. 'We had to bury it! We couldn't let it out!'

His words were nonsensical. He was rambling, tumbling over

every syllable, but there was sincerity, too, as if he genuinely believed what he was saying. She was eager for him to tell her more, to tell her everything, but somebody clattered into her. She looked up, outraged.

'Do you mind?'

It was Davi. He was doing some sort of crazed, robotic dance routine. When she shoved him away and turned back to Karin, she saw he had fallen into a deep sleep.

It was frustrating, but she thought she had probably got all she was going to get out of him anyway. It was okay. She had enough to work with. All it took was a little research into Karin's bank accounts to find out where he'd spent his money in the past three months. It didn't take her long to spot the two hundred pounds he'd paid out to a little bed and breakfast in Penwyllt, or the three hundred and fifty pounds he'd spent on caving equipment hire.

She activated her Bluetooth headset.

'Gunthar,' she said, tucking her hair behind her ears. 'I need you to go on a little field trip to Wales. I suggest you book your flights immediately'

Sunday, 25th June:

Sittingbourne, Kent

Paul sat in Phil the landlord's flat and watched as the old boy, who was in his mid-sixties and overweight, struggled to work his antiquated laptop.

'It'll be on here somewhere,' he said, wiping sweat from his chin. 'I never delete anything.'

I bet, Paul thought, wondering whether he also had secret cameras placed in each of the rooms. The thought of the sweaty old pervert masturbating while watching him and Jules getting down and dirty made him want to heave.

'The past two days, you say?' Phil said, turning to Paul, his glasses perched on the end of his nose.

'Yeah. Friday and Saturday.'

'It might take me a little while. You wanna go and put the kettle on?'

Paul obliged and headed towards the kitchen. The worktops were covered in empty Chinese takeaway containers and pizza boxes, and the sink was piled high with unwashed dishes. He filled the kettle from a tap that hung limply from a loose fitting and recalled Julie's frantic phone call from earlier that morning. He'd almost forgotten about it, what with Manny's dramatic arrival, the shocking revelation about Wade, and then the frantic dual he'd fought with the neighbour's cat straight afterwards. Jules had sounded harried, upset, perhaps even a little scared. He thought she should have been back home already, which worried him. He checked his phone but there were no messages, no missed calls. He was just about to dial her number when Phil hollered from the other room.

'Here it is!' he yelled. 'What a bloody thieving so and so.'

Paul raced back into the room to see a figure entering his flat, but before his mind could piece together who it was, the screen went blank.

'Shit, sorry. Bloody VGA cable. It's always doing this.' Phil spun the monitor around and tightened the screws on the connector that joined the screen to the base station. The monitor came back to life, but the video had rolled on, and the corridor outside his flat was empty once again.

'There's no-one there, now!' Paul cried. 'Phil, come on! Can't you run it back?'

'No need. You'll get a better look this way. Whoever broke into your flat has to leave at some point, and unless he or she goes out the window, they'll have to come back through here. When they do, the camera will get a good shot of their face. Just be patient, young Padawan.'

Paul groaned. Was this bloke really giving him lectures on patience? The fat letch spent twenty-three hours of every single day just sitting there in his room, playing computer games and eating his bodyweight in cholesterol. How he'd survived sixty plus years without having at least a minor heart attack was beyond him.

'The door's opening,' Phil said, leaning forward and practically drooling with anticipation. 'This is the moment, Paul. This is it!'

'Get out the way,' Paul said, pushing Phil's giant torso to one side. 'I can't see anything.'

'Hey, stop shoving.'

When the door swung inwards, and the dark figure emerged from within the shadows, Paul couldn't believe it. The face was unmistakeable, as was the slim frame and distinctive gait. It was Wade. Wade had broken into his home.

'Son of a bitch.'

'You know him, I presume.'

Paul gave a curt nod.

'There's something else,' Phil continued. 'I noticed it as I was scrolling backwards. It looked a little weird, but we get all sorts of weird up here. Maybe it'll make sense to you.'

'Okay. Let's see it.'

'Yeah, just give me a minute.'

Paul was still trying to process everything. They'd given Wade the Amrita, and also provided him with plenty of doses to last him while they were away in Norway. There was no reason for Wade to get so desperate that he would do the unthinkable and break into Paul's flat. Obviously, he hadn't known that he and Manny had already relocated the freezers to their unit at Storage Explosion on the other side of town, which Paul thought would explain the disappointment on the guy's face as he exited the apartment. He recalled the details of Wade's murder and wondered whether this had anything to do with it. It didn't make any sense. Nothing was making any sense.

'There!' Phil yelled. 'There he is. See?'

Paul bent down and glared at the screen. There was someone else. This other man's face was barely distinguishable in the shadows, but Paul thought he recognised him, nevertheless. He was standing at the end of the corridor in the semi-darkness, apparently watching the door of his flat. He had an almost perfectly round head, with a bald pate and grotesquely crooked nose. He looked like a neanderthal knuckle-dragger which, from what Paul knew about him, was exactly what he was. The guy went by the name of Rami, and he'd been linked to a number of violent incidents that had occurred in the town over the past couple of years. Somehow he'd managed to stay out of the nick. Rumour had it that the goon was now a hired hand and worked solely for a guy that supplied all the local dealers with their narcotics; a villain that Paul tended to stay well clear of.

Rami Malinowski wasn't a man to mess with. And, more worryingly, neither was Ted Barker.

Sunday, 25th June:
Sittingbourne, Kent

Julie sat down on the sofa as her head flopped into her hands. She was so tired. She felt like she could sleep for days, maybe weeks.

The room smelled like Paul. There was the scent of beer, burnt toast and the musky aroma of cheap body spray. His underwear was hung limply over the radiator. An empty packet of crisps lay on the floor beside the bin, tiny morsels of dried potato spilling from its gaping mouth. The TV remote was tucked between the arm of the sofa and a cushion. He had been there but then he had gone. And why was that? Why the hell was that? She'd told him she was coming straight there. She'd told him about what had happened in the cave. He should be there, eager to find out what had gone on, to comfort her, to make sure she was okay. It was just so like him, only ever thinking of himself. What about what she needed? What about giving a shit about anything else other than what was going on in his own personal little bubble?

She yawned. She was so desperately tired. She hadn't slept in almost two days. Her eyelids felt like they were lined with sandpaper. She couldn't help herself. She had to rest. She stretched her arms, curled into a ball, and before she knew it, she dozed off.

She dreamed of black, dripping creatures dragging themselves through narrow cracks in the rock, their smooth bodies coated in a yellow and black ooze. Other creatures erupted from the swirling eddies, their sleek, muscular bodies fanned out, their many eyes unblinking and cruel. They came at her, moving through the mist with a speed that belied their awesome bulk, descending on her, crushing her. She awoke with a start, her face pressed into the cushions, warm drool pooled under her chin.

She turned her head to the side to see a man sitting on the armchair opposite. She instantly pulled herself upright.

'Who the hell are you?' she croaked.

The man cocked his head to one side, a grin curling at one corner of his mouth. 'Where's Paul?'

'I don't know. And even if I did, why should I tell you? How the hell did you even get in here?'

The man laughed. 'I don't want no trouble, lady. I'm just looking for something. Something I need. I know your boyfriend has it.'

'Then do yourself a solid. Go ask him.'

'Why do you think I'm here?'

She held out a hand, presenting the meagre contents of the room. 'As you can see, Paul doesn't have a lot.'

'Oh, but he does, doesn't he. He has something that nobody else has, something that will change the lives of an awful lot of people.'

Julie's brain started to connect the dots. 'What…are you talking about?

'You know about it, too, don't you? I thought you did. Well, maybe you can help me, Julie. Is it Julie? Or do you prefer Jules?'

'I'd prefer that you don't speak to me at all,' she hissed. 'But I'm guessing that's not an option.'

The man stood, offered her his hand. 'I feel like we've got off to a bad start. Name's Ted Barker, local businessman.'

Suddenly everything came back into sharp focus. She knew of Ted Barker, alright. What had Paul got himself into? 'Local drug dealer more like.'

'Ooh, you know how to hurt a man with your words, don't

you, Jules?'

'I can do much more than that, mate.'

He sat on the sofa beside her. 'Shove up a bit, love. Let's you and me get better acquainted.'

She jerked away. 'Don't you dare touch me.'

'Woah, I have no bad intentions, sweetheart. I just want your help.'

'Go to hell.'

He smiled. 'Well, I've pretty much got my place booked there already, but I'm hoping if I get my hands on some of your boyfriend's merchandise, then perhaps my arrival can be delayed for a while.'

It was obvious that Ted knew all about the Amrita, but the question was, how?

'Before you ask me,' she said, trying to sound authoritative but failing dismally. 'I don't know where it is. I just got back from a few days away, and I think Paul's moved it.'

'Funny,' he replied. 'That's what Wade said.'

'Wade?' She shook her head. 'If…if you've already spoken to Wade, why do you need to talk to Paul?'

Ted's expression hardened. 'I guess you haven't heard the sad news.'

'Heard? Heard what?'

'Wade's dead, darling. Murdered.'

Her breath caught in her throat. Was this guy serious? Wade? Murdered? By who? 'It was you, wasn't it? You killed him.'

Ted held up his hands. 'Hey, not guilty.'

'Liar.'

'I'm not here to plead my innocence, sweetheart.'

Julie thought fast. 'Look, Ted, I don't know anything. I swear. The stuff was here and now it's not. Paul could have moved it while I've been away. I don't know. I really don't.'

He glared at her. 'You better not be lying to me, darling.'

She thought of Paul, of the lies he had told her about the Cave of the Black Spring. He had kept so much from her. He had cajoled her into allowing her father to take some freaky alien gunk which had eventually led her to drag Ellie into that godawful, hellish place. Sure, the trip had been her fault, but Paul, with his hair-brained, half-baked schemes, had been the catalyst. What did she owe him? Nothing, that was the truth of it. And yet, she still couldn't find it in herself to betray him.

'I'm not lying.'

Ted held her gaze for a painfully long moment. Her gut twisted into tiny knots inside her. Sharp bile rose in her throat, hot and sour. She thought he was going to kill her right there on the sofa, but instead, he reached into his pocket and pulled out a phone. She let out a breath as he scrolled through his contacts.

'Rami,' he said, his dark eyes never leaving her. 'I've got someone here who could be useful to our cause…Yeah, if you could, mate. I'm at Karin's place…That's right, I followed her in. Yeah, I know. Some people…Okay, that's a great idea. I suggest we make her feel at home. She could be with us for quite a while.'

Sunday, 25th June:

University of Canterbury, Canterbury, Kent

Renee sat in the lab and carefully grabbed the tiny vial filled with red liquid from the stainless-steel trolley. The sample had cost her quite a bit of her monthly salary from the coffee shop, but she'd thought it was worth every penny. She had to know how powerful the Amrita was, if not for her, then for those that were suffering. Apparently, blood samples were far more difficult to come by these days, particularly when you were looking for unhealthy specimens, but she knew a guy, and he knew another guy, and somehow they'd managed to get her almost exactly what she needed in a matter of hours. The subject was dead anyway, so she didn't think she was breaking any ethical boundaries. She knew the university governors wouldn't see it like that, but this was in the name of science. It could overturn years of medical studies in a heartbeat.

She eyed the needle. Patient X10Y41. The little glass cylinder contained the blood of a colorectal cancer sufferer, stage four. She had a petri dish filled with a sample of the Amrita on the bench. She slowly slotted it beneath the lens of her microscope. Her mouth was like dust. Her fingers jittered and danced.

She eyed the other students in the lab. She knew they were busy carrying out their own experiments, but even so, every time one of them brushed past her, the pulse in her neck thrummed a little bit louder. When the lab door opened, it was if someone was kicking a metal drum. She knew she had to control herself. A good scientist had to be able to temper their nerves.

She pushed the needle of the syringe into the sealed lid of the vial and drew the contaminated blood into the barrel. She glared at it. It was red like any other specimen, but she knew this was different. It contained high levels of carcinoembryonic antigen (CEA) which was a tumour marker for cancer—in this case, colon cancer. Bad glycoproteins were swimming around in the blood, and it was these proteins that Renee was planning to observe. Her working hypothesis was that if the Amrita was able to reduce the amount of CEA in the blood, an antigen that the human body stopped creating just before birth but that re-appeared in some cancer sufferers, then in theory, it could do the unimaginable and cure cancer. It was a long shot, and a speculative theory at best, but she just had to know.

She approached the microscope, holding the syringe tightly in her hand. Her eyes pressed against the rubber eyepiece as she peered at the crystalline structures within the compound. The organic cells were irregularly star shaped, and they glistened with a brilliant, sparkling luminance as they jostled with each other, often joining together and then separating. She watched as the tip of her syringe came into view, and then the blood sample trickled from the end, mingling with the Amrita. She found herself involuntarily holding her breath.

At first, the red blood and multi-coloured crystals held their own separate positions, the cells maintaining their shape as the mixture made a raspberry ripple style pattern within the yellow liquid. The CEA proteins were clearly visible in the blood, but the Amrita crystals initially made no attempt to approach them. She felt a bitter snap of disappointment. Perhaps she had been wrong.

'What do you have there, Douglas?'

Renee sat back sharply and looked up at Professor Wayling, a tall man in his late sixties who had long, grey hair, a goatee and a silver nose-ring.

'I'm just doing some experiments on the reaction of blood within crystalline compounds, sir. It's for my paper.'

The professor's eyes narrowed as he eyed her over the rim of his round-framed spectacles.

'A strange experiment, Douglas. What's your hypothesis?'

'It's an odd one, sir, if you don't mind me saying.'

'Hey, it's your experiment. If you're okay with it being a little strange, then why should you worry what I think? Come on, lay it on me.'

The syringe containing the illicit blood specimen burned hot in her fingers.

'I…I'm looking into cleaning solutions, sir.'

'Cleaning solutions?'

'Yes, mineral compounds that could, if mixed properly, instantly remove tough stains such as red wine, cooking oil and…and…' She stumbled over her words. Her mouth felt like it was filled with cotton. The professor's eyes were on her. Sweat formed at the nape of her neck. She couldn't think. Everything was jumbled.

'Blood?' he offered.

'Yes, blood,' she yelped. 'I wanted to see if this concoction I have created could literally erase bloodstains.'

'That's a rather off-the-wall project, wouldn't you say?'

'I did tell you.' She forced a smile. 'It's a side-project of mine. That's why I came in so early this morning, just to see if my hypothesis was worth pursuing.'

'And is it?' he asked.

'Is it what?'

'Is it worth pursuing?'

Renee felt the immediate need to get up and flee her professor's constant barrage of questions, but she held her ground. She felt sure he knew what she was up to. She bit down on her bottom lip and counted to five.

'I don't know…yet.'

He folded his arms, his heavy brow triangulating above his piercing eyes. She was instantly transported back to her childhood home in the Dordogne, being scolded by her mamie for once again leaving the kitchen in a mess. She came to the realisation that she would have to fess up and tell him what she was doing, which she knew would lead to her being suspended from her studies, or worse still, kicked out of the university entirely.

Eventually the professor offered a small nod of approval. 'Well, let me know how you get on. I'm intrigued, if a little surprised.'

'Of course, Professor!'

As he moved to the next bench, she let out a long, silent breath. The whole exchange had left her feeling exhausted. It had been close. It had been way too close.

She sat there, still as a mouse, waiting patiently until he was sufficiently occupied with another student before slowly lowering her head to the microscope's eyepiece. What she saw made her heart literally stop beating.

The CEA. It was gone.

Monday, 26th June:
Heathrow Airport T3, London

It was a little before 9.30 am when Gunthar Strøm's British Airways flight touched down on the tarmac at London Heathrow's bustling Terminal 3. The flight was completely full which made the whole journey feel more than a little claustrophobic. However, Elysian Field's policy of flying all executives business class made the experience slightly less nauseating. Gunthar collected his carry-on bag, exited the aircraft, and proceeded through immigration in less than twenty minutes. Pleased with his progress, he headed for the rental car booth.

Keys in hand, he located his vehicle in the carpark—a barely cleaned VW Passat—and squeezed into the driver's seat. He was a tall man at a little over six-seven, and broad across the shoulders, and consequently he found travelling a painful experience. There was never enough legroom, and hardly ever the width to allow him to sit in a comfortable position. The whole flight had been an exercise in endurance. To take his mind off his discomfort, he had used the onboard wi-fi to fully trace Paul Karin and Manmeet Davi's movements on the weekend of the 27th and 28th May. Karin's card had been used to acquire fuel and two Burger King meals at the Membury Service Station located on the M4 motorway early on the 27th, and Davi had spent twenty-four pounds on his debit card at a pub in Swindon called the Rare Gent a few hours later. Petra had already informed Gunthar of the bed and breakfast the pair had stayed overnight in, which was located in the village of Penwyllt, and so he logged onto the property's website and booked himself a single room with breakfast.

The drive from Heathrow to the village was long and tedious. Gunthar had always hated driving on the British road network. The traffic was always horrendous, the roads were poorly maintained, and the quality of the service stations on route was mediocre at best. He grabbed a lukewarm coffee and a chicken salad sandwich at Swindon, which barely sated his appetite, and braced himself for another two hours behind the wheel while trying to not get himself killed by homicidal motorists.

When he reached the Prince of Wales Bridge, a feat of magnificent engineering that managed to impress his usually stoic cynicism, he started to feel a little more at ease. He had never enjoyed spending time in England. His parents had chosen to send their young son to a private boarding school in the UK until he was in his late teens, and those years did not hold happy memories for him. His mother and father had been wealthy beyond comprehension. Haakon Glücksburg was Norwegian royalty, twenty-sixth in line to the throne, but that didn't mean he wasn't a bad parent. If anything, his wife was worse. Gunthar had been sent off to boarding school as soon as he reached the required age, and consequently he could barely remember the family home in Berkshire. He had spent so little time there.

His years at Queen Mary's had been tumultuous. He had been persistently bullied, ridiculed for his Scandinavian heritage, and ostracised for his almost milky-white complexion and beanpole frame. For that reason alone, he had decided to enrol in the school's boxing team, a sport he'd followed only occasionally. Very early on, he found he had quite the knack for it. He enjoyed the almost balletic movement, the artistry involved in timing the perfect shot, and the need for near supernatural clairvoyance in avoiding the opponent's punches. He found it was the ideal pressure release for his pent-up anger and volatile aggression. Gradually his body matured, and pretty soon he had filled his impressive frame and was boxing as a cruiserweight in the regional championships. When he knocked out his overweight opponent in the county final, he finally felt like he had the vindication he deserved for the years of torment, bullying and neglect. His jubilation was tainted, however, when he realised his parents hadn't even shown up to watch him compete. He hated them for that, hated them for the abandonment, for the absence of any visible affection, and for the lack of self-worth he felt every time he looked at himself in the bathroom mirror.

When he returned home that Christmas, the year of his sixteenth birthday, he decided enough was enough. He ate dinner with them, picking at the meagre portion of veal and creamed potatoes served by the in-house chef, watched a little TV, and talked for an hour or more with the staff. Then, when he was sure his parents had drifted off to sleep in their separate beds, he killed them both with a pickaxe he'd found in his father's garage. He didn't try to cover up his tracks. He was proud of what he'd done. They'd deserved it.

He spent five years in Her Majesty's Young Offenders Institute for the worst juvenile offenders the country had to offer. He spent that time honing his boxing skills and learning a new sport – Jiu Jitsu. He excelled at both and fought off allcomers to win both the centre's heavyweight boxing competition, as well as the Mixed Martial Arts cage fighting championship. He found that his years learning how to box made him an excellent striker in the octagon, and Jiu Jitsu gave him the brutal ground skills needed to excel at the sport.

It was this that brought him to the attention of Petra's scouts, and when he was extradited back to Norway upon reaching his twenty-first birthday, Elysian Field paid the guards responsible for transferring him to Oslo's maximum-security prison to stop off at a truck stop, unlock the rear doors of the van, and look the other way while he made his escape. Petra's team had picked him up via helicopter and whisked him to Galdhøpiggen where they provided him a new identity and a new life. He never looked back. Elysian Field was exactly the kind of organisation that he needed. It had given him a purpose, a mission, and a way in which to use his finely honed skills. He'd only had to kill three times since joining the fold, but each time he had executed his orders with skill and precision. The natural high it gave him was better than any sexual encounter he had ever experienced. He never once regretted joining Petra and her team, and until now, he had never returned to the UK.

As he pulled into the tiny car park in front of Ty Selah Lodge, he knew exactly who he was and what he needed to do. His past was just a bitter memory. His present, however, was staring him in the face. Karin and Davi had been headed to the Cave of the Black Spring. He was as sure of that as he was certain that his birthname had been Olav Glücksburg, thirty-sixth in line to the Norwegian throne. That had all been such a long time ago, and right now he knew he had to focus on the job in hand. He had to find the source of the Amrita, and if anyone deemed it necessary to stand in his way, he was authorised to use maximum force. Gunthar felt something akin to happiness blossom in his chest. It was these types of jobs that made it all worthwhile.

Monday, 26th June:
Sittingbourne, Kent

Paul sat down on his couch, wincing as his daily dose of Amrita slipped down his gullet. He was worried. Jules hadn't shown up, despite telling him she was merely an hour away from home the morning prior, and now her phone had been permanently switched off. He cursed himself for not agreeing to Jules's request to download the tracking app on his phone so that they would always know where the other was. At the time, he thought it was an outrageous invasion of his privacy, and he told her as much. Now the argument seemed pathetic.

He'd called her mother who'd told him that they hadn't heard from her in a few days, but he decided to downplay his concern, telling her that he thought she'd made the decision to spend an extra couple of nights at wherever the hell she'd disappeared to. He realised he didn't even know where she'd been the whole time he'd been in Norway, and it also dawned on him that he hadn't tried to make contact with her while he was there. What sort of a shit boyfriend was he? Firstly, refusing to download the stupid app, secondly, not even considering her suggestion that they move in together, and thirdly, treating her like she didn't even exist.

He thought again about Phil the landlord's CCTV footage, the grainy image of Wade leaving his flat and the even less clear image of Ted Barker's henchman, Rami, standing in the dimly lit corridor. The whole thing left him feeling uneasy. He hadn't let Manny know about what he'd seen just yet. He didn't want to light a fire under that particular stack of kindling. Manny was too volatile, too unpredictable. Going in all guns blazing against a criminal like Ted Barker was apt to get you a broken nose or worse.

He thumbed through his emails, looking for an update from Petra or one of her employees. He couldn't recall much about their conversation at the contract signing party, but he felt sure he'd disclosed more than he'd intended to. The more he thought about it, the more it seemed to him that the whole thing had been carefully orchestrated by Petra, and that he and Manny had fallen for it like two naïve apprentices. He just hoped the patent that his uncle had filed was legally enforceable, otherwise there was every possibility they would be kissing their fortunes goodbye. He couldn't let that happen. He wouldn't. They'd already gone through so much to get this far. He wasn't about to let it all go.

His phone pinged.

Jules: Paul, it's me.

It was a WhatsApp message from his girlfriend. He let out a huge sigh of relief while hastily thumbing a response.

PK: Hi, I thought you'd gone AWOL.

Jules: Yeah, sorry. Got a little sidetracked.

PK: Where are you?

Jules: I found out some stuff about the Amrita. It's important.

PK: What stuff?

Jules: Can't say over WhatsApp. Can you meet?

PK: What? Right now?

Jules: Yes please. It's urgent.

He glared at the phone. She seemed different. When they'd last spoke, she'd been upset, in a state of panic, but now she was all business.

PK: Why didn't you call yesterday?

Jules: I told you, I got sidetracked.

PK: By who? I don't understand.

Jules: Don't worry. I'll fill you in when we meet.

This was going nowhere. He had an idea. He hit the video call icon and waited for her to pick up. He needed to see her face to be sure she wasn't playing some sort of dumb prank. When the call didn't connect, he stared at the screen. What the hell was she playing at?

Jules: Sorry, connection isn't good.

PK: Where are you?

Jules: The Rifleman.

The Rifleman was a pub he and Jules used to frequent in Leysdown-on-Sea before the pandemic. The landlady had closed its doors during lockdown, and as far is he was aware, she had never re-opened them.

PK: Why the hell are you all the way out there?

Jules: Privacy.

PK: Jules, I don't like this. Why don't you just come home?

Jules: Here's an idea. Why don't you break the habit of a lifetime and do something I ask?

He pursed his lips, mentally deflecting the jibe. He had to admit, Jules's last reply did sound like the girl he knew.

PK: Okay. Give me half an hour.

Jules: Make it twenty minutes.

Monday, 26th June:

Ospringe Road, Faversham, Kent

Roger Harbor arrived home from his allotment at around two in the afternoon. It had been a hot one, making the job of weeding the long, narrow plot a lot harder than it should have been. He didn't care. He was still so grateful that he could do it all. Being able to recall what he had achieved afterwards made it all the more rewarding. He didn't remember much about the crippling dementia that had afflicted him for so many months, particularly the latter stages as the disease became more and more rampant in his body, but what Julie and Barbara had told him had shaken him to his boots. He'd been no more than a year away from dying—he was now very sure of that—and yet, after his daily doses of the yellow medicine Julie called the Amrita, his mind was now perfectly fit and healthy. He felt like a new man, and a much younger model, too.

He had always been wary of his daughter's partners. She had a less than particular taste in men. Paul Karin was no exception. He was attention seeking, self-obsessed, and rarely treated Julie with the same level of devotion that she deserved. He guessed it was natural for a father to feel that way. He and his wife had conceived her, Barbara had given birth to her, and the two of them had spent the past near thirty years tending to her every whim. That sounded wrong, but it was the truth. It wasn't like they had spoiled Julie—she certainly didn't get everything she asked for—but they had always managed to be there for her when she needed them. Roger saw that as his job. He wanted to be Julie's hero, her guardian angel. The irony was, when the chips were down, she had been a hero to him. She had literally saved him from a fate far worse than death.

The house was empty. He knew Barbara was still at work and wouldn't finish her shift at the opticians until just after five p.m. That was a shame. He preferred it when she was at home with him, but he also knew that she'd had to increase her hours after he'd contracted the disease. Their finances had taken a hit when he'd been forced to retire from his job at the estate agent when his memory had started to lapse. He hadn't even thought about returning to work yet. The truth was, he wasn't sure he had the confidence. Who could say whether his new healthy mind would remain in its current condition? They just didn't know. Julie had admitted as much to him. The drug that Paul and his friend were developing was still in its infant stages, and they'd taken a risk in allowing him to trial it. He was the human equivalent of a lab rat.

He headed for the kitchen and put the kettle on. He was parched. He treasured something as simple as making a cup of tea. He had a new perspective on everything. Life was now coming at him in technicolour. He'd never take anything for granted, ever again.

It was when he opened the cupboard to reach for the teabags that he heard it. It was a noise that was out of place; a wet, slippery sound, like a towel being dragged through a puddle. He spun round, but it was okay. He was alone. He'd half expected to come face to face with the undead corpse of a fisherman, a bloodied hook in one hand and the head of a viciously gorged victim in the other. When all he was confronted with was the kitchen table, he let out a breath. He knew he was being stupid. The lingering disease was still playing tricks on his mind. Barbara would be home soon, and then the house would feel normal again.

When he finished making his cuppa, he grabbed two gingernut

biscuits and headed for the living room. Sure, the sweet, buttery treats were bad for his cholesterol and his blood sugar, but what the hell. He'd come back from the dead, after all. Didn't he deserve the odd luxury now and again? He slumped onto the sofa and grabbed the remote, but when he hit the standby button, nothing happened. The TV just glared back at him, its blank screen like an unblinking eye.

'Well, that's weird,' he said, before heading to the wall socket and turning the TV off and on again.

He sat back down and tried again, and this time the TV blinked into action. He grinned as a re-run of The Fall Guy leapt onto the screen. Lee Majors and Heather Thomas were doing their best to get away from a gang of armed men. When the TV blinked off again it caught him by surprise.

'Jesus bloody Christ!' he yelled as he stood up and bashed the side of the monitor. This time, nothing happened. He resigned himself to defeat. 'Like we can afford a new TV,' he said, slamming the remote onto the coffee table. 'Of all the bleeding luck.'

When he turned to pick up the phone and call his wife, he noticed the shadow lurking in the corner of the room. It was barely perceptible, but it was so out of place, he couldn't miss it. It was long and narrow and pressed into the wall like a thin sheet of paper. Water dripped from it, as if the absence of light had made that part of the room so damp that liquid was literally seeping from the plaster. He moved tentatively towards it, but he backed away sharply when the shadow shifted. It crept with a slithering malevolence, devouring the light socket, consuming the picture frames, and then stretching like elastic towards the armchair. When a single yellow eye appeared from within the darkness, Roger heard himself cry out.

'What are you?'

The shadow didn't answer. It simply continued to move and grow, bending and shifting until slim protrusions began to appear from its bulky mass, as did a pulsing, amorphous lump that revealed indented features: nostrils, a wide slit of a mouth, teardrop shaped ears. A long tentacle-like limb snaked across the doorframe and slithered along the carpet until it was mere centimetres from his unsteady legs. When its tip touched his thigh, he jerked away, shock spurring him into action.

'You're not real,' he said, climbing over the sofa towards the living room window. 'You're just a product of my illness. You're not real to me!'

The shadow gradually grew, standing upright, unfurling like a grotesque orchid, rising to over seven feet tall with features as black as the ocean. Unblinking, yellow eyes glared at him with hatred and revulsion, the force of which caused his bladder to let go as his knees buckled.

'The drugs didn't work,' he said with a grim realization, his voice full of despair. 'They didn't work.'

A snaking limb wrapped around his neck and torso, squeezing tighter and tighter until his vertebrae fractured. His distorted mouth urgently clamoured for oxygen as the blood vessels in his eyeballs burst. When he collapsed onto the floor in a crooked, tangled heap, he thought of only one thing. His daughter, Julie. She would be so disappointed.

Monday, 26th June:

Elysian Field HQ, Galdhøpiggen, Norway

Doctor Ida Strand stood behind the three-inch thick, reinforced glass window with her hands on the control levers. With a deft movement of her fingers, she began to manipulate the two robotic arms that hung from a metallic gimbal at the centre of the room. On a table, situated at the heart of the finely tuned piece of equipment, was a small dish filled with some of the unidentified material, dubbed the Amrita by its British inventors. To its right was another smaller dish holding a cloudy urine sample from a terminally ill victim of the Ebola virus.

Doctor Strand's assistant, junior scientist Jakob Keller, stood by her side, studying her every move.

'Do you believe what they say, Doctor Strand?' Keller asked.

'What is it that they say, Jakob?'

'That this Amrita can cure the incurable. That perhaps it can cure every deadly disease, every debilitating condition that has ever afflicted mankind.'

The doctor laughed, her gaze focused on the finger-like mechanism that was drawing the urine sample into a digitally controlled pipette. 'And, may I ask, who have you been talking to?'

Keller's cheeks bloomed pink. 'Just some of my colleagues in the dorm'

'Which ones?' She knew each of the junior scientists he was referring to. Gossiping was rife in the lower ranks.

'I'm afraid I can't name names.'

'I see.'

'I don't mean any disrespect. It's just that, well, you know, I don't want to get anybody into trouble.'

'I don't see how anyone can get into trouble speculating about something that is currently unproven.'

Keller's feet shuffled uncomfortably.

With the pipette now full, the doctor shot a sideways glance at her young assistant. He had been with the program for less than a year and was still as fresh faced as the day he first arrived. Elysian Field's academy program was one of the best of its kind in the northern hemisphere. It took the most talented young science students from schools all around Europe, gave them food and lodgings for three years, taught them the latest in medical science, and put them to work in their many labs. At the end of the program, the company selected the best twenty percent of its intake for senior scientist positions in Galdhøpiggen on very attractive salaries. For that reason alone, students clamoured to be on the program. Jakob had been at the top of his class in Ulm University, one of the more prestigious scientific schools located in the German province of Baden-Württemberg. He was a brilliant scientist but had proven to be a little too prone to chit-chat and speculation for Doctor Strand's liking. She knew she would have to knock that out of him if he was going to have a successful career in Galdhøpiggen. The one thing Petra Gunderson valued more than anything else—more than medical knowledge, world beating qualifications, and even scientific brilliance—was the ability to keep a secret. It was the very foundation that Elysian Field had been built upon.

'Look,' she said, 'it may have some healing properties. In fact, I'm sure it does, but scientifically, you must know it would be quite impossible to invent a panacea that could deal with all of humanity's many and varied conditions: the multitude of afflictions, diseases, viruses and disabilities. Such flights of fancy should only ever belong in the imaginations of authors, playwrights, and filmmakers.'

'If that's true,' Keller scoffed, 'then why are we testing it at all?'

The doctor shrugged. She'd been wondering the same thing herself ever since Petra's lapdog, Yazid, had handed her the assignment. Ten of Elysian Field's senior medical scientists had been called into the boardroom and had been provided with their instructions; test the new drug against the six deadliest viruses known to man: Bird Flu, the Marburg virus, Kiyasanur Forest virus, Crimea-Congo fever, Dengue fever, and the Ebola virus. Then and only then would they do what they always did—namely, test it on the residents of the Ambassade. That part of the process was their little secret, of course. Only the most senior scientists at Elysian Field knew about the human trials, but it really was quite ingenious, the two arms of Petra's organisation working in complete synchronicity. That was why Petra had branched out in the first place. She saw the opportunity in what she had created, coupled with the paranoia of a post-pandemic world. For years, radical animal rights activists had called for animal testing to be abolished and for the world's most dangerous criminals to be used as guinea pigs in their place, and here was Petra, jabbing her high paying, completely oblivious clientele with Elysian Field's latest experimental vaccines while the world looked on in ignorance.

Regardless of Elysian Field's practices, Dr Strand had thought the testing of the Amrita senseless and unrealistic. There was nothing out there that could tackle just one of those viral infections, let alone eliminate all six. She had been given a sample of Ebola, and her five colleagues had been given one of each of the remaining vials. Their tests were to be conducted at the same time, in the adjacent labs, and they were each to report on progress by the end of that very day. She thought it was ludicrous, but she knew better than to argue with Petra's orders.

'The boss has asked us to do this,' she said to Keller. 'And in case you hadn't noticed, she pays your wages.'

She smirked as the young scientist appeared to shrink at the sharp reminder. His thirst for a soundbite he could no doubt share over dinner with the other apprentices instantly diminished. Instead, he watched as she manoeuvred the pipette to less than two centimetres above the petri dish.

'Screen on,' she commanded. Keller tapped the keyboard that was built into the control panel. The LCD screen came to life, and the multi coloured, star-shaped cells sprang into view.

'Make sure we film the whole procedure, Jakob,' she said. 'I want detailed images of every significant incident.'

'Understood Doctor,' Keller replied, zooming in on a small cluster of cells directly beneath the pipette's suspended tip.

'Preparing to deploy two 0.05 millilitre drops of infected urine from sample XZ515. Recording commenced at approximately…' Doctor Strand checked her watch, '…11.17 a.m. Observations to include the reaction of Amrita cells to foreign antibody, modifications in typical behaviour of the attacking viral particles, and the ability or inability of the viral protein to infiltrate the cell structure of the subject material.' She took a breath and wondered how it had come to this. She had wanted to change the world through science, not waste her not insubstantial talents on debunking Holy Grail level nonsense. 'Okay, here we go.'

She gave the control trigger a gentle squeeze. The robotic hand deposited two discrete drops of urine onto the swirling, yellow mass. The impact was picked up by the microscope inside the lab, and a 4K high-definition image was immediately portrayed onto the large screen.

Doctor Strand watched as the Ebola proteins approached the Amrita crystals, initially swimming parallel to them and then moving randomly among the tens of cells that were visible through the microscope's highly magnified lens. The tiny yellow stars remained static, allowing the malicious particles to rub against them repeatedly. One of the Ebola cells became stuck to the outer surface of one of the stars, and its spike covered glycoprotein jacket began to tear a hole in the outer skin of the host cell. As it did so, the nucleoprotein within the virus started to move towards the small hole, its coil-like structure shrinking to a much smaller size, allowing it to squeeze through the tiny cavity. Its body moved with a hunger and urgency that she found quite intriguing.

'The Ebola is doing its thing,' Keller said. 'The Amrita, on the other hand, appears to be unmoved.'

'Quite,' she offered in reply. 'In a moment the Ebola will merge with the Amrita, and once that happens, the host cell will be truly and irreversibly infected.'

'I guess you were right, doctor,' Keller huffed. 'This really was a waste of time.'

She nodded, but she found little comfort in that. From what she'd heard, her boss had high hopes for her investment, but with her own scepticism confirmed, she would have to be the one to give Petra the bad news. She wondered if her colleagues had had better luck. She knew Petra hated negativity, and silently hoped one of the others had at least some success, perhaps enough to save her from a vicious tongue lashing.

The Ebola particle was now wholly inside the Amrita cell and its proteins were wrapping around the host cell's nucleus, constricting it as if it were a microbiological rat being consumed by a python. Gradually the two cells merged into one grotesque, mutated organism. One by one, the other cells succumbed to the

Ebola, and soon the whole Petri dish was completely over-run by the aggressive viral particles. The colour of the liquid darkened to an almost burnt orange, and then a grey cloud began to appear from within it, consuming the sample until it turned the colour of ash.

'I think we've seen enough here,' she said. 'For the record, the time is now 11.23 a.m. It has taken less than six minutes for the Ebola particles from sample XZ515 to entirely infect the Amrita cells. There also now appears to be a dark discolouration which is not entirely unusual for this kind of controlled test. The tested cells did not try to defend themselves in any way, wholly disproving the claim that this new substance is somehow able to combat all known pathogens. In the case of the Ebola virus, at least, this appears to be an incorrect statement.' She gestured to Keller. 'Experiment concludes at 11.24 a.m.'

Jakob halted the recording. 'What a disappointment.'

'I've had worse,' she replied. 'I'd get used to it if I were you. Science is full of let-downs and dead ends.'

As they left the lab, the doctor walked through what she was going to say to her boss. She decided that the best approach would be to get her own news in first, take her bitter pill and leave the other senior scientists to their own fate. She didn't like the idea of having to provide a shared report where Petra might be faced with six failures in a row. From her experience with her CEO, she suspected it would result in them all being fired. That was the outcome that terrified her the most. She needed her job. It was important to her family.

While she remained preoccupied in her own thoughts, she didn't see the liquid sample start to move within the dish or notice the colour as it shifted to a deep shade of crimson, intermingled with a snaking line of yellow. She also didn't see the petri dish start to shake violently, as if the metal table had turned into some sort of vibration platform, or spy the volume of liquid treble in an instant, the jelly-like material leaching over the sides of the dish and gradually forming an amorphous, ball-shaped blob. As that blob grew into a mishappen body that was so big it spilled from the table onto the floor, it began to shudder, its mass growing to dog-sized proportions with limbs that jutted at obtuse angles from a pulsing, muscular torso. When the newly formed entity stood on its hind legs and let out a horrifying shriek that was so piercing, it split the thick glass window in half, Doctor Strand was already standing before Petra Gunderson and delivering her report.

'It's about the Amrita,' she began. 'I'm afraid it's not good news.'

Monday, 26th June:
Sittingbourne, Kent

Manny stood in Wade's empty flat, the last of his friend's belongings safely packed in a cardboard box, ready to be delivered to his mum. It seemed like scarce possessions for a life that had held so much promise, but death was like that, wasn't it? Everyone was equal in the face of the grim reaper.

He still couldn't believe that his old school pal was gone. Sure, they hadn't been close since they'd left the education system, but they'd been tight when they were kids. Manny was always being picked on for being Sikh and fat, and Wade had been the butt of so many jokes about his hearing loss and thick glasses. When Manny had stuck up for Wade during one particularly bad spout of name-calling and petty shoving—getting himself a black eye and split lip in the process—they'd instantly forged a lasting friendship. They'd had each other's backs all through primary and secondary school, which had made Manny's time there feel a little less painful. It had been hard being Indian in a town that, at that time, had been over ninety percent white, but he could only imagine how difficult it was to navigate through a tough comprehensive without being able to see properly or hear what the teachers were saying.

Manny had met Paul later on, and it was no coincidence that it was about that time that he and Wade had drifted apart. He felt so guilty for that now, so shitty. If he could turn back time, he would go back and do things differently. He'd be a better friend. Now all of that seemed like such a long time ago and so inconsequential. Wade was dead; like, proper dead. It didn't matter how much he beat himself up or mulled over the past. He couldn't change the reality of the now. There was no going back.

As he hoisted the heavy box into his arms and headed for the door, he heard a soft tapping.

'Hello? Is anyone home?'

It was a female voice with a distinct accent. One that he recognised. When he approached the hallway, he was confronted by the sight of a petite redhead with smiling eyes.

'Hi. It's Renee, isn't it?' he said.

The woman grinned. 'Yes, it is. So nice of you to remember. Is Wade home?'

He slowly placed the box on the kitchen worktop. 'How do you know Wade?'

Renee explained she and Wade had met outside her university accommodation a couple of days prior, and that they'd had coffee together at her house. Manny thought the coincidence was more than a little suspicious.

'So, I guess you haven't heard,' he said.

'Heard what?'

'I'd offer you a seat, but as you can see, Wade's place is now completely empty.'

Renee's expression shifted. 'What's going on?'

He took a moment to compose himself. 'I'm afraid there's no easy way to say this. Wade is dead. He was killed by someone after a night out at a local pub. As far as I know, the police don't currently have any suspects.'

'What? No!' Renee staggered against the worktop. 'But I was with him just two days ago.'

'On the 24th?'

'Yes, on Saturday. I was literally in this flat.'

'You came here?'

Renee nodded.

'Why would you do that?'

She reached into the pocket of her jeans and pulled out a tissue. She dabbed at her tears. 'We made some more of the Amrita,' she said. 'From the dose that you gave Wade.'

Manny was taken aback. 'I don't understand.'

'Wade said you were out of the country for a while and he needed more, which is why he came to find me. I guess he heard you talking about me or something. Anyway, you only gave him a very small amount, and, coincidentally, I'd already been thinking about taking another look at it. You hardly gave me any time to do any experimentation, you know? To really conduct a thorough review? You have something truly groundbreaking here, Manmeet, and it's not fair that you're keeping it from the world. There are people suffering needlessly when you literally have a miracle under lock and key.'

He felt his blood boil. 'You had no right, Renee. Paul and I are trying to control how this thing is handled. Nobody knows what it can really do, or whether there are even any dangers.'

'Which is exactly why you should allow scientists to review it thoroughly, not show it to me and then take it away without allowing me to study it in detail.'

'That's where we were!' he yelled. 'When Wade was killed. We were negotiating a deal with a major medical organisation to do just that!'

Renee held a hand to her mouth. 'I see. I didn't realise.' She retrieved a pastel blue vape from her handbag. 'May I? It helps calm my nerves.'

'Knock yourself out. This place is being handed back over to the landlord in the next thirty minutes, so I don't really care what you do.'

She sucked on the plastic tube and blew out a white cloud of vapor. 'I can't believe he's gone. Who would do such a thing?'

Manny shrugged. He really had no idea, but if he got his hands on him, he'd kill the bastard. He owed Wade that much. 'Why are you here, Renee?' he asked. 'Was something going on between you and Wade?'

Renee's blush deepened. 'No, nothing like that. Well, maybe. Who knows?' she started to cry again. 'It's just that I had some news for him, but it doesn't seem to matter now. It doesn't seem as important.'

Manny found himself floundering. 'You could tell me, I guess. If it helps, I mean.'

She seemed to think it over, sucking furiously on her vape. 'It's about the Amrita. I did an unofficial experiment at the university. Strictly off the record of course.'

'Of course.'

'I tested its reaction to a carcinoembryonic antigen which identifies the presence of cancerous tumours in sufferers of certain cancers, particularly colon cancer.'

He was intrigued. 'Okay. And?'

'Nothing happened at first. I was distracted by my university professor, so I didn't see the actual event, but—'

'It cured it, didn't it?'

She grabbed him by the arms, and he flinched at her touch. 'It did more than that. It completely and utterly obliterated it.'

He fought to control himself. A cure for hearing loss and dementia was one thing, but a cure for cancer? That was game changing. If what Renee had found was true, he and Paul couldn't keep the Amrita from the world any longer. They had to tell someone.

'You're sure?' he asked.

'It's only one test, but on the strength of that single experiment, I would say that it's pretty certain.'

'Jesus bloody Christ.'

He ran options through his mind. They'd just signed a deal with Elysian Field which cut them out of a large slice of their profits, but once released to the general public, the cure for cancer was going to make them an absolute fortune, not to mention making a lot of people very, very happy. He needed to talk to Paul about getting Petra and her cronies to expedite the certificate. They needed this out there and fast.

His phone went off in his pocket. It was Wade's mother.

'Hi, Mrs Hughes. I'm just finishing up at the flat and then I'll bring everything over, if that's okay.'

There was the sound of sobbing, thick and damp.

'Mrs Hughes? Are you okay?'

'The police just called,' the distraught mother eventually managed to say. 'They've got the results from the autopsy.'

Manny steadied himself, praying that they'd found something that would lead them to Wade's killer. 'Go on.'

'Oh Manny. Why would he do such a thing?'

Manny glanced at Renee. 'Who, Mrs Hughes? Why would who do such a thing?'

There was the sound of more sobbing, followed by the wet snuffle of Mrs Hughes blowing her nose. 'My Wade,' she said. 'How could he? Why would he?'

'Mrs Hughes. Margot. I don't understand.'

There was a long pause before she continued. 'According to the police, nobody killed my son, Manny. There was no murderer.' She broke down then, her words barely audible. 'Wade…he…he killed himself.'

'What?' Manny couldn't believe what he was hearing. 'There must be some sort of mistake.'

'No, Manny. The police are certain. For some reason, my son, my little boy, he strangled himself to death.'

Monday, 26th June:

The Rifleman Pub, Leysdown-on-Sea, The Isle of Sheppey

Paul parked in the empty carpark of The Rifleman and switched off the engine. His eyes surveyed his surroundings, taking in the brown, weed infested wasteland that encircled the pub. The river Swale rolled silently in the distance, the village of Conyer just across the water, a series of barges and well-weathered fishing vessels littering its muddy banks. Behind him, the long, narrow road that led back to civilisation wound through trees and shrubs.

The sight of the pub with its boarded-up windows and graffiti strewn front door made Paul feel pretty sad. The Rifleman had been such a bustling, lively haunt, bringing visitors from all over Kent during its heyday. The food had been good, if a little pricey, and there had been a great selection of lagers and craft ales. He and Julie had come out at least twice a month before the pandemic, and they'd even had their first date there; one that ended with a clumsy fumble in the back of his Vauxhall Corsa before realising that the punters sitting in the beer garden were all getting a good look. He let his mind dwell on the memory. It had been a simpler, happier time, before he'd even heard of the subterranean cave network with the funny name nestled in the Brecon Beacons.

Suddenly there was a tap on his window. He looked up, and instantly he felt his heart slam violently against his chest. It was somebody he recognised. Somebody he'd last seen standing in the corridor outside his flat. Rami signalled for Paul to lower his window, a request he respectfully declined.

'I don't know you,' he said while discretely checking that the doors of the vehicle were locked. 'What do you want?'

'It's about Julie,' Rami replied in a thick, eastern European accent. 'I've been asked to take you to her.'

Paul gripped the steering wheel. *Take him to her?* His pulse began to gallop. 'Where is she?'

'In there.'

Paul eyed the building, wondering what was happening to Julie at that very second. 'Well, she can come out here then, can't she.'

'Sorry pal, no can do.'

'What the hell does that mean?'

'Just what I said. She's inside having a chat with my boss, and I'm under strict instructions to make sure you join them.'

Paul shook his head, speechless. He'd always vehemently tried to stay out of trouble. He didn't break any laws—well, nothing serious anyway—he didn't mix with the wrong sort of people, and he'd fought hard to hold down a steady nine-to-five job with a reputable company. His life was about as passive as was reasonably possible. Sure, he'd now opened the door to an illegal enterprise in the Norwegian mountains, but this wasn't them. This wasn't anything close to them.

'Look, mate, are you getting out of the car or what?'

'I ain't your mate,' he spat, reaching for his phone. 'I don't know who you are or what you've done to Julie, but I'm sure the police would like to hear about this.'

'Oh, for fuck's sake.'

Rami stooped down, his bald head the only thing visible in Paul's side window, and for a moment, Paul thought the big guy had disappeared. He peered over the edge, just in time to see a rust covered crowbar coming towards him, shattering the window and sending thousands of tiny, diamond shaped shards of glass slamming into his face and chest. He raised his arm to protect himself before a meaty forearm and hefty shoulder followed the metal bar through the newly formed opening and grabbed him around the throat.

'This isn't optional, mój przyjaciel,' the man yelled. 'You're coming in, whether you like it or not.'

Paul gripped the seat and tried to prevent himself from being forcefully evacuated through the shattered window, but the man was way too strong and had the significant advantage of leverage. As his body was violently pulled from the car, and shards of jagged glass tore chunks from his exposed abdomen, he felt something in his right shoulder give. He howled in agony as his face connected with sharp gravel and his legs spilled over his body, forcing him to roll over in an awkward, spine-breaking backflip. As he lay face down in the dirt, his shoulder screamed in agony and blood oozed from his ripped stomach. He felt strong hands grab him beneath his armpits.

'There,' Rami said. 'That's better.' He hauled Paul to his feet and slapped him hard across the face. 'You ever disobey me like that again you skurwysyn, and you'll end up in that river, a concrete block tied around your fucking neck. You get me?'

Paul nodded before he felt the sharp sting of the man's palm across his cheek once more.

'Answer me, dupek,' he said. 'And use my proper title, too.'

Paul's cheek was hot and his right arm hung limply from a dislocated shoulder socket. 'Your proper title? I don't understand.'

There was another hard slap, and Paul's head jerked painfully to the side. 'I don't understand, *sir*,' Rami insisted. 'As you've been so bloody rude, that's what you can call me from now on.'

Paul heard the creak of hinges as a door opened behind him,

followed by the sound of a man yelling.

'You're playing with him, Rami!' this new voice yelled. 'You've had your fun. Now stop fucking about and bring him inside.'

Rami spun Paul around to face the pub, causing a fresh flame of agony to blossom in his shoulder and chest. He clenched his teeth, waiting for the pain to subside. After a few moments of excruciating discomfort, he recovered his composure. Sweat dripped from his forehead and into his eyes as he looked up and saw a man standing in the doorway; a man whose reputation Paul was well aware of. He was exactly the type of trouble Paul had spent his life trying to avoid. The problem was, this time, trouble had come looking for him.

'Come in, Paul,' Ted Barker said, Julie standing by his side, her face a scowl of defiance. 'I've put the kettle on.'

Monday, 26th June:

Ogof Ffynnon Ddu (Cave of the Black Spring), South Wales

Gunthar Strøm sat on the rock ledge overlooking the glistening underwater pool that shimmered beneath his feet. He took a bite from a bar of dark, bitter chocolate and perused his unusual surroundings. Blue and green rock, a shimmering lake of serenely still, clear water, and a jagged fissure in the cave wall to his left. This place was on no map and didn't exist in the network diagram he'd downloaded from the caving association website. It was truly a unique discovery, or, as his prison guard would say, a boil ripe for lancing.

The climb down had been treacherous but nothing that had particularly stretched his skills as a rock-climber. The only problem he'd had when initially arriving in the little Welsh village nestled in the Brecon Beacons—or as the fiercely patriotic Cymry natives now called it, Bannau Brycheiniog, a name which contained far too many consonants for Gunthar's liking—was that he hadn't known which entrance to the cave network the two Englishmen had entered, or in which direction they had travelled. The tunnels stretched for over fifty kilometres end to end, and while Gunthar would have gladly taken the time to investigate every crevice, every tributary, every tiny opening if he needed to, he was acutely aware of how much time a venture like that would take. He also knew Petra wanted results quickly, and he had no desire to stay in the UK any longer than was absolutely necessary. The air made his skin itch and his eyes sting.

Fortunately for him, he hadn't had to look far. The owner of Ty Selah Lodge, a woman in her late sixties with white, immaculately curled hair and a nervous twitch, remembered the two young men quite clearly.

'I thought it was odd,' she'd said, 'because they both looked as white as a pair of ghosts when they came back to collect their things. They'd originally planned on staying another night, but once they'd grabbed their bags, they shot off in quite a hurry. They'd paid up-front for the room, so I didn't care either way, but I was surprised they didn't at least try to barter for a refund. Most do.'

'Did they say what had spooked them,' Gunthar asked, trying to act as casual as possible. He picked at his bacon and eggs which were swimming in grease.

'No, not really,' she replied. 'Although they did mention that they'd stumbled upon a new cave. Can you believe that? The thousands of professional cavers that have scoured these tunnels over the years, and yet these two amateur potholers from England think they've somehow managed to discover a part of the OFD that has never been seen before. That did make me laugh.'

Gunthar feigned a chuckle, but in truth, his interest was piqued. 'It does sound pretty outlandish. It might be worth a look though, just so that it can be proven beyond doubt, or as you quite rightly suggest, debunked. Did they…happen to mention where it was that they'd allegedly found this new cave?'

The woman poured him another cup of coffee. 'You'll be wasting your time.'

Gunthar took the hint and pulled out his wallet. 'Well, fortunately I have a lot of it. I tell you what, how about I pay for another night myself? Just to see if I can't find what it is they think they discovered. I must say, I'm quite fascinated.'

He waved four, red fifty-pound notes in front of the woman

which amounted to more than twice the price of a night in the lodge.

'Well,' she said, her cheeks pink. 'Let me think, now. They were rambling like a couple of excited teenagers as they packed up their things, but I did overhear a little bit of their chatter.'

I bet you did, Gunthar thought. *I bet you listen in on a lot of things you know you shouldn't.* He pulled another fifty from his wallet and slid it across the table. 'Well, anything you can remember would be most helpful.'

She spooned three heaped teaspoons of sugar into her cup and stirred furiously. 'Yes, that's right. They said something about a waterfall, or a stream, or something.' She sipped her tea, casually pocketing the money. 'Mm…what was it again? Showers! That was it. Marble Showers. It's an underground waterfall that is really quite popular. They said there had been a newly formed crack in the rock, just before reaching the waterfall. I think they only mentioned it to me to see whether any of my other customers had spoken about it before, which of course they hadn't. It's hardly surprising as I don't for one minute think that it's for real.' She'd laughed out loud. 'I'm pretty sure they were both drunk on something by the time they made it back here, because they couldn't seem to stand still for more than a few seconds.'

That little insight was all that Gunthar needed. He'd already meticulously researched the various landmarks of the tunnel network, and he knew exactly where the famed Marble Showers were. He'd just needed to find the newly formed fissure, which he suspected would be a little tricky, but after an hour or more of walking up and down the tunnel, shining his headtorch into every dark blemish in the rockface, he'd spotted it.

Now, as he sat there on the rock ledge overlooking the pool, he grinned. 'Clever boys. You really are quite the surprise.'

It was an impressive chamber, and one that he thought really should be investigated by trained professionals. However, geology wasn't what he was there for, and he suspected Petra would want the find kept under wraps for as long as possible. He dropped to the floor and headed for the jagged opening. As he entered the tunnel mouth and walked carefully down the wet incline, the smell hit him. It was the scent of death, mingled with the choking stench of decaying fish. He reached into his backpack and pulled a handkerchief from inside, holding it to his nose.

The tunnel opened up into a much smaller chamber, and there on the ground lay what looked like some sort of giant sea creature, except its skin was grey and its torso resembled that of a flat fish. Whatever it was, it was dead. The flesh had started to pucker and split, and the edges of the fetid meat had begun to blacken and dry out, like beef jerky.

'Hello,' he said. 'What the devil are you?' He pulled a knife from his pocket and lifted one corner of the lifeless creature's body. The tissue was hard and festering, the muscular structure starting to retract and curl, but it was something else that caught Gunthar's attention. It was the sight of a human hand that gave him pause.

'Interesting,' he said, before donning a pair of latex gloves. 'What have you two boys been up to?'

As he dragged the large hulk across the rocks, grunting as he pulled its heavy mass from the water, more and more of the human body came into view. Almost immediately he could see it was female—between thirty and forty years of age by his estimate—and it was clear that she hadn't been dead long. While rigor mortis had started to set in, her skin was still mostly intact, and aside from the visible signs of organs decomposing and the veins turning dark and coarse, the woman could have just been lying asleep in the shallow pool.

With the body now fully visible, Gunthar bent down and rolled her over. Despite her crushed skull, he could see the woman had been pretty, with high cheekbones and a delicate chin. He wondered if she had a family, and if so, if they knew of her fate. The fact was, they would never find her down there, so far underground in a cave nobody except two amateur cavers knew existed. He would have to fix that. He didn't like the thought of the woman rotting down there, alone and with nobody to mourn her. It just wasn't right.

He ran his hands over her body to search for a cause of death. He was shocked at the sheer quantity of breaks and fractures in the woman's ribs, limbs and neck. The creature had crushed her to death, squeezing her within its gigantic torso until her bones had literally crumbled. Her eyes were riddled with burst capillaries, and black blood oozed from her nose, eyes and ears.

'I'm so sorry for what it did to you,' Gunthar offered, closing her eyelids.

His gaze turned to the water and the hint of a diluted yellow liquid swirling around the woman's body. He dipped his finger into the pool and inhaled. It smelled like pondwater mixed with aniseed. He stood and approached the motionless alien corpse.

'What in God's name are you?' he asked, before dropping to his knees and examining its bizarre structure. He grabbed his knife once more and carved away a fillet of some of the fresher meat. He held it up to the torchlight and watched as the grey flesh retracted against his touch. He bit into it and recoiled at the taste. It was like burnt ash mixed with sour milk. He discarded it and approached the creature's abdomen. Upon examination, he noticed half a dozen, twelve-inch-long gills located close to where its legs protruded. Gunthar used his knife to separate the gills, opening them up so that he could see beneath. He pulled at the meat, revealing two large, fleshy sacs. Both were the size of shopping bags. Within the tough but translucent skin swirled a thick, jelly like liquid. It was bright yellow.

'There you are,' he said, holding the balloon-like sac between his hands and picturing Petra's face as she told Karin their ill-fated deal was off. 'I found you.'

Monday, 26th June:
Sittingbourne, Kent

'I don't believe it,' Manny said, angrily tossing his phone onto the kitchen worktop where it clattered against the tiled wall. 'It can't be true. Why would Wade do that? Especially now. I mean, how would he even—'

'What exactly did the police say?' Renee asked. 'Did they disclose why they believe he did this?'

'They said something about the marks on his throat matching his own hands, the fingerprints too. He even had fragments of his own skin jammed under his fingernails.'

'And there you have it. It sounds pretty conclusive.'

'But even if he wanted to,' Manny continued, 'how would he even have the strength?' He wrapped his hands around his own throat and squeezed. 'I mean, it would be impossible, wouldn't it?'

'Firstly,' Renee replied, prizing his fingers away, 'don't do that. Secondly, maybe he was so upset, so distraught, that he found the strength from somewhere deep inside himself. You hear about these things, don't you? People lifting cars from victims of traffic accidents, or dragging rubble from landslide victims. If you want something badly enough, you'll find a way.'

'But you saw how he was, Renee. You saw him yesterday. You said he looked happy.'

Renee recalled Wade's laughter. It was so infectious. 'He did seem to be, but people who are suffering from depression are often very good at burying their real emotions. That's part of the problem, isn't it? That they can't express how they truly feel?'

'I don't buy it.' Manny said. 'Not Wade. Not the man I knew. We've been mates since we were kids, and even when we were getting the worst kind of abuse from people we went to school with—some of them supposedly our friends—he never let it get to him. He was always the life and soul, you know? The life and bloody soul.'

Renee thought about that. She'd only known Wade for a couple of days, but her version of Wade—the bubbly guy with the charming smile—seemed to match Manny's description almost too perfectly. Maybe something had happened to him, maybe he'd seen something, or perhaps since the last time she'd spoken to him, giving him her number—which was something she never did—he'd met someone who'd told him some terrible news. Maybe his eyesight or his hearing quality had deteriorated substantially? What if the effects of the Amrita had rapidly diminished in those hours since she'd left him standing in his doorway? What if it left him in a worse predicament than before? They say you couldn't miss something you'd never had, but surely once you were through Saint Peter's Gate, you could never imagine leaving the magical kingdom behind.

'What are you thinking?' Manny asked.

'I'm not sure.'

'Then tell me what you're not sure about.'

'Perhaps it regenerates and then degenerates.'

'I don't understand. Regenerates and then degenerates? What does that even mean?'

'It gives with one hand and takes with the other.'

'Will you stop talking in bloody riddles.'

She thought of the sample she had left in the lab, the carcinoembryonic antigen proteins that had literally been erased. What if the effects were temporary? What if what grew in their place was something stronger, something far more deadly? What if they weren't curing people at all? What if they were poisoning them?

'Have you given the Amrita to anybody else?' she asked.

'What do you mean?'

'You gave it to Wade, right? I assume you've also given it to others?'

Manny considered his answer.

'Quickly!' she insisted. 'This is important.'

'Other than Paul, the only other person we gave it to was Roger, Julie's father.'

She grabbed her keys. 'Where does he live?'

'Not far. Faversham.'

'Do you know the address?'

'I think I can find it, yeah.'

She took his hand and pulled him towards the door. 'Then that's where we're going.'

Monday, 27th June:
The Rifleman Pub, Leysdown-on-Sea, The Isle of Sheppey

Paul sat on a pub stool, his shoulder screaming at him for mercy. A slim trail of blood ran from his ear down the side of his neck. Julie sat across from him, the muscles in her jaw flexing. Her eyes were puffy and bloodshot as if she hadn't slept in days. He tried to give her a reassuring smile, but she refused to look at him, instead preferring to fix her stare on the door.

'Well, this is nice, isn't it,' Ted said, reclining in a booth scarred by cigarette burns and beer stains. 'Three of us together, chatting like we're old mates.'

'I'm sorry,' Paul said, trying to mask his pain. 'Have we met before?'

'Maybe in passing,' Ted replied. 'But I gotta be honest mate, I meet a lot of people, and your face ain't exactly memorable, if you know what I mean.'

'Cheers for the complement.'

'Oh, don't be like that. It's just one of those things. Some people have discerning features. You know? Like a scar, a hair lip, maybe an unusual mole. Not you, though. You're as plain as they come, like a blank page. Except you need a haircut. Aside from that, you could be anybody. I bet you don't even get picked up on CCTV. Invisible, Paul, that's what you are, which would be an asset in my line of work.'

'And what exactly is your line of work?' Paul asked, already knowing the answer.

'I'm on entrepreneur, Paul, like that space geezer, Elon Musk. I take an idea, I build on it, and then I execute.'

The way Ted drew out the last word made the hairs on Paul's neck stand on end. As if on cue, Rami cracked his knuckles.

'Why are we here, Ted? You've kidnapped Julie, and you've dragged me from my own car and had your guy kick the shit out of me. I'm guessing you don't just want a chinwag.'

Ted stood. 'I met your mate the other day,' he said, pacing the room. 'Wade. He told me all about his miracle cure, your miracle cure, Paul. The Amrita. That's Hindu, isn't it?'

Paul's stomach dropped. Wade had been sworn to secrecy.

'I don't know what you're talking about.'

Ted nodded at Rami, and the big guy's fist slammed into his jaw, sending him crashing to the floor. He screamed out as his shoulder connected with the hard wood. It was like a sharp jolt of electricity through his body, a fiery hot poker that spread from his arm into his throat.

'Okay,' he said, sweating profusely. 'Okay. Yeah, the Amrita. I know what you mean now.'

'Funny that,' Ted replied. 'Rami here does have a knack for making people remember things, don't you Rami?'

'What can I say, boss,' the giant gorilla replied. 'It's a talent.' He yanked Paul brusquely to his feet and shoved him back onto the stool.

'So anyway,' Ted continued. 'As I was saying, your mate Wade told me all about this Amrita and how it apparently fixed his eyes and ears, poor thing.'

'So Wade told us,' Paul replied. 'It was a surprise to us, too.'

'Now, now, Paul. Don't be disingenuous, otherwise Rami here might have to tweak your memory chip again. What I got from Wade was that you went to him, claiming you had a cure for literally everything, and offered him a free dose in exchange for him agreeing to sign some sort of disclaimer.'

'An NDA,' Paul said. 'Which he clearly didn't honour.'

Ted laughed, slipping behind Paul and patting him sharply on the shoulder. Paul bit down on his bottom lip, gripping the edge of the stool as he stifled a scream.

'You're not wrong there, old chum,' Ted said. 'He was about as free-wheeling as Lewis Hamilton in a Mercedes, was old Wade.'

Julie shuffled uncomfortably in her seat, playing with her hands. 'Why don't you just tell him what you want?' she spat. 'Get this over with.'

'And spoil the surprise, love?' Ted replied, turning to Paul. 'She's a bit of a killjoy, your missus, ain't she? Is she like that in the sack?'

Paul glared at him. He wasn't a violent man, but right then he wanted to slam his head into Ted's face and smash his nose to pieces.

'You see, Paul,' Ted continued. 'Your mate, Wade, agreed to get me a load of this Amrita for a fair price. Very fair, in fact, but guess what? He let me down. Came up with some cock and bull story about you and your mate being out of the country and not having access to your stock.'

Paul gritted his teeth. That's what he was up to. He was trying to sell this wannabe mafia don their stash of Amrita from right under their noses. The backstabbing bastard.

'Me and Rami here tried to force the issue with him a little bit,' Ted said, 'but then he went and got himself killed, leaving us out in the cold.'

Paul put two and two together. 'You killed him, didn't you? You killed Wade and now you're planning to kill me and Julie, too.'

Ted feigned shock. 'Not me, mon frere. We had nothing to do

with it. I mean, yeah, I had planned to lean on him some more, maybe use a bit of muscle, but kill him? Why would I do that?'

'Because he stood up to you.'

'Oh, believe me. If we'd got hold of him that night, he would have felt so much pain that he would have given me his own mum's pin number. But kill him? No, Wade's death was not beneficial to me at all.'

Paul tried to process everything. As much as he didn't trust Ted, he was right. It didn't make sense. But if Ted and his cronies hadn't killed Wade, then who had? Surely it couldn't have just been some random coincidence, some isolated event that just happened to occur on the exact same night that Ted had planned to torture him.

'But why grab Jules?' he asked. 'What has this got to do with her?'

Julie's head snapped up. He recalled their phone call, the terror in her voice. *'Why...tell me...Black Cave...Ellie...the thing.'* He'd been so dog-tired he hadn't connected the dots, but now it all seemed so obvious. The Black Cave. Julie had obviously done some digging of her own and found the underground network in the Welsh hills. He also knew Julie had a cousin called Ellie. Had she brought her in on it? If so, where was Ellie now, and what did she know?

'I was looking for you,' Ted said, interrupting his line of thought. 'And Julie here just showed up at your flat out of the blue.'

Paul kicked himself. He should have been there. He'd been so preoccupied with Wade's murder and finding out who had broken into his flat that he'd completely forgotten about his conversation with Julie that morning. If boyfriends were scored on a scale of one to ten, he was barely scraping the bottom of the meter.

'So,' Ted continued, 'I thought I'd grab myself a little

collateral, if you know what I mean. Give myself something to bargain with.'

'I wouldn't have bothered,' Julie said, practically hissing. 'He couldn't give a shit about what happens to me. Paul does whatever Paul wants, and to hell with the consequences.'

'Hey, that's not true,' Paul objected, but he could see Julie was upset.

'And yet here he is,' Ted laughed. 'Your knight in shining armour.' He grabbed Paul's shoulders in both hands and squeezed. The action sent fresh shards of agony through his body, and everything began to swim and fade.

'I want the Amrita, Paul,' Ted said, impatient and spiteful. 'I want it today.'

'Okay. I understand.'

'And if you fuck with me, if you try anything at all, you both die.'

Monday, 27th June:

Ospringe Road, Faversham, Kent

Renee stood outside a house Manny said he was almost sure belonged to Julie's parents. The little terraced place was immaculate, with bright yellow, wood framed windows, and chocolate brown rendering.

'Do you think anybody's home?' she asked.

'Only one way to find out,' Manny replied before knocking on the front door. He waited a few moments before knocking again, this time a little louder, followed by a sustained ringing of the bell. He shrugged. 'I guess not.'

Renee was still ruminating over her theory. She felt sure there was some truth in her hypothesis, but she needed to see Julie's father to be sure. She wanted to be wrong. She wanted so badly to believe that what they really had was the panacea for every deadly condition out there, but the revelation that Wade had killed himself threw everything up in the air. Something had made him desperate. Something had caused him to feel so much pain, so much angst, that the only way out was to literally suffocate himself to death.

'Let's try the back,' she said, walking further up the road and turning down a narrow alleyway.

'Wait!' Manny said. 'If they're not in, then—'

'I need to know,' Renee replied, sliding between two wheelie-bins and peering up at the buildings. 'It's important. Now, which one of these houses do you think it is?'

Manny stood with his hands on his hips and puffed out his

cheeks. 'Well, it was five houses along, so—' he raised his finger and counted. 'I'd say it's the one with the conservatory at the back.'

Renee nodded and hopped over the fence, pacing up the garden path towards the back door.

'Jesus, Renee,' Manny said. 'Isn't this breaking and entering?'

'Only if we break in.' She tried the handle to the back door and winked.

'I don't like this,' he groaned. 'Julie will not be happy.'

The house smelled of lavender and biscuits. It was so tidy, it put Renee's student digs to shame. The conservatory was empty, as was the neatly laid out kitchen-diner. A cupboard stood open to their right, as if somebody had grabbed something from inside in a hurry. She raised her eyebrows.

'What's through there?' she asked, pointing towards a white painted door.

'A hallway, I think, with the stairs to the left and the living room straight ahead.'

'Mr Harbor,' she called out. 'Are you home?'

There was no answer. She opened it, peering up at the top of the staircase before pushing the living room door open just a crack. Light spilled through the gap. She placed one eye against the opening and looked inside. The room was dominated by a large bay window and a three-seater sofa. The carpet was beige, the wallpaper floral. She opened the door fully. A biscuit barrel lay on its side on the coffee table, gingernut cookies spilled onto the floor. An almost full cup of tea sat on a coaster beside it, the drink growing cold.

'Somebody left in a hurry,' she said. She took another look, and to her horror, she spied a man's slipper jutting out from between the TV and sofa. 'Oh God. Manny, there's somebody on the floor.'

She ran around the table and crouched over the prone body. The man's eyes were staring sightlessly at the ceiling. His throat was a ghastly shade of purple and black with a long line of bloodied spittle coating his jaw.

'Is this—'

'Yeah,' Manny replied, breathless. 'That's Julie's dad, Roger.'

'Roger,' Renee said, speaking as loudly as she could. 'Roger, can you hear me?'

There was no answer.

'Is he breathing?' Manny asked. 'Renee, tell me he's alive?'

She pressed her cheek to Julie's father's mouth and waited, her fingers held against his wrist. She wanted to feel something, just the faintest murmur or the hint of a breath. She wanted him to be okay, for her theory to be all wrong.

'I'm sorry,' she said. 'Manny, I'm so sorry.'

'No. This can't be right. This can't be.'

'I'm afraid it is.'

'First Wade, now Mr Harbor. Both gone. There's been some sort of mistake. There must have been.'

Renee studied the dead man's throat, the dark indentations where his fingers had been pressed painfully into his flesh, a purple necktie where his hands had squeezed and squeezed until his life had been stifled and crushed. His eyes were bloodshot and at least one capillary had burst.

'I need to phone Paul,' Manny said, leaping to his feet. 'I need to let him know we have a problem.'

'A problem?' Renee cried. 'You think this is a problem?'

'Yeah. A big fucking one.'

'Manny, we need to call the police.'

'Not before I call Paul.'

'A man is dead! Julie's father is dead. We have to report this.'

He retrieved his phone and dialled, stood with it against his ear, breathing heavily, tapping one foot against the floor. After a few seconds, he hung up.

'Shit. Bloody thing went to voicemail.'

'Good,' Renee replied.

'What do you mean, good?'

She stood and went to the window, peering outside. 'Because now we can call an ambulance.'

'Renee, he doesn't need an ambulance. He's dead.'

'The police then.'

'You said we had the cure to cancer. You said the Amrita was a miracle. This isn't a miracle. It's a bloody catastrophe.'

'Woah!' Renee cried. 'Yes, I did say that, but you never gave me enough time to properly test it and find out what it was really capable of. I never expected you to let people ingest it without going through the proper channels first.'

'And, as I told you, we were. We even visited the labs. These people know what they're doing.'

'But Wade and Mr Harbor were your guinea pigs,' she said. 'You should never have let them take the Amrita before you had the results.'

'We don't know Mr Harbor killed himself.'

'Look at him, Manny. Look at his neck. Doesn't that look exactly like the police description of Wade's injuries?'

'Well, yeah, but—'

'Don't you think this is more than just a horrible coincidence? That not twenty-four hours after Wade is found dead, we have a second body with the same cause of death, and what's more, both victims were taking an untested drug?'

Manny's head dropped. 'It can't be that,' he said. 'How can it be?'

Renee thought of her sample in the lab. She'd left the Petri dish in the refrigerator where she'd planned to examine it the next day, just to make sure nothing strange happened. Well, *strange* had happened. *Strange* had most definitely entered the building, and what's more, it had brought its pal *fucked-up* along for the ride.

'We need to get to the labs,' she said. 'I need to see whether the sample has mutated.'

'Mutated?' Manny replied. 'What do you mean, mutated?'

'We're going to Canterbury,' she said, stepping over the body and heading towards the back door. 'You can call the police on the way.'

Monday, 27th June:

Ogof Ffynnon Ddu (Cave of the Black Spring), South Wales

Gunthar sat in his hotel room and studied the two internal organs he'd retracted from the creature in the underground pool. The skin, taut like a drum skin, appeared to be similar to the stomach lining of a cow but almost perfectly clear. The liquid inside was thick and bright yellow. He held the bag to the window and watched as it sparkled in the light. He'd had no preconceived notion of what the two men had discovered in the Cave of the Black Spring, but he certainly hadn't expected this. An organic material, grown within the glands of a bizarre monster. It really was quite the surprise.

He'd headed back to his room, eager to call Petra and fill her in on the details. The call had gone straight to voicemail. That was irregular. Petra always picked up. Perhaps there had been yet another incident in the Ambassade complex. It was hardly surprising. Violence in Elysian Field was an almost monthly occurrence, with one or more of the less docile clients unable to control themselves. Petra dealt with these incidents with the strictest measures possible. Nobody could be allowed to threaten the sanctity of the paradise she had built beneath the mountains. The principles were clear: abide by the rules, respect the clientele, and control all anti-social impulses.

He tossed his phone onto the bedside table. He had what he came for, and he planned to deliver it to his boss the very next day. He'd already booked his flight, which departed from

Heathrow at 7.30 a.m. the following morning. He knew that Petra would be very pleased with him, affording him a guilty pleasure for his troubles. She was nothing if not rewarding. He closed his eyes and dreamed of the things he would do to the gift she gave him. He relished the sensation, the expectation of the mind scrambling climax that was to come. He felt himself go hard beneath the thin material of his chinos. He imagined the faceless, nameless man writhing beneath him, the sweat on his torso, his hands squeezing a trembling throat, gently at first, but gradually increasing the pressure until the panic built. There would be much thrashing and kicking as the grim reality became apparent to his worthless victim, but he would ride his steed like a bucking bronco, maintaining his rhythm, thrusting deeper and deeper until there was nothing left to give.

There was a knock at the door, startling him from his daydream. He groaned inwardly before adjusting himself and returning the two yellow bags to his case.

'Yes?'

'It's only Angie.'

He stood and opened the door just a little. Mrs Griffiths stood there, her cheeks puffed out like tiny pillows.

'Well?' she asked. 'Did you find it?'

He attempted to quell his frustration. 'Find what?'

'The new cave. That was what you went looking for, wasn't it? Only, I had a couple of other cavers in this morning, and they told me there was absolutely no way there was an undiscovered tunnel in that cave network. Apparently, they've been potholing down there for years, and they know the whole thing like the backs of their hands. We had a good laugh about it.'

He eyed the hallway. 'No, I'm afraid to say I was unable to find anything.'

'I knew it.' She seemed pleased. 'Things like that don't just spring up out of the blue.'

'Quite.'

He should have closed the door at that point, should have let the conversation end there, but the woman's smug grin irritated him. He opened the door a little more, letting the light penetrate the shadows.

'Do you study history, Mrs Griffiths?'

She cocked her head. 'Do I…what?'

'History. Things that went on before: ancient texts, mythology, anthropology. The world that existed before we became the dominant species.'

She shook her head. 'I hardly get the time to read these days, what with the cleaning and the cooking, not to mention all the paperwork.'

'A pity. Scandinavian history, in particular, is really quite interesting. You see, there is much in the Nordic past that directly influenced the creation of what people now refer to as Great Britain.'

'I don't know that I'm following you.'

'I am Norwegian, Mrs Griffiths, and fiercely proud of it. I come from a well-respected line of Norse forbears. When I was a very young child, my nanny, or barnevakt as we called her, would tell me many folk stories, tales that had been passed down to her by her parents, and to them by her grandparents.

'You will know of the Norwegian fascination with trolls and goblins, I'm sure, but the stories my barnevakt would tell me were far more terrifying than any of those you may have heard.' He stepped into the hallway and leaned a little closer. 'She spoke of a creature that lived in the water, often in underground caves that nobody knew existed. It was able to shape-shift to fool its prey. It would hunt for young men and women, luring them into the darkness with a song, manipulating their minds with intoxicating words and enticing images, drawing them in until they were so near, so painfully close, that escape became an impossibility. The creature was called the Nokken, a malevolent water spirit. I dreamed of it every night, Mrs Griffiths. I often woke in the darkness, believing it was lying in my bed beside me, its hideous face mere inches from my own.'

The landlady gulped.

'Of course, as I grew older, I forgot all about my barnevakt and the stories she told me, but one night, while I was in my mountain cabin, making coffee and looking out into the wilderness, I heard that song, and I saw things that my young brain struggled to comprehend. There was a creature in the shadows, a shape-shifting monstrosity with a hateful glare that I will never, ever forget. Its very essence seeped into me, leaving me feeling dirty and soiled. There was a smell, too, an ungodly smell, like something had crawled out from some deep, festering hole in the mud, dragging itself towards my cabin with rotting arms and decaying legs. It was only when I switched on every light in the house that the shadow disappeared, and the stench drifted away with it.'

Her face turned pale. 'Do you think it was the Nokken?' she asked. 'Had it come for you?'

He let her words hang in the air. 'Perhaps. Perhaps not. I only tell you this story to illustrate to you that you should not close your mind off to possibility, Mrs Griffith. There is much more out there than we can even begin to understand. We are just passengers on this planet, and we are yet to meet all our travelling companions.'

She stood there, a tiny figure beneath his towering frame.

'Mr Strøm, I really don't know what—'

'I must go now,' he said. 'I have an urgent call to make before I turn in for the night.'

'But it's only half-past five. What about dinner?'

'I'm not hungry,' he replied, closing the door before she had a chance to ask any more stupid questions. He had already said more than he'd planned.

He stood there for a moment, taking in his stark surroundings and listening to the landlady's shuffling footsteps. He turned his nose up at the musty scent of his room, the off-brown bedsheets and the faded wallpaper. Through the window, dark clouds loomed overhead, the fine mist of a cold rain hanging in the air. His flight back to Oslo couldn't come soon enough.

Monday, 26th June:

Storage Explosion, Sittingbourne

Paul stood outside the lockup, his hands clutching a large bunch of keys, his anxiety like a hot poker between his ears. The bright corridor lights flickered. There was a heavy patter as torrential rain cascaded onto the corrugated roof. He knew that everything they had was behind the steel door. He also knew if he opened it, he would be giving up a fortune. A veritable pot of gold. His options were like elephants in Alaska. Scarce. Julie stood beside him, tentative but steadfast. The cold muzzle of a pistol was pressed into his lower back. He could almost feel the hot slice of lead as it ripped open his insides.

'You wanna do the honours, Paul?' Ted asked. 'Only, I was planning on catching Eastenders on the telly tonight.'

He looked down at the keys and then back up at Julie. She looked so fragile, so afraid. He'd let her down, he'd let them all down, and now they would have nothing to show for it except the bitter memory of the mistakes he'd made. An empty lockup and a belly full of anger. What was he supposed to do? Fight his way out of it? Negotiate?

'We have a patent pending,' he said, clutching at straws.

'You have a what?'

'A patent. It's a legal document that stops other people copying somebody else's invention for the purpose of making a profit.'

'Right,' Ted replied, raising an eyebrow. 'Of course. Go on.'

'I'm named, of course, Manny too, and we added Renee

because she discovered it.'

'Discovered what?'

'The secret ingredient.'

'The what?'

'The catalyst.' He was finding his rhythm. 'It's the thing that allows us to reproduce the Amrita in such vast quantities in such a short space of time.'

'I'm not getting you, mate.'

'You see, we only brought a small amount back with us. We didn't even know what we had back then, but we suspected it was something quite unique. The problem was, we only had enough to fill a biscuit barrel.'

'So you needed to make some more?'

'Right, and that was when Renee came in. We asked her to analyse what we'd found, and she came up with the idea of adding an ingredient to it to induce a reaction.'

Ted glanced at his watch. 'I'm guessing this is leading somewhere.'

'The Amrita isn't something they made,' Julie scowled. 'It's something they found. It doesn't matter how much you get out of this lockup, without the catalyst, eventually it will run out.'

'That's right,' Paul added. 'As I said, there's a secret ingredient. Which is protected by patent.'

There was a loud clap of thunder, and the lights went out, momentarily plunging them all into darkness. Ted grabbed Paul's arm, preventing him from making a move, and Rami drew his thick forearm across Julie's shoulders. They stood that way for a moment, listening to the machine-gun rattle of the rain overhead.

When the lights came back on, Ted grabbed hold of Paul's collar. 'So you're telling me you're the only people with the ability to legally reproduce this stuff?'

'That's right,' Paul replied. 'That's why we got this lockup, to hide away everything we produced from that initial batch. The patent's already in motion, too. I'm afraid there's no stopping it.'

Ted puffed out his cheeks. 'Problem is, sunshine, I'm not really one for following the rules. This patent sounds like a piece of officious, bureaucratic bullshit to me, a bit like the law preventing the private use of cannabis, or the one that makes the tobacco companies put stupid warning stickers all over fag packets. I really don't care whether I can legally produce this Amrita or not.' A fine spray of spittle leapt from his mouth and landed on Paul's forehead. 'I'm gonna do it anyway, and you're gonna help me.'

Paul dabbed at his face. 'Yeah, sure. I get it.'

'Now open this door before Rami gets even more restless and does something neither of us want to your pretty girlfriend.'

The keys almost slipped from Paul's hand as another sharp crack of thunder rocked the lockup and the fluorescent lights flickered once more. He rifled through them, eventually finding the one he was looking for. It was large with a long, thick blade. Ted glared at him as Rami's grip on Julie stiffened. He thought about running, chancing his arm in the storm, perhaps hoping that the two men would flounder in what would no doubt be a patchwork of deep puddles and slippery mud, but he didn't have a plan for Julie. If he left without her, she would almost certainly be killed. Once outside, he could call the police, but it would take them far too long to get there. Whichever way he looked at it, he was all out of options.

The lights went out again, and this time, Paul did drop the keys. There was a loud clang as they hit the concrete floor, accompanied by the deafening boom of thunder.

'Jesus!' Ted yelled, pushing Paul out of the way and stooping to grab them. He scrambled around in the darkness on his hands and knees, the pistol scraping against the floor. For a moment,

Paul thought that the keys had been lost, but then he heard Ted's excited grunt as he found them. 'Looks like I have to do everything around here,' he said.

They were just four silhouettes now, framed by the faint red glow of the emergency exit sign. He could hear Julie's stifled cry as Rami's grip tightened around her shoulders, and Ted's footsteps on the concrete as he shuffled towards the locked door. The sound of heavy rain became a timpani concerto, a thousand drumsticks hammering on rusted tin. He could just make out the metallic, scratching noise of the key scraping against the lock plate, and then the sharp clunk as it found its home.

'Hallelujah,' Ted yelled from within the darkness. 'At last, we're making progress.'

Paul felt his anger rising in his throat. Even though Wade was dead, he had been an idiot. If he hadn't told a drug dealer of all people about what they had in their grasp, their plan would still be proceeding full steam ahead. Elysian Field would get them the approval they needed, his uncle would get the patent certified, and then Paul would rock up at Harker's Pharmaceuticals, offering the multi-national drugs company the deal of a lifetime. Ten lifetimes. Instead, he was standing there in the darkness with a couple of lowlife hooligans, about to hand over the keys to a kingdom that hadn't even been built yet. He sensed Ted staring at him as he turned the key, pictured his smug grin. He hated him, he hated Rami, and he hated Wade. They could all go to hell.

The door opened, a black hole in a sea of swirling grey. The red glow couldn't penetrate the wall of total darkness that filled the narrow opening. There was an odd smell, like the scent of wet clothing that had become mould infested. He heard Julie gag behind him.

'I can't see a bloody thing,' Ted said, reaching for his phone. He stumbled in the darkness, the blackness sucking him in. His silhouette evaporated as it became at one with his surroundings. ‘Is there a light switch?’ he asked. ‘Tell me there’s a bloody light in here.’

That was when it happened. There was a muffled growl followed by a hissing, rattling sound. The dark began to mutate and move. Slim, climbing limbs reached out, tracing the perimeter of the opening. They reached across the concrete floor as though the material was distorting.

‘Boss,’ Rami said from behind him. ‘Something’s not right.’

Still searching for his phone, Ted walked further into the room. They heard him stumble into the first freezer.

‘It’s open,’ he said. ‘Nice.’

A cluster of yellow eyes appeared above him, speckled with black, like tiny, fluorescent spawn.

‘Paul,’ Julie gasped. ‘What is that?’

He couldn’t move. He could barely breathe. Everything came at him in waves, stolen memories like poison darts. The creature in his bed, the shadow in the kitchen, the thing that emerged from the cave’s dark mouth.

‘Wait a minute,’ Ted said, reaching into the freezer. ‘I’ve found something. Is this it?’ Paul heard the sound of Ted fishing around inside the open refrigeration unit and then swallowing. ‘Doesn’t taste great, does it. In fact, it tastes like shit.’

The eyes moved closer to him. Black, shadow fingers retracted from the door frame, slicing through the air like thin blades.

‘Boss,’ Rami said. ‘I think you need to get out of there.’ He released his grip on Julie and reached for his weapon, approaching the doorway with his legs spread wide. Paul managed to find his feet, and he stepped away. His fingers slid across Julie’s hand, and she responded, clutching him, her fingernails digging into his palm.

Rami raised his weapon but didn’t fire, seemingly unsure of

what he was aiming at. There was another loud crack of thunder and yet more rain.

'Is that all there is?' Ted said, his voice directionless and lost. 'If I find out you've played me, Karin, I'll put your body in the ground myself!'

An arm reached out from somewhere in the gloom and snared Rami's wrist, breaking the bone instantly. Rami screamed as the gun fell to the ground, discharging as it struck the concrete, creating a moment of startling clarity filled with acrid smoke, revealing a blackened face, a wide mouth with serrated fangs, a cluster of glowing eyes, and horrifying, squid-like tentacles.

Julie screamed as Paul pulled her away.

'What the hell?' Ted said, watching, dumbfounded, as Rami's body was encased in a dark, swarming shadow. The bodyguard yelled out, trying to beat it away, but the creature was relentless, squeezing and devouring. His screams rattled the walls, his voice wet with blood.

Paul reacted first, launching a foot at the doorway, trying to slam it shut. It rebounded, striking the unclasped padlock that lay across the latch, sending it clattering to the floor. Paul dropped to his knees and tried to block out the horrific sound of teeth tearing Rami's flesh. His fingers moved like spiders, frantically searching for the lock. The doorway stood ajar. He smelled the wetness, felt the warmth of hot breath and the saltiness of blood. Panic gripped him. He imagined the monster leaping from Rami's mutilated body and wrapping itself around his chest, digging its teeth into his trembling throat. Where was the lock? Where the hell was it?

'What's going on?' Ted shrieked. 'Rami, what the hell is going on out there?'

There was another bright flash as Ted fired his own gun, striking the plug socket beside Paul's ear. Everything became clear for a fraction of a second. Paul saw Rami's unblinking eyes, blood running from a gore-soaked flap that had once been his cheek. His body sat within a pool of slick crimson. The freezers stood open, a yellow ooze with black veins running down white, plastic shells. Ted was cowering in the corner, the smoking gun in his trembling hands. There was a shapeless, writhing thing crouching before him. It moved with the darkness, at once feline, but then slithering, reptilian, a collection of eyes, fangs and squirming limbs.

There was the acrid scent of live electricity, and Paul looked down to see a severed cable, its copper ends embedded within the yellow and black ooze, fizzing and simmering. There was a burning smell, like overcooked fish, followed by a flame, bright orange and sizzling. It crept across the floor, small at first, but then growing into a flickering, broiling heat, the temperature ferocious against Paul's skin.

He spied the padlock and grabbed it, his whole body frigid and pathetic. Julie helped lift him, and he reached for the door as the thing came at him, a long arm of blackness, its flesh elastic, rubber. The fire was at its back, illuminating its sleek, dark skin, its hellish face. A razor blade of a finger grazed his forearm, drawing blood. Paul cried out, but Julie was on him, slamming him against the door, closing it with a loud slam. The metal crushed the limb, severing it at what appeared to be an elbow. It fell to the ground where it shrivelled and bubbled, now no more than a dark puddle. Paul dropped the padlock again, but Julie caught it, hooking it through the clasp.

From inside the lockup, Paul heard Ted cry out.

'Don't leave me!' he yelled. 'Karin, let me out, you sick bastard! I'll die in here. The fire! That thing! Oh God!'

Paul couldn't breathe, couldn't think. Smoke was spilling out from beneath the door, grey and suffocating. It billowed and spread until it filled the corridor. The paint on the walls started to bubble and split as the temperature in the lockup rose to furnace levels. Everything was a jumble, a scattered montage of images and sounds, senseless and unstable. The Amrita. That thing. What the hell was it?

He heard himself choking as Julie's hand gripped his bicep. She pulled him away as something crashed against the door, jarring him back into reality.

'Come on!' she yelled. 'We're getting out of here!'

Monday, 26th June:

University of Canterbury, Canterbury, Kent

Renee pulled into the car park as the rain hammered down and lightning streaked across the sky. It was almost empty, which didn't surprise her. It was late. She was hoping that most of the staff had left for the day, and that those who were still around had vacated the labs. The students themselves would be headed for the bars, which is where she really wanted to be, but if her hunch about Wade and Roger Harbor was correct, they had a huge problem on their hands.

Manny had called Paul again as she'd manoeuvred the car through the heavy storm, but the call had gone straight to voicemail. Renee listened as he left a message.

'Paul, you need to call me back straight away. Wade, he killed himself. I know, it sounds unbelievable, but that's the truth of it. The police said so. I met Renee at his flat while I was clearing his things out for his mum, and she told me she had a theory about the Amrita. I'm not sure I even believe it even now, but we decided to check in on Julie's dad to see if he was okay. Paul, it's not good news. Roger, he's…I probably shouldn't say it over this damn thing, but by the time you hear this, the police will be at the house, and it will be all over the news. We're heading to Canterbury Uni to check a sample Renee has been working on. She thinks it may have…mutated or something. I don't know. Call me as soon as you pick this up, and don't consume any more of that shit. I mean it.'

They raced across the grounds and headed for the glass foyer.

She reached for her key card which hung on a green lanyard around her neck. With the door unlocked, they entered the building. The brightly lit area opened out onto two hallways. Renee took the door to their right and pulled Manny along with her as she ran towards a sign that read Science Department.

Thankfully, there was nobody around. She couldn't face another grilling from her professor or a random conversation with one of the other students. She didn't think she could mask her anxiety.

'What are we going to do when we get inside?' Manny asked. 'What are you even expecting to find?'

'I'm not sure,' she replied. 'But I'll know it when I see it.'

She used her lanyard to open the double doors that led to the labs, grabbing a white coat that hung in the entrance and handing it to Manny.

'You'll need to wear this,' she said, before grabbing a white cap and white, plastic overshoes. 'And these.'

She went to the lockers and reached for her keys. She stopped. There was something smeared on the metal frame, something dark. She touched it and instantly recoiled.

'Oh, oh,' she said, trying to focus her thoughts. 'C'est du sang. Mon Dieu, c'est du sang.'

'What is it?' Manny reached for her. 'Renee, I don't understand.'

'Look.'

She watched as his eyes moved to the crimson smear next to the blood splatters on the white tiles.

'Somebody cut themselves, maybe?' he offered.

'Let's hope so.' She grabbed her own coat from the locker before following the trail.

The drops of blood became more concentrated as they edged along the corridor, passing the professor's office and the student common room, both of which were empty. The spatters became a long line of blood that pooled around their feet.

'Okay, now that's a lot,' she said. 'Still think that's a cut?'

'I think this day is just getting weirder and weirder by the second.'

The door at the end of the corridor was covered in red handprints. Renee took a moment to ready herself before reaching for the handle. Blood ran from beneath the door, long snaking streams of red that filled the gaps between the tiles, forming tiny rivers of claret that gently flowed towards their feet.

'I don't like this.'

Manny grabbed her hand. 'Neither do I. Maybe we should call the police?'

'Again? How would that even look?'

'Well, I didn't leave my name last time, so, you know?'

She wrapped her fingers around the door handle and pulled, holding her breath, half expecting a mask-wearing axe-murderer to leap out and slam his bloodied blade repeatedly into her skull. She pulled the door towards her, revealing a lab bathed in darkness. At her feet, blood had begun to coagulate like thick jam.

'Mon Dieu,' she said once more. 'Qu'est-ce qui se passe ici?'

'You have to stop doing that,' Manny whispered. 'I don't speak French.'

Renee tried the light-switch to no avail. She stuck her head into the room and waited for her eyes to adjust. There was a glow coming from the lab equipment, but nothing else. There was no noise either, no sound, aside from the faint hum of the refrigerators.

Manny held out his phone and activated the torch.

'Here,' he said, handing it to her.

'You want to go first?' she asked.

'You know the lay of the land. I'd probably just end up

bumping into something or knocking over a piece of expensive equipment.'

She grunted and stepped over the blood, following the line of illuminated standby lights that ran ahead of her like cats' eyes. She knew where she had stored the sample. It was in the refrigerator at the end of the aisle, right behind her bench. She had to see if her theory was correct, but she hoped to God it wasn't.

There was a scraping, scratching noise from behind them and she whirled towards it, almost dropping the phone in the process.

'What was that?' Manny asked.

'I have no idea.'

She watched as he clenched his fists. 'This is getting bloody ridiculous.'

'Tell me about it. Don't worry, it was probably nothing.'

'Nothing doesn't make a noise like that. I'm gonna check it out.'

She grabbed his arm. 'No, that's exactly how people get themselves killed in the movies.'

'Renee, this isn't a movie. It isn't even Hollywood. We're in a lab in Canterbury where nothing ever happens.' His round face was like a full moon, off-white and ghostly in the harsh glow.

'Stay close then,' she said. 'Don't wander off.'

'Don't worry. I've got no intention of leaving you'

She watched as he disappeared into the shadows. Alone, she continued to move forwards, gingerly at first, holding the torch within sweaty, jittering fingers. She didn't know what lay ahead, but she couldn't shake the sight of the blood, alongside the image of Roger Harbor's dead body, the red and purple contusions around his throat, his eyes staring blankly at the ceiling.

Manny was some way behind her, moving from bench to bench. She stepped in something wet, and her foot slipped out from beneath her. She tried to use the lab table to hold herself upright, but her other foot stepped in the same puddle, and that too slid away, causing her to topple forwards. She heard Manny turn to her, but then there was another noise, like something covered in mucus clambering over a bench. The phone spilled from her hands as she fell to the ground, striking her head against something hard, causing bright stars to dance like fireflies.

'Renee!' Manny yelled, but she could barely see him. The phone had come to rest a few feet from her grasping fingers, and what it revealed made every fibre in her body scream out. Her cheek was lying in a sticky, thick pool of rapidly congealing blood, and her eyes were staring at the badly mutilated face of Professor Wayling, his round-framed spectacles lying askew against his torn skin, his mouth wide open, the tip of his beard soaked in crimson. Above him, the refrigerator door stood open, a long line of yellow and black liquid dripping from the petri dish, slipping towards the ground where dark slime stretched over her chair and bench, coating the lab equipment in a thick, congealed soup that hung across the gangway.

Manny emerged behind her, huffing and breathless.

'Holy shit,' he said. 'Is that—'

Renee nodded, unable to speak. She peered up at him and saw something that made her heart literally stop. A shadow monster stood behind him, a large, malformed body, tiny, yellow orbs, long limbs that slowly unfurled in the air. There was a rasping growl, an angry dog on steroids.

'Run,' she hissed as Manny slowly turned. 'We need to run.'

He reacted instantly, grabbing a chair and tossing it towards the creature, grabbing Renee and hauling her to her feet before almost stumbling over the professor's corpse.

'Go!' he said, pushing her. 'Now!'

'No, I—' She turned to see the beast launching itself across the gangway with the dexterity of a leopard. Manny ducked towards a bench and slid beneath it, avoiding the creature's talons as it slammed into the ground. She rounded the refrigerator and ran along the farthest wall, racing towards the fire escape.

There was a roar from behind her, piercing and hoarse like a hungry pack of hyenas. Manny grabbed a heavy microscope and hurled it at the creature. It danced out of the way before coming across the bench, moving with a speed that she thought impossible for its size. It was like a sea snake or a giant octopus, but with limbs that grew and then retracted, only to be replaced by other limbs that emerged from different places along its thick torso. It was unnatural, an abomination. She had never seen anything like it before.

Manny was backed into a corner with a large industrial oven by his lefthand side and a wall to his rear. The creature seemed to sense this, and it crouched in front of him, readying itself for its next assault. Manny glanced at Renee, his fists raised in defiance.

'Leave!' he yelled. 'Just go!'

Her eyes scoured the bench, looking for something, anything. She spied a keyboard, a mouse, a plastic beaker, a collection of pipettes and vials. She initially went for a syringe, hoping a jab from a needle would be enough to distract the thing, but then she saw it, sharp and glinting. A scalpel. She reached out, but her fingers slipped from it, almost knocking it to the floor. Eventually she found a purchase, pulling it into her palm. She raised it, ignoring her instinct to flee. With a reckless abandon she never knew she had in her, she ran towards it, driving the sharp blade into its side, twisting and pulling the scalpel upwards. Her hand was instantly smothered in black and yellow ooze, warm like chicken soup. It slipped between her fingers and slid down her arm. She recoiled as the monster shrieked, twisting its head towards her and thrashing its long, sinuous limbs. She was knocked backwards across the table by a flailing arm, and she went crashing to the floor, winded.

Manny ran, ducking beneath its sharp talons. He grabbed her and pulled her towards him.

'We have to get out of here,' he said. 'The fire escape.'

'No! We can't just leave that thing in here.'

She turned and spied the flash freezer they used to instantly chill some of the more sensitive biological samples. A series of complex pipes and cables were hooked into the rear of the apparatus, which were in turn connected to a group of metal cylinders.

'Come on,' she said, as an idea formed. 'This way.'

Behind them, the creature was turning, yellow slime pumping from the wound in its side. An arm slammed onto the bench nearest to them, sending metal and plastic equipment flying. Manny tossed anything he could find onto the floor, attempting to slow the monster's progress as it came barrelling towards them.

Renee reached the freezer first, but she tripped over a cord and went sprawling, tumbling over a chair, her arm twisting awkwardly beneath her. Manny couldn't halt his own momentum, and he crashed into her, tripping over her feet and smashing through a racking unit filled with tools and plastic trays. They lay there under an assorted mass of needles and beakers. The monster approached, an out of control truck with no brakes. They were in its sights, tangled in a collapsed heap.

'The pipe,' she said, pulling at Manny's sleeve. 'Unhook the pipe.'

He looked to his left, dazed and terrified. A series of bright silver cylinders stood beside the blue bulk of the freezer unit, black tubes connecting to a collection of couplings at its rear. Suddenly his eyes opened wide. He understood.

She could hear the beast's breath now. It was ragged and slow, a long, malicious drawl. It was so close, almost on top of them.

She wondered what it would feel like, death. Would her conscious self just be switched off like a TV, or would there be something else, something more? She might know soon enough. Her whole body trembled at the realization. She didn't want to die.

As the creature bore down on them, Manny's short, stubby fingers yanked at the rubber tube, twisting and pulling, frantically attempting to disconnect it. At first, Renee thought the plan was doomed to failure and the damn thing wouldn't budge, but then there was the slightest of hisses, a cold breath on her neck, and it came away with a snap, a plume of white smoke and liquid jettisoning from its open end. Manny rolled onto his front and directed the tube towards the pouncing monster, the jet of steaming liquid nitrogen connecting with its dark flesh, pushing it backwards, sending it staggering. There was a scream, shrill and deafening, as it tried to get away. Its limbs flailed and thrashed, its tail whipped round, sending yet more equipment flying, but then its body stiffened and became brittle. The creature was motionless, still. It was encased in a dense, white frost, but Manny refused to stop. He let the cylinder run dry before he dropped the hose to the floor, turning their attacker into a frozen slab of lifeless meat. It came crashing down, splitting a bench in two and sending chairs and equipment tumbling.

'Here,' Renee said, feeling every muscle in her exhausted body as she hauled the empty cylinder across the floor. 'Help me lift this.'

Manny turned to her and helped her raise it to chest height. She looked down at the thing that lay beneath them: eight feet in length, sleek like a salamander, half a dozen tentacled limbs protruding from a dark body, a tail covered in sharp ribs. Its frozen eyes stared at them, a clutch of tiny yellow orbs.

'Let's make sure it can't come back,' she said, spitting every word. They raised the heavy cylinder high above their heads, watching as the ice began to thaw and one of the yellow eyes shifted in their direction. They brought it down hard, smashing the creature's brittle skull into a thousand tiny shards.

Part Three: Elysian Field

Tuesday, 27th June:

Storage Explosion, Sittingbourne

Paul and Julie watched as the fire engines arrived. The blaze in the building was now so fierce that dancing flames peeked like nervous kittens through the slumped remains of the tin roof. The sprinkler system just couldn't keep up with the pace of the inferno. A thick cloud of soot and smoke billowed across the street, obscuring the traffic lights. A Transit van collided with a Mini Cooper, slamming it into the railings. The air was filled with an angry exchange, words fired off like projectiles. A group of kids watched from the pavement beside the Indian Takeaway, camera phones at the ready. What remained of the building was slowly succumbing to the fire, fifty or more rooms stacked shoulder height with people's heirlooms, keepsakes, memorabilia, all devoured by burning oxygen.

Paul checked the wound in his arm. It had stopped bleeding but it was painful. The tear in his skin was long and deep. Julie was shivering beside him. Neither of them had coats, and the storm had brought with it an ice-cold chill. He tried to pull her towards him, but she turned away, avoiding his attention. Her body was stiff, her arms wrapped around herself, an impenetrable shield.

'Do you think they're both dead?' he eventually asked as the first fire crew began to pump gallons of liquid over the towering flames.

'Yeah. Nobody could have walked out of that.' She averted her eyes before saying what they were both thinking. 'We locked him in there.'

'He was going to kill us.'

'It's still murder.'

She was right, of course. Wade was dead, and now Ted Barker and his muscle too. Everything was spinning out of control. People dying wasn't in the plan. It had never been in the plan. All he had ever wanted was to make some money out of a bizarre situation. That was all. Plain and simple. Nobody should have got hurt.

The thing in the lockup. The monster that had grown from inside the darkness. The open freezer, the yellow and black ooze, the tentacle wrapped around Rami's throat, the teeth sinking into his skin. Something had happened in there. The Amrita had changed somehow. Paul thought of the creature in the cave again, of Manny smashing a rock into its skull. They thought it had been mortally wounded, trapped behind a pile of stone and rubble. Maybe it had found a way out.

'You lied to me,' Julie said. 'You told me you'd just found the stuff.'

'We did.'

'You didn't tell me everything.'

'I told you what I knew.'

'You selected the bits that suited what you wanted me to believe.'

Her words were like wasp stings, sharp and hurtful. 'Help me out here, Jules. I don't know what you're talking about.'

'Don't lie to me, Paul!'

'I don't. I—'

She slapped him hard in the chest, shoving him away. 'I said, don't lie to me! We went there to the cave, we found the underground pool, we saw that monster, that…thing, and now she's dead!' She was angry, tearful, her words erupting from her mouth in hot bursts.

'I don't understand. Who's dead?'

'Ellie!'

'Your cousin? What does she have to do with any of this?'

'Because we didn't know, Paul! I didn't know. You never told me anything. I convinced her to come with me, to find out what the hell we had given to my father, and now she's—' The anger seemed to bleed from her. She bent over, her hands on her knees. She threw up, retching and heaving, her shoulders rolling as a thin line of bile spewed onto the floor.

'Jules, are you okay?' He tried to hold her, tried to help her, but she threw out an arm, hitting him in the stomach.

'Leave me alone!'

'I just want to help.'

'I don't need your help. I don't need anything from you.'

His pocket buzzed. He stepped away, unsure of what to say. He stared at the screen, still not taking everything in. What was Julie saying? How could Ellie have been killed? He tried to focus. He scanned his messages through bleary eyes. Manny had called him fifteen times.

He dialled his voicemail and held the phone to his ear. Manny was talking, but it was hard to make out what he was saying. He sounded out of breath. The roar of the fire engines drowned out his words. Paul stepped further away and hit 'replay message'. This time he heard him, every sharp, jabbing syllable. He staggered against the barrier. Wade's suicide. Julie's father. Was he dead? Is that what Manny had been trying to say? His stomach became a ferocious vat of acid. A power drill rattled in his chest as the ground beneath him became a rolling swell, rising and falling. He suddenly felt sick.

His phone pinged again. It was a WhatsApp message. Renee's red hair and grinning face peered up at him from her profile image.

We're at the Farthing Corner Services, Burger King. Need to see you ASAP. As in, straight away. Bad things are happening.

Paul read the message again, trying to take it all in. Information was coming at him like shrapnel. He wanted to duck, to hide. He couldn't shake what Manny had said about Julie's father. It felt so unreal, like a nightmare he couldn't escape from. He couldn't tell Jules. He couldn't be the one to give her the news. It would destroy her, their relationship too.

'We've got to go, Jules,' he said, his voice wavering. 'It's Renee and Manny.'

'I'm not going anywhere with you.' She was hunched over, her wet hair obscuring her face.

'It sounds important.'

'I need to check on my father.'

Her words were like punches, heavy blows he didn't have the energy to fend off. What could he say to her? It was too soon. He needed to hear it from Manny. He needed to hear the truth.

'Then I really think you should come with me. We have to find out what's going on here, and I think Renee and Manny might have some answers.'

He hated himself for the manipulation, for the thinly veiled lie, but he didn't know what else to do. He couldn't leave her crouching in the car park, knowing that inside the smouldering warehouse there was the crispy, blackened corpses of two drug dealers and a monster he could barely rationalise. They had to get ahead of this, for everyone's sake.

'You don't have a car,' she said.

He eyed Ted Barker's truck.

'No,' she objected. 'That's stealing.'

'What are our options?' He opened the door and found the key fob beneath the sun visor. 'It's not like they'll be needing it.'

She pushed him out of the way and headed for the passenger door. 'I'm only coming because I want to find out the truth. Afterwards, you drop me home, okay?'

He started the engine and stared at her, taking in her dark eyes, long hair, cheeks kissed with pink. She was about the best thing that had ever happened to him, and he'd messed it up. Only a miracle could save them now, and he was rapidly running out of those.

As the truck pulled away, a shadow stood among the trees, the flickering light from the roaring flames only partially illuminating its unreal features: a man's face, the remains of a human body, gorged skin encapsulated within a black, writhing sea of flesh and mutating limbs. It was hungry. It wanted. Its desire was unquenchable. The man inside the truck had some of what it needed. It slipped into the darkness and headed for the one place it knew the man would go. After all, it had been there before.

Tuesday, 27th June:

Farthing Corner Service Station, M2, nr Sittingbourne

Manny devoured his burger. He was ravenous, but even so, the greasy meat sat heavy and stodgy in his gut. His appetite and his skittishness fought against each other, a contradiction in his abdomen. He couldn't shake what he had seen. They had been so close to death. He could still fill the Grim Reaper's cold touch on the nape of his neck. If it hadn't been for Renee's quick thinking, they would still be there, no doubt lying next to her professor in a pool of their own blood and excrement. Cheese fell from his mouth as he took another huge bite, but he was forcing it down. He didn't want it. He didn't want anything. He eyed Renee. She was picking at a Chicken Royale, barely touching it.

'You need to eat,' he said. 'You've had a shock.'

'I'm not hungry.' She pushed the burger away.

'You need your energy.'

'You have it, I'm okay.'

'But Renee—'

'Oh, pour l'amour du ciel!' she cried. 'Please, you eat it. I don't want the bloody thing.'

A lorry driver on the table across from them looked up. Manny rolled his eyes theatrically.

'They should be here soon,' he said. 'Paul and Julie.'

'That's what I'm worried about.'

He glared at the table, knowing exactly what she meant. They had found his body. They had seen him lying there, and yet when it came down to it, they had walked away.

'They're here,' Renee said, watching as the door at the far end of the overpass opened.

Manny stood as Paul and Julie approached. He embraced them both.

'You want something?' he asked, cocking his head towards the counter.

Julie shook her head.

'No, thanks,' Paul replied. 'We've just come from the lockup.'

'Everything okay?'

Paul flinched at his question, and Manny realized everything was far from okay. 'It's gone. It's all gone.'

'I don't understand.'

'Ted Barker kidnapped me,' Julie said, her jaw clenched. 'Said he'd kill me if Paul didn't do what he asked.'

'Ted Barker? You mean *the* Ted Barker? The criminal? The drug dealer?' Manny tried to fit the pieces together in his head. 'What the hell has he got to do with any of this?'

'Seems like Wade told him all about the Amrita,' Paul replied. 'Told him everything. Ted being what he is, he saw the opportunity in it, the same way we did, except he was willing to cut some corners, some pretty big ones. Like actually paying for the stuff.'

'So, you took him to the lockup?'

'I had no choice.'

'Did he take it all?'

'It didn't go down like that.'

'What do you mean?'

'I'm not sure how to say it.'

'Well, try.' Manny urged.

'He's trying to tell you that…we didn't find exactly what we were expecting,' Julie said.

'What do you mean?'

'There was something in there. Some sort of creature, maybe an animal.' Julie paused, looked away. 'I don't know how to explain it.'

'What did it look like?' Renee asked.

'It's hard to describe.'

'Did it have strange - I don't know the right way to say this in English - strange, dead eyes. Lots of them?'

Paul cocked his head. 'How could you know that?'

Manny glanced at Renee. He nodded. They needed to share. They needed to tell them everything.

They sat there for more than thirty minutes, Manny and Renee revealing the truth about Wade's death, followed by a scrambled summary of what had gone down at the university. Renee described Professor Wayling's mutilated corpse and the creature in the shadows. Manny spoke about how they had almost been killed, avoiding death by using liquid nitrogen to turn the ungodly thing into an eight-foot ice lolly. Renee explained her theory about the Amrita's mutation, suggesting it could have been brought on by its activation with the diluted caffeine during the replication process, or even through it coming into contact with a contaminated blood sample. Perhaps, she theorised, either scenario was enough to bring the dormant cells to life, and that all the Amrita needed was a catalyst of some sorts, something to feed off.

The only part they omitted was the truth about Julie's father. Manny couldn't bring himself to tell Julie that. He just didn't have it in him.

'If Renee's right,' he said. 'We have to destroy everything we have left.'

'Well, that's easy,' Paul sniped. 'Because our stock in the lockup was torched, along with Ted and Rami.'

'But that's not all of it,' Renee said. 'You have some yourself, right?'

Paul shook his head. 'The stock at my flat is almost entirely gone, and Wade can't have had much left. We limited what we gave him, remember?'

'What about your father?' Renee asked Julie, causing Manny to half-choke on his Diet Coke.

'I've been giving him doses from Paul's stock,' Julie said. 'There's none at the house.'

Paul rested his elbows on the table, pushing his thumbs into his eyes. 'Then that just leaves—'

'Elysian Field,' Manny said. 'And they have a lot.'

Paul's head dropped into his hands. 'I know what you're thinking, but we can't do that.'

'We have to.'

'Why?'

'Because, if we don't, everybody in that complex is in danger.'

Paul exhaled sharply through his fingers. 'We don't know that.'

Manny slammed his hands on the table. 'Are you kidding? Did you listen to what we just told you? You've seen one of these things. It nearly killed you, and it bloody well almost killed the two of us, too. There's something evil going on here, Paul, and we have to put a stop to it.'

'You're saying that like you don't believe the Amrita has any benefits! Like there's no possibility it can be used to do good!'

'This stuff has the capability of killing a lot of people!' Manny yelled. 'Do you want that on your conscience? We know what happened to Wade, and we suspect we know what happened to Jules's fa—' He stopped himself.

'What were you going to say?' Julie asked.

'Nothing. I lost my thread.'

'No, you didn't.'

'Yes, I did.'

'Then I suggest you find it!' she said, raising her voice. 'Manny, what the hell were you about to say?'

He could feel his face becoming hotter and hotter as all the moisture evaporated from his mouth. Renee glared at the table.

'Manny,' Julie snapped, leaning across the table. 'You better tell me right now, or I swear, I'm going to scream.'

He felt himself shrinking into his chair, wishing a sink hole would open up in the ground. What was he supposed to do in this situation? Lie? Dodge the question like a skilled politician? Why wasn't Paul jumping in?

'We were too late,' Renee said, reaching for her vape before eyeing the No Smoking sign. 'We went there because of what happened to Wade.'

'What do you mean you were too late?' Julie asked. 'Where did you go?'

'Your—' Renee paused. 'Your parents' house.'

'My parents?' Julie turned to Paul. 'What is she trying to tell me?'

'Just hear her out,' Paul replied, urging Renee to continue.

'He was on the floor. There were marks around his neck, just like the ones the police said they found on Wade. He—' she turned to Manny.

'He choked himself to death, Jules,' Manny said, forcing the words out. 'I'm so, so sorry.'

'What?' Julie cried. 'You mean my—' She stood, her body trembling. 'My dad? You mean my *dad*?'

Paul leapt up, pulled her into him.

'My father? But he was fine, I saw him. Why would he—' Her voice cracked. She broke down, her shoulders shuddering, her fingers like sharp claws against her eyes.

Manny watched as Paul held her. His eyes met those of his friend. They both realised how bad this was. The pair of them had signed Julie's father's death warrant.

'I need to get out of here,' Julie cried, slamming her hands into Paul's chest.

'Jules! Wait a minute.'

'I said, I need to go!'

'But we're safer together.'

'Get your fucking hands off of me!'

She shoved him away, her eyes like bullets. She glared at the others before storming down the corridor, slamming into a magazine stall and crashing out the door.

'I should go after her,' Paul said, shaking his head in disbelief. 'He was dead, right? You're sure about that?'

'We're sure,' Manny replied. 'And those things are real, too, Paul. There's no denying them.' He grabbed his phone, opening a website with the image of an Airbus A380 on its homepage. 'I'm going to book us flights to Norway. All of us. We have to go back to Galdhøpiggen.'

'You do what you gotta do,' Paul said, flapping a hand. 'But right now, I've got bigger priorities.'

Tuesday, 27th June:

Sittingbourne, Kent

He tried to talk to Julie, tried to calm her down, but she was a mess, shrieking at him uncontrollably. He understood how she felt, of course he did, but how was he to know what was going to happen? It wasn't as if it had been predictable. The Amrita was a cure, a panacea for everything. He had been so sure of that, so utterly convinced. What had happened to Wade, Roger, and now Ted and Rami, had been an aberration, an abnormality.

He took her home, but when they got there, they found the police were still at the house, and a couple of journalists from the local rag had shown up too. He offered to go in with her, but she told him that he was the last person in the world she needed right now. She wanted her mum. He was on board with that, but he wanted to comfort her too, he wanted to be with her. She was in distress, she'd lost her dad, and now she was alienating him. He never said anything, but inside he was seething. It was completely unfair. She had been the one who had taken her cousin, Ellie, down into the cave. That wasn't on him. That couldn't be on him. And he had tried to save her dad, not hurt him. If it wasn't for the Amrita, the guy would have still been a dribbling, rambling mess.

He pulled away in Ted's truck, feeling neglected and hurt. He watched in the rearview mirror as Julie pushed past the journalists and the police officers. Her mum came outside. They hugged, sobbing into each other's arms. He hated seeing them like that. It wasn't right.

He headed home, planning on collecting his passport and

some clothes before driving to Gatwick. He wasn't thrilled about going back to Elysian Field, but he couldn't allow Manny to go there alone, all guns blazing. He walked up the stairs to his flat, expecting to find the door kicked in. Thankfully, the entranceway was intact.

The place was bathed in darkness, the only sign of Julie's kidnap a spilled cup of coffee.

He headed into his room and almost went tumbling over the goddam cat, Jesus. It was lying on the threshold, licking itself in hard-to-reach places. He stepped over it, calling it 'a fur covered pain in the backside,' before opening his top drawer, scrambling through his underwear, searching for his documents.

That was when he heard it; the tap, tap, tapping on the windowpane. He knew it was impossible because he was on the first floor.

Tap, tap, tap.

He looked at Jesus who had stopped doing what he was doing and was now standing on all fours, glaring at the blinds, his spine arched.

Paul stood, tense, a pair of socks in one hand and a pair of boxers in the other.

Tap, tap, tap-tap-tap.

He moved towards the window, unable to resist the temptation to look. He glanced at his bed which was still covered in glass and beer, and at the open drawer where his passport lay hidden. What was he doing? He knew he should just get out of there, but he couldn't help himself.

He grabbed one of the blinds. He could hardly move. He held his breath, listening to the percussive beat of fingertips on glass. He pictured the thing from the lockup, those horrible eyes, those limbs. He imagined it hanging from the window frame, a long curl of hard keratin, scratching and tapping.

He took a deep breath, counted back from three and pulled back the slats, shielding his eyes as moonlight poured into the room, bathing everything in a creamy skin.

There was nothing there. Nothing except the night sky. He shook his head, feeling like an idiot but knowing he'd definitely heard something. He looked at the cat.

'Can't you see what all this is doing to me, Jesus? I'm a wreck.'

The cat peered back at him, disinterested.

'Thanks for the vote of confidence.'

It yawned, raised its tail and departed.

'Yeah, I'm not much fun to talk to right now, am I?'

He turned back to the window, meaning to close the blinds, and that was when he saw him. Ted. He was standing on the street, looking through the side window of his truck. His face was covered in deep cuts, his clothes blackened from the smoke. He seemed to sense Paul looking at him, and he turned and looked straight into his room.

'Holy shit,' Paul cried out, diving behind the wall. How could Ted still be breathing? That room had been an inferno. How would he have even got out? Unless, of course, Julie hadn't hooked the padlock through the clasp properly.

He chanced another peek. Ted was still there, but now he was walking towards the building. In fact, he was heading straight for the entrance.

'Shit, shit, shit!'

Paul pulled his drawer clean out of the dresser and tipped its contents onto the floor, throwing pants, socks and till receipts in the air, searching frantically for his passport. He now desperately wanted to get out of the country. He caught his finger on a shard of glass and yelped, sucking furiously at the wound, tasting the sweet tang of his blood.

There was the sound of footsteps in the hallway outside as Paul continued his desperate search. He had seen what had happened in the lockup, had seen what that thing had become. He sifted through the remaining mess on the floor, but it was obvious his passport wasn't there.

Tap, tap, tap-tap-tap.

His head jerked up. Ted was standing outside his door now. He was close. Way too close. He pulled out the second drawer, but that one was filled with Julie's underwear and makeup. The third contained his T-shirts.

'Come on, come on.'

He tried every possible location, second guessing where he could have thrown his passport in his state of exhaustion when he'd arrived home from Norway. He guessed he could have tossed it anywhere.

Tap, tap, tap-tap-tap.

He held his breath, trying to calm himself down, but it was no use. Ted knew he'd left him there to die, and that meant he was a target. The pain in his shoulder still throbbed, but it was nothing compared to the guilt gnawing away at his insides. He had killed people, maybe not deliberately, but he knew that didn't matter one bit. Oppenheimer never served a life sentence, but his invention still evaporated over 200,000 living souls.

The handle began to rattle, and then the door started to shake in its frame, jarring him back to the urgency of his situation. The passport, the bloody passport. He knew it was in his room somewhere. He eyed his open suitcase and went to it, tipping everything onto the floor, rifling through his clothes, his travel documents. It wasn't there. He began to sweat profusely as panic set in. He couldn't waste any more time. He had to get away. He eyed the window, knowing it was his only means of escape, but also knowing there was a thirty-foot drop to the paving slabs below. What choice did he have? Ted was going to kill him, or at the very least, kick the crap out of him. Perhaps that was what he deserved. Perhaps he should just get it over and done with. Take his medicine. It wouldn't change anything, wouldn't make the regret go away, but maybe that was his punishment too.

The door exploded inwards as the lock disintegrated. A black shape lurched through the opening. It paused, sniffing the air.

Paul dived to the floor, covering his head with his hands, bracing himself for the sting of hard knuckles on his face and heavy boots in his ribs. He gasped. There under the bed, lying beside a stack of old comics and a photograph album his father had given him, lay his passport, covered in glass fragments.

He heard footsteps bounding down the hallway, the sound of raspy breaths and fists bashing against plasterboard. The passport was in Paul's hands, and then he was pushing himself upwards, leaping across his double divan, reaching out to the window lever, throwing it open and chancing a glance behind him as Ted came sprawling into his bedroom. His eyes were black, his top lip curled upwards. There was something else too, something about his movement, about how the shadows seemed to follow him.

Paul dropped backwards, hanging onto the window ledge with one hand, slipping and tumbling to the floor, his newly relocated shoulder smashing against the ground, crunching and popping as it slipped out of its socket once more.

Paul cried out, clutching his arm. He looked up, staring at Ted's shadow-face, snarling like a Bull Terrier. His hand extended, a thick finger gesturing, marking Paul like a leper.

Paul clenched his teeth and pulled himself to his feet. His stricken arm hung limply at his waist. He lurched to the truck as Ted jumped from the window, but he didn't look back. He grabbed the door and dived in, just as Ted slammed into the car, bashing the bonnet with his fists. His face was full of fury and desperation. He jumped onto the vehicle, smashing his head onto the windscreen repeatedly, fracturing his nose. Blood splattered on the glass. The wipers whirred into life, creating red, raspberry smears.

Paul fumbled for the key fob, hit the start button and gunned the engine, slamming it into reverse. He floored the accelerator and sped backwards, tossing Ted onto the tarmac before spinning the wheel and shifting into drive.

Behind him, Ted got to his feet. He stood at the kerbside, watching as the truck disappeared. Something crawled out from beneath his shirt, black and amorphous, fingers like rakes.

Wednesday, 28th June:

Gatwick Airport, Surrey

They sat in the airport terminal, waiting for their flight. Manny pushed greasy bacon and runny eggs around his plate, wanting to eat, but knowing his stomach was in no fit state to digest a full English with any degree of safety. Renee sat in front of him, slurping an orange juice and anxiously eyeing the concourse.

'Where is he?' she asked.

'He'll be here.'

'He should already be here.'

Manny knew she was right. They'd had to drive back to Canterbury to collect Renee's things, and yet they had still made it to the airport before Paul. He checked his phone, hoping for a message. There was nothing. He checked Paul's Facebook Messenger status, but it was inactive. Manny had already tried to call him three times, but the line had gone straight to voicemail.

'He had to take Julie back,' he said. 'That would have taken some time.'

'Not as long as this.'

'Maybe he went into the house with her.'

'You saw the way she looked at him,' she replied. 'She didn't want to be anywhere near him.'

Manny glared at his plate. If Julie blamed Paul for what happened, then he knew he had to shoulder his share of the responsibility, too. He and Paul had done this together. The two of them had made the decisions as a team. Sure, Paul could be convincing when he put his mind to it, but Manny was no pushover. He knew what was going on. There was no getting away from it. They had acted recklessly, without fear of consequence. They'd been lured by the promise of wealth and fame, and now five people were dead.

'Room for one more?' a woman asked.

'Hey, you,' Renee cried.

Manny looked up from his food. It was Julie. She looked dishevelled, her eyes red-rimmed, hair loose and untidy.

'Of course there is,' he said, awkwardly grabbing a chair from the next table. 'Here, take a seat.'

She slumped into it, her body collapsing in on itself. She looked exhausted, beaten.

A waitress approached.

'Coffee, please. Black.'

'I'm so sorry about your father,' Renee offered, fidgeting in her seat.

'Yeah,' Julie replied. 'Me too.'

Manny fingered his own mug, chasing the remains of ground coffee and leftover steamed milk, trying to think of the right words. He had to say something. He couldn't just leave it hanging. 'It wasn't just Paul, you know. I've been with him the whole time. I didn't stop him, didn't even try. We shouldn't have given that stuff to your dad, Jules. We just shouldn't have.'

Julie glared at him, bloodshot eyes, motionless like stones. Her fingers, white at the knuckles, gripped the edge of the table. The corners of her lips twitched.

'You know what I think?' she asked. 'You want to know what I really think?'

Manny glared at Renee. She was nervously fiddling with her rings.

'You've earned the right to say what you want to say,' he said.

'Yeah, I guess I have.'

The coffee arrived. Julie took a sip, wiping liquid from her dry lips. 'I think if anyone's to blame, it's me.'

'No, that's not true.'

'I ran out on my father. Did you know that?'

He shook his head.

'Couldn't handle being there with him, seeing him like that. Mum needed me, she even told me so, but I ignored her and just packed my things and left. Went to live with a friend, for God's sake, in a house that was way too small. I almost broke up with Paul over it because the stupid prat wouldn't let me move in with him. Can you believe that?' She shook her head, chewed her lip. 'But then you told me you had this wonderful new cure, and even though I knew it was too good to be true and that we were taking one hell of a risk, I went ahead and let you do it anyway.' She took another sip from her coffee and paused. 'When I think about it, the only reason I would have ever done something so stupid, so dangerous, was because I wanted to make my life easier. *My* life. Not my father's. Certainly not my mother's. My own. I thought, if this Amrita could truly cure my father's disease, then everything could go back to being as it was, and I could be the carefree, responsibility free, spoiled brat of a daughter I had always been. Daddy's little girl.'

Manny reached out to her, but she pulled away.

'You're not those things, Jules,' he said.

'Oh, yes I am. I'm all of those things and so much more.'

Manny let her words hang in the air. There was no point in arguing. She was suffering. Nothing he said could change that.

The airport speaker system shattered the silence, announcing that Flight DY1303 to Oslo was now boarding.

'We have to go,' he said to Julie. 'I'm so sorry to leave you like this.'

'What do you mean?' she said, throwing money for her coffee

onto the table.

'Renee and I are heading back to Norway.'

'We want to find out what this Amrita really is,' Renee said, grabbing her bag. 'After what's happened, we think the scientists that Manmeet and Paul have been in dialogue with could help us.'

Paul emerged from the adjacent concourse, breathing heavily, his cheeks red and puffy.

'Julie?' he cried. 'What are you doing here? I thought you were with your mum.'

'I was,' she said, hitching her bag over her shoulder. 'But if this thing really did kill my dad, then I have a right to know what's going on.'

Manny shook his head. 'So that means—'

'That's right,' she replied, marching towards the gate. 'I'm coming with you.'

Wednesday, 28th June:
Oslo Gardermoen Airport, Norway

They landed at mid-day and managed to get a cheap rental car; a four-year-old Ford Fiesta. Manny drove. The car was barely large enough to squeeze them all in, but space wasn't their priority. Paul sat in front and did his best to navigate while recounting the events of earlier that morning. He still couldn't make sense of it, how Ted could have escaped the fire.

'I reckon you had a lucky escape,' Manny said. 'That guy's an absolute nut-job.'

'Yeah, you're right,' Paul replied. 'But he was different to before.'

'What do you mean?'

'The way he was acting. It was as though…I don't know.'

'No, come on. Say it.'

'You know like that film? The one with Will Smith and Tommy Lee Jones?'

'Men in Black.'

'Right.'

'Which one?' Renee asked.

'What do you mean?'

'There's three of them,' she replied. 'Plus another one with Chris Hemsworth which wasn't as good.'

'He means the first one,' Julie offered. 'It's the only one we've seen.'

'Right,' Paul agreed. 'The first one. Well, you know the guy, the bad guy?'

'The guy with the bugs,' Renee said. 'He was funny.'

'Right, except this wasn't funny. Wasn't funny at all. You know how that guy was basically a skin suit on top of the alien.'

'Paul, that's gross,' Julie said.

'I know, but that was what he was. Ted was similar to that, but not the same.'

'How do you mean?'

'I don't know. I don't think he was a skin suit because he seemed to be fighting it, but…it was weird, like something was inside of him, controlling him.'

'You mean like a possession?' Manny asked.

'Maybe.'

'That sounds crazy,' Julie said. 'That's not even possible.'

'I know, but that's how he seemed Jules, believe me. He wasn't acting the way he was acting at the pub, or even when he had a gun on us at the lockup. He was different.'

'I don't understand,' Manny said. 'You think that thing in the lockup possessed him in some way? I mean, that doesn't sound believable, does it?'

'I'm not sure. He ingested the Amrita, right before that thing killed Rami. I think he was in a rush to see what it could do to him. Maybe he got more than he bargained for.' Paul pointed out the window. 'Turn left here.'

Manny swung the car onto the slip road and shook his head. 'People being controlled by the Amrita. I don't know. That's just weird.'

'It would explain what happened to Wade,' Renee said.

'Wait,' Julie said with a start. 'You think that's what happened to my dad, too. You think he was controlled by the stuff he was taking?'

'These cells mutate, Julie,' Renee replied. 'I've seen it myself. If the Amrita is ingested in the same or similar way, then I think there's every possibility that the host could be made to do things without being able to resist it. Perhaps your father and Wade fought against it, or maybe they were too weak to survive the transformation.'

Julie slumped against the back seat, her eyes fixed on a space way off in the distance.

Paul thought of the doses of Amrita he had been taking, of the visions he'd been having. He'd only been ingesting a very small amount, less than half of what they'd administered to Wade and Julie's father, but if what Renee said was right, any dose could be way too much. He'd tossed his inhaler not long after realizing his acute asthma had been cured, which meant he couldn't stop taking the Amrita, even if he wanted to. He'd told the others that his stocks had been depleted, but that had been a lie. He always carried it with him. The vials felt warm against his chest, hidden like contraband. What were his options? Without it, he could succumb to a severe asthma attack at any moment, one that might kill him. What harm would it do, anyway? He'd been okay so far, and the vials he'd kept for himself hadn't mutated as far as he was aware. He could put up with the odd hallucination and crippling nightmare. It would be fine. He was sure it would be fine. He just wouldn't tell anyone.

'This really is a beautiful country,' Renee said from the back seat. 'Just look at those mountains. They're gorgeous.'

'Where did you say this place was again?' Julie asked. 'I need to pee.'

Manny pointed towards the highest snow-capped peak. 'You're looking at it.'

Wednesday, 28th June:

Elysian Field HQ, Galdhøpiggen, Norway

Manny swung the car onto the wide plateau and turned off the engine. Ahead of them, the Jotunheimen mountain range stretched from east to west as far as the eye could see. A light dusting of snow drifted down from a grey, cotton sky. The thick white blanket covering the parking lot crunched like ice cubes beneath their feet.

'Oh, wow,' Renee cried. 'It reminds me of the French Alps.'

'It's cold,' Julie groaned.

'Yeah, it looks like a storm's coming,' Manny agreed. 'We'd best get inside.'

'You mean in there? In that place? It looks like an old shack.'

'It's not what it seems, Jules, trust us,' Paul replied. He opened the door, relishing the warm air. 'Come on, I'll see if I can find Gunthar.'

As the others followed, Paul headed straight to the kitchen.

'Nice,' Renee exclaimed, stepping inside. 'Comfy.'

'Doesn't look like the headquarters of a multi-national pharmaceutical company,' Julie sniped.

'That's because it isn't,' Paul replied, returning to the front room.

'You mean this isn't their headquarters, or that they're not a multi-national pharmaceutical company?'

'Let's just say Elysian Field aren't your usual FTSE 100 corporation.'

'Meaning?'

'Meaning they house criminals,' Manny muttered.

'They what?' Julie exclaimed. 'Oh, this just gets better and better.'

'You never mentioned this before, Manmeet,' Renee said. 'If I'd have known—'

'You'd have done what?' Paul asked, eyeing the stairway that led down to the basement. 'You wouldn't have come? That's fine, Renee. We never asked you to be here in the first place. This is a mess that Manny and I have to clean up. You wanna go sit in the car, be my guest.'

'Paul, that was out of order,' Manny interjected. 'They're right, we should have filled them in. We said no more secrets, and this is a pretty big one.'

Paul felt his anger spilling over. What more did these people want from him? A pound of flesh? He was doing the best he could.

'You're right,' he conceded. 'You all are. We should have said, but these are the people we entrusted the Amrita with, and whatever you might think of them and of the decisions we made, we can't change any of that now. What I do know is that the scientists down there have a stash of stuff we own, and they've been testing it for days. If anybody will know what we're dealing with here, they will. For now, I suggest we all just suck it up, keep our opinions to ourselves, and go find out what the hell is going on.'

Julie folded her arms as Renee glared out the window. Manny stood there looking awkward. Paul went to the staircase which wound downwards into a dark corridor. He pressed the intercom, expecting Gunthar's smooth, clipped tones, but instead there was nothing. After three attempts, and a hiss of muted static, he gave up.

'Perhaps he's playing host to some other guests,' he offered.

'You did call ahead, right?' Julie asked.

'Did you see me make a call?' Paul replied churlishly.

'Oh, you've got to be kidding me.'

'I don't even have Gunthar's number.'

'No, but you have Petra's. Tell me you have hers.'

'Yes, of course I do, but she's not the kind of person you just cold-call, Jules. She's a very busy woman.'

'Who happens to be in possession of a very dangerous chemical.' Julie threw her hands in the air. 'We've flown all this way, and we don't even have an appointment. Can you believe him?'

'I'll try it now,' Paul said, pulling his phone from the pocket of his jeans.

'Go on then,' Julie replied. 'Let's see how she reacts to four visitors from the UK dropping in unannounced.'

He found Petra in his contact list and hit dial, waiting as the network connected. The phone rang three times and then went straight to voicemail.

'Hey, Petra,' he said, trying to sound as casual as possible. 'It's Paul Karin here. Look, sorry for dropping in on you like this, but we're in the entrance cabin and Gunthar's not here. Anyway, we've got something important to discuss with you. It's about the Amrita, and it's kind of urgent. I know you're probably super busy, but I'd be really grateful if you'd give us some of your time. You can reach me on this number. Thanks again. Really appreciate it. Er…we'll wait right here. Cheers.'

'Way to go,' Julie said. 'That ought to do it.'

'She'll see us,' he said, fighting to control his temper. 'She will. She'll have to.'

'And what if she doesn't?'

Paul shrugged and glared at Manny. 'You wanna help me out here, pal?'

'I agree with Paul,' Manny offered, sounding unconvinced. 'We just need to speak to someone with authority, explain the situation.'

'And how do we do that?' Julie asked. 'There's nobody here.'

'Then we go find them,' Manny replied, suddenly finding his bullishness. 'And we make sure they bloody well listen.'

*

When they reached the bottom of the staircase, Paul led them along a corridor towards the living quarters. He felt sure that Gunthar would be in one of the many rooms, although his absence had surprised him. The place was so professionally run, it seemed odd that the cabin would be left unattended. Okay, so the little shack was a hidden entrance high up in the mountains, the location of which was fiercely guarded by all those involved, but Petra had seemed so cautious, so protective of her enterprise, that he couldn't imagine her allowing the hut to be left so exposed.

He ushered the others into an adjacent corridor where the doors to eight rooms were inset into a stone wall. Paul tried each door in turn, giving them a gentle nudge, followed by a loud rap. After realising they were all locked, he headed towards the communal kitchen at the end of the annex, situated up a set of narrow steps. When they entered the dark room, the lights automatically sprang into life, revealing a set of ten tables, a large central island, and an array of stoves, cooking implements and food trays. The place smelled of lamb stew.

'Very nice,' Renee said, lifting the lid on one of the trays. 'Nothing's cooking though.'

'No Gunthar here either,' Manny added, opening the door to the storage room. 'The lights are on but nobody's home.'

Paul studied each of the tables in turn, running his finger

across a chrome surface. The place was immaculately clean, as it was during their first visit, but the deathly silence bothered him. From the corner of his eye, he spotted a shadow in the furthest corner, lurking just above the cupboard that stored the cups and saucers. It looked out of place, an ink spot in a sea of gleaming metal and crisply painted walls.

'I could live here,' Renee said, reclining on one of the loungers. 'This is better than my own front room.'

'You live in university digs,' Manny replied. 'I've been in some of those places. Even a squat in the east-end would be an upgrade.'

'Oh, *case-toi*,' she cried, shooting him a grin. 'Our place is not like that at all. We have high standards, you know?'

Paul drowned out the voices as he watched the shadow. It was moving, inching forwards before stopping abruptly, and then edging forwards again. It was like a spider with a wide, flat body. Tiny legs seemed to be pulling it across the wall, slowly at first, but then faster. Much faster. It was growing, stretching and distorting, its black form bubbling at the centre as if it were boiling under the heat of the spotlights.

'I bet your place is piled high with empty bottles of wine, pizza boxes and cigarette butts,' Manny continued.

'Hey,' Renee retorted, holding out her vape. 'Look at this. Just look at it! I run a tight ship, believe me.'

Paul couldn't take his eyes off the undulating darkness, the thing that was now creeping over the edge of the cupboard and slipping like oil down the white door. He could see what appeared to be fingers now, long and flexing, the beginnings of claws, a stretching, reaching leg that bent downwards towards the worktop. It was growing, becoming too large. He was transfixed, unable to move, unable to blink.

'You okay, Paul?' Julie asked, jolting him awake.

'What? Yeah, yeah.' He looked at her. 'Yeah, I'm fine.'

'You look distracted. I think we all need to focus here.'

'Right, yeah. You're right. And I am.' He shot a sideways glance at the corner of the room. The shadow had disappeared. 'I'm totally focussed.'

'That's good,' she replied. 'Because this place is giving me the creeps. Can we go?'

'Just a minute.' He checked his watch. 'I just need to use the loo.'

'What? You mean, now?'

'Yeah, Jules,' he said, holding his bladder. 'When a man's gotta go, he's gotta go.'

He ducked into one of the unisex toilets and closed the door, sliding the lock home before slumping onto the seat. His mind was racing. What had he just seen? Was it real, or was it just another crazy hallucination? He hadn't had any sleep after all, and so much had happened. Was it any wonder he was seeing things? He reached into his jacket pocket and slipped out a yellow vial. He held it up. The viscous liquid clung to the edge of the plastic. Satisfied that nothing had changed, he unscrewed the lid, pinched his nose and tipped the contents into his mouth. He swallowed instantly, wincing at the sour taste. His throat was filled with a heat that seemed to follow the liquid all the way down. His stomach blossomed with a mellow warmth. With that done, he turned, unzipped his fly and forced out a miniscule amount of urine.

'Okay,' he said, hiding his guilt as he closed the door behind him. 'Let's go and see what these scientists have to say for themselves.'

*

They walked along the long hallway and headed towards the stone door.

'How are we going to get in?' Manny whispered as they neared.

'What do you mean?'

'Don't you remember what Gunthar did?' Manny replied. 'He placed his eye against a scanner.'

'Right. And?'

'We don't have Gunthar's eye, and we're not supposed to be here, remember?'

Paul hadn't thought that far ahead. He'd been acting on instinct, hoping that fate and blind luck would be enough to get them where they needed to go.

'Well,' he said. 'I guess we'll just have to ring the doorbell.'

'You don't have a key, do you?' Julie asked from behind them. 'You don't know how to get in.'

'I don't know what you're talking about,' Paul said, pushing the green button that sat just beneath the gleaming lens of the scanner. 'This is how we got in last time.'

'Yeah, right.'

Paul bit his bottom lip, fighting his desire to react.

'They're not answering, are they?' Julie sneered. 'Which isn't a surprise, because they didn't answer before, either.'

'Just give it a minute,' Paul replied, chancing a glance at Manny. 'They'll let us in.'

They stood that way, Paul watching the door, Renee nervously drawing on her vape, Julie tapping her foot. He wondered what the hell he needed to do to get a break. After a few moments of anxiety fuelled silence, there was the sound of a high-pitched electronic ping, the dry slip of metal against metal, and then a click as the door popped inwards.

'It's open,' Paul said, grinning. 'See, I told you. I bloody well told you.'

He pushed hard against its heavy bulk and took a breath as they walked into the foyer. The whole place was bathed in dark shadows.

'What the hell?' he said, attempting to take everything in.

The oak desk was unmanned and the large TV screens above it hung like dark windows. Overhead, the crystal chandelier looked like a giant spacecraft hovering in a black sky. There were now just two empty seats where the security guards had been, a single cup tipped onto its side.

'Is…is it usually like this?' Renee asked.

Manny shook his head.

'So, this is odd?'

'Very.'

'Maybe it's a national holiday,' Paul offered. 'Or a staff meeting.'

'You don't stand down the security for a staff meeting, Paul,' Julie replied. 'This place looks like its closed. Like, permanently.'

Paul approached the desk, walking slowly across the tiles, half expecting the lights to come on at any moment.

'I don't get it,' he said, peering behind the desk. It was vacant. Literally vacant. There was a half-consumed bottle of green juice by one of the disconnected laptops and a cinnamon bun that hadn't even been touched on the other desk. 'It's like they just got up and walked out.'

'I don't think they've been gone too long, judging by this spilled coffee,' Renee replied, dipping her finger into a puddle of brown liquid. 'A couple of days, maybe three.'

'That doesn't make sense either,' Manny added. 'It would mean that whatever happened, it took place not long after our departure.'

'Maybe they knew what they had,' Julie said.

'What do you mean?' Paul asked.

'Well, you said so yourself. You all thought this Amrita was some kind of world beating drug that would make you millions, maybe billions of pounds. Perhaps Petra saw that, took what you gave her, and sold it to the highest bidder.'

'You mean, she stole it?' Manny replied.

'Stranger things have happened.'

'No, no, *no*,' Paul repeated, running Julie's accusation through his brain. 'She wouldn't do that.'

'Wouldn't she?' Julie asked. 'You said she was an astute businesswoman. She would have known the value of the Amrita, even before you stupidly left her a sample and told her how to replicate it. What was going to stop her from manufacturing as much of the stuff as she could and launching it onto the open market before you could lay claim to it.'

'But we have a patent pending,' Manny said. 'We're protected legally.'

'I don't think people like Petra Gunderson give two shits about patents and the legality of mass marketing an unapproved drug,' Julie replied. 'After all, didn't you come here to get it certified through the back door?'

Paul's stomach was churning. It made sense. It made so much sense. They had been played in the worst possible way. Petra had lured them both in like lambs to the slaughter, filling their heads with promises she had no intention of keeping, sending them back to England with their brains buzzing.

'That bitch,' he mouthed, feeling his self-belief crumbling like an overbaked cake.

'Maybe we should just head back,' Manny said, nodding slowly. 'Perhaps this trip has just been a complete waste of time.'

'Yeah,' Paul reluctantly agreed, feeling like the world's biggest clown. 'Maybe we should just get out of here. Call Uncle

Barnaby. See whether he can do anything.'

'Wait!' Renee interrupted. 'Aren't you all forgetting something? Manmeet, don't you remember the monster that nearly killed us? What about what we saw in the lab? The mutated samples? Paul and Julie, you said there was something in that lockup that you couldn't explain, something terrifying. We have to tell Petra what we know, no matter what her intentions are. She's sitting on a ticking timebomb here.'

'Look around you, Renee,' Paul said, deflated. 'She's not here. Nobody's here.'

'We don't know that,' Renee replied. 'We can't possibly know that.'

'Then where the hell are they?'

Renee strode towards the glass doors, her jaw twitching. 'Well, that's exactly what we need to find out.'

*

She sat in the darkness, her hand holding the photograph, its frame in pieces on the floor, fragments of glass embedded painfully in her palm. She picked at them, extracting thin slivers as blood trickled down her wrist, pooling at her elbow. Her husband's smiling face looked up at her from the bloodied image, her young son, the dimples in his cheeks like kisses from heaven. They would be at the school waiting for her, Thomas, riddled with worry, her son, Ethan, wondering where his dear *mor* was.

She had been too quick to rush out of the lab, too hasty in reaching her misguided conclusions. It had been so obvious, so predictable, but she had been blind to the possibility. Years studying her profession, the hours spent gaining her degree, working her way up through the hierarchy, impressing boss after thankless boss. What had it all been for if not for this? She was paid to be certain, to be sure of her results, to let the science guide her. She had been so worried about her own neck that she had put everybody else's on the line, the hatchet lurking above them, an executioner's blade, ready to slice, chop and sever.

She had never seen anything like it before, never witnessed any existing organism that could mutate so rapidly. The lab had been bullet proof, secure, and yet that thing had made short work of the strengthened glass partition. And the door. Oh God, the door.

There was a sharp ping from the laptop. She glared at the screen, confused, as if the sound was entirely alien to her. Four people standing in the corridor: two men, two women. She paused to consider whether she should let them in. The place was a hunting ground, a kill zone, but maybe they could help. Maybe that's why they were here. Her finger hovered over the keypad. God help her. She hit *Open Main Door*.

Hunkered down in the shadows, she attempted to stop shaking. At her feet, Keller's motionless, unrelenting eyes glared back at her, his neck twisted obscenely. She turned her face away, the saltiness of dried tears on her lips.

They would find her. Somebody had to find her.

*

They entered the conference room where Paul and Manny had shaken hands with the devil. It was empty. The place looked exactly how they'd left it, as if the cleaners had never arrived. The crumbs from Manny's pastry lay scattered on the table, the remaining croissants slowly hardening on the tray by the door.

'Looks like this place has been left vacant since we left,' Paul said, placing a cup in the machine. 'Coffee anyone?'

'Paul!' Julie cried. 'Don't we have more pressing things to

worry about?'

'They stole our invention, Jules,' he said, waiting for the steamed milk to finish gushing from the nozzle. 'They at least owe me a decaf.'

Renee arrived at his side. 'I'll have a cappuccino. Double strength. Unlike you, I need the caffeine.'

He hit the button and turned to the others. 'They can't have just upped and left.'

'Well, it sure looks that way.' Julie replied.

'Well, I'm telling you that's impossible.'

'You're thinking of the other residents. The people in the Ambassade,' Manny offered.

Paul nodded. 'There are dozens of them. There's no way that Petra could have shut this whole operation down so quickly. There would be transport to arrange, contracts to terminate, money to transfer, and then there would be the small matter of relocating a whole underground network's worth of criminals. Where would they even go?'

'Back into society?' Renee offered.

'You must be kidding,' Julie replied. 'There are more than enough criminals on the streets, without adding dozens more.'

'Exactly,' Paul said. 'They must still be here somewhere.'

'But why the silence?' Renee asked. 'Why does it look like these people just evaporated.'

'The residential block is separated from the offices,' Paul replied. 'Just because this area is empty, doesn't mean the Ambassade will be.'

'You think we should head there first?' Manny asked. 'See if one of them knows what's going on?'

'I think it's a good place to start.'

'Great idea,' Julie sniped. 'Visit the thugs, murderers and drug dealers.'

'Do you have a better idea?' Paul asked.

'How about we leave? This place is creeping me out.'

Renee stepped in. 'I still think we need to find out what happened to the Amrita. We have no idea what they've done with it.'

Julie whirled on her, her lips pulled back. 'Can't you see? They've taken it. Whatever deal these guys thought they'd agreed to, it's over. Done with. There's no point hanging around. Let's just get the hell out of here. I have a mother at home who's grieving over her dead husband, my *father*, and that's where I should be. Not skulking around down here, trying to find someone who clearly doesn't want to be found.'

'You showed up unannounced, remember,' Paul said. 'Nobody asked you to come. Manny and I had this in hand.'

'Oh, yeah, I forgot,' she scowled, pressing the heels of her palms into her eyes. 'You had the whole situation under control, what with my kidnap, the murders, the suicides, the fire at the lockup, the mess these guys made at the university, and the drug dealer who showed up at your flat.'

'Christ, Jules. I don't know what you want from me here.'

'I don't want anything from you, Paul! In fact, you're the last person I want to be anywhere near right now. Ellie and my dad are dead. Dead! Do you understand that? Do you realise exactly what you've done to my family, what you've done to me?'

'Ellie's death wasn't my fault!'

'What do you mean?'

'You dragged her down into that cave, Julie! You convinced her to come with you on that crazy, completely mental expedition.'

'Because you weren't honest with me!'

'What the hell is that supposed to mean?'

'You made me give my own father that crap without even

telling me where you got it from!'

'You knew where Manny and I had been!'

'Yes, but I didn't know you'd spooned it out of some alien creature's intestines!'

'Then why did you let us do it?'

'Because I was desperate! Because my dad was alive, but he really wasn't! Because my mom was drowning under a terrible emotional burden! And because I was scared, Paul! I was so scared!'

He turned away, unable to face her, knowing that it was an argument he couldn't afford to win, that he didn't have the right to win. He kicked over a chair and slammed his hand onto the cake tray, crushing hard chocolate and brittle pastry beneath his palm.

Only Renee held Paul's gaze, unblinking, her eyes soaking up the tension like a mop. They stood that way, knowing there was only one way this situation could play out. Leaving was not an option. She took a long, determined drag on her vape and exhaled through her nose.

'I'm sorry Julie. But I agree with Paul and Manmeet on this one. If there's any chance the Amrita is still here, we have to find it. We must prevent what happened to your dad and the others from happening to anybody else.'

Julie let out a long breath, dabbing at a tear. 'Whatever. I don't even care anymore.'

Renee placed a hand on her shoulder, squeezed it gently. After a moment of silence, she turned to the door. 'Okay then. If someone wants to lead the way, I suggest we get moving. Dépêchez-vous.'

*

He sat in his room, wiping blood from his hands, trying to come to terms with a life that he once cherished, now transformed. It was a problem, but not an insurmountable one. The one thing he had learned through his drama-tragedy of a life was that things could change in an instant, in a micro-second, and there was absolutely nothing you could do about it. He had taught himself to never be comfortable, to never let the malaise of absolute satisfaction get hold of him. Understand, react, adapt, his personal mantra. Do not become a part of something you cannot immediately leave behind. Do not create ties that cannot be severed. Above all, never, ever fall in love, because love is a flawed emotion that completely obscures objectivity.

What he found when he had arrived home from his field trip to the UK had surprised him. Things had taken a dramatic turn, a catastrophic twist. He had moved instantly, found a place to regroup, to think. He knew that Elysian Field housed dozens of dangerous criminals, but he also knew that none of them were capable of causing the chaotic destruction he had seen laid out before him like a Francisco De Goya painting. He was also aware that the labs had been engaging with any number of bizarre activities since Petra had decided to expand the company's portfolio into the pharmaceutical industry, and despite Gunthar's reservations, she had shown herself to be an astute businesswoman with an eye for detail, and therefore he had gone along with it, quietly and without argument. Nevertheless, as he sat there, crouched in the security tunnel, running every possible scenario through to its ultimate conclusion like a super-computer trying to unravel the mathematical conundrums of the universe, it was this area of the company's activities that troubled him the most. They had made mistakes before, bad mistakes, and so this new event, this brand new apocalyptic happening, was well within the realms of possibility.

If Gunthar was forced to lay his chips on the table, he would bet everything he had that it had something to do with the thing in the cave. He didn't understand what he had found, not yet, and in his experience, it was the things that he didn't understand that usually came back to bite him. He also knew that not being aware of everything about an adversary was a sure-fire way to get blindsided. He wouldn't allow that. He was a meticulous, well researched problem solver, and that was what he planned to do. Solve this latest riddle.

After an hour or more, he selected the most appropriate way forward, and he headed out, keeping to the shadows, moving swiftly through the underground tunnels, only rising to the surface when he was within striking distance of his destination.

When the concierge, Yaz, had emerged from the storeroom, bleeding heavily from a wound in his side and yelling for help, Gunthar had not paused to consider his reaction. The boy was callously and stupidly giving their position away, and that could not be tolerated. He had driven his blade into his slim throat, severing his vocal cords as well as his carotid artery. The surprised look in Petra's lacky's light brown eyes had almost been comical. Gunthar might have allowed himself a laugh had it not been for the screeching sounds that echoed down the long corridor, signalling the arrival of something unnatural.

He had dropped Yaz to the floor, splattering blood across the white tile, and moved with haste, slipping through the door to his apartment just as he spied the dark, writhing form of a thing he had seen once before.

Breathless, he had slid his door closed, listening at the slippery, scraping sound of the creature moving on the other side of the wall, pausing in the corridor, tapping gently against the door, hissing like a viper, its presence poisoning the atmosphere. He held his breath, feeling the acidic burn of unease rising in his gullet, relishing the intensity of it.

When it moved away, Gunthar slipped to the floor, sliding slowly and carefully, closing his eyes, listening as the wet, slurping sound faded into nothingness.

He had been sitting there in silence ever since, observing the yellow, crystalline liquid swirling in the organic sacs that lay between his legs. It was the link between the underground pool and the carnage that now decorated the halls of Elysian Field. The Englishmen had brought the exotic fluid to Petra, and in doing so, had ignited a spark that could not be extinguished. That single belief led him to his next life affirming conclusion, even though he was forming a judgment through instinct and intuition rather than science. What was the point of science anyway, when a person with years of training in their field could make such simple mistakes? Now was not the time for experiments and calculations. Understand, react, adapt.

He had recognised the creature. Its slipperiness had given it away, its dank, pungent odour. Just like a calling card, it had disclosed itself in a way that only a creature of such beauty, such majestic serenity could. The Nokken had visited him once more.

He reached for his knife with one hand and the syringe that lay in his lap with the other, and he did the one thing he had dreamed about all his life, ever since he had been shipped away to boarding school and abandoned by the pathetic vessels that had once called themselves his parents.

He began his transformation.

*

Paul led them along the corridor, second guessing the way to the Ambassade. He could sense the atmosphere darkening amongst them, each of them painfully aware of the devastation they had left behind. What were they even doing there, thousands of miles from home, aimlessly stumbling through an underground hideout, searching for some sort of answer when they had no idea what was waiting for them?

Julie could barely look at him, let alone speak to him, and when she did, it was full of so much malice, so much seething animosity. He'd ruined the only relationship he'd ever really cared about, and for what? To get ripped off by some glamorous Scandinavian with a god-complex? They'd been played, Petra had played them, and she hadn't even had the decency to gloat about it. She'd just disappeared, evaporated, leaving them reeling, cast adrift in a world they weren't prepared for.

'There it is,' Manny cried. 'There. See? I'm sure that's it.'

The corridor to their left seemed to drive further into the belly of the mountain, culminating in a set of dark tinted sliding doors that Paul recognised. The last time he had seen them, he'd been off his head, barely able to walk straight, but he recalled his reflexion in the glass, Petra's hand on his shoulder.

'Okay,' he said. 'These people are dangerous, so I suggest you don't look any of them in the eye. Leave the talking to me and Manny.'

'Manny and I,' Renee said.

'Sorry?'

'It's just your English,' she replied. 'It's worse than my French.'

'Yeah, well I never claimed to be literate. What I do know is that through those doors are some very nasty people who would rather their presence here be kept a secret.'

'Hence, we suggest you stay in the background,' Manny added, eyeing Renee. 'For your safety, we mean.'

Julie huffed loudly before looking away.

'I'm trying to make things right, here,' Paul said to her. 'I'm doing the best I can.'

'Too little, too late,' she replied.

'Come on,' he said calmly, realizing any argument from him was bound to make things worse. 'Let's find out what these people know.'

As they approached, the doors began to slide open, but the mechanism seized, leaving an inch-wide gap.

'A bit odd,' Manny said.

Paul pulled one of the doors, which barely moved. 'Probably needs oiling. Maybe the caretaker took off with Petra and the others.'

He peered through the gap. It revealed another corridor, which in turn was intersected by a third corridor, beyond which were a set of swing doors.

'Looks pretty quiet,' he said. 'Here, help me pull these apart.'

Renee was the first to help out, grabbing one side while Paul yanked the other.

'Mechanism's pretty stuck,' she said. 'Maybe if we rock it a little.'

Manny grabbed the upper part of the door and slid it backwards and forwards as Renee stooped down and did the same at the bottom.

'Jules, you want to help here?' Paul asked.

She joined Renee on the ground. 'You look like you're perfectly capable of breaking this stupid contraption all by yourself.'

Slowly but surely, the glass panels shifted, and before long, they had created a space big enough for one person to squeeze through.

'There,' Paul said. 'Wasn't so hard, was it?'

Manny took a moment to catch his breath. 'No, but you have to wonder why the door's been left like that.'

'You think too much,' Paul replied, turning himself sideways and sliding through the gap. 'They probably have someone on it. Just haven't gotten around to fixing it yet.'

'Well, they are criminals after all,' Julie added, following him. 'Why worry about whether the doors work properly when they've got drugs to peddle and people to kill?'

Renee was the next to pass through. 'Maybe keep those kinds of thoughts to yourself from now on. They probably won't go down too well with this audience.'

'That's a good point,' Manny said, following behind.

They walked along the corridor, checking the doors as they went. Almost all of them were locked, except for one halfway down that stood ajar.

'Hello!' Paul called out. 'Anybody home?' When there was no answer, he tried to push the door open, but it wouldn't budge.

'What is it with you and doors today?' Julie sniped, pushing him out of the way and trying it for herself. 'Feels like something's been jammed up against it.' Her hand went to her nostrils. 'Woah, do you smell that?'

Renee chanced a whiff. 'Maybe the refrigerator's out.'

'Or the drains,' Manny offered.

'Either way,' Paul said. 'The caretaker's going to have his hands full today. Come on, let's not hang around. That stink's turning my stomach inside out.'

They left the unlatched door behind and crossed the intersecting corridor. It stretched either side of them for thirty metres.

'This place is huge,' Julie said. 'How many people did you say were housed here again?'

'Petra was a little elusive on the topic,' Paul replied, 'but it was well over seventy. Maybe a hundred.'

'All paying a heavy price for the privilege, I bet,' Renee said.

'You could see why the people who run this place see it as a financially attractive proposition. I mean, who's even doing this?'

'But it wasn't enough,' Paul spat. 'I mean, why else would she branch out into the pharmaceutical industry and then run off with the first decent invention that lands on her desk? She was in line to make a hefty amount of money from the deal that we signed, but she obviously wanted it all.'

Renee shrugged. 'It seems to me that this Petra is a woman who wants more than just table scraps.'

'You're not kidding,' he hissed. 'She wants the ingredients, the recipe, the cooking instructions, and on top of that, she wants to eat it.'

Julie gestured towards the corridor. 'We can stand here and bitch about how much smarter this woman is than the four of us combined, but if we really want to know what went down here, we have to find somebody to ask, right? Isn't that why we didn't just leave when I suggested it?'

'On that point, at least, I think we can agree,' Paul said. She was right. Getting angry about being duped wasn't helping their cause. 'Let's get moving.'

As he pushed through the next set of doors, a smell hit him. It was like rotten cabbage mixed with festering water.

'Jesus,' he said, reeling away. 'They really need to get these drains sorted out.'

Julie gagged. 'What the hell is that?'

'Smells like decomposition of some sort,' Renee replied, blowing out her cheeks. 'Maybe the rubbish bins need emptying.'

'This is supposed to be a high-class resort, isn't it?' Julie asked. 'Can't they pay someone to do that?'

Manny pointed towards a spot on the wall further along the corridor. 'What's that? Do you see it?'

Renee went to the dark smear that stretched from the next set of doors to the centre of the wall. She held a hand to it, gingerly sliding a finger across the stain before holding it to her nose. 'That's blood.'

'Blood?' Julie cried. 'There's blood on the walls?'

'Yes. Quite a lot of it, too.'

'No way,' Manny groaned. 'This isn't good, Paul. This really isn't good.'

Paul inspected the three-inch deep stretch of dark crimson. He eyed the rest of the wall. There were dense patches of spatter marks that sprayed outward from the door. 'Could be anything.'

'What? Are you kidding?' Julie replied. 'Somebody has literally bled to death here.'

'Maybe there was a fight,' he offered. 'These people are criminals, Jules. I bet they fight all the time.'

'And that smell? You think that's from a fight, too?'

'I don't know. Maybe.'

She threw out her hands. 'You're deluded, Paul. You know that, right? I mean, I always knew you could convince yourself of anything if you thought the rewards were big enough, but this? This is insane. Manny, can't you talk some sense into him?'

Manny went to the door. 'It's just like what we found at the university. There's blood on the handle and all down the edge of the frame. Here, look.' He turned to them. 'And just like at the university, if we want to find out what's going on, we're going to have to go inside.'

Their discussion faltered, his words hanging like a flitting ghost between them. Inside was bad. Inside was where the blood was seeping out from.

'He's right,' Renee agreed. 'We've come this far. We have to see it through.'

'If you think I'm going in there, knowing what we know,' Julie replied. 'Then you're obviously as crazy as he is.'

Renee gasped, insulted.

'So what would you have us do?' Paul asked. 'Just leave.'

'Yes!' she cried. 'That's exactly what I'm suggesting. Look, Renee, I know you're concerned about the Amrita and what it can do, but we can't let that get in the way of common sense. Until that thing came into our lives, we were happy. All of us. Sure, maybe our lives weren't perfect, and maybe we had illnesses or sick relatives, things we were having to live with, but we were doing just that. Living with them. If we go through that door and face up to whatever horrendous truth is lying in wait for us, then we can never go back. Things can never return to the way they were. You get that, right? There's no reboot option. The stuff that's happened to us, it's been awful. I lost my dad and cousin, so I should know, but I would rather go back to that, go back to the grief, to my mother who is in pieces, bury my dead father, knowing that I'll always harbour the guilt, that I'll always wake up in the middle of the night with the weight of responsibility on my shoulders.' She paused, fighting back the tears. 'But if there's any hope that one day that pain will become a little less, and that maybe you and I, Paul, that maybe you and I can get through this, maybe even patch things up eventually, I don't know,' she took his hand, her fingers cold against his palm. 'Then we can't go in there. We just can't.'

Paul watched as her shoulders heaved and her lips trembled. He loved her, or at least he thought he did. He'd never really got around to rationalising his emotions before, but he knew he felt something he'd never experienced. Not with anybody. Not even with his parents, which was hardly surprising given how useless they both were. But these emotions he felt were real and they were palpable. He knew that. He had wanted to build a life with her, even settle down one day, buy a house, become a responsible adult, who knows, maybe even get married, but things had changed; there was no denying that. The world he knew now was not the world he thought he understood. How could he forget everything he had seen, everything that had happened in the past few months?

'I'm sorry, Jules,' he said, regretting every word, but meaning it, too. 'I can't let this go.'

Tears welled in her eyes as the dimple in her chin quivered. He wanted to hold her, to hug her, but then her jaw clenched tightly, and her eyes became narrow black slits. She spoke without emotion. 'Then I guess you and I have nothing more to say.' She turned to the others. 'If anyone wants to come with me, I'm going home. I'm getting the fuck away from this place, right now.'

She stood there, waiting, her expression a mixture of cold defiance and desperate hope, and for a moment, Paul thought Renee might go with her—part of him hoped she would, if only to ensure Julie made it back safely—but then the scientist's eyes fell to the floor, almost apologetically.

'Well, fuck the lot of you,' Julie spat, walking away. 'I hope you find whatever it is you're looking for.'

*

Something was in the aircon duct. She could hear it. It sounded like pennies in a can, metallic, scratching. Her whole body shuddered, her mind unable to bear the thought of something dragging itself towards her through the narrow tubing, breathless and hungry.

She cowered on the toilet seat, her knees pulled up to her chin, her feet on the rim. She had abandoned her workplace, terrified that the grotesque, unfathomable thing might return to finish the job. She thought she might find sanctuary in the office of the one person who was supposed to be in control of everything, who was supposed to have installed failsafe systems to ensure this kind of thing couldn't happen. What she had seen had shattered her illusion of security. The creature had already been here. She had been too late.

There was no way out, no way past them. Her only hope was that someone would save her, that someone had somehow contacted the outside world, that right now the police were on route, or better still, the military were arriving in numbers, heavily armed. They would need to be. These things were strong, quick and highly evolved. Their bodies seemed to defy physics, to stretch the boundaries of biology. She had never seen a living, breathing entity with the ability to shape-shift so readily before. Sure, there were animals that could do it; the mimic octopus for example, which could change colour and use its long, jointless legs to help it imitate any number of predators, but none that could literally enlarge or shrink from within itself, grow limbs in an instant, and literally metamorphosise before your very eyes.

'Go away,' she whispered beneath her breath as the clanking noise continued. 'Please, go away.'

She needed a cigarette. Shit, she needed a drink. Anything to calm her shredded nerves. She reached for her lighter, her name inscribed into the glimmering steel.

To Ida, from your lapdog, Thomas x

She fought back the tears. He would be so worried about her. Perhaps he would contact the police, but it would make no difference. She'd been forced to keep the location of Elysian Field a secret, even from him, and there wasn't any way she could get a message to him. There were no mobile phones allowed on the premises, and even if there were, there was no network and no god-damn Wi-Fi. They were cut off from the rest of society, the protocol so ingrained that even a request to make a call in an emergency could get you fired, and right now, Petra's deep seated, stubbornly persistent paranoia could prove to be their undoing.

She thought of the cells in the petri dish, of how they had reacted to heat, the way they had become energized, multiplying when caffeine was added. She glared at her lighter. Maybe, she thought, just maybe.

Above her, something scratched at the steel inside the tubing, trying to burrow into the metal, penetrate it, tear a hole right through it. She watched, her blood cold, her mind imagining a dark finger emerging, twisting and probing,

She shut her eyes. She needed to do something. She couldn't be a victim. She would not allow herself to be a headline in the national news.

In the bathroom cabinet she rummaged through boxes of medicine and lotions. She knew what she needed. She just prayed she could find it.

*

Paul entered the Caldarium recreation complex. He pressed his hand against a part of the door that wasn't smeared with blood and took in his surroundings. His stomach lurched.

'Oh God.'

Manny was behind him. 'What the fuck?'

Renee turned away, her hand to her mouth, eyes wide like portholes.

There was more blood, much more blood, and bodies too. Tens of them. Dozens. Throats carved, heads cleaved in, chests butterflied open, innards spilled onto the floor. The pool was a bright red lake, the jacuzzies spilling over with scarlet foam, the mechanisms still whirring, pumping sinew and gore through fizzing jets. The sunbeds were scattered, toppled and destroyed. Some of the lamps overhead had been smashed, covering the floor with tiny pieces of crushed glass. Lifeless hands reached for an escape route that wasn't there, agonised mouths hung open, frozen in terrified screams that could never be heard. Above them, a flayed body hung from a sign, blood oozing in thin strands, pooling beneath it in a slick puddle of gloopy red. Paul realized it was the tattooed guy who had taken a dislike to them when they had first arrived. Tiggy. He didn't look so mean now. By the far door, a pair of legs lay severed, the top half of the body jammed between the door and the frame, bloodied tendrils soft against the floor. More blood spattered the walls, some of it reaching the ceiling.

'What are we going to do?' Manny said, his voice thin, reedy. 'We can't just stand here.'

'Give me a second,' Paul replied. His overloaded brain was still trying to glue together the pieces of what he was looking at.

'We have to get to the lab,' Renee said. 'Somehow we have to stop this thing.'

'But how?' Manny replied. 'We don't even know what we're up against. Look how many people it's killed already, and there's only three of us.'

'We have to get to the source,' Renee said. 'Destroy it. It's the only way.'

Manny turned to her. 'You think this is to do with the Amrita? You think it caused all of this?

'I think the creature we encountered grew out of my experiment, the controlled test I carried out with the cancer cells. If the scientists here have carried out similar experiments, then I think it's entirely possible that a mutated form of the compound could have manifested itself within Elysian Field. Maybe more than one.'

'Shit,' Manny said, wringing his hands together. 'You mean this could be our fault? We could have brought something into this building that killed all these people?'

Renee's eyes fell to the ground.

'I don't buy it,' Paul said with his back to them. 'Nah, that doesn't seem like a logical explanation to me. More likely that this was caused by one of their own.'

'What?' Renee replied. 'I mean, I know that I'm making a leap from one isolated instance to whatever the hell this is, but look at these people, Paul. They weren't victims of a homicidal maniac with a knife. They've been literally torn to shreds. Are you trying to tell me that one of the residents could have done this?'

'No,' Paul replied. 'Obviously not. But a few of them? A small army? Perhaps. Maybe it wasn't someone staying at Elysian Field at all. Maybe the locals found out about what was going on down here and decided to take some action.'

'That's possible,' Manny agreed, seemingly grasping at what appeared to be a more logical explanation. 'Yeah, I could see that.'

Renee went to one of the closest victims, a woman in her thirties whose insides lay in a tangled mess around her throat. She dropped to her knees and carefully examined her.

'You see this?' she asked, pointing to a separated area of skin beneath her breasts. 'You see the way the wound is jagged, the tissue stretched. This isn't a clean incision or even a jagged rip made by a serrated weapon. This is a tear. This woman's abdomen was literally pulled open and her insides ripped from her.'

'You can't be sure of that,' Paul replied. 'Not without the right equipment. The killer could have been a maniac, possibly in a rage. Any number of variables could have led to that outcome.'

Renee stood and wiped the blood from her hands onto her jeans. 'You're right. That would be possible once, maybe twice.

But there must be thirty bodies in here, and they're all the same. This isn't an attack by a human. This was a rampaging animal, a creature with extraordinary strength, powerful jaws and a huge amount of energy.'

Manny continued to shake his head. 'If you're right, we need to get out of here.'

'No!' Renee cried. 'We need to destroy it.'

'But how?'

'I don't know. Not yet.'

There was movement from behind them, and suddenly the doors opened, the solid timber crashing against the wall. Paul was the first to react, stepping between them,

'Who the hell are you?'

A man stood there, tall, well over six feet with a milky white complexion, blonde hair and beard. His hands were covered in blood. Crimson spatters decorated his chest and neck.

'Gunthar?' Manny cried. 'Mate, we've been looking for you everywhere.'

The tall Norwegian's expression darkened, his bright blue eyes flitting.

Paul went to him. 'What the hell happened here?'

Gunthar grunted, the corners of his mouth twitching, his eyes drawn towards the shadows. For a moment he hesitated, seeming to spy something against the far wall, but then his attention switched back to the three of them.

'You need to leave,' he said. 'Quickly. They already know you're here.' He backed out through the door, pulling it closed.

'Wait!' Manny yelled. 'What do you mean?' He turned to the others. 'What does he mean?'

There was no answer, no sound, just the bubbling, spitting hiss of the jacuzzi throwing crimson ink blots onto the floor.

'I've had enough of this shit,' Paul said, grabbing Manny's

arm. 'Come on. We need to talk to this guy.'

They rushed down the corridor with Gunthar's silhouette twenty metres ahead of them. He glanced over his shoulder as he rounded the corner. Paul kept pace with him, running everything back through his head. The scores of dead bodies, the blood, the suicides. Nothing made any sense, none of it.

Manny paused at the crossroads. 'He went that way. I think.'

Paul took a moment to consider their options. 'You're sure?'

'Not really.'

'As in, you don't know?'

'As in, I'm not sure.'

Paul cocked his head. 'You want to take the left one and I'll take the right?'

'We could do that. Or we could stick together.'

'Why would we do that.'

'You know? Backup.'

'Manny, we don't need backup,' Paul growled, growing impatient. 'It's just Gunthar. I'll literally be right here.' He waited for a response. 'Well?'

'Well, what?'

'Oh, Jesus bloody Christ, does it have to be this hard? Do you want to go left or right?'

Manny didn't look comfortable with either option. 'Er…what about Renee? We left her on her own back there, you know?'

'She'll be fine. She's a big girl. Come on. Left or right? You have to choose one, and preferably this century.'

'Then left, I guess.'

'Cool,' Paul strode off. 'Shout if you find him.'

'What do you mean, shout?'

'Shout as in shout. You know?' Paul glanced over his shoulder. 'Scream your bloody guts out if you have to.'

*

Julie was furious, spitting with rage. Her boyfriend was such an arse, such a complete tit. He was so bloody minded, so tunnel visioned. He couldn't see the real truth if it kicked him in the nut-sack. Something terrifying, something horrific was happening, and they were standing slap bang in the middle of it. People didn't just bleed out all over a corridor like that and then smear it up the walls and door. That wasn't an everyday, run of the mill occurrence. If Paul couldn't see that, then he was a bigger imbecile than she gave him credit for.

The thing she couldn't rationalise in her own head was that the French woman, Renee, had refused to leave. She just couldn't understand her logic. Sure, it was admirable that she wanted to destroy what remained of the yellow gunge they'd brought back from the cave, but didn't she realise they were in serious danger? The risk wasn't worth the reward. Julie had a dead father, all because she had taken a similar gamble, and look how that had played out. They were going to get themselves killed—she was in no doubt about that—but what could she do? If they wanted to play at being action heroes, she would leave them to it. She wasn't about to end up the same way.

She felt abandoned, she felt let down, but no matter how pissed she was, she couldn't shake the thought of the three of them back there, wandering around with targets on their backs. Sure, Paul was an idiot, but he was her idiot, and Manny and Renee didn't deserve to be thrown to the lions just because her boyfriend could never admit he was wrong.

And what about the people that ran the place? Petra? The other guy, Gunthar? Where were they in all of this? For all she knew, Petra was still skulking in her office, racking up numbers on a spreadsheet while she figured out how many billions of dollars she could make convincing seven billion people to buy her new drug.

She became more and more angry as she thought about the deceit and the game playing. Petra had known exactly who she was dealing with, and she'd known exactly how to play them. Now people were dead, and more people were going to die. That didn't sit well with her. Petra needed to be shown the error of her ways. If Julie could convince her, woman to woman, then perhaps this whole thing could be stopped. She couldn't bear the thought of another daughter losing her father, or a wife losing her husband. Too much gut-wrenching pain, too much heartache.

She made a snap decision and took the next left. Above the corridor was a brass plaque embossed with a black arrow that pointed towards a row of wide glass doors.

The sign read, *Senior Management*.

*

'Hi honey, I'm home,' Paul said, entering the unlocked room. The space was dark and smelled of Lynx body spray. He tried a light switch, but when nothing happened, he realised the lights and sockets were connected to an energy saving system that needed a key card to activate the power. He fumbled around on the small desk beside the TV, but all he found was a packet of cigarettes and a half-eaten Snickers bar.

He checked the small bathroom and chanced a glance under the bed, but it was pretty obvious that whoever had been in there had vacated the place in a hurry.

He went to leave but stopped. It hung like a veil in front of him. The shadow. It moved and weaved within and around itself like a giant, living web. He stepped backwards, stumbling over something, crashing against a tall lamp. The darkness moved again, the thin strands joining together, forming a long, flexing limb as it slithered across the ceiling, as if its very blackness was conjoined with the plaster, but also apart from it.

He ran a palm across his face, tried to wipe away the horrifying vision. It didn't disappear. If anything, it grew bigger.

He backed away towards the bathroom as the darkness took shape, solidifying, gaining musculature, a structure. He tried to shout, but the only sound that escaped from his parched throat was a dry, heaving cough. He stood with one leg in the bedroom, the other in the bathroom, his eyes searching for a weapon. The room was so dark that all he could locate was a toothbrush and a bar of partially depleted soap.

The thing was almost fully formed now, long and lithe, its skin completely black, its body covered in a fine hair, limbs long and serpentine, its fingers like serrated blades.

Paul was frozen to the spot, unable to move his feet, his eyes burning. An arm reached for him, moving through the air rapidly. It touched his throat with cold, damp skin. He tried to pull himself away, but its grip was too strong. It slithered around his neck, tiny suckers kissing his throat. He opened his mouth to call out, but another thin, vine-like appendage thrust itself between his lips, its slippery wetness bitter and salty. It glided between his teeth and across his tongue, its tip caressing his larynx. Paul's gag reflex kicked in and he retched, his oesophagus instantly filled with bile and acidic gas. The other arm squeezed his throat as the creature moved closer, its beak-like mouth opening wide as a pink tongue dripped with yellow saliva.

Paul couldn't breathe. It was now more than an inch into his windpipe and the arm around his neck was squeezing so tightly, he could feel his vertebrae literally crumbling. He tried to lash out with his feet, but it was if he had no feeling in his limbs. Nothing was operating as it should. He was shutting down. Everything was a blur, a faded image through murky water. He was falling now, slipping through a tiny hole, his body liquified. He felt everything and nothing. Submission was his only option, and he accepted it gratefully. He couldn't stand the pain. He had to make it stop.

'What the hell are you doing, man,' a voice said, swimming towards him from a deep abyss. 'Open your fingers. My God, you're stronger than you look.'

Paul could see the pinkness of his own eyelids and felt the warmth of fresh tears on his skin.

'That's it,' the man said. 'Just relax. Let your arms go limp. That's it.'

Time seemed to slip by. He was dreaming. Someone calling out to him. He could see Julie. She was back home. She had made it there safely. She was with her father, and somehow, he was alive again.

'He's not dead!' she yelled. 'Paul, he didn't die. He's not dead!'

He suddenly felt hope rising within him. If Roger wasn't dead, perhaps that meant that it all had been some sort of big misunderstanding. Maybe the Amrita wasn't poisonous after all. Maybe he'd been right all along.

He went to her, trying to find a way into the house, but there was no door. He peered through the window and watched as Julie spoke to her dad. They were laughing and joking as if the whole month had been just some dreadful, ridiculous delusion. He tapped on the glass, trying to draw her attention, but neither of them heard him.

'Julie!' he shouted. 'It's me. Let me in!'

She shot him a casual glance, but it was as if she was staring at a wall. Her eyes were swimming in her head, her expression deadpan. Her father sipped tea from a China cup, but something slipped from his lips. Yellow ooze. Behind Paul there was a hiss, as if air was escaping from a balloon, and he felt himself being pulled backwards.

'Wait!' he cried. 'Wait, I need to get to Julie. I have to get to her. She's in danger!'

'Take this,' the unfamiliar voice said. Paul's eyes snapped open. He could still see Julie sitting there, oblivious of the thing that was now growing from her father's mouth, the black, dripping monstrosity that was spawning from him. The image began to fade as another face came into view. A man's face. Dark skin, black hair, chocolate brown eyes.

'Who are you?' Paul asked. 'Where am I?'

'We're in my room,' the man replied, a thick accent. Indian or Pakistani. 'You were having some sort of episode.'

Paul recalled the thing in his throat, the slippery tendril around his neck. He tried to stand.

'Woah,' the man said. 'Try not to move too fast. Your blood pressure's pretty low. You might pass out. Here, sip this.'

Paul took a glass filled with clear liquid.

'It's okay,' the man said through a thin smile. 'It's just water.'

'Who are you?'

'I'm Rajveer Kholi. You can call me Raj. I work here at Elysian.'

'For Petra?'

'Among others. I'm a pharmaceutical scientist.'

'So you work in the labs?'

Raj nodded.

'Then have you seen—'

The man's expression shifted. He glanced at the door. 'We need to keep it down. They could hear us.'

'Who?'

Raj stood. 'I came back to collect some things. We need to get out of here. If they find us—'

'No,' Paul said, wiping water from his lips. 'My friends are here.'

'Then we need to go and find them. They could be in danger.'

'You mean, from the Amrita?'

Raj turned to him. 'What do you know about that?'

'As much as anybody. We were the ones who discovered it.'

'You brought it here?'

Paul nodded.

'I'm guessing you also came up with the name. Do you know what Amrita means?'

Paul shrugged. 'My friend, Manny, named it.'

'It's a Hindu word for immortality, but this thing you brought to us, it doesn't help people achieve that. It does the opposite. It brings death.' Raj shook his head, picked at a hangnail. 'I've never seen anything like it before. At first, we thought it was some sort of panacea, a miracle cure if you can believe that. I was tasked with trialling it against a particularly nasty strain of Rotavirus, and at first the results looked promising. I even reported to Petra that I thought there was mileage in carrying out more tests, using a wider array of samples and different doses of the Amrita. Sometimes, as scientists, we see what we want to see. Perhaps I was blinded by that.' He paused. 'Others returned negative results, while a few suggested that until we knew the genomic construct of this new material, that any and all hypotheses should be considered speculative as best.'

'But some of you did believe the Amrita could cure the incurable?'

Raj seemed to ignore the question. 'We left the samples overnight and planned to put together a more rigorous testing sequence the next day. Only, the next day never came.'

'What do you mean?'

'With my assistant, Agnetha, we headed to my lab, expecting

to assess the samples from the day before and report our findings to the head of the unit. Only, when we got there, the lab had been completely destroyed.'

'As in?'

'As in, totally ripped apart. The equipment was crushed, the electricity disabled, and the plexiglass window had been literally ripped in half.'

'That's impossible,' Paul said, but he couldn't shake the thought of the creature in the lockup and Rami's mutilated remains.

'I know,' Raj replied. 'It should be. That window is three inches thick. Bulletproof. There's nothing I know of that could pull it apart like that. We headed to the main lab where most of the pharmaceutical staff work. They would have just started that morning's shift. I have friends on the shop floor, some of them are my family. My niece, Janeah, was on the rota that day. It was me who got her the job.'

Paul recalled the bodies torn open in the Caldarium. So much blood.

'They were dead, weren't they?' he said. 'Murdered.'

'Not all of them. Some were still breathing, but barely. I'd never seen anything like it. I understand death, I've dealt with patient mortality many times, but this was something way behind my comprehension. It was everywhere, the blood. People were screaming for their lives, others were crying out in agony. It was just terrible.'

Paul shuddered.

'Janeah was lying by her workbench,' Raj continued. 'She was face down. Her neck looked all wrong. I checked her pulse.' He paused to collect himself. 'She was only twenty, had her birthday just last month. She'd been working here for less than three weeks. She should have been at home with her family, my brother and his wife. With her sisters.'

Paul touched his arm awkwardly, not knowing what to say.

'I'm sorry,' he offered, but his words sounded pointless. 'I'm so sorry.'

'Don't be,' Raj replied. 'Yeah, you brought it to us, but we unleashed it.'

'So, where's Petra in all of this?' Paul's thoughts shifted to Julie and where she was right at that very moment. Had she got out? Was she on her way back to the airport?

'I haven't seen her since I gave her my report.'

'What about the security staff? The other directors?'

'If they have any sense, they'll be long gone.'

'We can't just abandon this thing down here,' Paul said. 'Aren't you worried what might happen if it gets out?'

'No,' he said. 'That can't happen. It's impossible.'

'I don't understand. How can you be so sure?'

Raj's hand went to his pocket.

'I said I came back to collect some things.' He retrieved something small and red. He placed it on the side table.

'A thumb drive?' Paul asked. 'What good's that going to do?'

'A couple of years ago, not long after we started in on the vaccine program, we had an unfortunate incident.'

'Go on.'

'Don't worry. It wasn't pandemic proportions, but one of the guys didn't follow protocol when handling the infected specimens.'

'You mean a sample of one of the viruses.'

'Yes. The Machupo virus. It can lay dormant for days, so at first, nobody knew anything untoward had happened. Then the lab assistant, Rufus, started to get headaches, really bad ones, and eventually he contracted a fever. Again, nobody thought anything of it, and so the onsite doctor prescribed him some penicillin and a week of bed rest. The problem was, within four days of what we now know as the incident, severe nausea became severe haemorrhaging, and two days after that, Rufus died.'

'Oh shit. I'm sorry.'

'Don't be. It was his own fault, and what's more, by the time we'd realised what was going on, three other members of staff had contracted the virus, and we were forced into a complete shut down and a full evac of the labs. It was a bloody nightmare. The whole place needed a deep clean, which meant all the experiments we had been conducting were scrapped. We lost a month's worth of long days and hard work, just like that.'

Paul raised an eyebrow.

'Shortly after the facility was reopened, Petra tasked us with creating a failsafe in the event there was ever another breach.'

'You mean, like a doomsday scenario?'

'Right. Exactly. We got lucky with the Machupo event. Contact with Rufus had been limited. However, if he had carried on working in the labs, if he had socialised with friends or family, we could have been faced with a COVID19 type episode, and we know how that played out.'

'So, this thumb drive?' Paul asked, glancing at the tiny plastic memory device.

'We had an external firm develop this, and then we had a contractor come on site and make the necessary structural adjustments.'

Paul wondered what he meant by structural. They were deep within a 2,500-metre-tall mountain in a facility that was only known by its employees and its highly secretive client base.

'All of the directors were given one of these,' Raj continued, pointing at the memory stick. 'The senior lab staff, too. We were given strict instructions and made to sign a legally binding document.'

'To protect the work that goes on down here?'

'No. Well, yes, but that's not what the thumb drive is for.'

'Sorry. I'm not following you.'

Raj picked up the tiny, red object.

'Think of this as a key,' he said. 'The lock for which is held in the central computer system that's located in the heart of the facility. All you need is this and a unique number sequence that each of us were tasked with memorising.'

Paul felt his throat tighten. 'And what does this…key unlock.'

'It unlocks hell,' Raj said, leaning forward, his elbows propped on his knees. 'Complete and utter annihilation.'

*

Manny walked gingerly along the corridor, wondering what the hell he was supposed to do if the giant Norwegian oak launched himself at him. He wasn't exactly built for speed. He wasn't much of a fighter either. Neither of them were. They were chasing a guy who looked like he worked out every day and ate whole chickens for breakfast. In the boxing world, it would have been ruled a mismatch.

He wondered how Renee was doing. He'd never really paid much attention to Paul's ex before, but ever since they'd almost fallen into each other at Wade's flat, he thought there'd been a connection. Of course, that was nothing new. He was the kind of guy who fell in love at the drop of a hat, a serial romanticist. His mother was always telling him he fell too hard, and she was probably right. He'd been about as successful in the dating arena as a poker player with no chips. Paul had always been the one who got the girl. Manny had never really known him without a pretty woman on his arm. He, on the other hand, tended to get friend-zoned faster than a whippet on roller skates. Renee seemed different. She had smiling eyes, and she even laughed at his jokes. She'd touched his hand when they were chatting, an act which had sent little shockwaves up his arm. He could almost hear his mother's voice; 'You're getting older now, Manmeet. When are you going to make your father and I grandparents? You would make such a wonderful husband and an excellent dad. Why not let us see if we can set something up for you? Our friends' daughter, Yashveer, has just finished college, and she is a very, very pretty girl. She would be perfect for you.' He didn't want that. He didn't want any part of it. After everything that had happened, it was Renee's face he couldn't get out of his head, not the image of some family friend he had never met. He'd made up his mind. When they got out of this—if they got out of this—he was going to ask her out. That thought was enough to make him so scared he wanted to puke, even more so than the encounter with the creature that had almost killed them, but he would do it. Or, at least, he thought he would.

He decided he was just going to give the corridor a cursory check and then get back to the Caldarium. Renee was on her own in a room full of dead bodies, and she was probably freaking out. Maybe being the hero would be a good look for him. He hoped he would wear it well.

Just then, he noticed something. The door up ahead was slightly open, and he stood there staring at it. There was a blood pattern by the handle in the shape of a palm. He couldn't be certain, but the size of the handprint certainly looked similar to a man of Gunthar's build.

'Hello,' he called out. 'Is that you, Gunthar? It's Manmeet Davi. Er, Manny. I just want to talk.'

There was a deafening silence from inside the room. The whole corridor seemed eerily quiet. He tried again.

'Hey. I don't know what's going on here, or what the hell

happened to those people back there, but we're stronger as a team, right? There's three of us, and with you as part of our group, we stand a much better chance of getting through this, don't you think?'

Still there was nothing, and Manny began to get the impression he was speaking to an empty apartment. Perhaps he was wasting his time. Gunthar had probably got spooked seeing the three of them back there like that, and he'd hidden somewhere. He did work down there, after all, and he probably knew all the secret corridors, all the hiding places. They stood very little chance of finding him.

'Paul,' he yelled over his shoulder. 'You done up there? I'm thinking of heading back.'

When the blow to the back of his neck came, it caught him completely off guard. He didn't hear his head crack against the hard floor either, the warm blood seeping from his right ear as he slipped into unconsciousness, and he certainly didn't feel the sharp dig of the strong hands that dragged him backwards into the dark entranceway. As the door closed silently, there came a growling, piercing screech from somewhere along the passageway.

They were coming.

*

Renee stood in silence, motionless among the disembodied limbs, dangling intestines and festering cadavers. The smell was repugnant, a mixture of copper and out-of-date meat, like a deli counter in the middle of a power cut. She moved towards the wall, making herself as small as possible. The shadows in the room were freaking her out. So was the pool, which resembled the world's largest vat of pinot noir.

Manmeet and Paul had been gone for what seemed like an hour. She knew it either meant they were reasoning it out with the big Norwegian dude, or something had gone horribly wrong. Either way, she was a sitting duck for whoever had killed all these people. She had a choice to make. She could continue to wait around like a wallflower in an abattoir, terrified of the sound of her own uneven breathing, or she could do the one thing that she knew had to be done. She'd been saying it all along.

She waited for a moment, glaring at the door, willing it to swing inwards, desperately hoping to see Manmeet's chubby, brown face peering through the bloodied glass. There was nothing.

She didn't want to die in Norway. Shit, she didn't want to die at all. She liked her life, loved her studies. She wished she'd never laid eyes on Paul Karin or that bloody yellow gunk. If only her curiosity hadn't got the better of her. If only Wade hadn't come looking for her. If only she hadn't shown up at the flat and bumped into Manmeet. If only. If only.

Her heart was running laps in her chest. She tried to calm herself by thinking of home, of her mamie, the angel who had raised her single handedly.

She had been born in Sarlat-le-Caneda, a picturesque town in the Dordogne valley, to upper-middle class parents. Her father had been a respected lawyer, her mother, a successful author of middle grade fiction. Renee was the third daughter. Her twin sisters, Charlotte and Delphine, were several years older than her. By all accounts, Renee's conception had been a happy surprise. She was born on the 25th of July 1999.

She should have had the classic upbringing. She should have had an ordinary life. She should have been able to Facetime her parents and her sisters back home and tell them how well she was doing with her PhD, discuss boy problems and laugh about how crazy the English were. She'd never been able to do any of that. She'd never known her mother and father, nor Charlotte and Delphine. She'd been at home with her mamie while her family boarded the supersonic jet destined for New York at Charles de Gaulle airport, her mother scheduled to meet with her new North American publisher. She and Renee's father planned to show their two eldest daughters the sights and smells of Manhattan. Renee, however, had been far too young to travel. When that fated Air France flight hit debris on the tarmac, and its shredded tyre struck the fuel tank, causing a ball of flame to erupt from the rear of the Concorde, Renee was probably having her nappy changed or eating frosting from one of the cakes her mamie had baked. They say fate has a funny way of squaring the circle or joining the dots. Her parents and sisters died on the 25th of July at 11.30am, the exact time and date of her first birthday.

With baby Renee all alone in the world, her mother's mother took the reins. She had lost her own husband two years prior to a massive heart attack, and consequently she was a woman of limited means, but what she lacked in wealth, she more than made up for in fortitude and courage. Renee never wanted for anything and had always felt loved. When she left high school and decided to further her studies in England, her mamie had been overjoyed, even though she knew that her granddaughter's departure meant she would be left alone in a town that for some time now had been slowly passing her by.

They were so close. They talked every day. Renee shared everything with her, no matter how embarrassing or how personal. She'd told her about the Amrita, even though she wasn't supposed to. She'd even told her about Wade. There was nothing her mamie liked to hear more than news of Renee's pending dates. Of course, she didn't know that Wade had been killed, that her and her new friend, Manmeet, had almost been obliterated by a giant, multi tentacled monster, or that she was now in Norway, deep within the belly of a mountain, trying her best not to tread on the rotting remains of a harboured criminal. Renee would have to deliver the details of her adventures later on. She only hoped she got the chance.

As seconds became minutes, and minutes became tens of minutes, she decided to act. Something had gone wrong, she was sure of it. That meant she was on her own, a thought that sent her mind racing. She gulped in deep, ragged breaths, trying to ignore the fetid stench of the toxic air. She eyed the door. What if Manmeet had been killed? She pictured her new friend's broad grin, the dimples in his cheeks. He'd been a lifeline since they'd found out about Wade. If it hadn't been for him, they would have both been pulverised by that perverse abnormality in the university labs. The thought of him lying dead or wounded made her want to scream. She had to put a stop to it, to use all her years of education. Nobody else could get hurt. There could be no more death. Her conscience was already at breaking point.

She became aware of her foot tapping against the floor and her hands fidgeting anxiously in her pockets. Her cheeks were hot. She glared at the doorway once more. Nobody was coming. She needed to find the labs. If the freezing cold was the one thing that those fucking monsters couldn't stand, then she had a plan. She just prayed that it would work.

*

Julie stood in the reception area of the directors' offices. To her right lay the office of the Head of Operations, a lady named Geraldine Sahlberg. The lights were off and the door appeared to be locked. Ahead of her was the office for the Finance Director, a man named Karl Torvik. That door was locked too, but Julie didn't care. She wasn't interested in anybody else. She wanted to confront the person at the head of the snake, the CEO, Petra Gunderson, the woman who she was sure had tried to rip them off. She was also certain that if anybody knew what was going on, it would be her. Thankfully, the door to her office stood ajar.

She walked into the room. A standing lamp occupied one corner, bathing the large space with long black silhouettes that stretched across the walls like shadow puppets. An ornamental figurine became a giant, kraken-like creature, the desk-tidy an unevenly built castle. Even the shadows of the dozens of books that stood like trophies on the desk became huge, soaring monoliths against the beige décor.

She saw the blood in an instant. The floor was covered with it, splatters of darkness seeping into the cream-coloured carpet. She stepped around it, trying her best to avoid the stickiness of coagulated gore clinging to the soles of her shoes. She felt sick. Her stomach was doing somersaults and her heart was like an assault rifle, firing fifty shots per second.

A leg protruded from beneath the desk. The skin was the colour of soft cheese. A mid-heeled, polished black pump lay beside a bare foot, bent awkwardly at the ankle. She didn't want to look, but she couldn't help herself. She despised rubberneckers, people who gazed in morbid curiosity at the scene of a car accident, and yet here she was with her eyes glued to a bloodied leg. She walked slowly and carefully, taking care not to make too much sound. Her ears were filled with the persistent, ribcage pounding kick drum of her heart. She was trembling. She could barely keep her hands still. As she neared, the hem of a skirt became visible, a hip, followed by the crimson spattered, pale blue of a cotton blouse.

'Petra?' she said as her voice cracked. 'Petra? Is that you?'

There was no movement, no noise, only the muffled sound of

her shoes pressing into the carpet. She wanted to turn and leave. She wanted to run, head back to the cabin, get inside the car and drive as fast as she could back to Gardermoen airport. She hadn't wanted any part of this. She hadn't wanted to come to Elysian Field. She'd never wanted to give her father that shit in the first place. And yet, here she was, in it up to her eyeballs, trying her hardest not to get any blood on her shoes, but completely and inexorably drawn to what she was now sure was Petra Gunderson's dead body.

The woman's face gradually came into view. The skin had been peeled back to reveal dark pink flesh, sinuous muscle tissue, exposed and torn. Petra's eyeballs were almost cartoon-like; off-white orbs dissected by a patchwork of blood vessels. Her pupils were tiny, peering at a spot on the ceiling that she undoubtedly never saw. Her mouth was open, her tongue hanging between crimson teeth. Her abdomen was ravaged, the skin stretched and torn, the organs inside pulled apart.

Julie felt light-headed. Everything was swimming and dancing. Her legs felt like they were somebody else's. She reached out for the wall to prevent herself from falling. Her fingers tried to find purchase against the plaster, but they found something sticky instead. She gazed at her fingertips. They were covered in blood. Petra's blood. She recoiled, trying to wipe the stickiness away as if it were just dirt, but her jeans became soiled with it, infected.

'I need to get out of here,' she repeated over and over in a hissing, foaming whisper. She couldn't be there any longer. She felt claustrophobia gnawing at her brain, her anxiety like a boiling kettle, its jet of hot steam scorching her lungs.

There was a sound like a snarling, tumbling screech, followed by something moving in the corridor outside. It was a noise like a hammer slamming into wet earth. Her eyes went to the window.

There was a darkness out there, a thick shadow. She huddled into a corner, her arms curled into her like claws. Her breath was coming in short gasps now. She couldn't focus. The terror consumed her. She was going to die, she was certain. She would never see daylight again. She should have stayed with Paul and the others, stayed in a group where she could be protected. Now her temper, her hot-headedness, had led her here. To this.

'Come with me,' a voice said, pulling her towards an open doorway.

'What? Wait.'

'No time,' the woman continued. 'If you don't come now, you'll end up like her.'

They were dropping to the ground into a second, smaller room, slipping beneath a large object, withdrawn into a tiny, suffocating gap.

'I can't,' Julie said as something moved in the office beyond, giant fingers tracing the wall with a sucking, squelching eagerness.

'Shh,' the woman said, a finger to her lips as she pulled the hatch closed. Darkness enveloped them like a tomb, and everything outside turned into a pounding crescendo of rage.

*

There was a throbbing pain in Manny's head. He felt like he was in the throes of one of the world's worst hangovers, almost as bad as the one he'd had the day after his cousin Navinder's wedding. He tried to open his eyes, but his eyelids felt insanely heavy, like cast iron doors held in place by badly rusted hinges.

'I need a glass of water,' he said through what seemed like a mouthful of sand.

'What's that?' a voice replied. 'Did you say something?'

'Drink,' Manny repeated. 'Water. I need water.'

There was the hiss of a tap running, followed by the light clinking of a glass which was then pressed against his lips, the coolness like a welcome salve. He gulped a mouthful, followed by another, letting the water run down his chin and neck.

'Thanks,' he said, gradually opening his eyes and peering up at the blurred outline of a tall, broad-chested man with a neatly trimmed beard. 'Gunthar,' he said. 'Wh…what happened?'

The Norwegian held a finger to his lips. 'They're listening,' he whispered.

'Who?'

Gunthar turned and washed out the glass. Manny tried to move his hands but realised they were bound behind his back with cable ties.

'You hit me,' he said. 'What the hell?'

'I asked you to keep the noise down,' Gunthar hissed. 'Don't make me hit you again.'

'I just wanted to talk to you. Why are my hands tied? Gunthar, what's going on?'

The Norwegian pulled a chair towards him and sat down, directly facing him. Manny sat sprawled beneath him, legs splayed out on the floor.

'You and Karin have been naughty boys,' Gunthar said, pointing a finger. 'You were not honest with us.'

'I don't know what you're talking about.'

'I think you do.'

Manny felt his pulse quicken. 'No, honestly. I have no idea.'

'I met Angie. She remembered the two of you very well.'

Angie, Manny thought, running the name through his scrambled memory banks. Who the hell is Angie?

'You don't recall her?' Gunthar asked. 'Annoying woman. Irritating. Asks a lot of questions.'

Manny shook his head, confused. He'd met a lot of annoying people in his life.

'Ty Selah Lodge,' Gunthar said, his breath hot. 'Ah, you remember that place, don't you. After all, it's a short drive from Ogof Ffynnon Ddu, or as the English say, the Cave of the Black Spring.'

'How did you—'

'Oh, come on now, Manmeet. Your movements are not so difficult to trace. It's not as though the pair of you covered your tracks. Any fool could have found out where you had skulked off to.'

'I don't understand what that's got to do with this,' Manny said, objecting as forcefully as he could. 'It doesn't explain why you knocked me unconscious and tied me to this radiator. Whatever's happened here, we need to help each other, not fight.'

'The underground pool is really quite beautiful, isn't it,' Gunthar said. 'So full of colours, so untouched by humans, and so still. Not even a ripple on its glass surface. I could have stood there for hours, watching the light shift.'

Manny nodded, buying time, trying to figure out what Gunthar knew. 'People say those caves are some of the most jaw dropping in Europe. Tourists come from all over.'

'I'm sure. Although very few people have ventured so far beneath the established route, have they?'

'What…do you mean?'

'I'm guessing no more than a handful,' Gunthar continued. 'Maybe only three men and two women in all.'

Manny felt like he was on the ropes. 'Look, Gunthar. I really don't know where you're going with this.'

'I've seen a lot of things in my life, Manmeet. So many things: the stunning peaks of the Lofoten Islands; the troll wall of Frokostplassen; the shimmering, ethereal lights in the sky above

Tromsø. But I have never seen anything like that which I encountered at the foot of that jagged fissure; the thing that bore no resemblance to any living entity, the human body that lay beneath it.'

Manny's saliva threatened to choke him. 'A body?'

'Yes. A woman's body. Crushed to death.'

'Jesus!'

'It wasn't easy to find, this new passageway within the rock. I'm guessing you came across it by chance, as did the two females. I, on the other hand, had to scour every inch of that section of the network, armed with just the information given to me by that woman, Angie, and even then, I very nearly missed it.'

Manny tugged at the cable ties. This wasn't good. This wasn't good at all.

'A giant, undiscovered, marine creature. I was fascinated. It was like an enormous squid, cross bred with a ray of some sort, but with the eyes of an arachnid. I'm guessing it was alive when you found it, and still breathing when it was discovered by the two women.'

'Look, Gunthar, I know what you're about to say, but we didn't know, I swear.'

'Oh, but you did, didn't you.' Gunthar's lips became a thin crease. 'You knew exactly what you were doing. You knew that this material you brought to us was unknown to science. You knew that it had strange properties. And you also knew its alien source. Yet you proceeded with a plan, driven by greed, to distribute it to the whole world, to feed it to the mouths of every man, woman and child, to the sick and the desperate, the poor and the needy. To literally spoon feed it to the masses, even though you knew the risks.'

'That wasn't my idea.'

'But you went along with it.'

'Yes, but I didn't think—'

'Nobody thinks when vast sums of money are involved, Manmeet. Especially when the potential for wealth is beyond their wildest dreams.'

Manny's tongue felt like a ball of cotton in his mouth. Gunthar was right. He'd let Paul drive the ship, to steer them towards this inevitable catastrophe, but who was he kidding? He'd been lured by the money, too.

'I don't blame you,' Gunthar continued. 'I might have even done the same. And if Petra didn't have such an inquisitive nature, we may have never even found out where the Amrita came from.'

He reached behind him and fumbled around in the darkness. He pulled out a large, bladder like object. The yellow, viscous liquid swirled within it.

'You brought it back,' Manny gasped.

'Of course. I wanted Petra to see for herself the source of your so-called invention.'

'You planned to cut us out of the deal,' Manny sniped. 'Julie was right.'

'Maybe. I'm sure that was very much in Petra's thoughts. I mean, what were you actually bringing to the table?'

'We were nearly killed down there.'

'But you weren't, and that young lady was. Does that mean her family has some rights to your discovery, too?'

Manny shook his head. He didn't know what to think any more. This wasn't what he'd signed up for. If he'd have known what was going to happen, he would have walked away and forgotten all about the OFD. This was a world of shit he didn't need.

'Imagine my surprise when I returned to Galdhøpiggen to find that,' Gunthar said, gesturing towards the door. 'The chaos. Everything Petra built, in flames, the whole enterprise in ruins.'

'We didn't know what would happen,' Manny replied. 'How could we?'

'You should never have brought it back. Sometimes, secrets do not want to be found.'

'But it had so much potential.'

'On that point we are in agreement,' Gunthar said, smiling, his pupils shifting slightly.

'What are you going to do with me?'

'I've been thinking about that,' Gunthar replied. 'My instinct is to let them decide.'

'Them?' Manny's unease grew steadily in his chest.

'The Nokken,' Gunthar replied. 'The creature's from the lake. You stole from them, and so I think it's only right they sentence you.'

Manny pulled at his binds. The Nokken? What the hell was a Nokken? 'Look, Gunthar. Let's be reasonable, here. We took something we shouldn't have, and we did some bad things with it, but that doesn't mean we can't put it right. That bag you have, the samples in the labs, we just need to destroy them. That's why we came back here. We realized we'd unleashed something terrible, something evil, and we travelled all this way to put it right.'

Gunthar's forearms flexed as his head jerked. 'That ship has sailed, I'm afraid. Look around you. They are alive. They roam this building like hell hounds, each of them searching for their next meal. You've seen what they've done, the people they've killed. They cannot be destroyed.'

'That's not true. Renee and I, we killed one back in England. We froze it in dry nitrogen and shattered it into a million pieces. It's the cold, you see. I don't think they can withstand the cold.'

Gunthar's eyes shifted to the bladder beside him. 'Destroying one of them is one thing, but there are tens of them out there,

Manmeet. Maybe more.'

Manny gulped. Tens of them? Killing one had been almost impossible. Killing ten? A dozen? The thought terrified him. 'But we can destroy them,' he replied, his conviction like wet mud in his voice. 'We can make this right. I want to make it right.'

Gunthar stood. He looked huge, as if his body mass had grown by ten percent. There was something about his skin, too, as though its surface had been replaced with something coarse and hard, a jagged criss-cross pattern stretching across his arms and face. Dark veins throbbed in his neck and forehead, and his fingers grew in length, their tips like tiny mouths. His long tongue protruded, greedily licking at strands of yellow saliva that oozed across his teeth.

'There's no going back from this,' Gunthar said. 'The die has been cast.'

'No! I don't believe that.'

'The only way to survive is to appease them.'

'What the hell are you talking about? How can you appease something that you don't even understand?'

'Oh, I understand them,' Gunthar replied, snapping the cable ties and effortlessly dragging Manny to his feet, leaning towards him, eyes like sulphurous holes. 'I understand completely.'

*

Renee crept along the corridor, her senses pinging like a supermarket checkout. Every sound, every soft echo of her carefully placed footsteps, made her anxious, skittish. There was more blood, smeared along the walls like art deco. She stepped over a congealing puddle of it, half expecting a body to be hanging from the ceiling. The lights flickered as if someone was playing with the switch. She knew she was crazy. She was heading towards the danger, not away from it. Whatever had killed all those people in the Caldarium had clearly come this way, and it had brought one of the bodies along for the ride.

Something scurried above her, a scratching, scraping sound, like rodents running along the air conditioning duct. She froze. The noise was followed by a screeching howl from further up ahead, like the grunting bark of a fox coupled with the desperate squawk of a seagull. Everything inside her was telling her to get out of there. She couldn't defeat this thing, whatever it was. She had been inches from death not so long ago had it not been for a slice of good fortune. Did she really think she could repeat the same trick twice? The last time she wasn't alone. She was with Manny in a place she understood. Now she didn't even know where he was. This was all so fucked up, so asylum-level insane, but she just had to try. She would never forgive herself, never be able to look at herself in the mirror again. This hell they'd stumbled upon needed to be annihilated.

'Come on, Renee,' she whispered to herself. 'You can do this.'

The door to the lab complex lay before her, a red light blinking above it. *Experiment in Progress*, it said. *Do Not Enter*. There was a wet crimson stripe on the reinforced glass, a bloodied handprint beside it. The door lay open, the eye-scanner shattered.

The sound of something large moving towards her came from the ducting to her right, followed by a hissing breath beneath her feet. She was unarmed. She had nothing to defend herself with. She knew if she didn't find what she was looking for, she would become nothing more than a seal caught within the snapping jaws of a Great White. At this moment, her death was an inevitability, as sure a bet as the swarming of bees at springtime. She needed to change that. She needed to find a way.

She reached for a fire extinguisher that hung from a hook beside her. It felt like a barrier, at least. It felt like something.

She approached the doorway, the nozzle of the extinguisher held out in front of her like the muzzle of a rifle. She peered inside. Dark shadows moved among the equipment, dream-like bodies that gained shape and then dissipated, only to appear somewhere else, growing from the ground like gnarly, twisted brambles. There was another screech from behind her and she whirled around, her breath like a storm, swirling and dense. The end of the corridor was bathed in a stifling gloom, the light fleeing from the darkness. The thick, soupy shadows moved towards each other, as if attracted by some magnetic force, and they became gelatinous, viscous, as long tentacles slithered along the floor like oily tendrils. She backed away towards the door, finding comfort in knowing she had a means of escape, but then there was a high-pitched squawk from within the labs behind her, snarling and hurtful.

'Stay the fuck away from me,' she said as the amorphous darkness approached. She couldn't get a read on it. For a moment, it was human in shape, with long, loping limbs like a neanderthal, but then it seemed to shift into a giant, upright cephalopod with squirming tentacles and a powerful, razor-sharp beak. Its eyes were unwavering, a tight clutch of yellow spheres with black, slotted pupils that moved within jellified orbs. It hissed, pulled in an asthmatic breath, gurgled a shrill cry like air escaping from a fractured pipe. 'Get away!' she yelled, the nozzle of the hose aimed at the creature's undulating face. 'I'm warning you!'

A figure began to emerge from the shadows, becoming an unholy squirming thing. Renee pressed her body against the door, trying to mould herself into the steel panelling, hoping without logic that its hard exterior would protect her.

The creature screeched again, and this time the sound travelled through her bones, sending tiny shockwaves through her skull. She felt it in her teeth and fingernails. Even her eyeballs seemed to tremble at the ear-splitting cacophony.

She ran through the room, kicking the next door open as the corridor became a dark tube of descending terror. She couldn't bear to look at it any longer. It wanted her. She could feel it.

She pushed the door closed behind her and locked it from the inside, engaging the bolt before stepping away. The creature's tentacled limbs slipped against the glass, its suckers licking at the blood that painted its smooth surface. Its eyes were upon her then, cat-like, the emotionless glare of a hungry predator.

She staggered backwards, the extinguisher hanging from her limp grasp. She stumbled into a workbench, knocking folders and steel containers onto the ground, the jarring clatter echoing from the walls. She whirled around, expecting another creature to be beside her, but there was nothing but the incessant, mind-fogging flickering, the strobing light intensifying her emotional nausea.

Something had happened there. Something bad. Blood dripped from the bench and pooled at her feet. A body, torn from the throat downwards, lay between the workstations, a hand hanging from the legs of a toppled chair, fingers reaching for something unseen.

She stifled a scream, holding a hand to her mouth as the creature at the door rattled its hinges. She continued to move, stepping over the body as if it were nothing, ashamed and terrified, her revulsion coming in waves. She knew the only way to help was to do what she had planned, but the horrors were so visceral, so monstrous, that she felt her sanity slowly slipping away from her. It was as though the glue that held everything in place had become nothing more than ageing sticky tape, worn and peeling.

The lab was small, a side room that led to another larger area that lay behind another door. She went to it, peering through the window, her breath now just shallow sobs in her throat. There was a scalpel on the bench beside her. She pocketed it, knowing it was far too small to inflict any real damage, but desperately wanting the security of its sharp edge.

She opened the door just a little and felt the warmth of the musty air on her face and the stench of more blood and decaying flesh. There was another shriek from up ahead, but it was in the distance, a sound muffled by her own hammering heart.

There were a dozen or more benches in this room, surrounded by large racks filled with plastic trays that contained biological samples. A woman's broken body lay against the far wall, her hazy eyes peering at Renee, her head bent at an obscenely acute angle. On the other side of the room, a man sat on the floor, his eyes closed as if he were sleeping, his abdomen torn open. She didn't know how much more gore her mind could take.

'Get out of here,' the man said through bloodied lips, one eye now open, the other a dark slit.

Renee went to him. 'You're alive. Keep it together. I can help you.'

'I…don't…think so,' he said. 'Ripped…me open…lots of blood.'

'There must be something I can use,' she said, scouring the room. She felt the man's pulse. It was hardly there at all.

'Just…leave,' he said, bubbles of blood in his mouth. 'Get…out.'

Something slammed into the door behind her. Up ahead there was another sneering, rattling screech. He gripped her arm. His fingers felt like plasticine.

'They're…coming.'

He let out a long, rasping breath and slipped away as if he had never really been there at all.

'No, wait,' she said, but she knew he had gone. She reached out and closed his eye.

There was another loud crash from the first lab, and she moved swiftly through the room, keeping as low to the ground as possible. A shadow flitted at the window. The door behind her creaked open and a coiling limb curled through the gap like a tongue. She ducked down behind a bench and held her breath. The limb extended through the room, slipping over tabletops, caressing monitors and cabling. She shuffled forward on bent knees. Her hands were shaking. The door to the main lab extended to her left, and she slid toward it, never looking over her shoulder. Something fell to the ground, but she didn't stop. She wouldn't let herself. She was barely breathing. She couldn't make a sound, couldn't give herself away.

A window to her left became a black hole. Her eyes shot to it involuntarily. A sea of yellow orbs glared at her. Their grotesque pupils instantly became dilated, little black pools of hatred, and then there was a louder crash as the serpentine limb erupted towards her, showering glass and utensils all over her body. She jumped up, no longer concerned about hiding. Her legs moved like quicksilver, and then she was sliding in a puddle of crimson goo, blood coating her clothes. Yet another battered, broken body lay discarded in front of her, and she leapt over it, barely looking down at the ripped torso. She crashed into the door just as soft suckers kissed the base of her neck.

'Get off me!' she screamed as she crashed through the exit, slamming it shut behind her.

There was a muted green glare from an emergency light. *This is it*, she thought. *This is what I've been looking for.*

There were at least a hundred benches in there, organised in neat lines, each covered in black and yellow ooze. The ground beneath her feet was thick with a pungent, wet stickiness. Mist hung in the air, the dampness clinging to her. She peered through the swirling vapour. The rear wall was gone. Whatever had once occupied the tall partition was now just a sea of tangled, shapeless darkness. Snaking, twisting limbs squirmed along its huge expanse like a thousand writhing worms. A large, dark entity lay at its centre; a hooked beak covered in serrated teeth, an orb containing hundreds of eyes, a metallic, plasticised body that hugged the wall, a giant heart that oozed yellow gunge, black protrusions along its torso, dripping with slime. It glowed with a strange, dull-green intensity. The ground around it was wet, ankle deep in liquid. A crack split the ceiling overhead, mountain water running down the walls. Giant silhouettes moved ahead of the creature, morphing and shifting within the mist. One moment they were there, and then they vanished as the darkness pulled at them, drawing them in. The terrifying scene was hard to focus on. It was like a moving picture. Nothing remained static. Everything was dancing and strobing. Talons raked at the walls, carving insane, random patterns in the plaster, but then they too were gone, and sucker-like cups appeared, clinging to the wall like lichen.

As she stared, transfixed, the creature began to shudder and twist. When she stifled a scream, the eyes opened, black slits of marble dividing a throbbing, undulating ocean of yellow. The shriek that filled the room was like the sound of dry metal gears grinding together, coupled with the wet, bubbling slump of a mud slide. The silhouettes turned to her, spied her standing there in the darkness. She felt completely exposed, a field mouse caught beneath the glare of a hungry kestrel. She knew then that it was a trap. She had been lured in, ushered willingly into the monsters' hive, tempted by her own naivety. She couldn't defeat these things on her own. There was no way. What the hell had she been thinking?

'Merde,' she whispered under her breath. 'Putain de merde.'

*

Julie lay there, rationing her breaths to one every ten seconds. The woman beside her looked ashen, her whole face milky and slick. The noise outside had quietened to a few dull thuds, but Julie had no intention of moving. There was no way of knowing. They were crammed beneath the bathtub with nothing but a thin sheet of plastic panelling protecting them from the outside world. They were hardly safe.

She glanced at the other woman's lab coat which was spattered with red. The helm was torn and more blood decorated her blouse. She appeared to be wounded. Her name badge was imprinted with three bloodied words.

Dr. Ida Strand

She was an attractive woman that Julie placed somewhere in her late forties. Brown, shoulder length hair, dark eyes framed by petite spectacles, freckles on her cheeks and forehead, long nose. Shallow lines danced at the edges of her mouth, her lips pursed tightly together.

The sounds outside were getting quieter and less frequent. Julie nodded to the doctor. Whatever was out there, it appeared to be leaving.

They waited for another fifteen minutes. Eventually, Julie reached out towards the panel, but the doctor grabbed her arm, shaking her head. Julie raised an eyebrow, pulled her hand away. She couldn't stay there any longer. The creature would be back, she was sure of that. It knew they were still alive. It had sensed them. They had to move.

She pressed her body against the panel and pushed. It came loose with a soft pop. She closed her eyes as cool air raced into the enclosed space through a narrow gap. She could breathe again. She maneuvered the partition back and forth until it came free, and then laid it gently onto the ground, breathing out as she released it.

'Come on,' she whispered. 'I think it's okay.'

She pulled herself out into the open, scraping her spine against a nail, its rusted tip clawing at skin. She rose gingerly to her feet, dabbing at the fresh wound. She approached the door and peered out into the office. A shadowy figure emerged from behind the desk, tall and humanoid. Her breath was like a hot stone in her throat, her panic visceral and sharp, but then she realised she was looking at her own shadow.

'It's gone,' she said without turning.

'You're sure.'

'The office is empty.'

'What about the foyer?'

Julie moved towards the window and chanced a peek. Black ooze streaked the carpet. The water dispenser had been sent tumbling to the ground. There was a fist sized hole in a partition, its edges jagged and damp. Otherwise, the area was clean. 'That's good, too.'

The doctor came up behind her, her bare feet silent on the blood-soaked ground. 'That's the third time. The next time we won't be so lucky.'

'Thank you,' Julie said, facing her, 'for rescuing me. That could have been me lying there.' She turned her eyes towards the deceased CEO's bloodied remains.

'Who are you?' the doctor asked. 'Why are you here?'

'Julie Harbor. I'm with Paul Karin and Manmeet Davi.'

'The Amrita?'

'That's right.'

The doctor took a seat, her arms pulled into her body like broken wings. 'I wish you'd never brought it here.'

'I know.' Julie's words were like bile in her mouth. 'I wish it had never been found.'

'Found?'

'In the Cave of the Black Spring.'

'Where the hell is that?'

'It's an underground tunnel network in South Wales. I went there after I'd realised something wasn't right.'

'I don't understand.'

'Ellie died,' Julie said, wringing her hands together like a wet cloth. 'Oh God, her body's still down there. I can't even think about that now. My dad, he killed himself after we cured his disease. That stuff is poison, Ida. It's cancer.'

The doctor stood. 'Listen. I need to know how you and your friends found it. Everything. We've unleashed something here that modern science doesn't understand. If we're to have any chance of stopping it, I need to know every detail, no matter how insignificant it might seem.'

Julie shook her head. 'It won't make any difference.'

'It might.'

'It's alien. Can't you see that?'

'No, not alien.' The doctor eyed the damage in the corridor. 'It breathes our air, feeds on protein, bleeds just like we do. That means it's carbon based, which also means it can be destroyed.' She reached into her pocket, pulled out her engraved Zippo lighter and handed it to Julie. 'There's some disinfecting fluid in the bathroom, some nail polish remover, too.'

Julie eyed the inscription. The lighter had been a gift from someone close to Ida. She flipped the lid and thumbed the flint, relishing the heat on her fingertips.

'I don't get it,' she said. 'What are you saying?'

'Fire,' Ida replied, her eyes flickering in the flame's orange glow. 'I say we incinerate these fuckers.'

*

Manny shuffled along the service corridor, Gunthar's hands at his back. His wrists hurt. The sharp plastic was cutting into his skin, drawing blood. He could feel the warmth of it as it slipped between his fingers.

'Where are we going?'

'You'll see.'

'I'd rather know now.'

'Shut up.' Gunthar shoved him forward. He could hear the big guy's breath, sharp and wheezy.

'You took some of that shit, didn't you?' he said. 'You brought it back with you, realized what had happened here and decided to fight fire with fire.'

'Keep your theories to yourself,' Gunthar replied.

'I know exactly what that stuff does. It was Paul and I who found it, remember?'

'You didn't know what you had.'

'No, we didn't, and that's been the problem all along.'

'I see things now,' Gunthar said. 'I didn't before. All these years, fighting against my natural urges, rallying against my blood line. It has been an opportunity missed.'

Manny pulled a little harder against his restraints. 'You're not making any sense.'

'My parents were royalty. Monarchical. My family still sit in prominent positions of power within the Norwegian hierarchy.'

'Right. Good for you. Do you want me to bow or something?' Manny felt his skin tearing beneath the plastic straps as he twisted his palms.

'I've spent many years being incarcerated, trying to become something else, something better, when all along my destiny has been staring me directly in the face.'

'In prison? You?' Manny exclaimed.

'Yes.'

'What did you do?'

Gunthar's tone remained passive. 'I killed my parents.'

'As in murdered?'

'They were not nice people.'

'You killed your own mother and father? How bad could they have been?'

Gunthar slipped his arm around Manny's throat and pulled tightly. 'Don't question my motives. You weren't there.'

'Okay. I'm sorry. You're right. Who am I to judge?'

Gunthar relaxed his grip. 'Petra saw my potential.'

'As a killer?'

'As an ally. Powerful people require powerful protection. Petra was never the sort of person to turn away a rough diamond.'

Manny continued to stall, allowing his blood to lubricate the coarse plastic as he attempted to slip the edge of his palm through the tight straps. 'So, given everything that's happened, what are you planning to do now?'

'Reinstate who I am. Re-assert myself in my rightful position.'

'But how? You're a criminal on the run, right? No matter what the reasons were, the Norwegian authorities must still be looking for you.'

They were nearing an intersection in the service tunnel.

'To the left,' Gunthar said. 'We're nearly there.'

He turned down a dark passage. The emergency lighting flickered overhead, red and black, black and red.

'I have a brother,' Gunthar continued. 'A twin.'

'You never mentioned him.'

'He's a snivelling rat. A *drittunge*. A *sutrekopp*.'

'I assume that means you don't like him.'

'He bowed to my father's will and left me to take the brunt of his contempt.'

'And he's still alive?'

'He resides in the big house and relishes the royal lifestyle. He wants for nothing.'

'You're jealous of him.' Manny flinched as he heard something clawing on the floor above them.

'I don't even think of him. He is not worthy of my energy. He is no more than a stain on my legacy.'

'But he's part of your plan.'

'His seat will be vacated, yes.'

'Which means you plan to kill him and somehow take his name.'

'It's not his name!' Gunthar yelled, his voice raspy and wet. 'I was born first. I sucked on my mother's teat before him. I was superior to him in education, in sport, in intellect. I endured puberty before he did, masturbated into a dirty sock before he'd even realized what an erection was, and fucked my first conquest before he'd had the guts to approach the opposite sex. He is like a distortion in the mirror, a faded shadow on the wall.'

Manny felt his palm starting to slip through his restraints. He worked his raw skin against them, twisting right and left, pivoting his wrist until one hand came free. The feeling slowly returned to his arm as pin pricks of painful heat erupted in his fingertips. 'And yet you're trapped down here while he's out there.'

Their conversation was cut short by a deafening squawk, followed by the sound of something sucking against the door.

'We're here,' Gunthar said. 'It's time for you to meet them.'

'Meet who?'

The giant Norwegian opened the hatch as the stench of swamp water and blood filled the tunnel.

'The Nokken.'

*

'It's a little farther,' Raj said, leading the way. 'We just need to follow these cables. They're part of the service loop that connects all the systems. Elysian Field is basically one giant super-computer. The locks, the air con, the lights, the power, everything; all controlled by an AI algorithm. Petra really broke new ground in allowing relatively untested technology to run her state-of-the-art facility.'

'Which explains why she was so happy to take on the Amrita without truly understanding it,' Paul said, following behind. 'She likes to take risks.'

'She prefers to call it running the gauntlet,' Raj replied.

'Maybe none of this would have happened if she'd turned us away. Did you ever think about that?'

'Or if you'd never brought it to her in the first place? Yes.'

There was a sharp hiss somewhere behind them, followed by the sound of metal clattering.

'We need to hurry,' Raj said. 'We don't have much time.' They approached a ladder that led to a hatch overhead. 'It's up there.'

'Wait,' Paul said. 'What if they're up there waiting for us?'

'Do you think they could be?'

'I don't know, but do you really want to take the chance?'

He glared at the circular opening. It was barely big enough for them to pass through.

'The only other way to reach the computer room is through the labs,' Raj replied. 'But that way is far too dangerous.'

Paul thought of the others. They were out there somewhere, trying to stay alive. He had a responsibility to do something. Maybe this was the only way.

Raj grabbed his arm. 'We need to decide.'

He shook his head, trying to stay focussed. The ladder was

cold to the touch.

'We have to go,' Raj said. 'They're close. They're really close.'

Paul pulled himself upwards.

'I'm going,' he said. 'You follow me.'

He made it as far as the third rung before it emerged from the shadows, long and sleek like a salamander, its glistening skin the colour of dark slate. Furled limbs emerged from its body, embedded with sharp, thorny talons, interspersed with sucker mouths and squirming tongues. Its beak was lined with dozens of teeth in multiple rows that moved like a chainsaw, and in the centre of its face was a clutch of yellow eyes divided by black slits. It hissed like a snake, crouching in the darkness.

'Hurry!' Rav screamed. 'Move!'

Paul grabbed the hatch. It was heavy, too heavy. He shoved, using his legs and lower back, straining with everything he had. It barely moved. His shoulders burned with the exertion. The thing screeched again.

'Oh God!' Rav yelled, but Paul didn't look down. He tried again. His own terror was escalating, causing his muscles to tense up. That thing, that smell. He stepped onto the next rung and used his legs as leverage. Eventually the hatch moved, but only barely. He knew he had no time to waste. He pushed harder, and this time the hatch pivoted, flipping onto the ground. He found his footing and used his arms to pull himself upwards. The floor was covered in yellow slime, but he didn't care. He slid across it, using it to smooth his path. They had to get away. With his legs now all the way through, he turned and held out a hand to the doctor.

'Come on!' he yelled. 'Now!'

Rav peered up at him, the whites of his eyes like snowdrops in the darkness. Something lashed out at his feet, but he kicked it away.

'Get away from me!' Rav screamed, rummaging for something in his jacket. 'Trinity, one, six, zero, seven,' he said, clambering onto the first rung and pulling himself up to the second. His hand was no more than an inch from Paul's. 'Remember it. It's important.'

'Come on. We've got this.'

There was another screech, and now the thing was below him, a writhing mass of hair and skin. Rav looked down and screamed.

'It's coming for me!' Rav yelled. 'It's going to get me!'

Paul leaned further into the hole. His fingers grazed the doctor's forearm. 'No, it won't. I promise. Just keep moving!'

Rav's hand grasped the next rung. He was almost there. Below him, the creature snarled and spat. The doctor clenched his teeth and lurched upwards, his arm stretching desperately, fingers clawing at thin air. Paul leaned through the hole. He grasped the doctor's hand and squeezed, gripping him tightly, knowing he couldn't let go. The muscles in his neck became taut and strained as he pulled with all the energy he had left, using his feet as pistons.

'Nearly there!' he cried. 'Just a little further.'

'Nearly there,' Rav repeated. 'Nearly—'

There was a tearing sound, followed by the bubbling slip of liquid and skin. The colour drained from Rav's face and his mouth contorted into a terrified grimace.

'It's got me. Paul! Help! It's got hold of my legs!'

'I've got you, buddy. Don't worry.' Paul pulled harder, reaching out and grabbing Rav's forearm with both hands. He could feel him shifting towards him.

There was another sound like something heavy hitting the ground, and then a long, looping tentacle reached through the hatch and wrapped itself around the doctor's throat.

'Paul!' Rav cried. Blood ran from the corner of his mouth. 'I can't feel my legs.'

'No!' Paul yelled, grabbing the doctor's shoulder, dragging him through the hatch, but then something seemed to snap, like an elastic band torn in half, and Paul fell backwards, bashing his head against the wall. His senses were dulled but he could feel Rav's hand in his own.

'You made it,' he said, before kicking the hatch closed. 'We made it.'

His shirt was warm and damp as he looked down. There was blood on him. He glared with maddening eyes at the doctor's arm, and realised something was wrong. There was nothing beyond the shoulder, as if somebody had erased the rest of the doctor's body.

He pushed the limb away from him, bone and muscle giving way to fleshy tendrils. 'Doctor!' he yelled. 'Doctor!'

He stood, stunned into inertia, glaring at the hatch. It shuddered as something connected with it from below, jerking it upwards. His skin turned cold. He caught a glimpse of the creature's eyes before the hatch closed once more. He leapt on it, reaching for the lock. It shuddered again, almost tossing him onto his back, but he slipped over it, forcing his whole bodyweight toward the ground. He scrambled for the mechanism, fumbling like a teenage kid on prom night. There was another more powerful surge, followed by a deafening shriek. Paul cried out, more in fear than anything else, before slamming the latch home.

He tumbled onto his back, feeling the softness of cold fingertips at his brow, and then he realised they were attached to Rav's disembodied arms. He yelled and rolled away before spying the thumb drive in the doctor's palm. He reached out and touched it. It ran with blood and sweat. He held it to the light. Scratched into its black surfaced was the word 'Doomsday.' His face contorted with concentration as he tried to recall Rav's garbled words. It was something about Trinity. He sat there, trying to catch his breath. It would come to him. He was sure it would.

The doctor had given them a lifeline. He had the software, and pretty soon he would have the access code. All he needed to do now was find the computer.

*

Renee kept her head down as she scrambled along the wall. They had to have one. It had to be here. Ahead of her, another door led to a secondary corridor, but outside she could see the darkness moving, followed by the flicker of black skin and raking claws. She turned on her heels and shuffled backwards. The mist hung heavy in the air like cigarette smoke. The floor and walls were covered in black sludge. It reeked of the sewer and the sea. The stench made her gag.

A bench lay ahead of her, and she scrambled beneath it, using the darkness to conceal her movements. She realised they hadn't spotted her yet, which was a miracle. They hadn't attacked her, and that meant something.

There were three of them. As a scientist she couldn't help but marvel at their biological composition. Each was different, but at times the same. Their bodies seemed to be able to shapeshift with ease. It was as though at the cellular level, they weren't quite glued together, as if the inter-molecular force that held everything in place was able to detach and then re-attach in an instant. They were terrifying but graceful, horrific but captivating. She didn't know what to think or how to react. She simply knew they had to be stopped. The Amrita had to be destroyed. There was no other outcome that made sense.

She reached the end of the workbench and paused. Above her, thick cables ran towards the wall. There was a dark indentation in the surface of it, rectangular and stark. She saw what looked like a yellow warning sign, but it was partially obscured by tendrilous ooze. She inched forwards, but she was aware she was now in the open. If any one of them turned their gaze towards her, she would be done for.

She felt her pulse hammering in her throat. She knew she had to move, but her legs felt numb. In fact, her whole body was beginning to stiffen. Her hands were trembling. She had never wanted to puff on her vape so much in all her life. How she yearned to be back in her university digs with no responsibility and absolutely zero accountability. Better than that, she yearned for her mamie, her life back home in France.

Her nails clawed the ground, slipping against the ooze. Her feet slipped behind her, struggling to find purchase. Around her, the mist sucked at her skin as if it were a living entity. She drew in a breath and turned her nose up at the noxious stench. She had to head towards the door. This was what she was risking her life for.

She turned and saw one of them. It was moving among the equipment, a dark grey, hulking mass. Its face was squashed inwards, like the mouth of a fly trap, dozens of yellow and black eyes pressed together as if secured by cellophane. It breathed through gill-like holes in its torso. Its mouth resembled a sharp tear in its skin. Rows of rapidly moving, slime coated teeth were nestled behind charcoal lips. Limbs grew and retracted from its body, tentacles with suckers and talons alternating along its squirming flesh. It turned its eyes towards her, and she shrunk into the mist, her breath like a tight ball in her lungs.

'Have to move, have to move,' she repeated over and over.

There was another squawking cry, as if an eagle was being brutally crushed, and then she was off, a flash of T-shirt and denim as she scurried across the walkway. She saw the slipperiness of the wall, the dark solitude of the cavity, and then nothing else. She didn't glance to her right. She dare not look at the distorted, twisting creature that sat within the writhing sea of limbs, knowing that if she did, it would probably sense her, and then those fleshy, squirming arms would reach for her, sucking and cutting.

She slid into the opening, pushing herself against the door, wanting desperately to morph into it, to hide her beating heart. There was the sound of scratching and wetness. Slime dripped from the rim of the cavity. Her eyes became fluttering butterflies. There was something on the wall above her. The tip of a tentacle appeared at the edge of the depression. A suckered tip crept along the threshold, prodding, searching. Hooked talons carved ravines in the wall, spilling yellow gunge onto the ground at her feet. She bit down on her lip, pressing her tongue to the roof of her mouth. Her breath was hot in her chest. Her hand crept along the door behind her, her fingers desperately scouring the slippery surface for a handle, a button, anything. Above her, the tentacle probed. It was beside her now, edging towards the frame. Her neck was frozen, her head like a cinderblock on her shoulders. She exhaled through her nose, slowly and deliberately. She had to draw breath. She was suffocating. Another tentacle appeared from above. It hung in the air, a python from a tree. It jabbed at the mist, almost grazing her cheek. Her fingers worked faster now, clambering across the metal surface like a Huntsman spider. A third tentacle, this time from her right. She was surrounded. She couldn't move. Dark limbs had encased her in the cavity, and now she was trapped with a locked door at her back and the creature at her front. Her skin was like daggers snow. Everything was sharp, everything was highly tuned. She felt like she could erupt at any moment. The fear was molten rock in her chest. She had made a terrible mistake. She should have left Elysian Field with Julie.

Right now, she could have been in a car, racing towards the airport.

Her fingernail caught the edge of something raised. A screw? A flake of paint? Her scouring digits chased towards it. Her thumb struck a protrusion, her ring finger a horizontal bar. She felt hope slip into her gullet. Her palm enveloped the handle, her fingers embraced it. She paused, her eyes staring at the tentacles as they moved around her in a silent dance. They were close now, so close. Her hand depressed the lever, so slow it was hardly perceptible. She dare not make a sound. She knew one of those things would hear her and then there would be no escape. There was a grunt and a slippery crunch as the thing on the wall descended. She imagined its yellow grape-eyes emerging from the mist. She pictured its torn hole of a mouth. She smelled its repugnant breath. She imagined its teeth closing around her throat, the crimson erupting from her, the warmth of her own essence marinating her skin.

There was a sharp movement and then her body slipped inwards. Her feet moved like slippers on linoleum. A sliver of darkness appeared to her right. She went to it, allowing it to haul her towards it. The talons had found her now, the space she had existed in, but she was no longer there. She was sliding into the black, shutting herself inside a cocoon. As she allowed the latch to slip back into place, the arms found the tiny window. Their suckers pressed through the ooze and onto the glass. If they had eyes, they would have been staring directly at her. She threw herself against the wall and slid slowly to the ground. Hot tears fell from her cheeks like acid.

*

They entered a large hall, its walls painted cream and its tiled ceiling interspersed with bright, fluorescent lighting panels. The floor was littered with stacked tables and plastic chairs. A stainless-steel counter lined the far wall, shining cabinets and large ovens sat behind it. A man's body was slumped over a table-top, a pool of blood where his mouth hung open.

'What is this place?' Julie asked.

'It's the staff canteen,' Doctor Strand replied.

'Why are we here?'

'Because it's on the way.'

There was a water dispenser by the counter and Julie helped herself to a glass. Her throat felt like cement. The doctor went to one of the cabinets and pulled out a slice of cherry pie. She grabbed it with a surprising urgency, tearing a biscuit sized chunk stuffed with red fruit. She filled her mouth greedily.

'Here,' she said, spitting crumbs and juice. 'Have some.'

'How can you eat at a time like this?'

'I haven't eaten anything in two days,' she said, taking another bite. 'We need our strength. Seriously, you should have some.'

Julie looked down at her clothes. She was covered in grime and sweat. She felt disgusting. 'Couldn't we have stopped by the shower room?' she asked, her nose turned up.

The doctor wiped cherry juice from her lips. 'I figured sustenance was more important.'

Julie thought about it. She was kind of hungry. She eyed the cabinet. There was a croissant that looked like it had her name on it. She opened the door and reached inside. She could almost taste the buttery filo pastry dissolving on her tongue. Her stomach let out a loud growl of approval as her fingers found the hard crust of the slightly stale cake, but then the wall became a dark, emerging thing. She staggered backwards, tripping over the dead man's legs. The creature came over the counter like a panther, a talon slicing a hole in her shirt as she fell. She twisted onto her side as a mass of wet skin and dark hair came crashing down beside her. It turned, yellow drool dripping onto her face, the stink of its meat-breath burning her eyes, but then she heard the doctor's scream. The monster moved swiftly towards the sound, leaving her breathless, unable to speak.

She didn't see the creature as it engulfed the scientist. She didn't hear Ida's blood-filled cries, or the sound of her body being torn into ravaged, shredded pieces. Her mind was consumed by one thought only, and that was the desperate need to get away. She crawled over the dead man's body, her hands slipping in his greasy blood. She kicked with her feet, dragging herself across the floor, keeping the steel counter between herself and the thing with the horrifying eyes and the sharp claws. She grabbed a paring knife that lay on the ground, but it felt like nothing more than a pencil in her hands. Her breath was trembling gasps. She could barely focus on what she was doing. Her terror squeezed her throat, constricted her lungs. She felt dizzy, as if she were drifting. She wanted to throw up. She wanted to curl into a ball and cry until everything went black.

The sound of thrashing and gorging abruptly stopped and the room fell silent. She bit down on her hand to stop herself from screaming. She knew it would come searching for her. She heard it turn and felt the thud of its heavy mass moving across the floor. It was behind her, lurking on the other side of the counter. She knew if it peered over the top, she would be dead in an instant. She scoured the kitchen for somewhere to hide. The desire for a croissant now felt like such a stupid, pathetic mistake. She was going to be killed over a French pastry.

The little square door lay ajar. She wondered. It was the sort of place her parents would have told her never to go, but this situation was so different from a Sunday afternoon dinner. This was the only hiding place that came even remotely close to safety.

As the creature dropped onto the ground beside her, she held her breath. She was thankful for her diet. The belly of the oven was a tight squeeze, but she made it inside and quietly closed the door. She just hoped that it didn't see the smear of blood on the handle.

*

Manny stood in the giant lab, his jaw hanging. This wasn't the spotlessly clean, gleaming workshop he recalled. This was a dark, glistening place, bathed in a dull green light, filled with strange things, odd things. He saw the huge swirling mass of limbs and eyes on the rear wall, the weaving, writhing appendages that tumbled over each other like eels, the metallic skin, the strange black, oozing protrusions, the eery glow that emanated from its body. He'd seen it before in the cave, or something like it. How could it have come back? It was impossible.

'What the hell is this?' he asked.

'The hive,' Gunthar replied. 'This is where they are born.'

Manny heard his words, but they sounded ridiculous. A hive? Was that what they had stumbled into in the OFD, a breeding ground, a hidden lair, revealed to them by some sort of shift in the bedrock? Was this monster a replica of the creature they had found in the pool, barely conscious, its flesh already starting to rot. And the thing that came at them from the darkness? Was that one of its children, a decaying, starving version of the things that Gunthar referred to as the Nokken? Had he and Paul inadvertently rescued a dying species, given it a means to rejuvenate itself?

Gunthar raised a flask to his lips and sipped. His eyes flickered like the fluttering pages of a book.

'What are you doing?'

'I am becoming.'

'Becoming what?'

'The Nokken.' Gunthar held out the flask and Manny smelt the familiar sickly-sweet aroma. 'Join me.'

'No thanks.'

'They'll kill you if you don't.'

Manny saw the creatures hanging from the walls. 'I think I'll take my chances.'

'Very well.'

Gunthar ushered him into the centre of the room. The movement caused the Nokken to turn their grotesque heads. Manny tensed, held his breath. They were unreal, unnatural. They resembled every monster he had ever seen in a horror movie but were like none of them at all. Nothing about them remained static. It was almost impossible to focus on them. Just when his confused brain decided where the limbs were or where the grotesque eyes should be, everything disassembled and reassembled, as if they were a constantly moving puzzle. These creatures had more bulk than the withered monster he had cracked over the head in the caves. They were younger, stronger.

There was another shriek, and on the far wall, hundreds of eyes opened. Manny stared at them. The swirling yellow was hypnotic; a spinning, thrashing vortex. He wanted to head towards them, even though his head was telling him that he needed to run for his life.

The Nokken spat and barked. The one nearest to him opened its mouth and leered at him. What were they waiting for? He was right in front of them.

There was a grunting, gasping sound from behind him. He managed to turn his head away to see Gunthar hunched over, his body shuddering as elastic drool spilled from his blackened lips. His skin had turned a pallid sepia. He looked like a faded version of himself. His huge hands grasped at a space six inches in front of his eyes. He was babbling something into the darkness, glaring at the unblinking eyes.

Manny turned his head towards the spot on the far wall where the Nokken had congregated. There was a ghost within the window of a door. A mouth moved. Soft fingers touched the glass. Familiar eyes peered out at him, filled with the sparkle of recognition. He gasped. He would have recognised her image anywhere. His moment of relief was swiftly replaced by a gut-wrenching dread. It was Renee. She was trapped.

'Come here, you fuckers!' Manny hollered, reacting before his mind had a chance to catch up. 'Why don't you pick on somebody your own size!'

Gunthar was on all fours now, his fingers clawing at the ground. His spine hunched over as he retched and coughed. He turned his head, his face a twisted, screwed-up ball. His eyes were black and enflamed, hot coals in a dark pit.

'You are my gift to them,' he said.

Manny shook his words away. All he could think of was Renee. He turned to her. Her hand was against the glass, her skin like milk. He had to get her out of there.

The Nokken fell to the ground. They had seen him, marking him, making him a target. Maybe that was a good thing. If he could draw them away, Renee had a chance.

He bounded across a workbench and ran towards the far wall, turning and screaming over his shoulder.

'Come on!' he yelled, his heart pounding. 'This way! I'm over here!'

He could hear them; the scrape of their talons on the ground, their screeching, hissing cries. He clattered into a lab trolley which sent tweezers, scalpels and clamps flying. He cut his shin on the leg of a table and smashed into an autoclave. None of that was important. All that mattered was luring those things away. He kept moving. He glanced over his shoulder. One of them was on his tail, the others either side of him. Ahead, the yellow eyes glared and the giant beak snapped open. He saw an arm whip towards him like a leash. It slammed into his cheek, knocking him sideways. He felt the blood on his skin. He grabbed a computer monitor and tossed it in their direction, heard it smash uselessly on the ground. Behind him, something reached for his legs. A talon dug at his calf, tearing his jeans and ripping his flesh. He cried out.

'Get away from me!'

He heard a door open.

'Manmeet!' Renee cried, now standing in the open. 'This way! Bring them this way!'

Her words sounded like insanity. She wanted him to lead them to her?

'No! You need to get away!'

'The cryogens!' she yelled. 'Remember? They can't handle the cold. This is a cryogenic chamber. We have to get them inside!'

A glimmer of hope flickered. Of course. That was how they had killed that bastard before. He felt a surge of adrenaline. She had a plan. Renee had a plan.

Ahead of him, the wall of limbs became a sea of stretching, flexing arms. He ducked as one suckered tentacle tore through the air. Another slammed down from above, shattering a table in half as he skipped to his left. The Nokken came at him in a pincer movement from either side, but he dived to the ground, slipping in groundwater as he bodysurfed beneath a table. They slammed into each other, clattering and tumbling. He watched as they became one misshapen blob, their limbs caught up in a tangled flurry. He afforded himself a wry smile, but then he was up, running breathless along the rear wall. Renee was ahead of him, gesturing towards the open door. He knew he needed to get the Nokken inside, but he had no idea how.

From his left, Gunthar was moving, running towards Renee. His body bulged with black pustules.

'Renee!' Manny yelled. 'Watch out!'

She turned too late. Gunthar was on her, his hands grabbing at her chest and throat. He lifted her up as if she were nothing and tossed her into the air. She screamed as she flew backwards, her body smashing into the wall with a sickening thud. He grabbed a heavy racking unit and raised it over his head, his mouth a snarling ball of rage. Beneath him, Renee was lying there, dazed and disorientated.

'No!' Manny cried, charging into Gunthar's exposed stomach. The Norwegian let out a grunt as they went tumbling to the ground. Manny threw his forearm into Gunthar's face before grabbing his head and slamming it against the floor. The Norwegian was insanely strong and he pushed him away, sending him sprawling, cracking his own head against the ground. Renee appeared from nowhere and clawed at Gunthar's face, digging her nails into his cheeks.

'Bitch!' Gunthar screamed, slamming the palm of his hand into her jaw.

'Get off her,' Manny yelled as he leapt to his feet. The creatures were coming now. Two were heading straight towards them. The third was racing across the ceiling overhead. He had no time to think. He just had to act. He grabbed a table leg from a destroyed bench and lunged at Gunthar. The Norwegian's face bulged and twisted. Manny could see squirming darkness beneath his elastic skin. His lips were black and split, his tongue like a charred ember.

'You cannot win this, Manny,' he said. 'You are out of your depth here.'

'It's not about winning. It's about stopping them.'

'They cannot be stopped. You must have known that the first day you laid eyes on them.'

'But we trapped them in the cave.'

'You brought a piece of them back with you. Their lifeblood. It swims in my veins. I can feel them inside me now, changing me. I will be immortal, an undying vessel.'

'You're just a freak!'

Manny swung the leg of the table just as a black, vine-like arm erupted from Gunthar's chest. It slammed into Manny's face, sending him reeling. He fell backwards, his legs flailing. Renee caught him as he stumbled, wrapping her arms around his shoulders. Gunthar's body jerked robotically as more black limbs emerged from his splitting skin.

'Look!' the Norwegian screamed. 'Look at what I am becoming!'

'It's killing you!' Renee yelled.

'No! I am evolving!'

There was a horrifying scream as the first creature dropped from the ceiling, crashing into Renee, knocking her to the ground like a bowling pin. Manny struck it with his makeshift weapon, but it whirled on him, lashing out with elastic arms. It wrapped its giant tentacles around his body and squeezed. He clawed at it with flailing fingers as he tried to wrench himself away.

Renee got to her feet and grabbed the remains of a metal lamp. She tore off the head and jabbed the slim strut into the creature's flesh, piercing the skin. Black and yellow liquid spurted from the wound. It screeched, releasing Manny as it turned on her. Its yellow eyes glared at her with an unyielding hatred. She backed away, holding the metal spike like a dagger.

Another creature came crashing through the nearest table, and a third swept aside an analysing enclosure before rounding on

Gunthar.

'I am you!' he hollered. 'We are here together.'

Manny staggered backwards, holding a chair in his hands as a makeshift shield. Renee moved beside him as the Nokken followed, mimicking her steps. They were surrounded. There was no escape.

'What do we do?' she asked.

'I don't know.'

'The cryo chamber?'

'Yes, but how?'

Manny glared at the doorway. It may as well have been in another country.

Gunthar stood among them. Black limbs hung from his body like the legs of a spider, intersected with puckered suckers and hooked claws. His eyes were dark pebbles, his mouth a grey crease. Black veins criss-crossed his pallid body. His shirt was ripped open at his midriff, his skin torn apart and flaccid. His mouth emitted a jabbering, bubbling sound. A lecherous grin stretched across his face. His beard and hair dripped with yellow ooze

'We are hungry,' he said. 'We must feed.'

'Sorry, pal,' Manny replied. 'But we're not on the menu.'

A black tongue slipped across Gunthar's lips. 'I'm afraid you don't get to choose.'

Manny glanced at Renee. She looked so small, so terrified, but so utterly beautiful. He wanted to reach out and take her in his arms. Something had happened to him back at Wade's apartment, something chemical, something unbreakable, but maybe it was too late. He realised she didn't feel the same way about him—how could she—but what did that matter? He loved her. He had never been more sure of anything in his life. They had a connection. A bond. He would do anything for her.

'Don't worry,' he said.

'Worry? I'm bloody terrified.'

'Yeah, well, me too, actually.'

'Manmeet, they're going to kill us.'

He forced a smile. 'It's okay. I think I have a plan.' He turned to Gunthar and pointed to his gut. 'I'm the one you want. There's more meat on me.'

'You will both die.'

'Yeah, but me first.'

Renee glared at him. 'What?'

'Why muck about with chicken wings when you can have a nice meaty kofta? Am I right?'

The Nokken crept forward on stuttering limbs. His throat felt like a narrow tube that restricted his breathing. What was he doing? They came closer and closer. The stench was unreal. He wanted to push them away, throw the light switch and embrace the darkness. These were the nightmares that had terrorised him as a kid. Reality wasn't supposed to be like this. This was a graphic novel, a Netflix series, a fucking eighties B-movie.

Every single one of their yellow and black eyes were focussed on him. He had their attention. He felt like he was being studied, like he was a lab specimen. He wanted to throw up, he wanted to scream, but he knew he had to hold himself together. There was a job to be done. If his whole life amounted to this one final act, then so be it.

'Whatever happens,' he said to Renee, 'don't hesitate. Once I move, you go. Do you hear me?'

'Manmeet. No.'

'I mean it. This is the only way. You run, and you don't look back. You promise me?'

Her eyes glistened with tears. 'But I can't.'

'You have to.'

'No. Please, no.'

They were so close now. So close. Within touching distance.

'I can't let you do this alone,' she said as she wiped snot from her lip. 'We'll do it together.'

'That's not happening.' Without warning, he pushed her hard, sending her tumbling behind a large oven. He turned and lashed out wildly, striking Gunthar in the chin before spinning on his heels and running as hard as he could. 'You want me, motherfuckers, then you're gonna have to catch me!'

The door was less than ten metres away, but it may as well have been a mile. He could hear them tearing up the ground behind him. They'd taken the bate, but he needed to make it into the chamber before them. He couldn't bear to think of those things turning on Renee. His plan had to work. It just had to.

*

Paul crept along the service tunnel, taking care not to make a sound. He couldn't shake the image of the doctor's severed arms. He could still feel his lifeless fingers, like latex replicas, warm and soft. Nothing felt real anymore. It was as though he'd slipped into some alternate reality. Norway had become Narnia, or Middle Earth, or some other crazy, fictional realm. He wished he'd never even heard of Galdhøpiggen or the Cave of the Black Spring.

The thumb drive felt like a tiny, plastic capsule in his hand. It was the only thing he had left that could even come close to stopping what he and Manny had started. These things had to be destroyed. He couldn't see it at first, but now he could. They couldn't be allowed to exist.

He had no way of contacting the others, no way of knowing if they were still alive. He let out a long breath. At least Julie had got away. He was sure she'd made it. She was strong. She wouldn't let anything get in her way. Her escape was the one good thing in a long list of catastrophes. Nothing he did seemed right anymore. He had always been so confident, so cock-sure of himself, but now everything he touched seemed to turn to shit.

Every clang of the pipework, every hiss of a steam vent, made his whole-body jerk. He knew the creature that had killed the doctor would be coming for him. It knew he was here. If he didn't find the computer room fast, he was in trouble. Big trouble.

The service tunnel ended at an intersection, and he approached it with caution. He had no idea what could be lurking around the corner.

There was a sound like someone scraping the silver from a scratch card. He paused, his breath like propane in his lungs. The noise stopped just as abruptly as it had started. Something moved in the corner of the corridor, and he jerked his head towards it. Shadows crept in at the edges of his vision. The space was closing in on him. His body felt like it was encased in a clear plastic cube. The claustrophobia was intense, suffocating him. He raised his hands to his face, but they looked like opaque overlays on a flittering backdrop. Something moved beneath his skin, round bugs with sharp antennas and bulging eyes. He clawed at them, trying to scrape them off him like unwanted tattoos. His fingernails grew long and curved. His eyes felt too big for his head. He dropped to his knees as the thumb drive went skittering across the metal grate. He didn't care. His heart became a steam engine, his breath hot and damp. He needed water, some sort of lubrication. He was so dry. His skin became tin foil against his flesh. He lay there, breathless, feeling like he was having a heart attack. That had to be the explanation. All the stress, all the horrors he had witnessed. He was going to die there in the bowels of the mountain, and nobody would ever know. By the time people came, his body would be nothing more than dusty bones and leathery skin.

Eyes glared up at him from beneath his prone body. Their festering gaze drifted over him like an MRI scanner. A gasp caught in his throat. Something protruded from within the grate and caressed his abdomen. The skin was damp and slick. He rolled onto his side, trying to escape its tepid toxicity but failing.

There was a piercing hiss as something screamed, and the terrifying sound jerked him back to life. He reached for the thumb drive which was now teetering on the edge of a drain. He couldn't lose it.

He clambered to his knees, batting at the tip of a tentacle that was straining to reach him. The grate began to shake violently as the thing on the lower level started to holler and snarl.

'Get away!' he screamed. 'Get the fuck away!'

His sweat-soaked fingers grasped for the thumb drive, but it slipped away from his hands, edging closer and closer to the gaping grille. The creature grabbed his ankle, and sharp, teeth-like protrusions cut into his shin.

'No!' he hollered. 'Get off me!'

He turned and punched the black, squirming thing. Everything swam as his vision became a whirlpool of light and colours. He grabbed the wall, but everything felt hot to the touch. He pictured the cave, the giant creature in the underground pool. Somehow, it was alive. It was calling to him in a language that wasn't human.

He shook his head in an attempt to shift the fever that had taken hold of him. He wanted no part of it. Everything was a dream. It was all just one big mirage.

'This isn't real,' he heard himself saying over and over again. 'This isn't real, this isn't real. It's all just make-believe.'

He couldn't remember what he was planning to do next. He couldn't recall why he was there in the first place. He remembered his friend, Manny, but he didn't understand why. They had been close once, hadn't they? They did something important together.

There was a sign up ahead, a series of letters and words that appeared jumbled and confused. He saw the squirming, snarling monster beneath his feet, and his own hands that appeared to be melting like butter. He had no idea how to use them or what they were for.

More foreign words fizzed in his head in a voice that sounded like whale song.

His palms found his ears and he shook his head.

'No, no, no! Stop talking to me! I don't understand you!'

He staggered forward, his feet clattering together as his legs became gelatinous and weak. He stumbled, falling to his knees once more as sharp teeth snapped at the metal grate. A needle-like protrusion jabbed into his palm, and he felt the hot flow of crimson. He snatched his hand away and sucked at the blood. As the coppery taste slipped into his gullet, he spied the thumb drive. It was now perilously close to being gone for good. He recalled the doctor's terrified face as he hung from the hatch, the code he had screamed at him.

Trinity, one, six, zero, seven.

He looked up at the sign, and now all the letters were in order, making perfect sense. An arrow pointed to his left.

Computer Room.

He clutched the thumb drive and stood, pausing to let his splitting headache calm to a dull throb.

'Let's get this done,' he said, staggering along the corridor. He could hear the grate shaking violently behind him. The monster hadn't given up. It was coming for him.

He hurried towards the doorway and tried the handle. It didn't budge. The rattling continued, followed by the sound of metal shearing. He tried the handle again. Still, it didn't move. He kicked the door in frustration.

'Open!' he yelled. 'For God's sake, give me a fucking break.'

The creature screeched as everything became a fuzzy blur. He was cornered. He was a rodent, he was food. The python was slithering toward him, its mouth open, tongue flitting. He kicked the door again, but he knew it was no use. It was locked, and he didn't have the key. Nothing could save him.

The creature's writhing limbs stretched around the corner, followed by the hulking, shadowy mass of its sleek body. He knew he couldn't fight it. He would be dead in seconds. He turned to the door and slammed his palms against it, crying out, screaming at the metal. Sweat poured from his face. Drool hung like elastic from his lips; he watched as it fell onto his fingers. He glared at the handle. Something occurred to him. In his panic, he'd been pushing it down, but what if that wasn't right? What if the handle needed to be pulled.

There was a frustrated whinny from behind him, followed by the sound of wet feet on metal grating. It came running towards him. He gripped the metal bar, but his sweaty palms slipped against the plastic cover. He tried again, this time clamping his fingers tightly. He pulled upwards. There was resistance, but he leaned into it, gritting his teeth and letting out a coarse, rasping snarl. The monster was so close now. He anticipated its claws sinking into his spine, and its jagged teeth tearing at his throat. Before he knew it, he was tumbling inward and turning round to see the beast lunging towards him.

'Not this time!' he hollered, putting his shoulder against the door and slamming it shut, severing a two-foot length of squirming tentacle that reached reflexively for him.

He slipped to the floor as the monster slammed its body into the steel frame.

He lay there breathless, his chest heaving in and out like thick bellows.

Ahead of him lay banks of computer terminals and CCTV screens, all showing high definition, full colour images from all over Elysian Field. He stood and approached them. Maybe he could save the others after all. If he could only find them, then perhaps this wasn't the end.

Maybe there was a way.

*

Julie waited in the darkness. At first, there was a sound like a dog sniffing frantically for treats, followed by the damp slippiness of something creeping across the metallic casing. She held her hand to her chest, trying to dampen the thump of her hammering heart. She took in slow, deliberate breaths. She felt lightheaded. The cold steel of the oven floor was like ice against her spine. Her body shook, partly through the cold, but mainly through sheer terror. She was centimetres from an alien creature she couldn't even begin to understand, perhaps only millimetres. The only thing between herself and a violent, bloody death was the thin, glistening wall of her metal coffin.

There was no sound from Ida. She was dead. There was no way the doctor could have survived such a savage attack. The sound of her body being torn open had made Julie's stomach flip. She still tasted the bile on her tongue.

Dozens of sharp claws tap, tap, tapped against the oven door. She drew herself away, her fear like a ball of twine in her throat. The creature hissed, and she held her hands to her mouth instinctively, stifling a scream. It sensed her. Perhaps it didn't know exactly where she was, but it knew she wasn't far. The shallow space was filled with a sucking, puckering sound. She pictured the monster's tentacled arms wrapped tightly around her tiny tomb, its eyes glaring at the thin gap between the two oven doors. It was toying with her.

Her mind became a roaring flame of uncertainty behind her eyes. She was hot, she was stifling. She was slowly suffocating. She needed to get out. She couldn't just lay there like a stuffed turkey waiting to be carved open. She had to do something.

The tapping intensified, as did the wet sound of a dripping tongue on cold steel. It was all around her: at her back, by her feet, beside her head. She was like moth larvae in a cocoon, except rather than blossoming from a chrysalis, she would simply be crushed to death like her cousin, Ellie; like the lifelong friend she had left behind like a coward.

Her hand brushed against a bulge in her pocket, and her fingers slipped tentatively inside. She found the smooth metal casing of the doctor's Zippo lighter nestled in the soft folds of the material. For some reason she had kept it. She read the inscription, '*To Ida, from your lapdog, Thomas x.*' She thought of Ida's family, sitting at home, waiting for her to return. She wasn't coming. She never would. Tears welled in her eyes. Her thoughts drifted to Paul, the version of him she had fallen in love with; the stupidly sarcastic, often hilarious guy who made her smile. She missed him, even after everything.

Ida's plan had been to use fire against the creatures, but the doctor had the bottle of disinfecting fluid in her coat pocket. Without it, the lighter was no good. Julie wanted to slam her hand against the metal frame, to cry out. Her fingers found the rear wall of the oven, and she came across something unusual. It was metal ducting that led to a cavity lined with sharp, tube-like protrusions. Her eyes narrowed. She had been convinced she was hiding inside an electric oven, but instead it was gas. Gas could be a weapon. Her mind formulated a plan.

She listened keenly, waiting to hear what the creature did next.

The tapping had slowed. She pressed her ear to the wall. Something slipped by on the outside. She felt tiny vibrations course through the steel and ripple against her cheek. It was withdrawing. She pressed her hand to the sliver of light between the two doors. A shadow moved across the opening. A smell wafted in on the slight breeze, pungent and salty. It was leaving. It hadn't sensed her after all.

She gripped the lighter, letting her thumb caress the wheel. Warm fingers of hope slipped around her larynx. She just had to wait a little longer.

There was the sound of something hitting the ground, and then the rattle of metal implements scattering, followed by the swishing drag of something being pulled. She saw it slip past. It had the chef's body. It was taking him somewhere.

She pushed gently against the door and allowed herself the narrowest of peeks. Up ahead, the dead man's boots were disappearing behind the counter in a trail of smeared blood. He was being dragged to the eating area. The irony was not lost on her. There was a wet, shredding sound, followed by the dripping, slop of liquid on tile. She held her nose. The scent was copper and offal.

She peered up at the large round knobs that rose from the edge of the hob. She turned every one of them up to full, relishing the damp sock-like stench of the gas. There was a pile of dish cloths placed in a neat stack on a lower shelf, and she grabbed one, stuffing its flannel length through her belt. She slipped backwards, staying close to the ground. The counter was the only hiding place. It was only a few feet, but it felt like an ocean. She knew where the exit from the canteen was. To get to it, she would have to reveal her position. That meant she would have less than a few seconds to escape before the thing was upon her.

She pulled herself across the cold floor. The chef's blood had formed a slowly coagulating oil-slick beneath her. She stifled a gag. She hated blood. The gurgling, snapping noises from the canteen added to her nausea. The caustic acidity of her stomach fluids rose in her throat. She clamped her teeth and blew out her cheeks as a little sick escaped into her mouth. She let it slip from her lips silently. She felt more on the way, so she quickened her pace.

She had less than a metre of her hiding place left. She could clearly see the window to the corridor now and the hinges of the doorway to the left of it. That was her means of escape. It was so close. She had to get there, she just had to. The stench of gas was getting stronger and stronger. It made her feel giddy.

She raised her knees and pushed herself up to a crouch. The squelching, snapping sounds stopped. That meant the creature had finished its meal, which also meant it was no longer distracted. She held a hand to her nose, trying to block out the rotten-egg reek of the fumes. She glanced at the lighter in her hands. One flick and the whole room would be engulfed in a giant ball of flames. If that thing caught her, that was exactly what she would do. Kill herself along with it. Anything was better than that disgusting, squelching yap.

She heard the puckering sound of approaching tentacles once more. It had remembered her. The thing was coming back to finish what it had started. She had to move.

Cooking implements fell on top of her from above as the creature mounted the steel work surface. It let out a piercing shriek. She ran, sprinting for the door as it turned and spotted her. Something brushed against her spine, drawing blood as her feet pounded on the ground. She didn't care about the pain. She didn't care about the noise. The door was so close. She was so close.

Something wrapped around her foot and pulled, sending her skidding across the ground, the Zippo lighter clattering loudly against the wall. She turned and saw it approaching; its black, sleek shape, a thick tentacle coiled tightly around her ankle. She tried to kick it away with her other foot, but it pulled tighter, its curled talons digging into her flesh. She screamed out as the sharp claws found bone. Blood poured from her wounds, soaking the leg of her torn jeans.

The creature loomed over her, crimson gore hanging from its dark slit of a mouth. It pulled her towards it as her hands tried to find some sort of purchase on the smooth ground. It was no use. There was nothing to hold on to. She eyed the lighter which was agonisingly out of reach. The pain in her leg was unbearable.

'Fuck you,' she spat. 'Fuck all of you.'

As the creature threw back its head and roared, her hand touched on something cool and smooth. Her head snapped towards it as her breath caught in her throat. She sucked in air as her fingers curled around the steel handle of the paring knife. It had been sent tumbling across the floor when the creature had rushed her. She raised the blade over her head in both hands and brought it down on its dark grey limb, severing it.

The monster flailed as she leapt to her feet, scooping her Zippo lighter in her free hand as she dragged her wounded leg behind her. She gripped the door and threw it open, racing into the corridor and slamming the door shut. The creature clattered into it, cracking the toughened glass. She stepped away and ignited a flame, raising it to the hanging edge of the dish cloth and letting the fire spread. As the monster hammered at the window, she waited for the glass to shatter. It was a savage creature, enraged, consumed by hunger. It wanted her. It would not stop until it had her. She had to destroy it.

She eyed the doctor's body in the distance. She was a pulpy mess of blood and tissue.

'Sorry, Ida,' she said as the window gave way and the creature began to clamber through the hole. She stepped back and tossed the burning dish cloth towards what remained of the canteen, diving for cover as it fizzed past the monster's glaring eyes.

There was a loud roar as the gas ignited, followed by an explosion so powerful that it tossed her into the air like a rag doll. The last thing she saw was the flaming, writhing torso of the thing, its many flailing arms and dozens of boiling eyes.

*

Renee watched from the floor as Manny raced for the doorway. The creatures were close behind him and gaining fast. He had pushed her away to save her. He was sacrificing himself. She was filled with so many tortured emotions. Grief. Fear. Gratitude.

She didn't think he was going to make it. They were closing the distance, and they were much quicker than he was. Just when it looked like he was going to be caught, his body clattered into the door, and he threw himself inside. The creatures raced in after him, but he skipped to the right with an almost balletic agility and let them race past him as he slipped behind the door. He peered out at her through the tiny observation window.

'Manmeet!' she screamed, laughter rising in her throat. He'd done it. He'd got them to follow him inside. She stood and raced over to him, to help him to escape, but then the door began to close. She could see the look in his eyes. He wasn't leaving.

She pushed against the door, desperately trying to open it as the creatures approached him. 'Manmeet! Manny! Please, no!'

He pointed towards a panel set into the outside wall as a tentacle wrapped around his throat. He didn't look afraid. It was as though he had resigned himself to this one dreadful finale. She couldn't let it end this way. She wouldn't.

'No. I can't!'

He mouthed the words, 'do it,' just as another tentacle appeared around his waist.

She shook her head, unable to comply, but then she watched as he was hauled backwards, and the window was filled with a dozen yellow eyes. She screamed. The door began to shudder, but she regained her composure in time to slam her hand against the locking mechanism just as it rattled against its hinges. There was a sucking, hissing sound as the room beyond became pressurised.

She wiped tears from her eyes and glared at the screen. There were three options on the panel: drying, pre-cooling and deep freeze. She caught a sob in her throat. She couldn't do it. She just couldn't. The yellow eyes slipped away, and she caught sight of Manny. He was trying to fight them off, but they were too strong. She couldn't bear to look. She stepped away, her hands held to her face, fingers intwined in her hair. She knew she couldn't let them rip him apart. She couldn't let him suffer like that. She had no option. There was no way out. She approached the panel, raised a trembling finger to a deep blue square labelled '*Deep Freeze*', and pressed down. There was a hiss as liquid nitrogen was pumped into the cooling jets, and then the temperature on the display began to drop in ten-degree increments.

'Sorry Manmeet,' she sobbed, her face pressed to the glass. 'I'm so sorry.'

The creatures turned to her, their torsos stiffening. Manny slumped to the floor, already losing consciousness. He looked up at her, doe eyes filled with sadness, but something else, too. Affection, perhaps. Joy. The tears came then. She was killing him.

'Sorry' she mouthed. 'I'm so sorry.'

Manny shrugged, shot her a wry smile. Pink drool slipped from the corner of his mouth. She wanted to go to him, to drag him out of there, but then a sharp talon pierced his abdomen like a spear, and black blood erupted from the wound.

'No!' she yelled. 'Please, no!'

The window was covered in a foggy sheen as a tentacle slammed against it repeatedly. The creatures were desperate. They knew what was happening.

'You're dying, you fuckers!' she screamed, her words masked by her own heaving cries. 'You're finished!'

As a long limb slammed against the door, the black flesh shattered into tiny, shard-like pieces.

Gunthar let out a horrified cry behind her. 'What have you done?'

She whirled on him. 'I just saved your ass. Manmeet is dead because of you.'

The eyes glared at her from the rear wall. Dozens of writhing limbs swirled around it like nettles. Something fell from within the tangled web, followed by another slowly expanding shape. As the darkness took form, Gunthar began to laugh.

'Your friend died for nothing,' he said. 'You've achieved nothing.'

Her mouth hung open, her jaw slack. Another dark object fell to the ground. They grew like blackened trees, their bodies unfurling. From within their rippling flesh, the slippery, clambering limbs sprouted. Their eyes appeared at the centre, tiny clusters of yellow hatred.

'It can't be,' she said. 'This can't be.'

'Oh, but it can,' Gunthar replied. 'It really can.'

*

Paul saw her. It had taken him a while, scouring through every security camera feed, peering at dark corridors and empty, blood-spattered rooms, but it was her, alright. He would know her anywhere. She was lying on the ground, an inferno engulfing the room behind her, the corridor a swirling mess of black smoke and ash. There was a dark, smouldering tangle of limbs and crispy flesh beside her feet.

He reached for the push-button display and hit the intercom connected to the southern corridor.

'Julie,' he said. 'Julie, can you hear me? Please tell me you're okay.'

No answer.

She shouldn't have been there. She should have been long gone. She had said she was leaving. She'd been so angry, so pissed at him. He couldn't imagine why she would have stayed.

'Julie. Please, Julie. Please get up.'

What had he been thinking? He should have gone after her. He should have left with her. That would have been the right thing to do, wouldn't it? He'd been so blinded by his need to find out what was happening with Petra that he'd let Julie just walk away, knowing something bad was going down. That was on him. Everything was on him.

'Julie,' he whispered into the microphone, gripping it with white knuckles. 'I'm sorry about your dad. I am. It was my fault. I know that now. If I could take it back, I would. I'm sorry about what happened at the lockup, too. You should never have been there. I should never have let those thugs lay their hands on you. And, most of all, I'm sorry about us. I'm sorry about ruining everything. You're the best thing that's ever happened to me.'

He gripped the edge of the desk and let his head fall. His hands were covered in blood, his clothes too. What had he become? What had happened to him? It was as if he was somebody else, a person he didn't recognise or have any affinity with. He'd risked the lives of everybody he'd ever cared about—Manny, Renee, and now Julie—and for what? For his own inflated ego? For his depleted sense of self-worth? His own parents hadn't cared what he'd got up to, so why should he? After their divorce, he had become a spare part, a key that no longer matched the locks of their new family homes. He'd been excess. He'd been a nuisance. Manny had been the one who'd pulled him out of his senseless, sightless journey towards oblivion, and yet he'd treated him like shit. Julie, too. Even Renee had been a better friend than he'd ever deserved.

Maybe that was it. Maybe that was why he was so egotistical, so selfish. Perhaps he was just trying to prove something to someone, anyone. Prove how good he was, how successful. Not that his parents would care—they'd moved on a long time ago—but that didn't stop him wanting to show them, to show that he wasn't just an expendable commodity. And what had his little crusade achieved? He'd hurt everybody, dragged them all down into the gutter with him.

He clenched his jaw and ground his teeth together. He couldn't let it end like this. He had to do something. He tossed the thumb drive onto the desk. It was worthless to him without his friends.

A sharp pain wracked his body and he toppled sideways. He tried to grab the chair, but his hands faltered. Foam bubbled at his lips as his head connected with the ground. He lunged and reached for the edge of the table. His body was shaking involuntarily. His skin bulged and rippled as though his muscles were about to tear through flesh and tissue. Long black vines hung from the ceiling. He glared at them. They were slithering. There was a loud ringing in his ears like an alarm was going off in his head. He retched as black vomit erupted from his lips. He rolled onto his side and curled into a tight ball. His face felt numb. His mouth went lax, and his lower lip hung against his chin. Was he having a stroke? A heart attack? It felt like his whole body wanted to turn itself inside out.

'No,' he hissed. 'Not now. I can't die like this.'

He couldn't breathe. His throat was closing fast. His lungs craved oxygen. It was his asthma. The episode in the tunnel must have brought it on. He tried to control his spasming arm. He focussed on pulling his fingers towards the pocket of his jacket. What he needed was just inside. He realised that taking even more of it was wrong, he knew that it had caused everything to go so catastrophically badly, but he couldn't allow himself to die there on the floor while Julie was out there, unconscious while the whole place was burning.

His peripheral vision was slowly disappearing. A tunnel of darkness was closing in on him. He knew he didn't have long. His hand slipped onto his abdomen. He focussed on his fingers. They inched further along like the legs of a crab, slowly creeping across his stomach. The tiny capsule was just there, mere inches away. He could feel it against his skin. He thrashed out with his legs as panic set in. His chest convulsed and his back arched, and then the capsule slipped out, tumbling towards the ground. His eyes flitted towards it, but he could barely move. It was right there within easy reach, if only reaching was easy. With some effort, he managed to roll onto his side and stretch out his tongue, pushing it as far as it would go, causing the muscles in his mouth to spasm. He tasted the capsule's bitter plastic exterior. He was seconds away from passing out. He could feel everything beginning to fade. He didn't have long. In one final effort, he dragged the slim vessel towards his lips, sucking it into his mouth before clamping it between his teeth and biting down.

As his throat was filled with the sour, acidic tang of the Amrita, everything slipped away.

*

Julie's head was filled with a familiar voice.

Julie. Please, Julie. Please get up.

Everything ached. Her whole body was a bruise. She tried to force her eyelids open, but they were so heavy.

I'm sorry about everything. You're the best thing that's ever happened to me.

Light leached into her eyes. She felt a burning heat on her back. The smell of smoke and fire assaulted her senses as her mind flipped into survival mode. She was instantly awake. She remembered the burning cloth, the shattered glass. There was a smouldering pile of burnt meat beside her. She pushed herself away from it.

'Oh God, oh God.'

It was dead. The creature was nothing more than crispy flesh and withered limbs.

'Paul!' she yelled. 'I'm here!'

She pulled herself to her feet. She knew she had heard his voice. There was no mistaking his Kentish accent, the semi-cockney way he omitted half the consonants. He had to be somewhere close. Maybe he hadn't seen her.

The cafeteria was gone, obliterated. The room was a mess of fallen beams and mangled tables. The kitchen still burned. Blistering heat scorched her skin as she backed away, her hand against her forehead, shielding her eyes. She allowed herself a smile of victory, although it was a hollow one. Ida's plan had worked. She had killed one of them.

She doubled over and let out a hacking cough. The smoke was becoming thick and acrid. She had to get away. The corridor led to another set of double doors, and she staggered towards them. Paul had to be through there. He just had to be.

Her emotions were so torn. Maybe it was the grief. She had lost people she loved—her cousin, her dad—in such horrendous circumstances, and now she was in the middle of a war with alien creatures that were intent on killing them all. She couldn't make sense of how she felt or why. One minute she felt distraught, the next angry, other times she missed Paul like he was the only person in the world who could make everything seem okay.

He had been a prat. No, worse than that, he had acted selfishly, negligently, but that didn't mean she didn't love him. He'd had no way of knowing what the Amrita was, nobody had, not even his ex, Renee, and she was a full on, no shit scientist. Sure, Julie had lost her temper, but wasn't that to be expected? She'd lost more than anybody. Didn't she have a right to be pissed?

She reached the door and opened it. The room beyond looked like a chill-out area for the staff. There was a huge, seventy-inch TV screen mounted on the far wall, a large semi-circular pink sofa that filled the centre of the room, an Xbox in the corner, a smattering of bean bags and coffee tables. Julie would have found the bright, circular space a welcome relief had it not been for the dead body on the couch.

She approached the corpse with caution. The woman's head was slanted to one side, and her neck was torn open, the right side of her body soaked in blood and gore. Behind her, a door hung from its hinges, its surface coated in yellow slime. The corridor beyond was a swimming pool of darkness. One of the creatures had been in the room, killed the woman and exited through that door, but she had no way of knowing if it was gone for good or whether it was still out there, watching her every move.

She backed away as cold fingers of terror gripped her heart. She couldn't face one of them again. She just couldn't.

She thought about cowering behind the sofa and waiting for help to come, but then she realised Galdhøpiggen was Elysian Field's top-secret facility. Nobody was coming because nobody knew they were there.

She glared at the door. The darkness was a deep chasm. She

couldn't face it. She slumped onto the couch and buried her head in her hands. She tried to focus, but she was so tired. Across from her, the dead woman glared at her through semi-closed eyelids. She whispered with dark grey lips.

'Julie, is that you?'

Julie's head snapped up. It was her father's voice. 'Dad?'

'Why did you do it, Jules? Why did you make me take that stuff?'

She felt the tears coming. 'I didn't know, Dad. I swear. I didn't.'

The woman jerked forward, her mouth hanging open. 'It was poison. You made me drink poison.'

'We thought it would make you well again.'

'Well, guess what, princess? It didn't.' The woman lurched at her and collapsed onto the floor. Her head lifted and she began to crawl towards her, leaving a bloodied smear on the ground.

'You killed me, you bitch. You left me to die in my own piss.'

Julie pulled her legs away and slid towards the rear of the sofa.

'You're not my dad.'

'And you're no daughter of mine, you ten-penny slag. I know all about you and what you do. You fuck anything with a pulse.' The woman clambered onto the sofa, her partially severed head hanging grotesquely to the right.

'What the hell are you?' Julie cried, spilling onto the ground behind the couch.

'Why, I'm your father, Jules. Don't you remember? Have you forgotten about your good old dad? Is that all that I mean to you?'

The woman's corpse leered down at her, but Julie couldn't move. Her fear had solidified her. She was an ice sculpture, a glacier. Dead arms reached for her as a long line of bloodied drool fell from the woman's lips.

'No,' Julie said. 'Stay away from me.'

'Come on, Julie. Come on. Just give me a little kiss and this will all go away.'

'You're not my dad!'

'It's me. Can you hear me?'

'I don't want to listen to you. I don't want to look at you!'

'Julie, it's me. It's Paul.'

Her eyes fluttered open. She was back on the sofa, her head lolled to one side. The woman's corpse was once again sitting motionless across from her.

'Oh, thank God,' the voice said. 'Julie, it's me. Nod if you can hear me?'

She turned her head. It was Paul, but where the hell was he?

'I'm in the computer room, Jules. I'm looking at you through the security camera located in the far corner. If you look up and to your left, you should be able to see it.'

She was confused, disorientated. Could this be true? Could Paul have found her?

'Paul, I'm sorry about what I said. I didn't mean it. I just want us all to get out of here. There was this thing back there, and it trapped me in the oven, but I managed to use Ida's lighter to—'

'Jules, it's no good. I can't hear you. The sound on this thing is only one way. I can talk to you, but you can't talk to me.'

She shook her head. This was crazy.

'Look,' he continued. 'I've got access to all the security cameras in Elysian Field. I think I can guide you to me while making sure you avoid those things. You just have to trust me, okay?'

She nodded. It sounded like it could work.

'You see that door ahead of you?'

She looked at the black hole of darkness.

'You need to go through there.'

She shook her head. 'No, I can't. I can't see anything. What if one of those things is down there?'

'Julie, I can't hear you, remember?'

She gestured towards the door and shook her head again.

'I know it's not ideal,' he said, 'but the other way is blocked. You don't have to worry, I swear. They're not down there.'

She paused to think about it. If Paul could see what was going on, perhaps it was safe. She stood and approached the exit. It smelled gross. She peered into the gloom. The corridor was long.

'About halfway down, there's a hatch to the left. You need to take that. It leads to a service corridor.'

Julie stepped over the broken door and slipped into the darkness. She could smell blood and festering water. She trod on something soft and wet, and she jerked away.

'I can still see you,' Paul continued, his voice now coming through speakers that were embedded in the ceiling. 'The cameras have night vision. It's okay. The way ahead is still clear.'

She walked on, her hand tracing the wall to her left.

'I don't like this,' she said, realising she was talking to herself. 'You'd better be right about this, Paul. I swear, if you're not—'

'Keep going,' he said. 'You're almost there.'

Something scurried across her feet, and she screamed. Tiny glistening eyes peered up at her before disappearing into the shadows.

'Rat,' she said. 'It was just a rat.'

'Woah,' Paul exclaimed. 'Didn't see that coming.'

She cursed under her breath and focused on placing one foot in front of the other. It was all she could do. Despite what had happened, she knew she had to trust him. She was literally stumbling around in the darkness, like a miner without a headlamp. She had no control of what was happening to her. If one of those things crept up on her, she would have absolutely no idea. It was that simple.

'You're doing great,' Paul continued. 'You're doing awesome, Jules.'

She didn't feel awesome. She felt anything but. She had witnessed the brutal murder of the doctor, been trapped in an oven by a creature that wanted to rip her throat out, and held a conversation with a corpse who was masquerading as her dead father.

'Just a little further.'

Her hand brushed against something and she pulled it away, holding it out in front of her. She couldn't see anything, but she could feel it. It was running down her arm. The damp stickiness of blood.

'Okay, you're going to want to duck down a little—' Paul began to say, but it was too late. As she moved her head, something slipped against her face: moist and soft with strands of hanging slickness. It was a hand. She'd walked into a dangling arm. She reacted without thinking, jerking away and screaming.

'Shh,' Paul said. 'Jules, keep it down. They could hear you.'

She covered her mouth but gagged as her throat filled with the coppery taste of cold blood from the dismembered limb. She retched and spat onto the floor, holding her belly as her stomach cramped.

There was a loud screech from up ahead and her heart leapt in her chest.

'You need to move,' Paul said, his tone shifting. 'It's one of them. It's coming towards you.'

His words were like brittle shards of glass. She peered along the corridor, but everything was a sheet of utter black. She heard something slamming against the walls, followed by another hissing scream. She reached out, but in all the panic, she had completely lost her bearings. She didn't even know if she was facing the right way. Her senses were scrambled.

'It's to your right now, Jules,' Paul said. 'Just reach out your hands. Come on! Hurry!'

She was so confused; she couldn't remember which hand was her right. There was another shrieking cry, this time much closer.

'Shit, shit,' she said, waggling her fingers. 'Righty, writey. Righty, writey.'

She found the wall, turned to it and held both hands against its surface, searching for something resembling a door.

'A little to your left,' Paul urged.

She edged along the perimeter. Her fingers came into contact with yet more blood. She clenched her teeth and continued to move. She could hear the tap, tap, tapping of claws against the hard floor. She wanted to scream, to run, to get the hell out of there. The wall felt endless. There was nothing, no features, just a damp sheen of sickening gore. The creature was so close now, she could sense it. She pictured it; its monstrous, inhuman face inches from her own. Those eyes, that sordid mouth, its slick wetness. She could almost taste its fetid breath. There was no escape. She was floundering in the darkness with a beast at her back. She wanted to disappear, to become nothing but molecules. Her only solace was the sound of Paul's voice, but she knew he could be anywhere.

'Talk to me,' she whispered under her breath, her panic like lead, hanging heavily on every syllable. 'Please Paul, talk to me.'

'Keep moving. You're so close now.'

There was another cry, followed by the sound of something sharp scraping against metal. She pressed her face to the wall and stifled a scream. She tried to become as flat as possible, like a mollusc clinging to a shipwreck.

She reached out, pulling herself against the cold surface, and that was when her hand touched something. It was a raised rim. She caught a gasp in her throat and slowly moved her fingers along its edge, a glimmer of hope burning like a slowly flickering candle in her gut. There was a depression in the surface, and she moved her hand towards it. Something was by her side now. She could sense it. It was watching her like a cat watching a winged bird. She knew it could strike at any second. If she made any sudden movements, she was dead.

She could feel the heat of her blood in her face and on her body. Everything inside her was animated and frantic. She thought she was about to explode.

Her fingers found a protrusion and she slipped her hand around it. It was a handle. Her tongue was ash in her mouth. She knew she would have to be quick. If the door opened at all, and there was no guarantee of that, then she would have to slip inside in an instant and then close it rapidly behind her. Hopefully it locked. God, she hoped it locked.

'Jules,' Paul said, but she could hear the terror in his voice. 'I love you.'

Don't give up on me yet, she thought. *This isn't over.*

The creature hissed, and she could smell the dank odour of its essence. She yanked the handle out of desperation, heard a soft click as the latch disengaged, and then she pulled.

There was a breath of air as the door opened. She moved, but not before the creature came for her. Its long, twisting limb was around her waist in an instant, slipping around her like the thick, muscular torso of a python. She screamed and dug her fingernails into its soft, mucus covered flesh. As her fingers found fluid and tissue, its grip relaxed momentarily, and she twisted her hips, shaking it off. Her hands found the edge of the door. She stepped inside, just as another serpentine limb reached for her wounded ankle. She cried out.

'No!' she yelled. 'You don't get to do this!'

She kicked out and slammed her calf into the frame of the

hatch. The creature screeched and released its grip, and she pulled herself into the opening. She turned, only to see her own reflection in a cluster of glimmering eyes. She was a ghost, an apparition. She reached for the handle as the thing opened its wide slit of a mouth and roared. Spittle showered her face and body as she screamed. It reached for her, but she pulled the door hard. A tentacle slapped against her face as metal ground against metal. There was a squelch as its flesh was crushed between two impenetrable surfaces, and she roared as she slammed the lock home.

'Yes!' she screamed. 'Yes. Take that you fucker! You don't mess with a girl from Faversham!'

She fell back against the door as the monster screamed from the other side. She could feel its frustration. It had been so close. She exhaled slowly as her body began to tremble and shudder with shock. She had won; not once, but twice. She'd killed one of them and maimed another. If she could do that, if she could achieve those two little triumphs, then there was no reason why she couldn't find Paul and the others and get the hell out of there. She never wanted to think about Norwegian mountains, yellow slime, salamander-like monsters or Welsh caves ever again. She wanted her home, she wanted her mum, and she wanted her quiet, boring life to resume. She would never complain about wiping down the bar or listening to yet another cover band singing Mr. Brightside again.

She flexed her fingers to get her blood pumping, afforded herself a little smile, and stepped into the gloom of the service tunnel.

She didn't see the shadow start to take form from within the ducting overhead, or hear Paul's frantic screams as he tried to warn her. She was still revelling in her victory. When the creature slipped silently around her body, wrapping her in its powerful, crushing limbs, she almost didn't notice. She was thinking about the life she and Paul could create for themselves: a house, holidays in Europe, maybe children. Her lungs became painfully constricted as two parallel rows of barbed teeth closed around her shoulders and neck, and suddenly she realised what was happening. Too late, her body went into survival mode, but there was no way out this time. She screamed and screamed until there was nothing left to scream for.

*

Renee ran like a crazy person through the labs, trying to put as much distance between herself and the army of murderous mutations as possible. Her plan had failed; her idea had been flawed from the start, and Manmeet had died because of it. Her whole hypothesis had been based on some crazy assumption that there could only be a few of them, that the quantity of Amrita that Elysian Field had been provided could only possibly create a handful of the creatures. She hadn't considered that they could now be self-sustaining, that they could have constructed their own means of reproduction, and that a hive system could grow organically in such a short space of time. It was a ludicrous fantasy, like something from a movie, but no matter how unreal it was, she couldn't argue with the proof. It was right there in front of her. One single entity, a queen-like being that could spawn monster after murderous monster. It didn't matter what she did or how many she killed. More of them would appear to take their place. It was a hopeless situation, an unwinnable game.

She thought of Manmeet. He had sacrificed himself for her without a second's consideration. Tears streamed down her face when she recalled what he did. He could have tried to save himself, but she knew the thought had never even crossed his mind. He had acted heroically, gallantly, but she could never repay him. He was gone, and she was alone. She desperately wanted to head back to the cryo-chamber to see if there was any way she could bring him back, but she knew there was no point. He had been frozen by temperatures the human body had never been designed to withstand. She wiped damp saltiness from her cheeks and took several deep breaths. If his death was to mean anything, she had to get away.

She entered a long corridor that she didn't recognise. The labs were behind her, and up ahead was a wide-open space behind two clear glass doors. She headed towards them, hoping to find someone who could help her. Julie had left, Manmeet was gone, and that meant the only other person in the complex was Paul, and she knew there was no guarantee he was still alive.

She entered a storage area. Plastic boxes surrounded her, stacked in shelving units that stretched to a ceiling some fifteen metres above her head. The large room was separated into half a dozen equally spaced aisles. She raced into one, just as the door behind her erupted inwards in a shower of shattered glass.

The air was filled with a duo of shrill screeches. She pushed her back to the shelves and held her breath. There were two of them. She moved along the aisle, glancing anxiously over her shoulder, half expecting one of them to come running towards her. She was trapped with no way out. She had to find another door.

There was a crash as a stack of boxes went tumbling from a couple of aisles over. She jittered, trying desperately to control her fear. She had to use her head. One wrong move and she would be hemmed in. The thought caused her mind to race. Her body was like a metal frame, welded in place. She closed her eyes as everything became a whir of noise and scrambled thoughts. She'd backed herself into a corner with no way to escape. She needed to think like a scientist and use the facts that presented themselves to her. If she headed to the end of the aisle she would be exposed, but if she stayed where she was, they would eventually find her. Her heart was racing. Fear encased her like a sarcophagus. She couldn't catch her breath. She raised her head and stifled a scream, but then a thought clarified in her head like butter. Maybe there was another way.

More boxes went tumbling, followed by a crescendo of shrill cries. Renee shut them out. She had to think. She grabbed the vertical strut and shook it. It didn't budge. It was solid enough. She placed her foot on the first shelf and pulled, hauling herself upwards. She moved silently to the second shelf and looked down. She was no more than two metres in the air, but it felt like a hundred. She moved again, mounting the third shelf, then the fourth. Soon she was more than six metres above the ground and peering down at the narrow concourse. Something was down there. It snaked between the shelves, flitting in and out, sending storage containers crashing to the ground. She held her breath and waited, praying that it didn't look up.

She shifted her body between two boxes and peered down at the walkway. The other creature was on the opposite side of the rack. It was moving slowly but deliberately. Its partner was making a hissing, snarling sound, trying to shake her loose. They weren't senseless predators at all. They were able to think, to communicate. She was no longer simply something to be killed. She was a prize.

She was on her knees, doubled over, sandwiched between the narrow shelves and storage boxes. She felt claustrophobic and sick. She knew she couldn't stay like this forever. At some point her muscles would cramp up, and she would give herself away. She considered her options: stay where she was and hope she could keep herself together, or move and risk making a sound, or worse still, sending something tumbling to the ground and completely revealing her location. Option two posed the biggest challenge, but it also presented the greatest prize.

She looked up. There was a grate covering a square hole. It was small, but she thought it was big enough for her to squeeze through. It was almost ten metres above her and to her right. She would have to clamber up another nine levels, head along the uppermost shelf and then lean over the edge to reach the grate, meaning her upper body would be hanging fifteen metres above the ground with nothing between her and the hard floor than thin air. It was dangerous, but it was something. Right now, with her options severely limited, something was better than nothing. Nothing meant an almost certain, agonising death. Something meant hope, and hope was good. She liked hope.

She felt a cramp gradually rising in her left calf, and she shifted her position. It didn't help. If anything, it made it worse. She shifted again, but the sudden movement caused a lightning bolt of pain to fizz from her ankle to her knee. She grunted, holding her hand to her mouth as a scream threatened. Below her, the creatures continued to search through the mountains of boxes and files. The floor was a mass of paper, plastic and metal. They were getting closer. Her cramp became a burning, scalding heat within her flesh. She couldn't bear it. She knew if she didn't do something, she would pass out from the agony. She gripped the edge of the box and gradually moved her left leg, but the pain was excruciating. She was sweating profusely and her whole body was trembling.

The creature on her right stopped moving and peered along the aisle. It had sensed something. It grabbed the shelf above its head and clambered upwards. She held her breath, but it made no difference. Everything was hurting now. She had to stretch her limbs. She moved her leg again, pushing it through the slim gap between the containers. A blinding shard of pain raced up her thigh, and she twisted sharply onto her side in an effort to release the pressure from her compressed joints.

'Motherfucker,' she whispered beneath her breath, bubbles of spittle spraying from her lips.

She pressed her buttocks onto the metal shelf and stretched both legs out. They were dangling over the other side of the racking unit, but she didn't care. The release was wonderful. The pain seemed to slip from her lower body like evaporating water. She flipped onto her stomach and saw the top of the creature's head. It was hanging from a spot four shelves below her. She had to do something.

With hot spots of feeling returning to her legs, she drew herself towards the edge of the shelf and peered at the grate. It was such a long way away. She looked down once more. The creature was motionless, listening. If she moved now, she might just have enough time. She paused. Maybe she could just stay where she was. Now the cramp had subsided, she felt much better. Perhaps complete inertia was better than the risk of exposing herself. She shifted her body to get a slightly better look, and that was when her knee caught a loose screw, and although she scrambled for it, her fingers clambering desperately for the spinning, metal projectile, it tipped over the edge and went tumbling through the air, end over end, until it clattered onto a metal surface and span onto the creature's spine.

She was moving, way before the monster looked up and spotted her. Her arms were like pistons, her legs like springs. She had already traversed three shelves before the creature began its furious pursuit, but it was far quicker than her. She heard the rattle of the aluminium and the tumbling, smashing clatter of box after box crashing against the floor. She was panting frantically, spittle and hot air ejecting from grimacing lips. Her left leg was still partially numb, but she drove through her hips, willing herself upwards.

Something snared her foot, but she kicked it away, and then something else slapped against her thigh. It was less than two shelves behind her, which she knew was far too close. She grabbed a box from above and pulled it towards her, sending it spinning past her right shoulder. It slammed into the creature's head, showering it with plates, dishes and cutlery.

'Yes!' she hollered, wincing as she looked down at the ground beneath her. One wrong move and she would be a broken pile of bones and meat.

There was a screaming, scratching sound from up ahead, and as she turned to face it, her expression twisted in horror. The second creature was now racing towards her from the opposite end of the aisle. What had seemed like an improbable mission was now almost impossible. She had one monster on her heels, and now a second one closing in.

'No!' she hollered. 'This isn't fair!'

She was three shelves from the top, but it seemed like such a long way. She tossed another box and then another, frantically trying to buy herself time. It didn't seem to be making a difference. They were so fast. She reached the next shelf, but her arms were throbbing and her legs were so tired. Falling seemed like the easier option. Perhaps then everything wouldn't ache. There was another scream from behind her, followed by a second louder screech from up ahead. She was about to be caught in a pincer movement with no way out, unless…

She eyed the gap between her and the stack of shelves opposite. It wasn't far, perhaps less than two metres. She thought it was possible, although if she made a mistake, she knew the results would be catastrophic. The thing behind her was almost upon her, and the other one would be on top of her in a matter of seconds. She had no choice. She had to do something. She eyed the distance and glared at the mash of smashed boxes over twelve metres beneath her. She was crying now. Her fear was deafening in her ears. It was now or never. She leaned forward, bent her knees and jumped, just as a long, squirming tentacle slammed into the metal shelving, and two sets of teeth snapped at the void she had just departed. She was airborne, her arms pinwheeling, her legs running in free space. Her mind made everything slow to a crawl. Yellow eyes glared up at her, and a black, swirling limb lashed at the air behind her. She heard the spitting, snapping screams, followed by her own hoarse cries. If she missed, she was dead, but she wasn't going to miss.

She hit the rack with a loud crash as her mouth smashed into the edge of a shelf, cracking one of her teeth. She didn't care. She'd made it, but she knew if she could make the jump, so could they. She had seconds to move. No, milliseconds. She drove upwards, racing across the last three shelves before either one of them had leapt across. She stood at the top, her fists raised defiantly, but she wasted no time in kicking box after box to the floor, running along the narrow expanse, standing, legs spread with the grate just ahead of her.

She leaned forward and immediately felt giddy. The ground was such a long, long way away. If she lost her balance, she would topple forwards, and then her efforts would be in vain. She didn't see any screw heads, which was good. If the grate was a push fit, perhaps she could prise it free. If she couldn't, all bets were off. She reached out, but her right foot slipped on a sheet of plastic and her legs almost went out from beneath her.

'Come on,' she said, steadying herself. 'You can do this.'

The first creature had almost reached the summit, which meant she had no time. She stretched out again, and this time made sure she had a surer footing. Her fingernail found the lip of the grate, but as she pushed the manicured tip into the slim gap between the ceiling and the plastic cover, her nail snapped off at the quick.

'Ow!' she hollered, pushing her finger between her lips and sucking the blood.

The creature was hauling itself upwards now. She had to move. She leaned across one last time, jammed her middle fingernail in the gap, and this time something clicked. With the crack now a millimetre, she slid her hand across, and within an instant, the grate came free and went spinning towards the ground. She squealed in triumph, but her victory was short lived. The monster was coming at her now, snarling and vicious.

She eyed the hole. If she was going to make it, she was going to have to jump, grab the edge and pull herself into the cavity. It was a tall ask. She moved her feet towards the rim and held her breath. The ground looked like a coffin. She pictured her fingers slipping from the edge and her body falling through the air, her head striking the hard floor and crumpling like a melon. She jumped without thinking. It was the best way. Her hands caught the lip of the ducting and her fingers found purchase, but her body felt so heavy. Her arms groaned in agony. She let out a bubbling croak as she strained to pull herself upwards. The creature glared at her from the top of the tall stack. She realized it was waiting for her to fall, but she wasn't going to. She wouldn't let herself. It didn't matter how much her body hurt, or how painfully tired she was; she was not going to give in. Nothing could stop her.

She strained with everything she had, thankful for the pull-ups she'd been forced to do at school. She had hated them. She could barely manage eight, nine at best, but that was okay. She only needed to do one now. One would be great. One would be fricking awesome. Every fibre in her arms felt like it was about to snap. She heard a sound like a dog growling, and she realised it was her. Her chin was slowly elevating, getting closer and closer to the lip of the cavity. Her legs flailed beneath her, running on an invisible treadmill that floated in space.

The darkness sucked her in, as if her mamie was up there in the narrow tubing, pulling with her frail arms, hauling her inch by inch into the tiny confines of the air conditioning duct. She slipped her elbow onto the metal surface and dragged her body across the sharp lip, grazing her stomach. She slumped forward, her mouth open, sweat pouring from her face. Her breath was like a hot jet, burning her throat. She drew her legs around her, bent at the knees, hugging herself into a tight sphere. Her tears fell as she peered into the darkness through watery eyes. She'd made it. She'd bloody made it.

*

'No! Please no! No, she can't be! She can't be…'

Paul couldn't bring himself to say the word. He glared at the screen through his tears. The image was a black, thrashing intensity. Beneath it, Julie's body lay in a bloodied heap. He hadn't seen it. He'd been so focussed on the creature coming towards her that he hadn't noticed the one behind the door. He'd led her straight into a trap, and now she was…dead. Julie was dead. Those three words were like icepicks in his heart. He was to blame. He'd found the Amrita, he'd convinced Wade and Julie's father to take it, he'd dragged the four of them to Galdhøpiggen, and now Julie was dead. Julie was…dead

It didn't matter that he'd survived an almost fatal asthma attack. He didn't want to be alive anymore. He didn't want to be anything. Everything he'd ever cared about was either destroyed or lost to him. He was destruction. He was desolation.

He eyed the thumb drive. It was on the desk. Anger gripped

him like a tight fist. Those vicious, murderous things had to be stopped. He'd brought them into this world, and he had to be the one to send them back to wherever the hell they'd come from. He plucked it between his fingers and glared at the banks of computer terminals.

The only thing he could see was Julie's body; her sightless, glaring eyes. Meeting and falling in love with him had been the biggest mistake of her life. He had failed her. He had failed all of them. He wouldn't fail them again. He didn't know if Manny or Renee were still alive, but he couldn't let his feelings for them cloud his judgement. If they had to be sacrificed, so be it. These things had to be destroyed.

He scoured the computer stations, located a keyboard on a slide-out shelf and hit the space bar several times. The large LCD screen sprang into life, emblazoned with the Elysian Field logo. He pushed the thumb drive home and waited for something to happen. A folder icon appeared, and he opened it. Inside was one single file entitled 'RUN DOOMSDAY'. He paused, realizing that if he went through with this, they would all be killed. There was no going back. He thought of his mother and father, of the wreck of a life for him they had left behind when they no longer wanted to fuck each other. He'd tried to rise above it, tried to make something of himself, but he'd always been the great pretender, a failure, masking his real self in a cloak of fake confidence and bravado. He'd talked himself out of trouble more times than he could remember, and convinced people with IQs much greater than his to take a chance on him. He'd been riding his luck for so long, he'd forgotten the single, most important truth. He was Paul Karin, the runt of the litter who wet the bed until he was fifteen years old. He was a loser, a never-been, a never would be. He pushed down on the mouse, pressing it so hard he thought the plastic housing might fracture. He watched through a veil of anger as a series of panels opened, overlapping each other like a deck of cards.

A dialogue box appeared.

Are you sure you want to run DOOMSDAY?

He clicked on the Yes icon.

Are you aware that the DOOMSDAY program is an end-game scenario?

Once more he clicked Yes.

Are you authorised to run the DOOMSDAY program?

'Enough with the questions,' he hissed, slamming his hand onto the mouse and sending it clattering noisily over the edge of the desk.

Enter authorisation code.

This is it, he thought. *This is how it all ends*. He held his hands over the keyboard and sucked air through his teeth. 'You fucker's asked for this.' He typed the code the doctor had given him, *Trinity1607*, into the white flashing box. 'No more mistakes.'

He hit enter and a digital countdown appeared.

30:00.00

Even before he had time to take it in, the numbers started to run down. He had thirty minutes to wait. It seemed like an eternity. Thirty minutes until his life was extinguished. The thought didn't seem real to him. It ignited no emotion. He was numb to his own death, something that was both tragic and sad. It had come down to this.

'Paul?'

He turned to face the entrance hatch. There was a plastic grate on the floor and a yawing square of darkness overhead. Standing beneath it was someone he had spent many long evenings with, poring over college papers and exam questions.

'Renee?'

'I thought you were dead.'

'Same.' He looked at her. She was bloodied and covered in dirt and slime. 'How did you…' he paused. 'Manny?'

She shook her head as her shoulders sagged. 'He's gone.' She eyed her surroundings. 'Did Julie get out?'

He could barely answer her. 'They got her, too.'

'Oh, Paul.' She wrapped her arms around him and pulled him close. 'I'm so sorry.'

He buried his face in her neck, feeling all the pain, all the grief pouring from him in rampaging waves. His best friend and his girlfriend, both gone. It was too much to take.

'Manmeet was a hero,' he heard Renee say. 'He saved me and killed three of them. I would be dead too if it wasn't for him.'

He gathered himself, wiping at his face with a grimy sleeve. 'He always wanted to be a knight in shining armour.'

She smiled through the tears. 'I guess he got his wish.' She peered over his shoulder at the flashing computer terminal. 'What's that.'

He followed her eyes. 'Oh shit,' he said. 'I almost forgot. I've triggered the facility's catastrophe protocol?'

'The what?'

He averted his eyes. 'Petra had it installed after she and her scientists started dabbling with deadly contagions.'

'You mean it's some sort of containment algorithm?'

'Of sorts,' he said.

'But wait,' she replied. 'How would that even work? Those things are everywhere. It's not like they're simply going crazy in the labs.'

'Right. I get that.'

'So what does this thing even do?'

He glared at the clock. They had twenty-six minutes remaining. 'It's a destruction sequence, Renee. This whole complex is rigged with explosives.'

Her mouth fell open. 'You mean we'll be killed?'

'Unless we get out of here within twenty-six minutes, yes. We'll be buried under hundreds of tonnes of rock and steel'

'Holy shit.'

'Yeah, that's about the sum of it.'

She turned to the door. 'Then what are we waiting for? We need to leave.'

He shook his head. 'I'm not going anywhere.'

'What? You have to be kidding.'

'I caused this whole sorry mess.'

'We all did,' she said, clutching his hand. 'Sure, you might have found the Amrita, but we all went along with it. Nobody forced us to investigate it. Nobody pushed us onto that plane.'

'But if I hadn't convinced everybody that this stuff was going to change peoples' lives for the better, Manny and Julie would still be alive.'

'That's a hypothetical theory you can't prove,' she said. 'And you know it.'

'Yeah,' he replied. 'But you know it's true.'

She tugged at him. 'I don't care what you say. You're coming with me.'

He pulled his hand away. 'I'm not. I've made my mind up. I'm staying here.'

She glared at him, her lips quivering. 'But I don't know the way, Paul. I can't find my way out on my own. You need to at least help me. Please. I can't be buried down here. I just can't.'

His jaw clenched. He didn't want to go anywhere, but he also didn't want more blood on his hands. Especially not Renee's.

'I'll show you to the foyer,' he said. 'But then you're on your own.'

'That's fine,' she replied, glaring at the clock. 'But we need to stop talking and start moving.'

Paul approached the hatch, listening for any signs of movement on the other side. There was nothing. He readied himself, gritting his teeth before turning the lock and opening the door. The service corridor was empty.

'They could be anywhere,' he said. 'We could be dead before the detonation occurs.'

'I'll take my chances,' Renee replied. 'If we stay here, we don't have any.'

He gestured for her to move. They walked quickly, moving back towards the ladder where the doctor had been killed. When they reached his severed arm, Renee turned away.

'What the hell?'

'It gets worse,' Paul said, opening the hatch. Beneath them, the doctor's body lay slashed and torn.

He heard Renee gasp. 'Who is that?'

'A friend,' Paul replied, descending the ladder. 'He's the one who gave me the thumb drive.'

They ran along the corridor, slipping through the service tunnel doorway and stepping out into the Ambassade.

'This place is like a rabbit warren,' she said.

Paul's eyes searched the corridor. 'Yeah, and it's full of foxes.'

'How much farther.'

He checked his watch. 'We should have time.'

They ran along the hallway which was bathed in shadows. Dark blood smeared the paintwork like chocolate. Panels were torn away from the walls and ceiling. Elysian Field had become a killing field, a morgue. What had once given criminals a safe shelter had become a murdering ground. It reeked of violence and death. It deserved to be annihilated.

Something scratched at the ceiling overhead and Renee gasped.

'I can hear them,' she said.

'Yeah, me too.'

'We need to hurry.'

'We're going as fast as we can.'

There was a shriek from above, followed by two more some way behind them.

'It's calling to the others,' Renee said, breathless and trembling. 'They can communicate with each other. I think these things are highly intelligent.'

'Let's not get too hung up on the science,' Paul replied. 'We're their lunch, remember?'

'How long?'

He checked his watch. 'Eleven minutes.'

'It's not enough time.'

'It'll be enough,' he said, but he wasn't sure.

They passed the office complex. He could see the sign to the executive suite to his left and the conference rooms to his right. He eyed the glass doors dead ahead. That was the foyer. That was where they needed to be.

Something crashed through the ceiling behind them, and he turned to see one of the creatures rising from the ground.

'Shit,' he said. 'They've found us.'

They doubled their efforts, but Paul could see how exhausted Renee was. She looked spent.

'Not much further,' he said, but the doorway looked so far away. He wasn't worried about himself—he was prepared to die anyway—but Renee? She didn't deserve any of this. He pulled her along behind him, but in the distance, he could see the creature was closing. There was no time.

He reached the doors and waited patiently for them to slide open.

'Come on!' he yelled as he and Renee slipped between the

narrow gap. He turned to lock them, but there was no mechanism, and in any case, the doors were glass. On the other side of the foyer, the large metal doors beckoned.

From above the desk, a creature dropped down from the ceiling. It snarled at them, its wide mouth leering and snapping. Behind them, their pursuer emerged. Its large limbs slammed into the ground, clawing at the stone tiles.

'Oh God,' Renee said.

'Let's move,' Paul urged. 'Come on. We can do this.'

They headed towards the exit as the creatures screeched. Paul could feel the weight of them on the ground. They were approaching fast. He only hoped the sensor in the door would let them through, otherwise they were finished.

As he reached for it, pulling Renee along behind him, the door became obscured by a darkness that crept in from the edges of his vision. His mouth was dry, and his head felt insanely heavy.

'Paul?' he heard Renee say, but her voice was swampy and muted. He suddenly wanted to hurt. He wanted to kill. He could taste the iron of blood on his tongue, and the soft swell of meat in his belly. He didn't notice the huge metal doors open, or Renee cry out as she slammed them closed, trapping the creatures inside.

'Come on,' she said. 'We only have a few minutes left.'

They approached the stairs to the cabin, but all Paul could feel was hatred and anger. Renee's voice irritated him. The feel of her hand in his was revolting to him. He wanted to tear her arm off. Her skin was a thin, putrid membrane, her muscle tissue soft and without merit. Even her brain was pure mush. She didn't deserve to get out. She didn't deserve to win.

They entered the cabin. Beyond the large, panoramic windows, the Jotunheimen mountain range was a snow-covered paradise, its peaks dusted in brilliant white. Renee approached them, pressing her hands against the glass.

'We made it,' she said, turning to him. 'We got out.'

He sensed a presence in the room, a powerful force that rattled his senses. He knew Gunthar was there with them even before he saw him.

'Bravo,' Gunthar said, his voice like a death rattle. 'You made it this far.'

Renee backed away towards the far wall. 'You! How did you find us?'

Dark limbs jutted from Gunthar's body like thick tubes. His face was riven with black sores and dark veins. 'It was a pretty simple calculation. You wanted to leave, and this is the only way out.' He forced a pained smile. 'That was some stunt you and Manmeet pulled back there in the labs. Very impressive. Of course, it was all a waste of time. We can't be destroyed.'

'Oh, but you can,' Renee replied. 'Manmeet killed three of those things all by himself. They're just flesh and blood, the same as any other living animal. They have the same vulnerabilities, the same frailties.'

'That's where you and I can't agree,' Gunthar said, continuing his approach. 'They are a species that has endured through this planet's ever-changing cycles. The existence of the human race is just a small blot on an everlasting timeline compared to the many millennia we have roamed the Earth.'

'We?' Renee screamed. 'What's with the we? You were human, too, remember? This change that's happening to you, it's unnatural. Look at yourself. They're killing you. Can't you see that?'

'I'm not dying. I am growing. I am becoming.'

'You're being overrun with a deadly contagion, Gunthar. You need help.'

'No,' he growled as another thick limb erupted from his spine. His body hunched over, his neck spasming as more pustules appeared, oozing with yellow and black sludge. 'I feel strong. I feel powerful.'

'Your blood cells are being invaded by a hostile disease. They are mutating into something your body cannot possibly withstand. Eventually, everything you once were, every ounce of the man you have been, will be completely destroyed.'

'You lie,' he spat, lurching towards her. 'You do not deserve to breathe the same air.'

Paul watched as Renee staggered backwards. He was confused. Nothing made sense to him. He felt an escalating anger bubbling in his gut, but deep down he was aware that his friend was in danger. He wanted to help her, but something was holding him back. There was a desperate struggle for power raging within him, and it was something he had no control over. He knew it was the Amrita. It was beginning to control him too.

'Get away from me!' Renee screamed.

'You must be stopped!' Gunthar roared. 'You have no right to exist.'

He lashed out, launching a rapidly unfurling limb in her direction. It cracked like a whip, striking the glass by Renee's head as she dived to her left. The window shattered, showering her with sharp pebbles. An ice-cold wind rushed into the cabin, almost knocking Paul off his feet. He watched as Renee crawled behind the sofa, her red hair just visible above the backrest. He checked his watch. They had less than two minutes to get off the mountain before everything went to hell.

'Paul!' Renee screamed. 'Help me!'

Gunthar was on top of her, his hulking frame obscuring her from Paul's view. He gripped her around her waist, lifting her into the air. She hung there, her feet dangling beneath her, pinwheeling and kicking.

'Get off of me!'

Paul stood gawping, not knowing what to do. He was still fighting against the darkness that was strangling him. He tried to focus on everything that had happened. He thought of Julie's body lying broken and bloodied, his best friend, Manny, racing into the cryo-chamber, knowing it meant certain death; he thought about the dozens of mutilated bodies in the Caldarium, and of the doctor's arm as it came away at the shoulder. He thought of his initial visit to Galdhøpiggen, and the contract Petra had convinced him to sign; he thought of the grotesque, foul smelling entity in the Cave of the Black Spring, and of the inhuman monster he and Manny had buried beneath the rubble.

'Paul! Help me!'

He pushed his demons aside, shoving them further and further into the darkness until some semblance of who he was managed to break through into the light; and then he was charging headlong towards Renee's attacker, screaming at the top of his lungs. He slammed into Gunthar, sending all three of them tumbling through the shattered glass and out onto the snow-covered car park. He felt the ice-cold wind and the damp freeze of the blizzard as a barrage of heavy snowflakes cascaded onto his chest and face. He saw Renee tumbling to the ground, and then Gunthar's malformed body as he rose from the blanket of white.

'What are you doing?' Gunthar screamed.

'I'm protecting my friend.'

'But you are one of us. She isn't.'

Renee pulled herself up, using the rear of their car for support. 'What the hell is he saying?'

'I don't know,' he lied. 'Honestly, I have no idea what this guy is talking about.'

'I can feel it,' Gunthar yelled above the bellowing wind. 'Their aura is emanating from you. You can sense it, too.'

Paul could. He could feel it moving within him like a snake. It nipped at his insides, wrapped itself around his intestines. He'd taken too much of the Amrita. Wade and Julie's father hadn't been strong enough, and it had killed them. Gunthar had embraced it, welcomed it, but now he was something else completely. He couldn't be like that. He couldn't be one of them. 'No!' he screamed. 'It's not true. I'm not like you. I'm not like those things. I won't be. I can't be!'

'You don't have any control,' Gunthar cried, his body convulsing as more black pustules erupted from his neck and chest. 'And neither do I. We are at one with them. We are evolving with them, creating something new and everlasting. We can be everything we have ever dreamed.'

'I don't dream of being like you and I certainly don't dream of being one of them. They kill, Gunthar. They destroy.'

'You're mistaken. They are much more than even I can ever understand. You unleashed them, Paul. You released them from beneath the Earth, from their eternity of sickening hunger, and for that they will forever be in your debt.'

'They killed Manny!'

'Because he tried to stop them!'

'They killed…' Paul's voice cracked. 'They killed Julie.'

'She was collateral damage.'

'I loved her!'

'She was beneath you!'

'She was everything! Don't you get that. She meant everything to me!'

'And yet without her, your potential can now truly be realised.'

Paul could feel the energy pulsing through him. His blood felt like it was boiling, and his skin was painfully raw. His head felt too heavy for his body, as if something was growing inside his skull.

'We have to get out of here!' Renee screamed. 'We have less than a minute!'

He whirled on her, feeling his own anger swelling in his gut. Her voice was like hot embers in his eyes. He wanted to lash out at it, to tear it from the air and rip it into tiny ant-sized pieces.

'Just go,' he hissed. 'The keys are behind the sun visor. Just get out of here!'

'What? No! We're going together!'

'You're not going anywhere,' Gunthar spat, his face tearing down the middle as black fingers emerged from his eye sockets. 'The unclean cannot leave the mountain.'

'I'm not coming!' Paul hollered at Renee. He was fighting every instinct he had to rip her head from her shoulders. 'Gunthar and I have unfinished business.'

'I'm not leaving without you!'

'Get the fuck out of here! Now!'

She must have seen something in his face that terrified her, because after a moment's hesitation, she threw the car door open. She looked back at him, her eyes red with tears, a dark bruise on her cheek.

'Go!' he growled as Gunthar wrapped a clawed tentacle around his throat.

'Kill her,' he said, although Gunthar's mouth no longer existed in human form. His face was now split in two, and a black, hooked beak jutted from where his forehead had once been. His words came to Paul like bubbles in his mind.

'I won't,' he said. 'She's my friend.'

Gunthar grabbed the vehicle as the engine roared into life, snaring the rear axle and lifting the back of the car from the ground.

'No!' Paul yelled in desperation. He kicked backward, throwing Gunthar off guard, and then struck him in the throat.

Gunthar cried out and then tossed him into the snow. Paul lay on his back, watching as Gunthar began to drag the car towards him. He could see Renee inside, a twisting knot of fear behind her eyes. He realised what Gunthar was planning to do. He was going to toss the car over the edge of the precipice. He rose to his knees and glanced at his watch. They hardly had any time left. He couldn't let this be the end. He had to make things right.

He crouched as all the hate that had been building inside him turned into a black sea of limbs and venom. He was within the hive. He was within the eyes. He could see everything. The creatures behind the locked door slamming into it repeatedly, their minds filled with so much unthinking hatred, clawing and gnashing, hanging from the ceiling like mutated bats, climbing the walls. He was within the mother, her motionless body lying in the underground pool. She became young again, and he was back inside the cavern. He was beneath the earth, hundreds of miles within its crust, a sea of molten rock roaring beneath him. Then he was above land, but the sky wasn't blue, it was a rusty orange, like terracotta. The earth was dry and scorched, the air a mixture of sulphur and ash. Giant creatures moved across the valley floor, only to be hunted down by more like him. They were running out of food. Their prey was dwindling. An explosion detonated some way off in the distance, and a giant plume rose in the sky. They were driven underground, deeper and deeper, searching for clean water and breathable air. The way back was blocked by the shifting planet. They were trapped.

There was a loud crack as the nose of the car struck the tarmac, snapping him back into focus.

'Release them,' Gunthar yelled. 'Let them out of there, or I will kill her.'

'No!' Paul replied, feeling the tug of his new blood, but knowing he had to resist for as long as he could. 'This ends now!'

He charged as a searing pain across his shoulders threatened to incapacitate him, and two blackened limbs erupted from his spine, tearing through skin and bone, ripping Gunthar from the ground. Gunthar turned, the cluster of yellow eyes that had emerged from his chest flitting back and forth, but it was too late. He could see what Paul was doing. He was heading for the edge of the platform and dragging Gunthar with him. Gunthar released the car as Renee gunned the accelerator, and it slammed into the ground, the rear bumper spinning into the blizzard as it raced away, disappearing from view as the air was filled with a deafening crack, and the ground beneath them began to split and collapse in on itself.

Paul yanked hard, hauling Gunthar's mutated body as he leapt from the edge of the rock face, the brilliant white of Galdhøpiggen's escarpment stretching beneath them. From above, Elysian Field erupted into a searing yellow ball of exploding metal and rock. Paul could hear his brethren screaming. They were desperate and without hope. He didn't care. The only image he saw as he and Gunthar raced towards the ground like a spinning, furious ball of rage was of Julie's dark, smiling eyes.

Saturday, 2nd July:

Pilgrims Way, Canterbury, Kent

Renee opened the front door. Her fingers felt alien to her, her body soft and sponge-like. She didn't feel at home in her skin. It was at least three sizes too big for her. She wanted to shrink, to contract. Exhaustion coated her eyes like cataracts. She felt weightless, formless.

A black shape came bounding towards her, a Springer Spaniel on amphetamines. She saw darkness and writhing limbs. She held up her hands defensively.

'Renee, it's me. It's only me.'

Rosa pulled her close, wrapping her in wiry arms. Her dark hair hung over them like a funeral shroud. Renee allowed herself to be absorbed. She needed a physical presence but wasn't sure whether this was it. She didn't cry. She didn't know if she could anymore.

Her housemate held her by her shoulders and peered into her eyes. 'What did the police say?'

'They asked a lot of questions.'

'Did you tell them everything?'

Renee paused. Of course she hadn't. She couldn't. She nodded anyway.

'That's good.' Rosa's eyes narrowed. 'What were you even doing in Norway?'

Renee shrugged. 'Holiday.'

'A bit last minute, wasn't it?'

'Paul's idea.'

'Renee, you knew how crazy that guy could get.'

'He was my friend.'

'Only when he wanted something.'

'Look, Rosa,' she snapped. 'I really can't deal with this right now. I'm walking around on literally no sleep.'

Her housemate released her. 'I'm so sorry. I'm just worried about you, that's all.'

'Don't be.' Renee slipped past her. She wanted to be alone. 'I'm shook up, but I'm fine. I just need some space.'

She wasn't. The police had told her that the Norwegian authorities might still want to speak to her. The idea terrified her. She couldn't go back there. She couldn't even bring herself to think about it. Manmeet, Julie, Paul, all gone. Every time she shut her eyes she saw those things, their soulless, unblinking stare and bloodied claws. It was like a nightmare, except it was endless. It played over and over in her mind, even when she was awake.

She saw Rosa's latest fling slumped on the sofa, and she ducked away from her smoke-filled gaze. She slipped into her bedroom, easing the door closed. She shot a cautious glance at her thing: her laptop, her clothing rack filled with charity shop chic, her well-weathered Docs. She dropped to her knees and rummaged for the tin box she kept under her bed. She opened it and plucked out a fistful of twenty-pound notes. She checked inside her bag for her passport.

She had been planning to stay, to use her studies as some kind of anaesthesia, but her encounter with Rosa had helped make up her mind. There was only one person who could even come close to making her feel whole again, and she lived in another country. She could almost smell the damp peat of the river, the crispness of the long grass. The Dordogne beckoned.

Epilogue:

Thursday, 3rd August:

St. Pancras, London

Paul Karin stepped off the train, his case tucked under his arm. St. Pancras station was bustling with commuters. He was anonymous there, just another ant in the nest. His invisibility suited him. He'd spent countless days giving statement after statement to the police about what had happened at Galdhøpiggen and how he'd managed to miraculously pull through, despite Renee telling them some weeks prior that he had been buried along with the others.

He'd concocted a story, of course, feeding them some line about an air pocket and the human spirit's unwavering will to survive. The truth was entirely different, but he had no plan to tell them that. They would never believe him anyway.

He'd made a stop on route. Temple. His uncle and aunt couldn't be allowed to get away with throwing them to the wolves like that. They hadn't suffered. He'd allowed them that one small mercy. He wasn't an animal, after all.

He followed a trail of eager bodies into the open, each of them shuffling with arms outstretched like zombies. The day was a brilliant white. The sun scorched his eyes. He stepped into the shade and breathed. He walked the street, staying close to the buildings. He picked up the scent of Chanel and body odour. A discarded fast-food bag lay at his feet, its disassembled contents cooking on the hot pavement. Cold coffee ran between the cracks, foamy milk laced with chocolate brown essence. He danced around it, dodging the belligerent cell phone junkies, swerving to avoid them as if he were on the fast slope at Chamonix.

Up ahead, his destination loomed. It rose up from the tarmac like a boil, ripe for lancing. He allowed himself a wry smile, idly fingering the catch of his case. He checked his watch. His meeting with David Harker was in less than an hour. It gave him ample time to rehearse his script. He had to get it right. They had big plans.

He eyed the 360-degree CCTV camera mounted above the street, scanned his surroundings, and landed on a nearby coffee shop. He would look and act normal, wait inside, but not before he collected. None of this worked without that one little deposit.

He spied him in the alleyway: black veins, jittering bones, anxious eyes.

'Hello Ted.'

'You're ready?' Ted Barker asked.

'I am.'

'You know what you have to do?'

'Of course. I'm not an idiot.'

'Didn't stop you killing the Norwegian.'

'That was before.'

'How do we know you won't try something stupid again?'

Paul hissed at him. 'Just give it to me, you cunt.'

As Ted relented, Paul backed towards the narrow gap between the bank and the overpriced deli. He felt the damp, slipperiness of the tentacle as Ted dropped the vial into his open palm. He sensed the power in his fingers. With all other supplies either destroyed or buried, this was the one thing he needed.

'Will it be enough?' Ted asked.

'This will do just fine.'

'Mass consumption?'

'Yes,' Paul replied, feeling the darkness bristle beneath his skin. 'We have the cure for everything, my friend. People will just eat it up.'

'And then?'

'Then it will be done.'

Paul began to move, slipping the vial into his case as he stepped through the coffee shop door. He felt good. Soon the Amrita would be in every bathroom cabinet in every home in the country. Eventually it would go global. Of course, as the transitions commenced, questions would be asked, but by then it would be too late. These people wanted to be cured of their ailments, but they would get so much more besides.

He approached the counter and beckoned the Barista. 'Americano. Black.'

'Will that be small or large, sir.'

He tapped his case and smiled. 'Go big or go home, right?'

A Note From The Author

The concept for this book came to me while I was driving on the M2, a little motorway which traverses a tiny section of north Kent, not far from where my wife and I live. I'm still not sure why this particular notion came to me on that particular day, but that's often the way with story ideas. They just creep up on you. Perhaps it was brought on by my frustration at how a few people managed to get very rich off the back of the COVID vaccines, or how some drug companies continue to rake in billions of pounds of profits from poorly tested medicines with side effects that ruin peoples' lives, but the story stuck with me. I didn't want to write a big satirical piece or undertake a serious deep dive into the alleged lack of moral integrity within the pharmaceutical industry, but I did want to explore—in a fictional setting, of course—what lengths people might go to if they truly felt they had a medicinal cure for every ailment known to humanity.

The idea sat in my head for a while where it started to take shape, growing little tentacled arms and tiny suckered fingers, and eventually I began to craft Paul Karin's story. At first, I flittered back and forth between a big sci-fi extravaganza and a claustrophobic horror, but as soon as I realised this novel couldn't be constrained to one specific sub-genre, it started to take on a life of its own.

I've taken liberties with the locations and the science, but I think I've got the details close enough to keep the story grounded in reality. What has always been paramount to me are the relationships, the emotional rollercoasters, the scares, and, of course, the story, the story, the story. After all, without those things, all you have is a collection of words and themes that really don't amount to much. If I'm off with the description of the lab equipment or the topography of the Brecon Beacons, please be assured these were honest mistakes.

I hope 'What Doesn't Cure You' makes you laugh, maybe shed a few tears, shout out loud, and most of all, jump out of your skin. This is the entertainment business, after all.

Until next time,

SD

About Stacey Dighton

Stacey Dighton is an author of horror and fantasy fiction. He lives with his wife in the south-east of England and has two adult children. He loves reading great fiction, listening to rock music, playing guitar and travelling – sometimes all at the same time.

Also by Stacey Dighton:

Pale Face and The Raven
The Hawk and The Raven
The Maidens of Fey and Other Dark Matter
The Faraway People

www.staceydightonstoryteller.com

Printed in Great Britain
by Amazon

57182193R00239